D1707211

GLORY

TO THE

HEROES

GLORY TO THE HEROES

Dean Proffitt

This novel is a work of fiction. All of the characters, organizations, and events portrayed in this novel are either products of the author's imagination or are used fictitiously.

GLORY TO THE HEROES. Copyright © 2023 by Dean Proffitt
All rights reserved.

No part of this book may be reproduced, or stored in a retrieval system, or transmitted in any form or by any means, electronic, mechanical, photocopying, recording, or otherwise, without express written permission of the publisher.

ISBN-13: 979-8-3958-1466-1

Cover design by: 99designs; Artist: ZAILE 88

Printed in the United States of America.

To Megan and Ryan.
You tolerated a lifetime of my reading,
And now the first step in writing.
Chase your dreams.

"What counts is not necessarily the size of the dog in the fight - it's the size of the fight in the dog."

- Arthur G. Lewis, *Book of the Royal Blue*

PROLOGUE

Some have called him an arrogant, stinking-rich, son of a bitch.

That was partially true, Ivan Rostov thought, particularly the arrogant and rich part. But a son-of-a bitch? Really? He didn't think so as he paused to look himself over in the gold-framed mirror, naked, with shaving cream on his face.

He rinsed the remaining creme from his hands and picked up the razor from its gold stand on the expansive marble vanity top.

"I guess Christmas in a 5,700 square foot villa overlooking Geneva and the lake wasn't good enough for her," he said out-loud to no one but himself.

He thought it was great - the sex was awesome. But the real New Year's Eve parties would be here in Moscow, and there was no way he was going to miss out. After all, he and his family (and also he and his friends of nearly 20 years) celebrated Novy God in this fabulous city together without exception. So he had to be here.

But calling him a son-of-bitch when he dropped her off at the train station for the trip back to Paris yesterday morning seemed a bit much. Off and on for just over a year now, he knew this relationship wasn't going anywhere - despite the physical benefits.

Half done, he focused on the dimpled chin, like a deep mogul on a ski slope, carefully working to ensure it was smooth as it could be. Tonight was going to be sensational. He loved this time of year - New Year's in Moscow is like no other celebration he'd ever attended.

The streets would be crowded, despite the freezing temperatures and the light powdery snow forecasted for the rest of the day, as people moved from one fabulous venue to the next. All the buildings in and for blocks around Red Square were decorated with bright festive lights strung along the roof lines, hanging from the awnings, and surrounding all the windows and doors. Street vendors sold warming borscht, pelmeni - even stroganoff - in steaming bowls to help fight the cold. Entertainers meandered through the crowds, acting and singing for adults and children alike. And Ded Moroz, or Grandfather Frost, with his long white beard, inevitably appeared at each place in his ground-length red or blue fur coat, walking with the aid of a long magic stick and holding a sack of little gifts for well-behaved children. Meeting him was one of his favorite childhood memories and lent excitement to being here even at this age.

There was something for every Muscovite, especially a rich, highly educated, aspiring young man like him.

He raised cupped hands full of water to his face, rinsed off the remaining lather, applied aftershave, then cologne, washed and dried his hands, and turned to the closet. Only the finest will do tonight. From the Proper Cloth tailors, he selected a plain front silk, long-sleeved dress shirt, trimmed out with 14-carat gold cufflinks and studs with single set diamonds (round brilliant cut, of course), black silk bow tie and cummerbund, and then the tuxedo from Anglo-Italian, the fine clothier on Weymouth Street in central London, just a mile north-northwest of Buckingham Palace. Prada's laced Oxfords were a perfect finish.

Arrogant? Yes. But he preferred the word *proud*. If even excessively so. For many years Russians of certain heritage went out of their way to hide it - particularly the higher classes of people. Understandable, given the penchant for communist commissions to label people of aristocratic descent as threats to the Soviet Union, where they found themselves labeled non-people who soon disappeared. Ivan found it ironic that his fifth great-grandfather, Full General Iakov Ivanavich Rostovtsev, whose work for Tsar Nicholas I earned his sons and their descendants the title of Count, did so through crafting and editing significant portions of the *Nazimov Rescripts*, the legislation institutionalized in 1861 that served to reform serfdom in the empire. In a sense, the General was working for the people as communism would claim to do some 56 years later. Of course, around the time of the revolution, those relatives dropped both the title and the Slavic suffix from the last name in an attempt at anonymity.

Now, in the last days of 2021, 160 years after being elevated to the aristocracy, (Count) Ivan Rostov tried to live his best, in a style reminiscent of aristocratic standards (even if he still dared not say the old title out loud). The fine cars, the estates and villas in five countries, the yacht berthed in a beautiful Italian port, the private aircraft, the many bank accounts, and the connections (both social and political) all illustrated his status, even if he couldn't legitimately claim a title in modern

Russia except to joke about the familial inheritance with a selected few friends.

Like most children, he knew nothing about these things when he was young. His father achieved much, born and raised in the Soviet Union. He was a businessman (soon widowed after Ivan's birth) whose trade embraced all aspects of weapons marketing and sales - first to government agents within the late Soviet military procurement system, and then internationally too, where the business skyrocketed, as did his wealth. Later, Ivan learned that his father was one of the first oligarchs in a system of power politics for the few.

Then he too died, and left everything to Ivan.

With the help of his father's lawyer, his father's money sent him to the best schools in Moscow and abroad. He attended law school and graduated cum laude, then hired by a prestigious law firm with offices in Geneva, New York, London, and Moscow.

His company sponsored his nomination, which was soon accepted, to join the Maurice R. Greenberg World Fellows Program at Yale University in New Haven, Connecticut. The four-month program allowed him to meet and interact with many other influential people in attendance, including fellow Russian Alexei Anatolievich Navalny.

Though not close, he had to admit that Alexei's beliefs and politics did motivate him to return to Russia, where he applied for and took a legal position with the Ministry of Defence in the Office of Deputy Minister of Defence of the Russian Federation for Material-Technical Support, first as a young policy attorney and eventually as the Lead Counsel for the Deputy Minister himself. Since taking that position, he found very little tolerance for reform.

Before the holiday break, he attended a series of upper level staff meetings where he repeatedly petitioned the Deputy Minister to prioritize distributing military equipment and other resources to the Russian Regular Army over other peripheral agencies deploying to Belarus. His insistence on prioritizing the Russian Army over paramilitary units made him unpopular in some circles. And this coming Monday was all about resuming these meetings at the MoD Building in Khamovniki District. He was well prepared - but it promised to be contentious. Though his role did not include setting policy or making decisions, Rostov found that the Deputy Director listened to him. He felt good about keeping some of the more militant elements in check.

"But enough of that," he thought. "It's New Year's Eve! I have places to go."

Fastening his Rolex, he walked across the antique Persian carpets to the double French doors, opened them wide to the harsh cold air, and stepped out onto the thin layer of snow on the balcony of his top-floor Premier Executive Suite and directly across the street to the Northwest was Teatralnaya Park, and beyond that rose the Bolshoi Theater where he had attended the ballet and many other productions in the past. Rostov turned to his left and cast his gaze over the neighboring rooftops to take in the entirety of Red Square and its famous surrounds - the nearby Revolution Square, then the old GUM Department Stores, to the Kremlin itself, and finally the 500-plus-year-old St. Basil's Cathedral in the distance. The buildings and the streets below him, were brilliantly lit for the New Year Celebrations.

He stepped back inside, closed the balcony doors, and walked purposefully towards the suite's double doors, grabbing his wool overcoat, scarf, gloves, and sable fur Cossack hat along the way. He stepped out into the hall and took the elevator (as old as the hotel itself, black metal with gold trim - an open cage assembly that descended majestically into the lobby below solely from his floor).

The noise from the lobby was evident as soon as he started the descent. And as always, when he stepped out of the elevator and arrived gloriously into the historic hotel's lobby, it was simply breathtaking. The expansive and marvelously polished marble floor, surrounded by square columns inlaid with fine artwork stretching (how far? 30 feet?) to the ceiling, crowded with travelers coming and going and bellhops (in sharp uniforms) hustling their bags into and out of the hotel. The beautiful clientele, dressed expensively for the evening, lingering in the lobby and at the bar, its expansive mirror behind the elaborate collection of alcohol reflecting and visually doubling the rich activity all around.

Tonight the lobby was breathtaking, embracing numerous oversized pots decorated with explosive arrangements of green, white, and red poinsettia and Christmas cactus schlumbergera, and evergreen boughs over-sprayed with fake snow. Each flower arrangement stood proudly on oversized marble tables around which the excited tide of humanity flowed here and there to wherever they were going, from the grand entrance to the front desk to the bar or the elaborately decorated ballroom or into the award-winning 5-Star Savva restaurant, complete with the original marble, two-tiered fountain in the center of the dining room underneath an immense arched leaded-glass ceiling.

This grand place, The Metropol Hotel, owns a fascinating history. It opened in 1905, like other grand hotels of the time such as the Waldorf Astoria in New York City and the Ritz in Paris. Over time it played host to the aristocracy of The Russian Empire, artists (writers, poets, and painters), then to bolsheviks, foreign reporters, government officials, and spies, then reformists, then modern, ambitious people of the Russian Federation. The Metropol Hotel reflects the very best of Russia, and it never fails to deliver.

After the revolution, it was closed by Vladimir Lenin himself in 1918, nationalized, and renamed the Second House of Soviets. It housed the many Soviet government officials in the new capitol, and the exquisite dining area served as a work center for hundreds of original policymakers for the new government working around the clock in the smoke-filled room drafting the many decrees and other official documents that formed the formal basis of the Union of Soviet Socialist Republics.

Ivan smiled. *This hotel brings out the best in me.*

As he walked past the opulent front desk, he nodded to the manager, Vasily (whom he'd known for years), "Good evening Vasily, our Metropol looks stunning tonight!"

"Thank you, sir. Will you be returning this evening?"

"Of course - before midnight, you can count on it. Must see the fireworks over Red Square from my balcony!"

And with that, he donned his coat and hat, exited through the front doors held open by two immaculately dressed doormen, and stepped off onto the sidewalk en route to join his enchanting friends - men and women - at the finest parties in the city. Despite the distractions, he had every intention of being back when he said. Who could pass up that spectacle? No, he'll be back.

"Preferably, not alone," he mused.

- - -

Hours later, he was pleased that despite the fine friends, the finer food, the drinks, and the champagne, he was walking back up the front steps (a bit unsteadily) at nearly quarter to midnight. Though he was alone, the night wasn't over. The exquisite lobby and the adjoining ballroom were overcrowded with lively, laughing party-goers, inviting him to stay. The noise was tremendous as live music from the ballroom and the bar bombarded the partiers as if the bands were competing with each other. There were plenty of beautiful people to join once he shed his outerwear, watched the fireworks, and then returned downstairs for what promised to be a late night indeed.

He was recounting the night's adventures so far, leaning against the rail at the back of the elevator, when the bell *DINGED* and the doors opened. He stood upright, stepped out of the elevator onto the plush carpet, turned left, and walked carefully to his door. Maybe he had a bit too much champagne already.

He reached for his wallet, removed the key card to trip the electronic lock, and extended the card to the sensor when he noticed soft, rapid sounds coming from behind him, out of the alcove that held the door to the room angled across the hall. As the lock clicked open, he turned his head just in time to take a crushing blow from one, then two men as they slammed against him and pushed their way violently into the room through the opened door.

Ivan tripped over his dropped overcoat and hat, stumbled, and fell to the floor, where big hands quickly grabbed him by the neck of his tuxedo and both arms, lifting him effortlessly up to his feet and rushing him straight across the room, knocking over two Louis XIV chairs on the way to the French doors. What was happening? He felt sick and confused.

"What on earth are you doing?" he shouted.

Not a word from the two men in dark clothes with masks over their faces, grunting as they slammed him against the doorjamb, one reaching for the handle, fumbling for a moment with the lock, then they pulled open the doors and rushed out onto the balcony.

And without delay or explanation, he found himself lifted and flung bodily over the railing, falling, screaming, the air rushing violently past his face as he approached 100 miles per hour just before the darkness took him.

- - -

The large, bald man, sitting alone in the Mercedes parked on Revolution Square across the street from The Metropol Hotel, heard the scream first, then looked up from his cell phone just in time to see a body slam onto the roof of a car parked outside the west side of the hotel, opposite him, across the street with a loud *THUD* that echoed between the buildings. The roof caved in as if made from tin foil. It was lucky no one was in the car. It didn't warrant a closer look.

He started the car.

While he was waiting, he had done some research on his phone. From that height, Rostov would have been going pretty fast - that was obvious by the size of the resting place he dug into the top of the car. The WiKi page defined human skin as "remarkably strong" - but everything else inside broke, pierced, dislodged, burst, pulped - as the body went from fast to an abrupt stop in a heartbeat. The fall happened so quickly he likely would not have processed what was happening in that short amount of time, let alone felt any pain.

"As they say," he thought, "It isn't the fall that kills you - it's that sudden stop." Heh-heh. He chuckled.

He turned on the lights, put the silver Premium S-Class with black tinted windows in gear, drove slowly straight ahead, and then turned the corner and disappeared around the block headed home.

1

KEY ASSET

Turkey was playing both sides of this conflict in Ukraine. Though a member of NATO, they played no role in the sanctions imposed by the West on Russia. While The Government of Turkey openly provides weapons to Ukraine for its defense, they still maintain normal business relations with Russia through ongoing trade by sea and air.

As far as anyone knew, Turkish Airlines Flight TK401 was just another cargo run delivering automotive parts of all types to St. Petersburg, the city known worldwide as the "Cultural Capital of Russia." Founded by Tsar Peter the Great in 1703, St. Petersburg served as the capital city of the Russian Empire for over 200 years until the Bolsheviks chose Moscow as the center of the People's Revolution in 1917. Today, the city boasts a rich history and hosts a class of wealthy uber-elites known as oligarchs - late 20th and 21st Century multi-millionaires and economic powerhouses. Some are just crooks. Some are empowered by government officials who were also on the take, and very few have some influence on the politicians in the Russian Federation. In calmer times, Carlos might be tempted to visit the historic glories of an old city, but not tonight or in the coming days. These were not calmer times.

Not once in nearly a decade of clandestine missions had Carlos ever traveled business class on the way to the fight. But he had to admit that it was nice to relax in these surroundings while he reviewed the details of the mission brief he just completed with the flight deck crew. While the Turkish goods onboard this cargo aircraft were routine for this run, his presence certainly was not.

This particular aircraft wasn't what it seemed. A highly modified Boeing 777F, its characteristics included more than the ability to haul 226,000 pounds of cargo, or that it had a full galley and business class seats, and the bunks for multiple crew. Lying inert far back in the belly of the aircraft, back behind fuselage station STA1886, in what was technically called the bulk cargo area, rested one of the blackest of black program acquisitions of the covert operations forces in years. This 777F was an Agency aircraft.

The aircraft was normally all white, but just last week it was secretly and expertly painted up with the Cobalt Blue and Lust Red trim colors of Turkish Airlines (the masquerade included appropriate serial numbers and duplicate maintenance records). Properly adorned, the aircraft was substituted for the company-owned plane thanks to the Turkish diplomatic duality - there was money in playing both sides. Of course this routinely scheduled cargo flight from Istanbul had a special crew who was fully versed in the special aircraft's hidden capabilities.

The captain got up from the left seat, stretched, and left the copilot in charge. Entering the business class accommodations, he caught Carlos's eye and said, "30 minutes. Loadmaster will be there waiting for you." Just 60 minutes to the drop, thought Carlos.

"I'll be ready," Carlos replied calmly before the big man passed quickly from view, aft of the bulkhead, between the pallets and cargo containers to perform a final inspection before the drop. Like the rest of the crew, the Agency-employed captain blended as an 'international', not unusual for non-Western airlines despite the rising pilot proficiency in most of the world's countries. This special crew was professional and distant, not wanting to know any of the details of the mission beyond what it took to drop him at the right place. Beyond the mission briefing recently completed, Carlos had barely talked with any of them in the three hours since departure.

Wearied and stung from a string of endless wars in Eritrea, Somalia, twice with Iraq, and finally the generation-spanning endurance test of Afghanistan, American foreign policy - or more accurately - the modus operandi of foreign policy was in upheaval. Many Americans no longer supported sending their kids (volunteers or not) to fight for the archaic diplomatic rules where warfare was just "the continuation of policy by other means." When he penned those words, how could the author and Prussian General Carl von Clausewitz have known that those words would shape international dispute resolution for centuries? But the modern electorate had had enough. There were home-front problems aplenty - polarized politics and extremism on both sides of the aisle negatively affecting polite discourse and problem-solving nationwide. There was police violence and the beginnings of long overdue police reforms, but there were also rising crime rates to be checked. And, of course, the pandemic.

So citizens were growing intolerant of the idea of the United States playing the role of an international police force - particularly when they understood only too well that the quick escalation to violence and associated losses was normally the result of political incompetence and inaction by the so-called statesmen and women the world over, who were frequently more allegiant to those holding most of the money than they were to the political ideals their governments espouse.

As a result, covert and clandestine operations, especially those with plausible deniability, were gaining favor again within the back halls of the US Government, where dedicated and professional leaders, soldiers, and intelligence officers focussed on doing the right thing as they looked out for the welfare and well being of Americans and the Constitution which they all swore to defend. Someone had to work the vital interests amidst the reckless rhetoric and resultant political turmoil caused by the nonsense spewed from the extreme left and right.

Of course, the focus on doing the right thing, covertly and clandestinely, needed help from industry. The Boeing Company was under exceptional public scrutiny in the aftermath of the 737MAX debacle, but sometimes it is easiest to hide in plain sight. Behind all the negative attention, the much acclaimed Boeing Phantom Works division was raking in black program dollars for one project after another in support of secretive operations. ARCHER PROJECT, convened several years prior to the presidential election in 2020, asked the triple-locked-down engineers, scientists, and managers in the

St. Louis Phantom Works vault, "How can we get a key asset into contested areas without being seen?" The problem with strict sanctions, international treaties, and high-tech means of observation and communications is that it is nearly impossible to go someplace sensitive and avoid detection.

The largest part of the ARCHER program was the secret conversion of a single jumbo Boeing 777F freighter. Derived from the commercially successful 777-200ER airliner, the 777F was designed to exploit an ever-expanding commercial freight market in support of the ever-increasing international business economy. The impatient buying public wanted their cheap, overseas-manufactured goods now, and air freight was the solution.

By any measure, this cavernous delivery van was huge, stretching two-thirds of a football field long with a wingspan slightly wider than its length. Weighing 159 tons empty, it could take on another 450,000 pounds of fuel and cargo - and travel over 5,500 nautical miles at 8.5 miles per minute. Amidst the sheer eye-stealing size of the aircraft, one could forgive anyone who failed to observe the subtle seam lines of new doors on the lower fuselage enclosing a space technically known as the bulk cargo compartment.

The modified bulk cargo space was called The Pit by the engineers. It was just 540 cubic feet in volume - measuring roughly 15 feet long, six feet wide, and six feet high. Normally reserved for loose or misshapen cargo that doesn't fit on pallets or in shipping containers, this modification was one of the most complex and expensive aircraft modifications ever made to an existing airframe. The objective was simple in principle: a rider needed to enter the pit from inside the

15

aircraft, access a special conveyance, and leave through the bottom of the aircraft. However, the engineering to make that happen was complex. The design had to accommodate segregated depressurization in the pit without effect in the aircraft itself, thus driving a modification of the existing pressure vessel - essentially inserting a pressure compartment within the structure of the original pressure vessel. They had to install suspension equipment, a rotary launcher rack, and a hydraulic ejection system. And finally, the engineers had to add discrete, fifteen-foot long, fast-action, hydraulically actuated double doors under the pit not unlike those found on bombers since bombs were first carried internally.

But it was the special conveyance in the pit that was the main purpose of the project: a highly classified single-person disposable vehicle. Like so many other aspects of his job, Carlos had to swear never to discuss the topic with anyone. It was so sensitive he only saw the training material once, and that was on an encrypted laptop kept in a controlled access vault in the George Bush Center for Intelligence at Langley (an odd name, Carlos thought). The special conveyance was called the Covert Ingress System, or CIS. No matter what you called it, Carlos knew the vehicle to be claustrophobic and a serious challenge to his desire to control his environment.

The riders called it The Sled because it was a rough ride. It was designed and built to provide protection and near-invisibility to a key asset (him) during a high-speed, night-time infiltration into contested areas. The well-known High-Altitude, Low-Opening parachute delivery method was good - but HALO only worked when you controlled the airspace and weren't worried about being detected, having the aircraft shot down, or alerting others on the ground of your approach. This system provided the invisibility needed to go deep into enemy territory - so long as you could masquerade as a scheduled, friendly, air cargo flight.

When he first saw the training material, Carlos realized that the reason they showed it to him only once was that you were just a passenger. You rode the sled to a point just before the intended Landing Zone, or LZ, where it would execute a terminal maneuver (another odd choice of words, he thought) and then initiate the low-altitude parachute deployment and landing. All automatic. All in the dark. There was nothing for you to do except control your anxiety.

The sled design was similar to the high-tech, high-performance science behind the finest Olympic bobsleighs. The sled was a 12-foot-long aerodynamically shaped complex cylinder, with a Craftcirrus lightweight polycarbonate 3D printed structure. It was skinned with carbon fiber composite material on the airfoil body and wings. It had a very low radar cross-section. Provisions were made for power, wireless connection to the aircraft intercom, onboard GPS navigation software, a miniature onboard guidance computer, an oxygen supply, and rider restraint. The vehicle was just over four and a half feet wide with the electric servo-powered eight-foot wings stowed in the wing/body filets along its length before ejection from the pit. Once out of the pit, and with separation from the launch aircraft assured, the high-aspect wings deploy nearly perpendicular to the fuselage. The resultant 20-foot wingspan resembles a glider and produces glide ratios better than 10:1. If the sled was released at the planned 20,000 feet above the ground it could glide just over thirty miles with minor course corrections to the LZ. Undetectable and unseen.

The top or back of the sled is nearly as open air as the open cockpit of the bobsleigh - with just a thin frangible aero sheet zippered along the perimeter of the seven-foot by three-foot extraction hole. That aero sheet also has a hole that perfectly fits around the exposed standard high-performance parachute that was attached to the prone, face-down rider inside.

Because of the soft top, the designers had to mount the sled on a rotary device. The rider had to don the parachute and other gear, board from above, and get strapped in face-down in the vehicle, at which point the loadmaster would rotate it around the horizontal axis 180 degrees so the strong "bottom" of the vehicle could take the hydraulic force of the ejection. As a result, the rider exits the aircraft lying on his or her back.

Once ejected from the pit, and after the wings deploy, the sled rotates right side up, seeks the optimum velocity for the necessary range, and automatically steers toward the LZ via GPS guidance. The navigation system constantly computes and flies the flight path necessary to arrive at 300 feet above the ground one half mile short of the LZ with sufficient airspeed to pitch up ten degrees nose high. Once the sled decelerates to 200 knots, the parachute automatically deploys, extracting the rider from the vehicle through the shattered aero shield. Not much training is required.

Carlos's alarm vibrated silently but persistently in his breast pocket, prompting him to get up and out of the plush seat. The alert emanated from a modified state-of-the-art, encrypted, Iridium satellite phone with data, voice, audio modulation, and a liquid crystal self-repairing display. Looking exactly like an iPhone XR, it had an iPhone OS clone with face recognition, then a hidden fingerprint touch point on the screen that accessed the actual classified SatPhone via his personal identification number.

He had 15 minutes to strap-in, 45 minutes left until the drop.

He was ready. Beyond the phone, he had a Russian MP-443 Grach double-action, short-recoil, semi-automatic pistol holstered inside his Premium Body Armor gray Viktory Gunfighter Sweater (over the top of the same company's long-sleeve black T-shirt with Level IIIA armor inserts). The pistol was not unknown to Carlos - he had fired thousands of rounds through this model in recent years on the range. But this was not one he would have chosen save for the confusion it would sow in Russian Federal Security Service investigators' minds when they determined the killing round would be from the very weapon issued to their own FSB agents and members of the various Russian special forces teams.

As he moved to the back of the aircraft he pulled on his Maliboo Hybrid Hooded Jacket (with easy-holster-access pockets) which had an expertly stitched rendition upon the left breast of the "The North Face" brand name and logo. Underneath his double rip-stop, Thinsulate-lined, dark gray heavy-duty cargo pants was a Spyderbite Equalizer self-defense combat knife strapped securely to his right thigh. The knife was razor sharp, and Carlos had proven it to be mean and effective when he had to be silent. His gear was topped off with Titanic HDX Elite gloves, a black watch cap, and subtle but completely effective black combat-style boots. Overall, his tactical outfit would gather no more attention on the street than any other similarly dressed and trendy millennial shopping downtown St. Petersburg for a new iPhone and an Iced White Chocolate Mocha.

The loadmaster was waiting for him at the open door of the pit and expertly assisted him with the high-performance parachute. Then, he helped secure and connect the protective smart helmet with a tiny one-inch square Tactical Augmented Reality eyepiece that displays a green altitude readout, a countdown reading of the time remaining to the terminal maneuver, and two markers - one a square symbol overlaying the LZ, and the other a triangle that would show on the Target of Interest. Finally, he helped attach the chest pack (with oxygen and communications quick disconnect feature on the webbing) that carried the last of his gear - a silencer, two 18-round magazines of Russian-made 9x19mm Parabellum ammunition, Night Vision Goggles, spare batteries, a single change of clothes, rubles, and a well-used Uniao Europeia Portugal Passaporte and various credit cards in the name of businessman Carlo Silva with appropriate stamps showing entry into Russia before the invasion.

"Good luck, man," the loadmaster said briefly with appreciable respect.

Carlos nodded his helmeted head, gave a brief thumbs-up, and stepped into the pit and into the sled. His chest pack settled into a depression under him as he lay face-down and pressed his feet and hands against the composite stirrups. Once in place, the loadmaster fastened the three electrically released restraining straps over him and zipped up the aero seal around the enclosure, ensuring the parachute protruded from the sled and secured it to the auto-deploy connection.

After a quick comm check, the loadmaster rotated the launcher to put Carlos's back down towards the exit doors. Watching the time, the loadmaster sealed the pit door. And then, after what he thought must seem like an eternity for the rider to lie there waiting, he pressed the button to depressurize the pit when the T-minus one minute light illuminated on the loadmaster's control panel.

Carlos took deep breaths and exhaled slowly, repeating this until he felt his heart rate calm. Ready.

A hydraulic whine and *BAM* the doors slammed open and before he could react to the noise, the sudden, abrupt hydraulic action of the ejection system against the upward-facing side of the sled pushed it and him out into the blackness and the minus-28 degree winter air at 20,000 feet above the ground. First there was violent turbulence, engine noise, wind noise, then steady as the wings extended to a full 20-foot spread - silent now except for the electric servo actuators as they rolled him around upright, then some positive G as they bit into the airstream to arrest the ballistic fall and transitioned to gliding flight. Carlos got his first view through the small plexiglass window forward and beneath his face. Suddenly, once stabilized in the descent, the navigation system turned the sled sharply 30-plus degrees to the right, and the LZ and the target came into sight in his eyepiece. All things were nominal.

These final four and a half minutes of the journey would take CIA officer Carlos Francis Pombar to the LZ on a frozen, partially snow-covered soccer pitch in Pavlovsk Park, 19 miles south-southeast of St. Petersburg. From the LZ in the small stadium, he will walk just over a third of a mile to Catherine the Great's Pavlovsk Palace and Museum. The opulent northern wing of that otherwise public place was the exclusive part-time domain of the one man whose elimination might enable saner people to persuade the President to end this senseless, invasive war in Ukraine before it spins dangerously out of control.

2

THE PRESIDENT'S EAR

It was getting late, and Yuri Demonov was exhausted. When they arrived, he dismissed the guards and sent his mistress Natal'ya to the bedroom adjoining the ornate, lavishly decorated, well-equipped ground floor study. But that was almost 45 minutes ago and she must be growing impatient. Such a waste - get away from the Kremlin for 24, maybe 36 hours to spend time with her, and now this endless stream of emails marked srochnyy.

Urgent. Everything was urgent these days, Yuri thought to himself, but our objectives were nearly within reach. If the damned generals could deliver what they promised, we would be closer to restoring glory to Mother Russia.

But patriotic fervor was wearing thin at this hour, even for him, especially with her waiting in the next room. Half empty now and having lost its ice-cold bite, his glass of exceedingly fine and expensive Russo-Baltique vodka was begging to be finished. As desirable for its refined, old-world flavor as it was for the 20-pound solid, pure gold case with the diamond-encrusted Russian Imperial double-headed eagle on top, he felt this extremely rare and ridiculously expensive spirit suited him perfectly. Celebrating was not appropriate yet, so one glass would have to do.

In fact, given the news, more drinking could be viewed as drowning one's sorrows.

This extraordinary residence was his version of a Russian Dacha - his country house in the woods. But in this case, the woods were part of the large public park associated with the great Catherine's Pavlovsk Palace. She commissioned this building in the late 18th century for her son and heir Pavel I, and his wife Mariya. Yuri thought to himself how the monarch must now be rolling in her grave to see that this palace was both a public museum *and* the part-time residence of the son of elementary school teachers, just one generation removed from Chechen peasant stock. But on the other hand, she might admire his arrogance, political savvy, and influential powers - similar to the talents she valued in the advisors she entertained in the royal court such as the brothers Grigory and Alexei Orlov.

He smiled for the first time all day. Yes. Just like them, he thought. As they had her ear, so too do I have the ear of Vladimir Vladimirovich Putin. Like no one else had.

His formal education included theater and economics, earning a Master's Degree in the latter from Moscow University in the late 1990s - an odd combination that made for the perfect skills when crafting the national story of Putin and The New Russia. His business career started in advertising and public relations for Bank Menetep, then he took management positions at Rostrom, finally landing a senior manager job at Alfa-Bank. At Alfa-Bank, he worked closely with senior officials who *allegedly* carried black cash to Putin; it was not long before they brought Yuri into that circle. While each of the wealthy oligarchs in the newly opportunistic post-Soviet nation associated with these companies had connections, ultimately, the only oligarchs that counted were those that gained the confidence of the future President of Russia, Vladimir Putin. These people were talented, had great wealth and power, and most importantly, loyalty.

Just after serving a short time as a director for public relations on the Russian public television ORT channel, he became the Deputy Chief of the Russian Presidential Administration - starting a close association with the then Premier Putin that culminated in 2013 with his appointment to be his Presidential Aide in the Presidential Executive Office. While in that position, he took on additional roles as the president's personal advisor on the situations in and policies crafted for Abkhazia, South Ossetia ... and Ukraine.

There are several flavors of oligarchs in post-Soviet Russia. The earliest modern wave arose in the late 20th century when the fall of the Soviet Union resulted in the legalization of private business ownership and wealth accumulation. Corruption in the Soviet Union was a staple - but its fall enabled all kinds of ugly criminal elements to purchase previous government-owned businesses for kopeks on the ruble and then grow their wealth exponentially through government contracting. First nationally, then internationally, they expanded their businesses, wealth, and power. This crowd was beholden to the politicians who helped make them - but their ability to influence those politicians was small and then all but erased with the rise of Putin. Today they still control unions, workforces, the businesses of entire cities, and local elections, but they play no direct role in Putin's politics.

Rising political figures in the new Russia picked the second variety of oligarchs. In the wildly expanding Russian economy, they grew exorbitantly rich - and were in bed with the rising politicians who enabled them. They had some limited access to those in government where they could openly give their opinions or suggest courses of action without the worry of sanctions.

But the most recent wave of oligarchs took on a more sinister and ominous tack. These make up a new inner circle who hold the political and financial power in government - cultivated, anointed, and tolerated as long as they were useful, by Putin himself.

This inner circle - called siloviks - are trusted current and former "people with shoulder marks" (slang for those coming from the many uniformed governmental enforcement agencies). These agencies include the Federal Security Service (known as the FSB), the Ministry of Internal Affairs, the Armed Forces, and the National Guard. They serve at the whim and mercy of the President of the Russian Federation. They were called for their service, when many of those at the highest levels of government, alarmed by the rising freedoms of a more liberal and modern society, felt there was a need for a circle of "strong arms" at the top, capable of maintaining order in the country.

Without national service, Yuri was not qualified to be a silovik. Nevertheless, he was a special oligarch - with real influence on the Russian leader that others could only wish for.

The Presidential Aide was a co-author and chief proponent of the new political ideology for Russia. Known as the Ideology of Putinism it is the social, political, and economic system of Russia formed expressly for the political leadership of Vladimir Putin. And the person most responsible for selling this image to the nation was Yuri Demonov. The siloviks may have the power, but as Yuri was so fond of saying, he had the president's ear.

In Russia, such power brings great risk. Not only could you fall out of favor with the president and find yourself forced to retire, be banished to a distant village, or even imprisoned (or worse), but you also invited jealousy and ill will from those that envied your exclusive access to power.

But for now, he was safe, as his envisioned view of Russian supremacy was the acknowledged purpose of Putin's Russia: Putin was the nation's hero, his power was supreme and it was Yuri's job to manipulate the press and the public to keep it sold. This government thrived on secrecy and excelled at manipulation of the press, and it practiced pan-Russian ultra-nationalism as the president worked tirelessly to push the country forward to its rightful place as the dominant nation in Europe and the world. It bordered on mysticism centered on Putin and supported by the Russian Orthodox Church.

Yuri was startled from his thoughts by the repeated *DINGING* of the new message alert tone. More messages. Yuri frowned and read the NEW MESSAGE highlights:

Subject: Leadership Fatalities. Six general officers dead - the last murdered when he was run over by a tank driven by some traitorous soldier! Yuri thought, "He should be shot, along with everyone in the tank. For good measure, they should take anyone suspicious in the entire unit."

Subject: Failed Logistics. Miles of stalled convoys - the spearhead of the northern army's advance! Out of gas, no food, sitting ducks on a road begging to be destroyed. "Idiotic planners - where was the logistics support?" he wondered. Even he understood logistics.

Subject: Enemy Resistance. Stronger than expected Ukrainian military and civilian resistance has blown up the military operation timeline. He thought, "Worthless Intelligence! So much for an easy five to six-day dispatch of the Ukrainians."

Subject: Casualties. Russian population alarmed by the alleged number of combat deaths - stories of deaths, injuries, and capture floated by the Western press and made available via social media. Losing public support. "Damn public opinion," as he took another drink. "Traitorous scum."

Subject: Combat Power Decreased. Many hundreds of tanks, APCs, and artillery and support vehicles were destroyed; the naval ship recently highlighted in Russian News was damaged while unloading at the dock! Already a total 10% reduction in combat power. Simply shocking.

Leadership failures, soldiers starving and lost, and dead soldiers gone uncounted and uncollected in numbers that cannot be advertised at home. Billions of rubles of military equipment were wasted. And video after video - dozens and dozens of them - posted to social media apps and running on international news outlets, all available to Ukrainians and Russians via the StarLink system despite the herculean effort of the Ministry of Information to control and deny access!

And now, in frustration, stalled generals pushed by the Kremlin for results resort to indiscriminate aerial, artillery, and rocket bombardment of whole cities and their stubborn Ukrainian peoples. Yuri didn't give one shit about the people except how news of their deaths and evacuations might drive public opinion. But our frustrated generals were fueling the Western images of an uncultured and incompetent Russia by resorting to wanton and unlimited violence. And it gains nothing but bad press.

This was Aleppo all over again - but with Twitter reporting every excess. "Maybe I should refresh this drink," Yuri thought. Then, "No, I should close this damn computer and go to her."

"Who would have thought the nation's cause could be betrayed by the military and intelligence community's failures during this time," he wondered.

They are the agencies who took billions of rubles and extolled the many scientific and technical breakthroughs that money supposedly bought in the tools of modern combat capability and effective information control that were failing to deliver! It was hard enough to control the modern Russian citizenry with their cell phones, social media apps, and ever-present access to international news. The people are lazy and over-informed, and mostly over-opinionated. It was hard enough to convince them that liberating Ukraine from Neo-Nazi oppression was something essential to Russian interests. But to feed the populace the very reason for their discontent - through our incompetence - was inexcusable.

Thank goodness Putin agreed to Yuri's plan to participate in the televised pep rally (as the Americans call it), with all the bands, the cheerleaders, the Patriotic Heroes, and red, blue, and white flags and bunting. That event put the president in public view for the first time in months leading up to the election. It generated the kind of patriotic fervor that might help the population suffer more willingly the upcoming deprivations and hardships consequential of the surprisingly harsh EU and NATO economic sanctions and other measures - all driven by the devils in America.

"The pep rally worked," he thought, "but even those bastards in Rossiya-1 state television managed to botch the signal with some kind of technical interruption of the transmission!"

He sighed. Was this going to work? He was beginning to wonder. But the president, the military, and the whole nation were now speeding down this path to glory that he helped instigate, and it will now happen no matter where sanctions or the unexpected belligerency of the Ukrainian people took it.

Those damned Ukrainians. It was supposed to be easy! If this doesn't end soon, escalating the rhetoric on special weapons may be necessary.

Yuri heard the bedroom door softly swing open against the plush carpet. He took a deep breath and regained some of his composure. Not wanting to leave it behind, he reached for the crystal glass with the last of the premium vodka, and with the beginnings of a smile, he turned slowly toward the adjoining bedroom, and her.

3

SOMETHING FELT AMISS

In the final moments of flight, just before the sled started the termination maneuver to pitch up and slow down, the green triangle hovering over the target in Carlos' eyepiece drifted out of sight to the right signifying he was passing the Palace and less than a mile or so from the LZ. For the first time, he got a good look at the lightly snow-covered ground glistening in the waning moon illumination - almost light enough to go without the Night Vision Goggles, but they will still be useful.

When the sled pitched up, the LZ drifted out the bottom of the eyepiece as it remained fixed on the flat white soccer pitch. Suddenly, three near-simultaneous reports as the restraining belts released then *WHUMP!* and a breaking-tearing sound as the parachute deployed and yanked Carlos through the aero seal and into the night. After the rapid deceleration and a couple of swings back and forth through the vertical, he looked up to see a perfectly intact, gray parachute with steerable panels deployed.

Looking down he found himself just past the midfield line on the soccer field - at least where he judged it to be if he could see it through the snow on the grass. He would be on the ground in seconds. He heard the crash of the sled past the far end of the field, in the woods beyond the parking lot - shattering the 3D printed frame and composite material into a thousand unrecognizable pieces of plastic, some wiring, a tiny oxygen bottle, four small electric motors, the navigation computer card, and a lithium-ion battery. The Russian-built electric motors had the Cyrillic script to add to the confusion of those who found the remains.

The landing was uneventful, like most of the several hundred parachute landings he had done previously. Carlos collapsed the chute, unbuckled the straps, stepped out of the harness, and then rolled it all up into a ball and carried it to the bleachers behind the east sideline and tossed it and his helmet into a snow-covered metal garbage can - he was careful not to disturb the snow on top.

It was silent in the small stadium. He quickly unpacked the NVGs from the chest pack, held them up to his eyes, and surveyed the stadium and its surrounds looking for any kind of heat - a person - possibly alerted to his arrival. Nothing. Just the soft, hushed, snowy field and the patchy ground fog one would expect at 02:00 Russia Time Zone 2 in 19 degrees Fahrenheit ambient air temperature. He located the watch cap in the pack and put it on, then extracted the buried carry straps and slung the pack around onto his back.

Next Carlos unzipped his jacket and cargo pants pockets to ensure easy access to the holstered Grach MP433 pistol and Equalizer knife. He quickly pulled out the pistol, installed the silencer, chambered a round, and reinserted it into the holster. It is hard enough to look inconspicuous walking around in the middle of the night - it is harder still while carrying an automatic pistol with a silencer in your hand.

Locating the southeast corner of the stadium, he set off at a steady fast walk toward the target. His trek exited the soccer pitch perimeter along a road that snaked off southeast through the stand of small, naked, deciduous trees surrounding the stadium. The waning gibbous moon offered plenty of light to navigate. But periodically he held up the NVGs to reveal any heat sources, first in front of him and then all the way around. He remained alone.

As he approached the arched, two-lane stone bridge across the Slavyanka River, he could see that the fresh light snow revealed no tracks of any kind. A quick jog up and over the rise of the bridge left it and the momentary exposure of crossing it behind him. Coming around a slight bend in the road to the left brought the large, two-century-old palace into view from the north-northwest - it was dark except for some external spotlights showcasing the grandeur of the original, west-facing, three-story building's facade. From that structure, the curved wings on each side arched away to the north and south forming a letter C, elongated like a horseshoe, with the open end pointed to the east. The only other visible light emanated from what was originally the imperial family's private chambers, now exclusively the periodic residence of Chief Advisor to the President, Yuri Demonov. Unexpectedly, what the plans showed to be the ground floor study, was illuminated. Were the lights left on? Doubtful. Was he still up working? Unlikely, given the distraction he was said to be here to enjoy in the first place. Odd - something felt amiss.

More importantly - where was the security detail? A man of this stature never travels without highly skilled bodyguards. Carlos was confident in handling whatever they had to offer but the first step in neutralizing a threat was finding it and they were nowhere to be seen. Just past the residence, not quite concealed around the corner and in front of the main entrance of Demonov's quarters, were two black SUVs parked facing east on a lane leading around the top of the C until it joined the central drive from the palace to the exit that led east to Sadovaya street. But again, the NVGs revealed no heat - neither body heat nor mechanical heat from a recently operating engine.

He slipped off the NVGs, let his eyes adjust to the dark, and started to the left of the residence, dodging slowly from one large ornamental shrub to another in the direction of the vehicles to check them out first. His feet crunched lightly in the well-below-freezing inch or two of snow. Several footsteps were crossing his line of advance from right to left - at least two people - that moved past the vehicles and beyond towards the east and out of sight.

As he approached the SUVs the windows showed appropriate light frost and a quick look inside each revealed no occupants - dead or alive. Moving up the steps to the main entrance on the right he tracked through many footsteps that had filled slightly with tonight's late snow. He went to the huge double front door, peered into the darkness of the entryway through the leaded glass, then carefully tested the ornamental door handle and found the door to be securely locked. No signs of forced entry.

There was also no sign of life.

He moved off the steps to his right and retraced the curious footprints back west towards the well-lit office at the back of the residence.

A final check with the NVGs revealed no heat sources to the north in the field or around any of the shrubbery, nor ahead of him as far forward until the wall of the palace bent around from the west to the south well past the residence. Carefully, Carlos advanced to the three oversized, glass doors that formed the whole wall of Demonov's study. The light from within cast itself out onto the white grounds, broken in shadows only where the odd trail of footsteps disturbed the light carpet of snow. As he closed the distance, he noticed that the center of the three doors was ajar - and he saw that the origin of the trail of footsteps was from within the room.

Edging silently to the side of the left-hand door, Carlos peered inside around the edge. There, sitting with his back to the doors in a large leather chair, swiveled slightly to the right, was what looked to be Demonov, laid back in the chair, motionless. He was in front of a laptop computer that appeared diminutive on an otherwise clear, very large, highly polished mahogany desk. The computer screen flared now and then with the randomly moving colorful Starburst screen saver. His arms dangled off each side of the chair, with an empty glass on the floor to his right, the lush dark red carpet appearing slightly wet. His head was back, seemingly asleep. There was no one else visible in the large room. Silently, Carlos crept in through the open door - feeling very exposed stepping from the night into all that light. Moving slowly to Demonov's right he saw what he already suspected to be the case - somebody already killed the man.

4

SECOND GUESS THE MISSION

Ignoring the body with the puncture wound on the outer edge of the right occipital lobe, Carlos worked quickly to clear the room, his pistol held securely with both gloved hands at the Center Axis Relock position, ready to use if needed, but not expected. After all, who would kill a man and then hang around just to see who showed up?

Removing all doubt of his condition, there to the left of the desk were the remnants of Demonov's left lower lobe and sinuses spattered all over the side table, printer, and the wall - typical of a well-placed single round to the head from a 1200 foot per second 9mm dumdum round at fairly close range.

Without hesitating, he moved on to clear the other side of the desk, behind each of the oversized sofas and tables, and the large closet before finally getting to the light switch on the wall opposite the glass doors. At last - with a flip of the switch - darkness again. He paused willing his eyes to adjust, looking back towards the desk and the dead man sitting there in front of the glass. He locked the door to the study behind him and listened for noises. Silence.

A soft warm light flickered from the open door to the left of the desk. Treading softly, he slowly crept across the heavy carpet, his breath condensing in front of him in the cold room.

Stepping through the opening and into the adjoining bedroom, lit and warmed comparatively by the dying embers from a fireplace framed by beautiful multi-colored tiles, he swept the room with the pistol and took in the inert female body on the platform-mounted, king-sized, four-posted bed, mostly covered with a rumpled up comforter, a pillow over her face. Her bluish feet stuck out the bottom, pointing in opposite directions, and her slightly bruised, slightly blue forearms and hands were laid out on either side of the pillow where they dropped after she surrendered to the suffocation. After checking the ensuite, and the spare-room-sized closet, he approached the bed and slowly pulled the pillow off her face to reveal the agonized face of a prematurely dead, attractive, 40-something woman. He closed her lifeless eyes, took a face-shot with the SatPhone camera, then covered her up again. He looked around for her night bag or purse, and having found it he was mildly surprised to find her Russian passport enclosed. Natal'ya Medvedevora. He took a picture of it then replaced the passport, left the remainder undisturbed, and returned to the study.

Demonov was as lifeless as ever - the right eye was gone and the left one bulged out from the hydrostatic pressure of the mushrooming round passing behind and underneath it before it exited the skull and traveled the short distance to crash into the side cabinet. A not-so-close-up photo was all that was required to document his demise.

Next, he turned to the laptop, powered it off, removed the mouse, and pocketed the security access ID card. He quickly searched Demonov and found his mobile phone inside his suit's breast pocket. Removing his backpack, he unzipped the top and slid the computer, security access ID card, and phone in beside his clothes and other gear then moved to the door. Now donning the NVGs he once again swept the field and surrounding area but found nothing. He stepped through the door, turned right, and started east to exit the area. Pausing only briefly as he neared the cold and empty SUVs, he soon worked his way around the arc of the north wing, entered the east-west central drive of the palace, and started the quarter-mile walk to the main road in a tunnel-like scene framed by tall evergreen trees lining either side of the lane.

At the end of the long drive, before the turn-circle at the crossroad, Carlos cut through the woods to the right and crossed the empty road that headed north-south where he walked into a parking lot for the tourist-favorite restaurant Street Cafe serving over-priced tea and light food (hours were 07:00 to 21:00, seven days a week). The owner was cooperative, allowing someone to park a beat-up, 2013 Lada Vesta hatchback overnight. One of the few remaining US embassy employees had left it yesterday afternoon in the far corner of the small lot, now lightly covered with snow. That same person would retrieve it later this morning at the train station.

All Carlos cared about was that the car was nothing special (to blend in) and that it had heat. He soon found that it met both requirements. Finding the keys on top of the left front tire (an old-fashioned, two-key set on a metal ring), he jumped in and started the car, turned on the heat, and left the lights off.

Quickly he pulled out his cell phone and prepared an encrypted text: Found the target down upon arrival. Unknown assailant. No security was present. In possession of laptop and phone. Egress initiated. SEND.

Carlos put the car in gear, turned on the lights, and left the parking lot turning north, then northeast. The roads were empty at this time of night. He paused only when crossing the Oleniy Most lake to toss the NVGs, the unused knife, the pistol, the silencer, and ammunition, into the dark waters. He placed Demonov's laptop, ID card, and phone in the trunk and extracted the small business travel bag with "his" stuff in it that was left there by the embassy employee. From there he took highway M-11 north, then merged with the R-23 and continued north for the easy 2-hour journey to St. Petersburg.

Two hours to second guess the mission. Precious ARCHER assets used and wasted. Who killed Demonov? Jealous oligarchs? Siloviks? It certainly wasn't his wife or his mistress. That was expert shooting. Was it Putin's bodyguards? Or someone less supportive of the regime? He simply couldn't know. Always a self-critic, he wondered what he could have done differently given what little he was presented and concluded he did the best he could do. Maybe the lover's identity will reveal something. Certainly, the geeks in the lab will get something out of the computer and the phone - if nothing else, exploitation of those data sources may be the only thing that makes the mission worthwhile. At least the target was eliminated.

Passing through downtown St. Petersburg's Central Business District, he crossed the Neva River on the Liteyniy bridge northbound in the fog to arrive at the Finlyandskiy railway station. He pulled into the parking lot and parked the car in a dark corner of the multi-tier parking garage whereupon he placed the keys back on top of the left front tire. From there he walked to the escalator and rode down to the ticket booths, after which Carlos Silva cleared Customs, walked to track nine, and caught the Allegro train number 781M that would depart for Helsinki at 06:00, just before sunrise. He hadn't been worried - the authorities were more interested in validating the exit credentials of the hundreds of Russians escaping their sanction-threatened economy than they were concerned about a Portuguese citizen trying to get home in the early morning hours.

5

A GOOD PLAN

Just as the Allegro train left the Finlyandskiy railway station 740 miles north, Ukrainian Army Maister Serzhant Petra Oleksander, the 34-year-old gun commander of 3rd Company, 30th Anti-Tank Artillery Battalion, 30th Mechanized Brigade, thought his lack of anxiety was most likely attributable to his exhaustion.

He and his unit had been in the field since before the invasion with the only time off being a rotation through a two-day training course on the newly received joint Swedish/UK Saab Bofors Dynamics Next Generation Light Anti-tank Weapon (NLAW) missiles. With his experience, and his team's recent training, he was the logical choice to lead the ambush.

The flat, squalid urban-type settlement of Ivankiv was not impressive looking in good times, and now, in the predawn twilight of a frozen February morning, it looked like a cold version of hell. Founded in 1589, only 54 miles north-northwest of Kyiv, none of the poorly aging mid-century post-war buildings were tall, and now most of those were knocked down, smoking, or otherwise lying in ruins around each other.

The Russians were out there - lost in the sub-freezing haze and monotony of gray - out there just past the Bolotna River slicing left to right before it empties into the larger, southbound Teteriv River to the east of the town of 10,000. Any moment now he expected the lead scout elements of the Russian Federation's 37th Separate Guards Motor Rifle Brigade to cross the little bridge over the Bolotna River and head south into the trap set by his rear-guard ambush team.

The plan seemed simple: surprise, entrap, attack, and withdraw. Punish them and slow the advance of the rest of the Russian brigade. But to succeed it had to execute like the symphony his wife Alena sometimes directed outside of Lviv when she wasn't teaching music.

And luck, always luck.

Three-quarters of a mile south of the bridge, the southbound two-lane hard-surfaced street Ivana Proskury crossed the east-west Khomenka street perpendicularly and continued south and then drifted southeast to join highway P02 to Kyiv. That intersection of the two roads contained the remains of a small business district to the west on each side of Khomenka Street, and a series of school buildings and playfields on the northeast block of the intersection that extended about a quarter mile to the east, the southern side of the property, bordering the street, was fenced in by an eight-foot concrete block wall. On the southeast corner (where most of his team was lying in wait) were the remains of a long manufacturing plant of modest two-story height, mostly roofless, bordered by a large worker's parking lot that extended approximately 1000' north to Khomenka street.

Travel to the west on Khomenka was blocked by debris - some of it brought down and enhanced by Ukrainian soldiers in the middle of the night to ensure it was impassable. Their efforts were hidden by the darkness and the noise of the intermittent Russian artillery fire from positions miles to the north.

Oleksandr had four anti-tank fire teams of five soldiers each, as well as two three-person air defense teams, and a four-person drone control team. Counting him, there were 31 soldiers. The fire teams had three Ukrainian-manufactured BTR-80UP-KR Infantry Fighting Vehicles (IFVs) hidden south of the factory, and the air defense and drone teams shared one nearer to their area well to the southwest of the intersection. They were all tired, wet, cold, and hungry after setting up fire positions all night. But they were upbeat - buoyed by the acquisition of new weapons that offered the promise of success against stronger forces.

First, the surprise would be when the Russians found any resistance at all in the battle-scarred town. The rest of their brigade had made a day-long, noisy show yesterday of retreating further south out of town - even playing a dangerous game of cat-and-mouse by firing artillery onto the northern edges of town from afar to show their distance to the enemy's artillery locating radar.

Next, they would spring the trap. When the lead element of the Russian scout column passed through the intersection, the drone team would attack the head and trail vehicles of the column with US-provided AeroVironment Switchblade 600 suicide drones - stranding the rest of the convoy between two burning hulks with the only out being a quick left turn and exit via the open Khomenka street taking them eastbound, between the school to the north and the factory to the south.

After weeks of suffering heavy losses in the long slog south, it was reported that one irate Russian tank driver of the brigade that faced them - the 37th - ran over and killed the Commander, Colonel Yuri Medvedev, blaming him for all the casualties. It was clear that many Russian soldiers were just not in the fight. Oleksandr hoped they would balk at the destruction in front of them and run east.

East, right into the main attack - the sights of his four anti-tank fire teams and their NLAW missiles. Fire Team 1 was split into two elements: FT-1.2 was deployed to the northwest of the intersection on the second floor of a roofless store to assist with part one of the ambush if the drones did not perform as planned. FT-1.1 was located in a destroyed single-floor building about 300 feet south of the intersection, on the east side of Ivana Proskury Street to prevent the enemy from continuing south. Once assured they were stopped, the team would pivot east through the wreckage of the building to help with the full attack on Khomenka Street as the enemy fled east.

The remaining three fire teams, FT-2, FT-3, and FT-4, were spread out, facing north, hunkered down in Bays 2, 10, and 18 of the 20 loading docks of the factory, looking across the wide parking lot. The shooting would start with FT-4 on the far right of Oleksandr's line as the leading enemy vehicle of the escaping column on Khomenka Street reached a point opposite Bay 18 - then the other teams would fire at the remaining armor until those units were destroyed or the team was out of rounds.

If the dreaded attack helicopters arrived on the scene they would be engaged by the two air defense teams equipped with the UK-provided Thales Air Defense Starstreak missiles. The teams, colocated with the Drone team, were dug in about a quarter of a mile southwest of the intersection to give them line-of-sight over the destroyed buildings to the expected engagement area.

When each element of the team fulfilled their role they would move to their concealed BTRs and exit south as quickly as possible to rejoin the brigade before any other Russians could cross the bridge.

A good plan, Oleksandr thought. Now if only the enemy would comply with it.

6

ANGRY RED DAWN

Russian Federation Army Starshiy Serzhant Stepan Popov was not happy. To keep warm, he was sitting just below the open commander's hatch of his T-72B3 main battle tank, its V-12 V9252F 1,132hp diesel engine idling, burning precious fuel, and going nowhere. The waiting made him angry. He was fed up with the cold, the lack of warm food; irritated with the other two members of the crew for their constant griping; frustrated with this damned snake-bitten brigade and its horrendous leadership, and unhappy with this fucking war. And now here he was about to jump off as part of the dreaded scout element and move even further from the limited logistics units at the rear to press harder for Kyiv.

His unit was not fairing well. After weeks in Belarus on military exercises, they were awakened with orders to reposition south. There was no warning, no preparations, no intelligence briefings, no threat assessments, no news, nothing. The first indications they had of entering Ukraine were the signs they saw welcoming them to their towns and cities with the Blue and Yellow flags, and the roads they traveled lined with burnt-out civilian vehicles with Ukrainian license plates. Now, just days into Putin's "Special Military Operation" there were signs of real trouble.

Killing the brigade commander was not good. The forced removal of more troops than just those of the tank that ran over him was indicative of how widespread the discontent might be. But more importantly, there were serious problems with their ability to fight. Not counting low morale, there were shortages of diesel, oil, and lubricants; of ammunition, food, and water, everything. What moron thought that six days of provisions and a minimal number of trucks and fuel bowsers would support an invasion? Or, more politically correct - a special military operation. Would we have better logistical support if it was called a war?

There was no routine maintenance being performed - even when stopped - as there was no maintenance equipment besides the minimum kept in storage bins on the left side of the tank and no spare parts! This machine can only take so much abuse, he thought.

Luckily, his gunner was able to conduct "battlefield resupply" by scavenging rounds from abandoned tanks along the way and his driver was good with his tools. They now carried all 45 rounds of 125mm main gun ammunition - the auto-loader tray and hull storage were full.

He loved this vehicle. Perhaps nobody but those who went before him and were now retired had more time in the T-72 tank than him. First deployed in the 1970s, these new iterations were far different from the originals. He felt his T-72B3 equipped with Kontact-5 Explosive Reactive Armor plates to defeat incoming High Explosive Anti-Tank (HEAT) rounds, and with the Shtora-1 Self Protection System, was a superior main battle tank. Weighing in at just 41 tons it measured over 31 feet in length from the rear bulkhead behind the engine to the tip of the 2A46 125mm smoothbore cannon barrel, and she could race headlong at the enemy at nearly 50mph. Using the stabilized fire control system with the automatic loader, a good gunner could fire three rounds at a target in less than 15 seconds all while on the move. It required only three men to make her one of the best land combat fighting machines ever: the commander, the driver, and the gunner. In his mind, there was no more satisfaction to be had than to be in command of this tank on the battlefield with the opportunity to destroy the enemy!

He frowned. To date that satisfaction has not been fully realized. This enemy, whenever the Ukrainians showed themselves, would jump out from behind a building, shoot at us, and disappear, rarely engaging in tank-on-tank combat. His grandfather was a young tanker in The Great Patriotic War. He proudly wore the Hero of the Soviet Union badge which he received in the Battle of Berlin his whole life. He was buried wearing it. Though Dedushka was long gone Popov idolized his grandfather and intended to live up to his example in combat. With that, he glanced up through the hatch to look at the brilliantly red State Flag of the Union of Soviet Socialist Republics that he attached earlier to the five-foot radio mast just behind his commander's hatch. It moved softly in the light breeze. Before his unit deployed, this was a special order online purchase to get the pre-1980 version with the yellow-outlined red star and yellow hammer and sickle emblem on both sides. The same version his grandfather would have fought under in Germany.

"So why are we sitting here?" he shouted, though no one could hear him over the noisy rumble of the diesel as he did not key the intercom button.

But the gunner sitting next to him in the cramped turret, short with a squeaky voice but an expert on the cannon, heard something for he did key the button and asked, "Senior Sergeant Popov, do you think they will cancel today's movement?"

"No Andre, be patient. The commanders will talk and talk some more, and then when it is light and way past our start time they will yell at us to get moving as if it was our fault that we are late."

The driver, an overweight and unkempt soldier named Ivan, keyed the intercom button only to laugh and say, "Those dumb bastards are going to get us all killed!"

"That's enough Ivan," Popov said.

No matter how hard the fans worked inside, the interior of the tank reeked of diesel fuel and their unwashed bodies. If they go much longer without a proper bath the enemy will smell us coming, he thought. He stood up through the hatch and the squat cupola with the armored gun shield and its 14.5mm machine gun. He noticed the angry red dawn as the sun's rays poked through the haze and smoke on the eastern horizon to his left as if scolding them for being late. So much for starting south before sunrise.

He looked aft past the two BTR-80s at the vehicle in the trail position - a BMP-3K Komandnyi command vehicle where he saw the scout team commander and his assistants dismounted and surrounded by senior staff officers.

Like the standard BMP-3 IFV at the front of the column, this was a low-profile, tracked vehicle, sporting a turret armed with a 100mm main gun, a 2A72 30mm automatic cannon, and a 7.62mm machine gun. Like his tank, both BMPs in the column were crewed by a vehicle commander, a gunner, and a driver. But unlike the troop-carrying vehicle out front, the Komandnyi version was equipped with additional navigation equipment, radios, and two extra whip antennas. And in place of the troops normally hunkered down in the main compartment, this one held only the scout team commander and two technical sergeants to assist with navigating and communicating.

The other IFV in the formation, the BTR-80, couldn't look more different from the BMPs though they too are operated by the same three-person crew and also hold seven soldiers in the cramped rear compartment. While the BMPs are tracked and heavily armed, the BTR-80s are 4-axle, 8-wheeled vehicles, mounting only a 14.5mm machine gun or the 2A72 30mm automatic cannon in a small turret aft of the driver and commander hatches. Both types of IFVs are capable of better than 45mph in the right conditions - but that speed rarely helped them in urban warfare. When directed, the squad of soldiers could deploy quickly from two doors at the rear of the compartment.

Unlike the T-72 tanks with their thick steel and ceramic composite armor, and the externally mounted explosive reactive armor and armored side skirts, the crew and troops in the two BMP-3s and the six BTR-80s were protected by only 35mm of aluminum alloy on all sides and the top. While this offered excellent protection against small arms fire, it provided no help to the soldiers when confronted with anything larger.

If the Komandnyi BMP was special, the scout team commander was far from it - a Starshiy Leytenant new to the unit and nervous, he was still getting extra help from the members of the brigade staff, their breath visibly clouding the cold air as they probably gave way more guidance than the young officer could handle. Senior Lieutenant Melnyk had promise but no experience and this was his first time as a team commander. His lack of experience showed not just in his young, smooth, pale face but also in the lack of information he passed to the 11 vehicle commanders gathered together earlier in the pre-dawn for the mission briefing.

All that Popov and the others knew about their mission was that they would cross the little bridge and head south on this narrow two-lane road in column formation, advance cautiously, maintain the assigned position behind the vehicle in front, and continue until we make contact with the enemy somewhere south of this dismal, half-destroyed village named Ivankiv. It wasn't entirely clear what the plan was after they "made contact."

Unfortunately, none of the accompanying infantry would be dismounted to probe out in front of the armor, leaving the tanks and IFVs to wander blindly into the enemy. It was as if the commanders had never read the lessons learned from armored combat in the decades previous. Not good, he thought.

Turning away from the officers and the three vehicles behind him, he looked to the front of the column at the head vehicle - also a BMP-3. Arranged closely behind it, was a T-72, followed by two BTRs, another T-72, then another two BTRs in front of his tank. Each of the three tank's long main gun barrels was pointed slightly left or right, alternating back through the formation. All of the vehicles wore the standard dark, forest green-black paint, streaked with mud, snow, and ice from the many days in the field. Many fenders, spray shields, side skirts, and other parts of the vehicles showed damage from rough use and combat. Each of the vehicles was adorned with the large, white "Z" symbols on the front, sides, and back - both a Northern Forces ID marking and a militarist Russian propaganda symbol allegedly showing support for the war.

The vehicles also had some type of white cloth or other material secured around the various gun barrels for additional differentiation from similar Ukrainian machines. Popov's gunner Andre had obtained a white (now dirty) bed sheet and fastened it around the mid-point of the huge gun barrel, its ends draping off slightly to either side.

They were all belching diesel fumes into the cold late-winter air increasing the morning haze and adding to the choking smells of yesterday's fires. Just eleven vehicles - three tanks, six BTRs, and two BMPs, would be moving off in front of the whole brigade who was idling somewhere out of sight several miles behind them.

Suddenly, the team's R-168-5UTE VHF radio net came to life - that it worked today was a minor miracle - with Leytenant Melnyk's voice, "37th Scouts, advance!" Popov looked aft to see the lieutenant emerge through the commander's hatch on the BMP-3K wearing his helmet with boom microphone and goggles. He may not be experienced, but at least he was standing there looking the part.

To his driver, he said, "Wake up Ivan, you slouch. We advance. Maintain 100 feet behind that piece of shit BTR in front of you!" Once the IFV in front of them finally started moving, Ivan upped the RPMs, engaged the first gear, and slowly the 96 treads of steel on the tracks began to smack the ground in turn, thumping rhythmically until the speed increased to a heavy rapid staccato beat, reverberating through the vehicle.

And into the wasteland of Ivankiv, they went.

7

ROAD BLOCKED

While he waited Oleksandr must have gone over the plan 50 times and could think of nothing to change. The men were good. And the weapons they held were superb. Truly, these weapons were equalizers for dismounted troops who must face the armor of the mighty Russian Bear. The morning air was crisp and cold, with a light breeze now picking up from the northeast. In the distance, he thought he could hear helicopters - but no sign of them yet. They were probably the biggest unknown this morning. Would they show? Would they fight or just turn and run? There was no knowing what...

"Maister Serzhant, they approach!" the FT-1 team lead interrupted on the encrypted tactical radio each member carried attached to his combat vest harness. Oleksandr roused himself in his hide alongside the men of FT-3 in Docking Bay 10 on the north side of the abandoned factory. The five-person fire teams had two shooters with two rounds each, along with three cover infantry with a light machine gun and small arms.

"Report," Oleksandr said calmly.

"First vehicles passing slowly over the bridge at this time - maybe a dozen vehicles total. Personnel carriers and tanks."

Petra considered the timing, then directed, "Drone team launch!" The electric-powered 50-pound drones had more than enough battery life to loiter until the enemy was in the right position.

"Delta-1 vyznav," the leader acknowledged.

"Delta-2 vyznav," repeated the second.

Drone teams 1 and 2, southwest of the intersection and separated from each other by about 100 yards, made ready to launch their single rounds of Switchblade model 600 anti-armor drones. Delta-1, Sergeant Kozak, would launch first.

The US-provided drones were relatively light, easy to transport and set up, and simple to operate after the appropriate training. Equipped with both electro-optical (EO) and infrared (IR) cameras with a digital data link to the portable controller, the operator was able to "see" the engagement, identify the targets, and command the kill which the drone would execute with a high explosive anti-tank (HEAT) warhead similar to that used in the Javelin anti-tank guided missile.

Each operator put power on the portable touchscreen tablet-based fire control system, commanded power to the drone in its portable carrying and launch case, performed a quick systems check, and with a green ready light, depressed the launch button.

With a *THUMP* and *WHOOSH* the Switchblade 600 was soft-launched from the tube starting the electric motor and instantly spinning up the propeller at the rear of the weapon. Simultaneously, three wing segments deployed - one just forward of the midpoint of the fuselage to form a straight wing, and a shorter horizontal tail set and a vertical tail snapped into place at the back of the drone. The high-lift wings quickly took the drone up to 500' altitude, whereupon the buzzing motor lazily established a cruise speed of 70mph.

En route to the intersection in town, Kozak soon scanned the convoy and reported, "Delta-1 counts 11 vehicles in the column with no other forces at the bridge."

He then commanded the drone to the geographic coordinates of the intersection where it took up a one-mile-wide orbit high overhead. Immediately, Kozak was able to make out the lead BMP-3 southbound on Ivana Proskury and kept it locked up with the 360-degree traverse of the EO/IR cameras during the orbit.

Delta-2 ran through the same steps and launched the second weapon. This drone's go-to coordinates were just south of the bridge over which the lead elements of the convoy were now passing. The operator located the trail vehicle in the view screen (which was still north of the bridge with one remaining BTR). The remainder of the column was already across. He couldn't help but notice with the IR camera that someone was standing in the commander's hatch of the BMP.

"Delta-1 on station."

Shortly after, "Delta-2 on station."

"Status."

"Lead vehicle is approximately 1/2 a klick north of the intersection. The entire column is across the bridge now with tight spacing between vehicles - tighter than they should be."

Oleksandr replied, "Delta-1 cleared to engage the head vehicle when he gets through the intersection. Delta-2, engage the tail vehicle as soon as possible after Delta-1's attack."

"Delta-1 kopiya," copied the leader.

"Delta-2 vyznav," acknowledged number 2.

As he crept cautiously out of the wrecked building to the side of the street, the FT-1.1 leader, Sergeant Kovalenko could now see the lead vehicle driving towards him down the middle of the road. He looked up, trying to locate the drone, but could not find it. The morning sky was turning a lighter shade of gray-blue. Not wanting to risk being seen he shuffled back to the shattered storefront, settled in behind the debris along with the two cover soldiers, picked up his NLAW, and waited.

Up the street towards the enemy and across the intersection to the northwest, Sergeant Moroz, the FT-1.2 element leader felt particularly vulnerable as he and his cover soldier were the farthest forward members of the ambush team. They could find themselves without a role - or they could be in the thick of it with their only escape route to cross Khomenka in front of a pissed-off enemy and evade south to rejoin the fire team. He didn't dare show his head above the north window sills to take a look at them for fear of tipping off someone in the convoy. So he stayed faithfully sitting next to the blown-out windows overlooking the intersection. He had carefully chosen the third window away from the intersection to ensure he would have the minimum arming range for the NLAW should he need to use it. He couldn't get over the feeling that the enemy was sneaking up on him.

Through the open roof behind him, he thought he heard helicopters - one or two but then they faded. They usually flew in pairs. He looked back across the floor strewn with broken glass and office furniture and briefly saw two Mi-28s about a mile apart in a turn back around to the north in what was probably a racetrack pattern oriented along the column's line of advance. "Headed the wrong way, boys," he said quietly.

It was getting noisy. Turning his attention back to his window, he soon saw the head BMP pass slowly through the intersection. The noise of the BMP and that of a T-72 following very closely made it impossible to hear the drone overhead. All of FT-1 waited anxiously for the explosion.

Sergeant Kozak watched the screen on the drone fire control system and maneuvered the Switchblade from the circular orbit to attack the BMP northbound in alignment with the street. The extra time it took to get the desired alignment allowed the target to advance fully through the intersection. Once he designated the target and commanded the attack, the drone turned in line with the road and dove at its maximum velocity of 110mph, aiming for the center mass of the vehicle.

Impatiently, Kovalenko stepped out of the building again and peaked at the intersection just in time to see the drone's HEAT warhead detonate right over the BMP, directing a two-inch diameter blast of molten chemical energy straight down onto and through the 35mm top armor. The effect was nearly instantaneous.

After the explosive *BANG* of the warhead and the piercing of the aluminum alloy, a convulsive expulsion of flaming contents of unrecognizable origin exited from every hatch on top and behind the vehicle as 100mm and lesser rounds detonated inside from the overpressure and heat. The right-hand track and running gear soon collapsed causing the BMP to lean over drunkenly, swerving slightly to the right to fully block the road as it burned out of control. Clearly, there were no survivors in that inferno.

Kovalenko thought, "That's all I've got," and ran inside to gather the two cover soldiers so they could reposition to the back of the building overlooking the industrial building's parking lot.

Meanwhile, with some alarm, Moroz saw that the T-72 did not stop immediately and was continuing down the road behind the BMP. He quickly stood, shouldered the 30-pound, three-foot-long NLAW launcher, and put the Trijicon TA41 sight to his eye. He shouted, "Clear!" for his partner's safety, steadied the V crosshair aiming reticle on the right rear quarter of the tank turret for the 2 to 3-second minimum count, and pulled the trigger. With a *WHOOSH* the soft-launch feature expelled the six-inch diameter warhead and rocket body at an easy 130 feet per second followed shortly by rocket launch and acceleration to 650 feet per second.

Preset to the Overfly Top Attack mode, the missile quickly closed the distance to the tank and detonated about three feet overhead the turret's thinner armor much the same way as the Switchblade warhead detonated over the BMP. In this case, the tank commander's hatch was open, and short moments after detonation a torrent of fire and smoke roared out the turret to a height of 30 to 40 feet as all the flammable material in the tank combusted as its entire load of 125mm shells spilled their contents and burned. The tank stopped in place, collapsing in a melting slag of metal as the diesel fuel from the right side tanks contributed to the conflagration. The southbound road was now completely blocked.

Moroz keyed the mic and said, "FT-1.2 reports BMP *and* T-72 destroyed south of the intersection. Road blocked." Just then, the first BTR turned left so Moroz added, "Column is headed your way." He and his cover soldier moved down to the bottom floor of the building and carefully crossed the street into the wrecked building on the south side to monitor the progress of the rest of the column.

Even before Moroz killed the T-72, Delta-2 designated the BMP-K in the tail position of the column as his target and directed the second Switchblade drone to attack. As the drone closed on the target the drone operator could see that the soldier was still standing exposed through the hatch, growing in size as the drone closed the distance. In the end, it wouldn't matter if he was exposed or buttoned up inside. He closed the tablet as the screen went blank. "Delta-2 reports tail vehicle destroyed."

Whether prompted by radio chatter, or coincidental with the end of their racetrack pattern, the air defense team saw the two Mi-28 Havoc attack helicopters fly a 180-degree turn to head back south. The pilots must have been shocked to see the totally changed scenario playing out in front of them now with burning vehicles at the front and at the end of the column they were supposed to protect. But Alpha-1 and -2, the air defense shooters, weren't concerned about what those pilots thought - they just wanted them closer.

Not that the Starstreak man-portable air defense missile couldn't handle the range - the helicopters were already closer than the missile's 4.3-mile max range. But closer meant it would be easier for the two shooters to keep their sights on the target through the missile's short time of flight.

They completed academic and simulator training across the border just two weeks ago with British SAS instructors - but they felt confident. Alpha-1 said on the tactical radio, "Alpha-1 targeted right," and Alpha-2 answered, "Alpha-2 targeted left." Alpha-1 already had his 4.5-foot, 30-pound launch tube, and missile controller up on his shoulder. Peering through the boxy aiming unit's optically stabilized sight he acquired the easternmost helicopter, designated it as the target, and tracked it for several seconds to provide the data necessary for the software to compute the missile trajectory. Then he pressed the launch button, and with a loud *THWUMP* the Starstreak soft-launched out of the tube, and then 13 feet out in front of him, the rocket motor fired with a screeching *ROAR* followed almost immediately by a loud *BANG!* as it went through the sound barrier.

In just moments the rocket boosted the three steerable, two-pound tungsten darts to 2800 feet per second - nearly Mach 4 - and then the rocket motor fell away. When released, each of the three darts flew in a triangular formation roughly five feet apart.

Meanwhile, Alpha-1 kept the optical sight on the target. At the back of each dart, a laser detector read the vertical and horizontal laser matrix projected by the shooter's aiming unit. The computer on each dart determined the difference between its position on the laser matrix and the pointed direction of the aiming unit's optical sight on the target and made the corrections to the flight controls to align the two - and hit the target.

Each tungsten dart carries nearly a pound of PBX-98 explosives with a contact fuze. The tungsten dart itself disintegrates upon detonation causing fragment damage to the aircraft - as if the kinetic energy of two pounds of steel at Mach 4 wasn't already enough destructive power.

When the darts hit the helicopter in the lower right front quarter it simply disintegrated. Both members of the tandem seated crew and the cockpit were shredded and behind them the rest of the fuselage with its fuel and two turboshaft engines exploded, the five rotor blades separated and flew off in different directions, and even some of the weapons load of cannon rounds and anti-tank missiles detonated. The fireball plummeted into the schoolyard on the north side of Khomenka Street trailing the aft boom and rotor and fire, smoke, and other debris down to the ground.

The eight seconds delay before Alpha-2 pressed the launch button allowed the other Havoc pilot to observe the carnage to his left and begin a hard turn to the right in an attempt to run away to the north. But the three darts closed the distance to the target in just four seconds - perfect timing to connect with the broadsided helicopter to knock the tail boom and rotor completely off the aircraft and send the remains bucking and flopping and gyrating to the ground where it, the ordnance, and the two-man crew blew up.

Oleksandr and the other Fire Team members hardly noticed the airborne destruction as the enemy column came around the corner.

8

MOVE, MOVE, MOVE!

Popov roared at the driver, "I said maintain 100 foot spacing Ivan! Don't bunch up like the rest of these clowns - slow down!" The column had never established tactical spacing since leaving the bridge and the BMP in the lead was not helping by crawling along. Popov stood up, poked his head through the hatch, and looked forward just in time to see a huge explosion at the front of the column - not all that far in front of him. Once he could take his eyes off the rising fireball, he turned to look aft just in time to see the lieutenant's silhouette vaporize as an unseen weapon detonated right over him and the vehicle. The BMP disgorged its contents in a fiery stream up through the commander's hatch and then immediately turned into a burning wreck blocking the narrow road. The only way for the survivors was forward.

The first BTR in the column was driven by a conscript. Inexperienced, he panicked at seeing the BMP and the T-72 explode in front of him and all he could think of was to find a way out - now! Even before the commander said a word he stepped hard on the accelerator, shot forward, and swung the wheel left to escape the carnage through the only possible exit at the best possible speed.

The second BTR barely hesitated before following. The second T-72 commander looked for something, anything - but found nothing to shoot at. Surely there was armor involved! He decided that he couldn't leave the BTRs unprotected - and he needed the infantry from those IFVs if he was to survive a close-in fight, so he ordered his driver to follow.

And then so too went the two BTRs in front of Popov. Now he yelled, "Speed up Ivan. Move, move, move!"

The final two BTRs accelerated to catch up with him.

9

THE GAUNTLET

Oleksandr thought, "Three vehicles destroyed. Eight to go." The lead BTR was now picking up speed eastbound on Khomenka followed closely by a second BTR, when a T-72 came into view from around the corner.

"Standby Fire Team 4," he said, as most of the column was entering the gauntlet. There was no answer required.

As the first BTR passed his position in Docking Bay 10 two more BTRs rounded the corner to his left gaining ground rapidly on the tank. Suddenly, out of the corner of his eye, a missile streaked out from the right at the lead BTR followed closely by the noise of its rocket motor. It detonated with a loud *BANG* above the speeding vehicle. The thin-skinned vehicle was no match as the warhead directed its energy downward into the compartment creating thousands of pieces of superheated shrapnel from the shattered aluminum armor, instantly over-pressurizing the interior and firing all combustible material - including people - into a fireball that exited the hatches on top and aft and through all the windows. The fuel tank situated in front of the driver and commander seats emptied its contents into the wreckage, further enflaming the destroyed vehicle. Some of the eight large road wheels were literally blown off the axles and sent bouncing or rolling onto the surrounding road and parking lot.

"Four down," he counted aloud.

The FT-3 gunner shouted, "Clear!" waited the required 2-3 seconds, and depressed the trigger. With a *WHUMP* the missile soft-launched out of the tube and then the rocket ignited and the missile streaked toward the T-72.

Nearly simultaneously, FT-2 fired their first missile at the BTR that was trailing the tank - the two missiles hit one after the other with predictable results. The tank veered right and came crashing to a stop, with flames glowing around the turret ring for a moment before the barrel dropped and the turret leaped off the vehicle and fell over upside down off the right front quarter. The force of the explosion sent fire and smoke boiling around the vehicle - made thicker by the explosions of fire and smoke from the trailing BTR.

Oleksandr said aloud to no one, "Six down - five left!"

As the BTR exploded and ground to a halt behind the tank, the trailing BTR nearly ran headlong into the aft end in the smoke. Jerking the wheel left to avoid the collision, the driver of the BTR ran square into the concrete block wall and climbed nearly 30 degrees up onto the debris and stuck there, spared for a moment as FT-2, -3, and -4 reloaded.

10

TIN DUCK AT THE CARNIVAL

Popov's driver Ivan morphed into a crazy man - taking the corner at great speed and almost losing control before accelerating east into the thick smoke that was the remains of the exploding vehicles that had gone before them.

"What the hell?" Popov screamed. How had this happened so fast? He was determined not to be shot like a tin duck at the carnival. He decided to act.

"Ivan, turn 45 degrees to the right, now, and accelerate to maximum speed."

As the tank lurched right and departed the road, Popov reached for the control panel of the Shtora-1 Self Protection System, turned the control switch to EMERGENCY, and hit the deploy button the moment they left the smoke of the fires. Not knowing what he was up against, he knew this action would energize the EO jammers and discharge all 14 grenade launchers mounted on the turret to deploy the aerosol screen designed to foil any laser range finders or laser guidance controls on anti-tank missiles.

The tank dipped down *hard* into the drainage ditch that ran along the road and flew up the other side, almost leaving the ground the momentum was so great. Flat again and accelerating on the other side Popov saw a missile launch right in front of him out of what appeared to be nearly the far end of a series of open doors in a long building.

"Gunner! Target missile site - direct front. Fire, *Fire!*" And with that, the great 125mm smoothbore gun preloaded with a HEAT round thundered and rocked the entire tank - even at this speed - and sent the round directly into the third bay from the end.

"Gunner! Same target - reload HE." Just before he shouted for Andre to fire, a missile streaked out of another bay in their direction but flew by harmlessly to the right side and behind the speeding T-72 tank. "Fire, ..."

11

AN ENRAGED ANIMAL

As FT-4 dispatched the second BTR on the far right with their second missile shot, Oleksandr was distracted by sudden movement and a show of color on the left. Bursting forth from the thick oily smoke of the burning tank and trailing BTR there emerged what one could only call an enraged animal as the racing T-72 fired off at least a dozen self-defense grenade launchers in a pyrotechnic fan that partially enshrouded the tank in a fog. Immediately it flew down and then up and out of a drainage ditch, before emerging again on a course aimed to engage his position with FT-3 or further to the right with FT-4. This machine was awesome - completely terrifying with its bold appearance. The white ID sheet at the barrel flared back in the wind at times appearing like the tank held a bone in its teeth or like it was the teeth of a dark grimacing skull. Its treads were sending gravel and sand and snow and low concrete parking blocks all over as it ramped up to maximum speed. Behind the turret on this dark behemoth flew - strikingly - the scarlet red banner of the Soviet Union. It was flying rigid and arrogant in the wind, the antenna bent back under the force.

The tank gun fired and the machine bucked on its speeding tracks, startling everyone with the supersonic *CRACK* of the passing round followed immediately by the thundering chest-shaking *BO-OOM* of the 125mm gun. It was clear now that he was firing on FT-4.

Without shouting a warning, the FT-3 gunner took a rushed shot at the tank with an NLAW. Understandably shaken, he did not let the sight settle for the required 2-3 seconds and the missile raced out and missed the tank to the left, passing harmlessly behind and detonating on the concrete wall on the far side of the road. Undeterred, the tank raced on, almost directly in front of Bay 10 now and roughly 200 feet out.

But from the far left, out of the low line of destroyed single-story buildings along the east side of Ivana Proskury streaked a missile fired by FT-1.1, left to right, that gave Fire Teams -2 and -3 a rare side view of an NLAW missile traveling 450mph at eye level. In an instant the missile detonated right over the charging T-72, its HEAT round driving a high-velocity superheated molten jet directly down through the top armor and into the tank. The tank visibly shuddered and heaved to a violent stop spinning slightly to the right until the main gun pointed directly at what Oleksandr thought was a spot directly between his own two eyes.

There was an orange-red glow at the base of the turret around the turret ring and fiery debris was spewing through the small hole at the top. The gun barrel lowered as if the tank was attempting to steady itself when terrifyingly it exploded upwards sending the 14-ton turret 30 feet in the air on a torrent of fire, twisting and spinning slowly, trailing fire and smoke and wreckage and body parts until it crashed to the ground between the tank and Bay 10, upright, somewhat flattened, barrel facing the other way, and oddly looking like a body does after falling from a great height. The open furnace that was the tank carcass continued to burn as the running gear and tracks on both sides collapsed and the fuel tanks emptied their precious diesel contents on the flames. The Soviet flag, mostly burned, fell off the radio mast and blew across the parking lot.

FT-2 broke the breathless fascination on the exploded tank with a missile shot from the left. This one reached out and destroyed the BTR that had turned onto the road behind the tank that just blew up in front of Oleksandr and FT-3. Counting the wrecks in front of him and adding the two BMPs and the T-72 at the beginning, the count was up to nine destroyed vehicles. "Two left."

At that moment, FT-3 fired their last round at the BTR that was stuck up on the wall and blew it and the wall to pieces. Some of the flaming wreckage fell forward into the school yard and the remainder settled in place - the back two wheels still connected by the axle bounced back out onto the parking lot.

To the FT-3 shooter, Oleksandr said, "One to go. Now where is it?"

West of the intersection, Sergeant Moroz stepped out into the street facing east, his new blue armband fluttering in the breeze, and watched as the last BTR finished the turn around the corner and paused at the sight of the wreckage and pandemonium in front of them. Moroz lifted the last NLAW to his shoulder, settled in on the eyepiece and stabilized the reticle on the back doors, and shot the vehicle right in the ass end at minimum range using Direct Attack mode. The round penetrated the right-hand door, just to the right of the center support post, passing well into the now over-pressurized compartment before detonating and combusting everything inside, exploding the turret off the roof and blowing wheels and tires off both sides.

Joined by his cover soldier, the man asked, "Why are there no bodies?"

"What's left of them is everywhere," Moroz said, "on everything." Understanding now, the soldier just nodded.

They carefully jogged forward, looked north on Ivana Proskury and Moroz reported, "The last vehicle in the column is destroyed. No other vehicles are coming from the north."

"Eleven," said Oleksandr.

"FT-4 report status," he said on the radio.

"A little deaf, shaken, but alive. The round passed high and through the aluminum walls of the bay before detonating on the other side."

"Excellent," Oleksandr said to himself.

He keyed the mic button again, and to all, he said, "Good job. All teams assemble at your vehicles and egress south."

As he turned, Soldat Bondar, one of the FT-3 cover soldiers, looked directly at him, pumped his fist, and said, "We showed those Russian bastards!"

Oleksandr paused, looked at him carefully, and said, "It is right to cheer our performance, but do not take joy in killing those soldiers. It will darken your soul." He patted the man on the shoulder, walked past him, through the factory, and out to the BTR, eager to rejoin the brigade en route to Bucha, and to get away from this killing field.

12

UNDER GREAT PRESSURE

Heavy-set, jowled, and bald-headed, his eyes bulged when he was angry and right now it was all he could do to keep them in his head while he waited on the phone. If anyone did see him they would know just by looking at him to stay away.

The headquarters building was not yet finished - he felt his temperature rise as he impatiently paced the floor even though the space was not heated.

"Pizdets!" he shouted in Russian in the cold, unfinished space to no one but the construction equipment.

He carried the secure satellite phone here only to have it fail to connect with his man near Kyiv. The system was down according to the military operator. Then, using his cell phone, his first call to go through went unanswered. Then the next call was picked up by the deputy only to say that the Group leader was not available. Now his phone rings and he picks up only to be told curtly, "Wait while the commander comes to the phone." That was 10 minutes ago.

Have they forgotten who they are dealing with here? There was much at stake right now and he was swimming in very dangerous waters. He promised so much and the Kremlin expects those promises to be kept. Certainly, you would think that they...

The static on the line was interrupted, "I am here. I'm sorry to make you wait. I was in a staff meeting with the battalion tactical group commander. He was... "

"I don't care what he was doing, do you understand?" the bald man exploded into the phone. "I expect you to answer immediately when I call! You do not work for him, you work for me!"

There was an awkward pause. It was the kind of pause associated with combat soldiers who are tolerating those who do not fight. You could almost see the contemptuous face from six hundred miles away.

The man on the phone replied, weary and somewhat irritated, "Sir, you directed me to work with these regular army dolts, and doing so requires me to act like I'm part of the team. You know that. I cannot just walk out on the commander and expect to be treated as an equal amongst his other officers." After weeks in the field, first in Belarus on exercises and now on this agonizingly slow, attrition-filled advance into northern Ukraine, he struggled to maintain his cold, calm demeanor.

More silence for a moment as the man in St. Petersburg gathered his thoughts and worked also to control his anger. He took in his breath and exhaled audibly before continuing.

"Are you alone?"

"Of course."

"There are many reports of problems - why are we not advancing? We should be on the outskirts of Kyiv by now. I hear that the Airborne is being decimated at Antonov Airport and Hostomel. Tell me what is going on!" It was a command.

"Nobody told the Ukrainians about our schedule. Apparently, they are not welcoming us with open arms," dared say the Group leader. "They appear motivated to fight well and they have...delayed things."

"Is the army fighting? What could those khokhols be doing to stall such a force?"

"We are stalled by the enemy, the weather, the roads, and our army's logistics stupidity," the man said through the static.

"But our forces are well equipped, correct?"

"Of course. We brought with us more trucks and supplies than the regular army - but getting them close to us takes time as they trail us along the same single road as the rest of the army travels. But our soldiers are warm, fed, and well-armed. They have fought well to date and they remain eager to fight."

"Of course they are Dimitri - they should be eager given the millions we and the Ministry of Defence have paid for their services. When will you advance?"

"Soon. The battalion has finally entered and cleared Ivankiv and tomorrow we expect to move on quickly to Hostomel and then Bucha and Irpin further south. Our special teams and the Kadyrovites will initiate their missions from there."

"Dimitri, pardon my anger earlier. I am under great pressure here. We need this to succeed. I told the President that he could count on us and our soldiers to motivate and drive the regular army - even to lead them to victory if necessary. You may not recognize just how much visibility we are under - failure cannot be tolerated - powerful men usually find others' heads upon which to lay blame."

Silence again.

Finally, Dimitri adds, "I am told the operation at Catherine's Palace was a success."

"Yes, he is gone. One more obstacle eliminated. But Dimitri, did your men have to kill the woman? I have known her for years. She was very brave."

"She was a whore. My men could not risk being compromised. As you said, there is much visibility on us and we cannot be outed by a witness who would be easily compromised in that kind of political business."

"I suppose you are right. Perhaps falling out of windows from tall buildings is a better technique. But in this case, we needed to sow a message of doubt and distrust amongst the siloviks and in that, I think we succeeded."

"I agree sir," said the Group leader to pacify his boss.

His victims weren't the only ones falling off tall buildings. One or two key people, yes, but not all of them. He suspected several within Putin's circle and others maneuvering to join that circle of doing similar things. He certainly wasn't responsible for the dozens who have fallen. Though he would like to know who was doing it to ease his anxiety.

Then, as if experiencing an amphetamine kick, he resumed his rant, "But again, let me be very clear about something Dimitri. There is a bigger threat here than the Ukrainians. Our presence is tolerated by powerful people only if we perform. You must exhort the most violent and extreme behaviors out of our troops to cement our security with the President and the Patriarch. You must get results." And with that, he stabbed a stubby finger at the phone and ended the call before Dimitri could respond.

He was sweating profusely in the frigid office space.

13

UNDISCIPLINED RUMINATION

C arlos peeled off the wet workout clothes and headed to the shower in his well-appointed embassy guest room. He'd worked out in the basement gym more in the last ten days just to pass the time than he could count. Since his arrival in Helsinki, Carlos sat idled and bored with little to do but work out and follow the progress of the war through secure situation briefings from Langley in the company of the station chief and sometimes even the ambassador.

Despite the initial assurance that there was another assignment pending, nothing materialized. Director of Operations Walker explained that the situation was very dynamic, and the administration was either unable to act decisively or unwilling to do so. And no one wanted to provoke the Russians. So he sat here.

Maybe not surprisingly, it took the tech geeks at the CIA and the NSA only a week to get into Demonov's computer and cell phone using the supercomputer Vesuvius (capable of executing 100 undecillion calculations at once - that's a "1" with 36 zeroes behind it). The Russian desk experts have been devouring the information ever since with no hint at what value any of it might be.

After a long, hot shower, he let himself have a glass of Buffalo Trace whiskey, neat, sat in the chair for a while, and revisited the train trip out of Russia.

There were lots of young families with fear and uncertainty in their eyes on that train. Those self-imposed refugees - Russians fleeing their own country under duress - had that same look to them as Carlos had seen in other faces in places like Columbia, Venezuela, Mexico, Niger, Chad, Syria, Northern Iraq, and Afghanistan. The circumstances in each place were different, but fear was fear just the same.

There was a young boy of six or seven, seated opposite from him on the train, looking lost and in need of comfort with tears in his eyes. Carlos knew little of giving comfort, but he certainly knew the feelings of being alone and helpless. He drifted off.

He was in a filthy dirt alley that passed for a road in the warren of dilapidated three and four-story tin, wood, and cardboard dwellings that they all called home. He was young - about the same age as the boy on the train. He was walking home and didn't even see the first punch from the older kid, nor could he defend himself from the other boys' punches and kicks once he fell to the ground. Scattered by a man's yell, the boys disappeared laughing around the corner.

He sensed someone standing near him, and a man's voice said in Spanish, "Levántate hijo. Estás bien." Get up. You'll be alright.

Carlos started to get up and felt strong hands on his arms as the man helped him to his feet. There were not many men in the barrios, let alone one who would take the time to help a child.

"*Sécate esas lágrimas y levántate como un hombre,*" he said in Spanish, "*They will continue to beat you until you stand up and act like a man.*"

As his crying was replaced with a sense of shame and embarrassment, he blurted out, "I can't fight them alone. There are many."

"But you can. You just don't know how yet."

"How can I fight many alone?"

"There are ways. First, you need to be more alert. There are dangers everywhere for those who daydream on these streets. You must pay attention to your surroundings."

"I didn't see them!"

"You were not looking for them. If you are alert you will be looking, if you wait to see them you will be a victim."

Carlos stared at him for a long time, thinking about what he heard. "*Gracias, senior.*" And he turned and ran towards home.

"I will see you again hombre."

After climbing the rudimentary stairs to their third-floor home his mamma was not overly sympathetic. She knelt, looked him over, and seeing nothing serious she held him briefly then worried about how she would clean the clothes tonight for *scuola cattolica* tomorrow. The nuns will not be happy with them if he shows up with a torn and dirty uniform.

"*Cosa ti è successo?*" she asked in her native Italian.

"The same boys from *Communa sette.* They don't like me."

"They don't respect you, *mio figlio.* Now go and get out of those clothes so I can fix them." That hurt.

Carlos didn't have a room. He and his younger sister and his mother all slept in the same room, their few belongings hanging on a taped-together clothes rack his mother had found in the alley

80

behind the Loma Hermosa department store. Their bedroom was partitioned off from the main room by an old tablecloth acting as a curtain. The main room was a kitchen, dining room, and living room all in one. There was one bare lightbulb hanging in each room, no running water, no bathroom (downstairs and outside), and no heat. The electricity was provided by the long extension cord that connected to the line that snaked down the stairs outside the door.

He found his other clothes - shorts, and a t-shirt - and quickly changed and went back through the curtain to eat something before going out to collect cardboard scrap to sell for the much-needed money for food.

His mother was once a maid who worked for wealthy people on or near Avenida 9 de Julio in the middle of the Autonomous City of Buenos Aires. He learned later that her work there stopped when he was born. And the hard times became even harder a few years later when his sister was born. Not that Carlos understood much at that age. But he did know that she loved him and that they had a home and some food. He knew nothing then about his father. And his absence is what made that man helping him in the alley so significant.

Startled awake, Carlos was a little surprised that he had nodded off in the chair. For him, this idle time was unpleasant. It led to undisciplined rumination. As a Type C personality with borderline Level 1 Autism characteristics, Carlos preferred to remain in complete control of his environment. He thrived on being accurate, rational, and independent, with a need to apply logic to everything he does. Something started must be finished.

Daydreams do not live within those constraints. He got up and moved to the bed to lie down. But sleep was elusive.

There were benefits to being borderline autistic - *though he knew nothing about autism or his strengths and weaknesses when growing up. He only knew what comforted him. A loner, with below-average physical stature and strength, he was frequently picked on by his peers. But within the isolation, he became an avid reader, a quick learner, and a good student who thrived under the discipline and order of the nuns at the nearby Pure Heart of Mary Parish. He still felt the sting of the ruler on his hands whenever he misbehaved. Perhaps the fact that Father Carlos Lopez had the same given name inspired him to perform, even if it didn't inspire him to be a very good Catholic. In that regard, the realities of Villa 31, one of the "Villas de Emergencia" baked a hardness in him that would influence the rest of his life.*

Also known as the Villa Miseria (misery, in Spanish), or just Villa for short, the more than 500 shanty towns throughout the city were inhabited by over 500,000 people. Villa 31 is known to this day as the most notorious slum in all of Buenos Aires. Not because any one of the villas is better or worse than the rest, but because of its location. Villa 31 was in the Retiro district, right next door to some of the wealthiest sections of the city and not so easily ignored. It was simple to walk Avenida 9 de Julio to get to the famous "Obelisk of Buenos Aires" where some of the poorest of Argentina mingled freely with the tourists. For many, it is... uncomfortable. At a minimum, it is an obvious and stark contrast between the haves and the have-nots that cannot be ignored.

The first people settled in the villa in the 1930s when poor Italian and other immigrants arrived from Europe to work the growing agricultural and food businesses but found no housing.

Carlos' mamma, Carmen Benitez, was of Italian descent. Though multi-lingual, she stubbornly clings to the language as a proud sign of respect for her heritage. Little had changed since her grandparents found themselves in the villa - maybe only the types of rudimentary materials used to construct the precarious multi-story dwellings. There was little running water in the villa, no gas, and most electricity was illegally tapped from nearby power sources with lines hanging precariously over roofs and snaked across alleys and along stairwells like theirs throughout the villa.

In all ways, Carlos remembered, Villa 31 was a desperate slum that took a toll on adults and children. Broken families, single parents, orphans - it was a place where women outnumbered the men by more than two to one and the absence of the men was palpable. Half of the villa population was under 24 years old. And most of those young people, with little chance of success, turned to crime and drugs. Fewer than a third of them graduate from high school.

The nights were always the worst in the villa. Bad things happened in the dark. Especially without a man at home. His sister slept well, but he and his mom were restless as she always seemed to have one eye open on the door alert for any trespasser.

When he turned seven years old he helped raise money by traveling out of the villa as a helper for the cartoneros, the name for those who went out every night to scavenge cardboard, plastic, and other recyclables from the trash bags and cans along the curbsides throughout the city. These men of all ages often worked from late afternoon to two in the morning or later. It was long, dirty work, and a long walk back home with only a few pesos paid by the recycling companies for their efforts. He shouldn't have been out at that age, but it helped mamma put food on the table once a day. The man in the alley who rescued him from the fight put a stop to his work as a cartonero, and soon he was the mentor that Carlos had been missing.

Sargento Ayudante Jorge Castillo was a career soldier in the Argentine Army who was medically retired as a senior sergeant - and abandoned by the system and the population after the end of the 1982 war for the Malvinas, or as the United Kingdom called it, the Falkland Islands. He was one of 1,657 wounded in a senseless war caused by the acting President of the Argentine Junta, General Leopoldo Galtieri, for nationalistic pride and prestige - and ego. Not unlike the current conflict in Ukraine.

Castillo was a senior non-commissioned officer, a previous special forces member, and a sniper who was decorated for actions during the Battle of Mount Longdon in the East Falklands. He was one of only 21 survivors from a platoon of 46 who forced the British 3rd Commando Brigade to withdraw from the mountain during a fight in horrible winter storm conditions. It was said that their withdrawal was largely due to his shooting - and the single shot kill of the British commanding officer, Lt Colonel Sir Robert Bellingham, CGC, DSC.

Carlos was cautiously navigating the dirt alley after school several weeks after the fight when the man in the alley spoke softly from the shadow of what turned out to be his ground-floor home, "Hombre, are you interested in learning how to fight?"

Startled, Carlos stopped and stared into the darkness of the man's front door and made one of those decisions that stay with you the rest of your life.

"Si señor, estoy." I am.

"Then be here tomorrow at 16:00 hours and be prepared to learn." With that, he coughed into a handkerchief and withdrew into the darkness of his home.

That encounter started three years of intense training in character, discipline, and hand-to-hand combat that served him well on the street and prepared him for more formal training later. The character and discipline training started immediately. Castillo was not easy on him and held him to high standards - in everything. He did not stand correctly, he knew no manners, and his voice was too high. He told Carlos he needed to look a person in the eye to truly see him and to know his intentions. It was relentless - for weeks nothing but strict behavioral training.

"How does this help me to fight?"

"This teaches you to be a man. It is the hardest part. Anyone can fight, but few of those ever learn to be a man. And it takes a man to know when and how to fight, and when to avoid it."

The training included meditation - something he struggled with each day as his mentor berated him for his inability to sit still or keep his eyes closed, or be silent for just five minutes. Then he began to realize that it allowed him the dedicated time, the peacefulness, to go inside his head and make things right for himself. He found that he had a better focus - he could be creative, imaginative, and analytical. It was restorative. He felt it made his brain stronger and that this new-found critical thinking gave him an edge over others who could not concentrate. His performance improved dramatically in school. He learned to speak Latin in addition to his native Italian and his adopted Spanish.

Then came the physical training. Later in his life, Carlos judged the real drill sergeants he met according to the standards and demands set by Sergeant Castillo. Some measured up, but most never did. Or at least he was never intimidated by them because he had experienced one of the best in the ex-soldier. He would sit on a mat in the corner of the empty room and tell Carlos what to do, getting up with some difficulty to correct his posture, place his hands appropriately, or play the role of sparring partner. His coughing continued at times, sometimes violently, and occasionally ending the session.

There was disciplined stretching - not just a slow cursory series of half-hearted moves one does before doing something else. This was stretching with your mind - assessing strength and weakness with a focus on healing. Then came calisthenics, agility, endurance, and strength training. All of it was exhausting work. But it came with water and extra food that Castillo provided for him so that he had the energy to train. It began to show. He found that without fighting anyone the people were looking at him differently just by what Castillo said was his manly carriage and behavior.

They trained like this for more than six months before he was introduced to self-defense and hand-to-hand combat techniques. There were no books, no tests, and no belts to win and wear. But later in life, he learned that those formalities were easily achieved from the methodical training the soldier provided and the skills Carlos developed.

This manhood training continued for nearly three years. As much as he tried Carlos could get very little personal information from his mentor. Sometimes there would be brief stories - he would speak of the ache of the loss of comrades or the absence of family. But never much, and he would not discuss his health or the ever-present coughing and the bloody spotting in the handkerchief.

Most interestingly, Castillo never said why he chose to do these things for Carlos - perhaps he saw himself in the younger boy. Perhaps he hoped to save one young man from the villa. But one day after school Carlos eagerly approached for another day of learning only to find that Castillo was no longer there, never to be seen again, with no explanation for the disappearance.

14

VIOLENT LOOKING MEN

Enough waiting. Ten days in the basement with nothing now to eat but corn meal and water. And no cigarettes! Despite his wife Alaina's protests (she was young, only 79, and argumentative) he was going out to the market for food. Or to where the market used to be. Even these Russians must have to eat something.

She walked with him part way up the cellar steps and begged him again not to go, and then forced him to take the cell phone her daughter had given them.

"Call if you need help," she said. But call who he thought, this is the only cell phone we have. But he took it anyway.

Slowly, painfully, Romi Menyuk took the last steps and lifted the two heavy wooden doors covering the entrance revealing the late afternoon winter sun, but also letting the cold winter air into the shelter. He hurried, best he could, so as not to provoke her complaints, closing the doors behind him.

When he turned around he did not recognize where he was though he was in his backyard. The two homes behind were burnt sticks, with only the chimneys standing, and the alley was strewn with the debris of those homes and vehicles and refuse of items dropped by people in a hurry.

There were bodies. Some in uniform, and some in civilian clothes. He hurried now around the house to the front yard facing Voksalna Street - a peaceful avenue in what once was a lovely housing area in Bucha, 16 miles from the capital city Kyiv. This was the first he dared come out since the terrible fighting two and a half weeks ago. The noise had been awful, but somehow the house and he and his wife survived in the cellar where they lived on their store of winter supplies.

He had not seen destruction like this since The Great War. Up and down the street as far as he could see were burnt-out vehicles of every description - cars, trucks, tanks, boxy armored vehicles (some with wheels and some tracked), and others of unknown description, all broken, melted, shattered, and rusted out. Surrounding them was the smaller detritus of war - rags, torn clothing, discarded boxes, containers, ration boxes, helmets, and other debris. And more bodies.

He moved out into the street and started towards where the market used to be. But at 94 years old it was very disorienting, made worse by the complete deconstruction and forced reimagining of his peaceful street.

He was a survivor. As a 13-year-old he and his mother were just two of thousands in Kyiv ordered by the Germans to assemble near the Viis'kove cemetery on 29 September 1941, with papers and valuables and traveling clothes to be resettled elsewhere. Instead, they were force-marched to a place called Babyn Yar to be killed. Systematically, for no reason at all but because they were Jews. He understood nothing but the terror of it all. Fathers, mothers, children, and babies, were all herded, pushed, and shouted at, the stragglers punched and beaten before being put back into the moving pack of people.

Babyn Yar was a large ravine to the west of the city. The Nazis initiated the terror of the Holocaust in this place just over 80 years ago. It became known as the "Holocaust by Bullets" as more than 33,000 Jews were led to the ravine's edges, forced to surrender what possessions they carried, stripped naked, and moved to the pit, where they stared directly into hell at the writhing bodies of those who preceded them, and were shot to fall in amongst them or shoved in and shot from above before the next wave of humanity flowed over the top of them. He and his mother were separated in the fall.

The gunfire seemed unending.

When he fell he was paralyzed with fear. He landed on warm, bloody bodies, some still moving, as bullets rained in from the edges of the pit striking people, dead and alive, all around him. He lay there, terrified, and they missed. And late that night he writhed out through the bodies and the dirt covering them all, to run the gauntlet between searching lights to reach the forest as Ensatzgruppen troopers looked for survivors. It lasted another full day. He hid in the woods, naked and filthy, until discovered later that week by Ukrainian partisans and taken away to safety.

He fought for nearly four years against the Nazi forces eventually seeing them run back to the ruins of Germany for a great reckoning. He never again saw anyone he knew from before that day.

And since then, he'd lived a good life, first in the Soviet Union and then in modern-day Ukraine. Married twice, with 6 children and more grandchildren than he could count, he was relatively healthy for his age, and rarely thought of those times. Until now.

He walked through the obstacle course haphazardly, stumbling and struggling to find his way. Perhaps he should go back...

From behind a wrecked vehicle on the sidewalk emerged two then three soldiers. At first, he thought they were SS, but no, that was then and this is now. These had to be...

"Ostanovi starika," the short one shouted gruffly in Russian for him to stop.

The tall one with the vodka bottle said, "What possible harm could this old man do, Yuri? Let him pass."

"Shut up pridurok; frisk him."

The third soldier stared vacantly from behind them - like he was somewhere else. Many uniformed bodies with white banners wrapped around their arms or legs lay stacked together in the yard by the house behind the wrecked vehicle.

The tall one set down the bottle and approached Romi casually as if to ask for a cigarette. He looked him up and down and then, startled, he reached out and grabbed the cell phone from his right hand. Romi forgot he was holding it, and said, "No - stop! That is my..." before the tall soldier back-handed him hard across the face knocking him to the ground.

The first soldier was now hovering over him too, and he ordered, "Tie his hands behind his back!" Quickly, he was rolled over onto his stomach, his stiff old arms yanked mercilessly behind his back, his hands secured with some sort of plastic material that rustled as the man leaning over him struggled to knot it tightly around his wrists.

Suddenly, he was yanked to a standing position with great pain in both shoulders and he shrieked, "Why are you doing this? I have done nothing wrong."

Ignoring him, the short bossy soldier ordered, "Take him to the others," whereupon he was grabbed by the elbow and pushed and shoved beneath a row of leafless lime trees walking next to the yellow and black curbstone then up a path and around the side of a second house whose front was full of holes as if a giant shotgun was fired against it.

In the back, he came face to face with a group of tough, violent-looking men in totally unmarked uniforms save for a black and red patch with a death's head on it. These men looked different from the soldiers on the street. The man sat at a table on the patio under a trellis covered with leafless vines, seated on a broken chair, with a meal sitting partially eaten in front of him. A small fire burned behind him in a cut-down barrel. He had the cell phone in his hands already.

"Are you an informant or a spy old man?" he said immediately in Russian.

Romi tried to stand straight and said, "Why, I am neither. I am only looking for food to take home to my wife."

"You have no use for this phone except to call in artillery strikes on our vehicles as you did to those in the street out front. Phones have been banned for weeks. I think you are a spy."

Then to another, he said, "Take him to join the others." And the man threw his phone against the wall smashing it to pieces.

And again, by the elbow, pushing and prodding, this time to a shed in the back where he was shoved roughly through the door and dropped to the dirt floor by a kick to the back of his knees. As his eyes adjusted to the dark, he had just enough time to notice the others in the room, many pairs of feet, all with hands tied behind their backs lying on the floor dead, before the shot came.

15

IL NORDEAMERICANO

Time moves so slowly with nothing to do. Carlos looked again at the clock - just 20 minutes since he laid down. He sighed and rolled over, bunching the pillow up under his head to favor an old neck injury.

Daydreaming again.

At 11 years old, he was struggling without Castillo's guidance and the purpose he gave to life. He did not forget the lessons - if anything his focus on the exercises and martial arts routines increased. But, as it was for most people in the villa, it seemed like there was no hope, no future.

Until the Church intervened in a way unimaginable.

One idle afternoon, he was involved with several other boys in stealing food for their families when the policia arrived. Unlike the other boys, Carlos did not run when they were discovered and he was alone to face them. The incident happened in the small vendor stalls right outside the Pure Heart of Mary Parish, and Father Carlos, being outside with the people, noticed the ruckus and joined the police to keep things from escalating. Father Carlos and the officers agreed that they would take him home to his mother so she could handle the situation - and so they could get the money to pay the vendors.

The apprehension, and the embarrassment of the confrontation with his mother, paled compared to what he learned when the police filled out their written report. Of course, he had no formal identification of any kind. The officer asked his mother for his full name and she said it was Carlos Francis Pombar - not Benitez. Stunned, he looked on in silence. Never before in his life had he heard that name. But then again, never in his life had he had reason to see his name spelled out in full as everyone from the Parish to others in the villa only called him Carlos.

Later that night, after his sister was asleep and they were alone, his mother told him about Il Nordeamericano, the man from the United States who she met before he was born. He learned much later that this man was at the house on Avenida 9 de Julio where she was working as a maid. She was young, the man was in distress because the master of the house, his father, had passed. And over a week, they found comfort in each other - him looking for solace from his grief and her looking for a tender escape with this intriguing man from the United States. In any case, the young Carlos only knew that after all this time the concept of a father finally had real meaning. Even if he did not expect him ever to be present in his life.

But the life-changing event occurred very soon after that revelation. The new Roman Catholic Archdiocese of Buenos Aires, Cardinal Jorge Mario Bergoglio, saw himself as a man of the people. He served the second-largest Catholic city in the world with nearly three million followers in 186 parishes and 183 missions. In addition to overseeing the many places of worship and his flock, he chose to visit the villas to bring attention to their plight and to give them hope. For years after, residents would still talk about the time they met the Cardinal, the future Pope Francis when he visited their parish in the villa. It was a moving and inspirational visit from someone so powerful.

The Cardinal was accompanied on these visits by the appropriate levels of the church from priests to parish leaders, as well as his immediate staff, maybe a local politician, a businessman or woman, or private citizens who worked with the churches or sat on the advisory council at the Buenos Aires Metropolitan Cathedral. Among the small group accompanying him to Villa 31 that day was an unofficial member of the council, a woman, widowed 12 years previously - but proud, assertive, and influential still. You could say she was regal. A striking beauty of indeterminate middle age whose poise and ability to work a room suggested some kind of ancestral nobility. She was independently wealthy, multi-lingual, and proudly served as an influential lay member of the Metropolitan Cathedral.

Carlos was assisting his namesake that day at the parish when Cardinal Bergoglio arrived. He was magnificent in his robes and accompaniment. It seemed so out of place in the villa, but his demeanor quickly put everyone at ease as the crowd grew larger in and outside the building.

As the entourage moved through the back of the parish to mingle with the people of the villa outside, Carlos noticed the woman right away. She greeted Father Carlos Lopez and introduced herself as Señora Lilia Pombar whereupon Father Carlos turned to him and announced with a smile, "It would be my pleasure to introduce you to my young assistant here today, Señor Carlos Francis Pombar. Isn't his last name a coincidence señora?!" he said. Her composure did not reflect the coincidence at all. Instead, she greeted Carlos politely, warmly, with a beautiful smile and then moved on with the Cardinal's party.

Carlos managed to say what a pleasure it was to meet her, "Es un placer conocerla señora," before she turned and followed the Cardinal.

And then he noticed that she saw a woman, his mother, standing by the door with a look of shock on her face.

Carmen Benitez had assembled her best clothes in hope of seeing the Cardinal. She had gone through the back gate of the parish grounds as she often did in the early years when she dropped Carlos off for school, and she found herself standing by the back door waiting at the front of the crowd outside. As the crowd surged forward in anticipation of the appearance of Cardinal Bergoglio she was pushed into the room. And that was when she saw her previous employer.

As was expected of a lady, Señora Pombar was gracious and kind, asking about her health and well-being, and "Won't you please come to the house to catch up?" Carmen barely remembered seeing the Cardinal at all.

Several weeks later, when Carlos came home from school his mother was waiting for him, sitting in the room at the table, again in her best clothes. After he changed into his shorts and t-shirt he joined her for something to eat before he went out to join the 'cartoneros'.

"You will not be doing that tonight," she said.

"But mamma, I don't mind, and we need the money," he said as he ate his empanadas.

"I went to see the person I used to work for on Avenida 9 de Julio today."

97

"Do you mean when you were a maid? Were they nice?"

"They were wonderful people. But she is alone. Her husband died many years ago - about a year before you were born." She looked uneasy.

Carlos put down his food and asked her if she was ok and he saw there were tears in her eyes.

But she cleared her throat and almost blurted out, "This person wants to help us, Carlos. She has offered me a job. And she wants you to live with her so that you can go to good schools and build a future for yourself. I think it is a good idea."

Shocked, he said, "No mamma, why would I leave you? I cannot."

"Carlos, listen to me. You must trust me on this." He sat back in his chair and looked at his hands as he tried to stop them from shaking.

"She is a good woman and has a big heart. Her extended family is overseas and she is alone. She can provide for you and for all of us. And there is one more thing. A very important thing..."

He looked at her not knowing what more could be said to convince him of why this was a good idea.

"You met her at the Parish. She is your abuela, my love," she said as she freely wept in front of him. "You are her grandson."

In the weeks ahead, the two women were smart about the transition. It made no sense to force the move too quickly. After all, they had all summer before school would start. And it would give both Carmen and Lilia time to make arrangements and adjust to this new reality. Carmen needed the time to slowly let go, and Lilia needed even more time to prepare to be a mother again.

She was not so foolish to think this would be easy. But she knew if she did not step in, then this child, her grandson, would have little to no chance in the world. Carmen was smart, she admitted, by naming him after the father. This was completely legal in Argentina and it would go far toward claiming dual Argentinian and United States citizenship. After all, if there was anywhere that one could have a "chance" in the world it would be in America.

Lilia took on this project in the same professional, determined way as she successfully ran so many other affairs for the church, community fundraisers, and the several women's groups of which she was a part. When Carlos arrived full-time in the fall he found himself under the wing of another style of drill sergeant. She had arranged private tutors, a private school, martial arts classes, and sporting clubs - all of which he was expected to participate in at a frenzied pace as if he was trying to catch up with someone. Luckily, Sergeant Castillo had properly prepared his mind and his body for such an ordeal.

And she was every bit of a grandmother to him as well. For the first time, he learned of family, family history, and his place in that story. Suddenly, he had a connection to his ancestors, a sense of being a part of something bigger than himself, his mamma and sister, and the villa. But he would not meet his father until much later.

One night after dinner, Abuela said, "You must respect the situation with your father for now. Meeting him will come in time when he is ready. After all, he doesn't know about you yet and it is not time to tell him or to burden him with that knowledge."

While he didn't understand, he didn't argue. What could he do about it? And what was he missing anyway? He had lived his life without a father this whole time so what would waiting longer mean? Nothing, he concluded. Life had never been better.

His mother was right, he thought. His Abuela was a good woman with a big heart. Her care and love for him were infinite. She provided a deep immersion in learning and life preparations, and ultimately she provided the opportunity that never would have come his way in Villa 31.

By the time he left for the United States to go to college, he was a citizen (after all, he was the legal son of a citizen who he learned was also a military officer; it was relatively easy for her to arrange citizenship with the embassy). He was a black belt or equivalent in Japanese Karate, Thailand Muay Thai, and Brazilian Jiu-Jitsu. He was fluent in Italian, Spanish, English, German, and Portuguese. He was schooled in everything from etiquette to transcendental meditation. And he had grown into an athletically proficient, yet unimposing figure of 5 foot 11 inches tall and 175 pounds, and as comfortable in athletic gear as he was in evening dress. And money was no longer a problem.

The problem was realized after the first semester of classes at Whittier College in downtown Los Angeles - he was overqualified and bored out of his mind. He didn't know if it was Sergeant Castillo, or if it was his distant father's example (rumored to have performed heroically in Bosnia and Serbia), but with the long war on terrorism still raging he soon found himself at the US Army recruiters office where he enlisted as a rifleman - Military Operational Specialty code 11B - and was soon after that a Ranger, Jump Qualified, HALO Qualified, a Scout Team Member, and then a graduate of the Sniper School. He excelled at every aspect of military life.

But his commander noticed his language skills (by then he spoke some Pashto and Persian after two long tours in Afghanistan) and he was involuntarily sent to the Defense Language School in Monterrey for Russian language training. And while there he was noticed and "recruited" by a senior Central Intelligence Agency officer who was also attending classes.

It was not long before interviews were arranged and he was asked if he would like to join something very special that could not be shared with him until after he agreed to join them. The interviews were not a challenge for him - and were conducted in multiple languages that highlighted his mastery of them. He also demonstrated a surprising level of education and intelligence for a young Army soldier. The Agency determined he was a perfect candidate.

Without any of the red tape normally associated with the military and the assignment system, Carlos found himself out of the Army, employed by the CIA, and en route to an undisclosed location in Virginia for processing and training. He met his contact at the Chain Bridge Road at Armstrong Street bus station in Fairfax, in front of public locker number 371 at noon, whereupon they whisked him away to weeks of training, followed by missions with ever-increasing levels of difficulty culminating in the sled ride late last month.

He had not yet made contact with his father. But he did tell his...

A sharp rap on the door brought him back. Up and moving to the door (with more caution than warranted in the embassy) he stopped short, and asked loudly, "Yes?"

"Sir, it is Lieutenant Abrahms. I was asked to inform you that you are invited to attend the evening situation briefing in an hour and a half in the main conference room."

"Got it. I'll be there. Thank you."

Just another meeting. This is really getting old.

16

FORCE TO RECKON WITH

It was quiet in his den in the large opulent mansion in the Tsentralny District of St. Petersburg. Near the Neva River, nestled amongst the museums and old palaces and churches, were fantastic houses only occupied by extremely wealthy and influential people. He was certainly one of them.

But once again, he found himself waiting near the phone for his man in Ukraine to call him. He understood the challenges - after all, Dmitri was the man in combat, not him. But it was frustrating nonetheless.

Obviously, things were not going well. This was clear even to the public. State TV, TASS, and The Moscow Times are stating that the special military operation was having challenges - and the Ministry of Information was racing to control the messaging to the people. With his access to Ministry of Defense information he knew it to be even worse. These were desperate times.

Luckily for him, it was up to the Kremlin to handle public opinion and to explain to both the public and others in the government why the situation in Ukraine was beneficial to Russia. But it was now clear that his Wagner Group was going to be key to the way forward. If only they could pull something good out of the current stalemate in Ukraine to better our position and solidify his standing with Putin.

To date, despite numerous attempts, the efforts to close on Kyiv were stymied by fierce resistance. And also by what appeared to be terrible Russian execution and logistics. He learned today that his Wagner troops in the north were caught under the guns of Ukrainian artillery in the towns north and west of Kyiv with horrendous casualties.

The delays experienced after crossing the border in places like Ivankiv allowed the Ukrainian Ground Forces to identify avenues of advance, preposition their heavy artillery, and pre-sight on known congestion areas without detection. Two enhanced Artillery Brigades, including the 44th and 36th, moved into place to the west and north of Kyiv. Three of the four battalions in each brigade were equipped with six-inch towed artillery pieces (the Russian-manufactured 2A65 MSTA-B and the 2A36 Hyacinth-B), and one battalion was equipped with the eight-inch 2S7 Pion self-propelled, tracked howitzer. In total, each brigade had 32 guns with ranges of 18 to 25 miles.

Special Forces teams worked in pairs to disable lead elements with ATGMs, and then they would radio coordinates to the Artillery command units. The units would also use drones to identify congested areas to target, and they benefited from civilians in occupied areas calling in strikes against specific targets - giving the Russians no place to hide. As one Russian soldier told his mother on an intercepted phone call placed on Facebook Videos, it was "raining artillery shells."

And worse - not one of the missions to decapitate the Ukrainian leadership had succeeded.

Meanwhile, the Russian Army is rumored to be contemplating a complete withdrawal from the north for a strategic repositioning to the east in support of the now "primary effort" to free the breakaway provinces of Donetsk and Luhansk. He was also glad he didn't have to sell the news to the public that the move against Kyiv was *not* the primary purpose of the special military operation.

The phone rang and he picked it up immediately.

"Dimitri here." There were explosions and sporadic gunfire in the background.

"Tell me what is happening."

The man drew a deep breath, then, "We must be quick. We believe the khokhols are using cell phone intercepts to locate targets of opportunity. I would not make this call on a cell phone except the encrypted radiophones do not work at all - they haven't fucking worked since we crossed the border."

"Fine. What is your situation?"

"It is not good. While we made initial advances as far south as Hostomel, our units were eventually stopped along the way, some nearly wiped out by Ukrainian artillery fire - guided no doubt by spies and informants reporting on our positions to Ukrainian authorities, even after we enacted extremely strict restrictions and severe punishments for those involved. The 141st Motorized Regiment of the Kadyrovites was nearly destroyed at Hostomel. It is rumored that the commanding general was killed. We did learn that they launched a mission against Zelenskiy before that but have heard nothing from them since. It seems our Chechen friends' best skills are limited to posting videos on social media and terrorizing the local population."

"But what of our attempts? Nothing?"

"Counting the Chechens, there have been nearly a dozen attempts to get him. The lack of reporting from those units does not speak well for their success."

"I will tell you that the bastard actor's presence on the world stage of the nightly news confirms your assessment."

More explosions. Closer. Silence for a moment.

"We have formed a team to make a final attempt that leaves tomorrow for the capital. I have picked the men myself. Some are made up of retreating Kadyrovites."

"Let's hope they succeed. This has been very disappointing. We need this! I have to warn you that the Ministry indicated yesterday that troops there could withdraw soon. Ensure that your forces are saved for future use in any way you can. I need the Group back here to reform and recruit more soldiers."

"The troops here in Bucha and further points south have fought with bravery and extreme violence. But be warned - there are excesses. Unavoidable given our situation. But our reputation here is strong amidst the regular Army's debacle."

"Thank you, Dmitri. We have been promised more financial and logistical support going forward. We will be the force to reckon with no matter what."

"We cannot be on the phone any longer. I must move." And this time Dmitri broke the connection.

17

TREACHEROUS DAYS AHEAD

Meanwhile, the White House Situation Room was anything but calm while the exhausted members of the National Security Council and their aides awaited the arrival of the President for this rare 10pm meeting.

The Situation Room was luxurious. Located in the basement of the White House, under the West Wing, its 5,525 square feet of space was composed of several video conference rooms, intelligence teamwork centers with secure multi-level classification data access, and the spacious, mahogany-walled conference room. The long table, and black leather adjustable swivel chairs alongside as well as against the walls on either side made it comfortable to wait for any meeting to start. And they'd been waiting here for a while now.

Those members invited tonight included the Vice President, the Secretaries of State, of the Treasury, of Defense, of Energy, and Homeland Security, the Attorney General, and the US representative to the United Nations. By the noise, it seemed everyone had something to say at once.

Stephen "Skip" Walker, the CIA Deputy Director of Operations, surveyed the room. For many of the staff working in the administration, the Ukraine invasion was never seriously considered a possibility until it happened - and now Putin's War was being served up as the cause of everything that had gone wrong in the first 15 months of this administration. It was convenient to blame Putin and his aggression for our domestic problems or inability to solve them, from the rising gas prices to food shortages to higher mortgage rates. And also for the declining popularity polls for elected officials.

The President's trip to Europe - some called it bold and purposefully symbolic - reflected the crisis state of affairs in Eastern Europe, and it was a gallant attempt to show American resolve in support of a united front with allies and Ukraine in the face of Russian aggression. While the general message was deemed successful, it was diminished by a series of gaffes from a man who generally speaks poorly from a teleprompter and even worse off script. The only person in the administration who performed more pathetically at public speaking was the Vice President herself. Upstairs, the White House Staff was in damage control mode.

First, the President alarmed world leaders with the comment to the press that the US would respond in kind to rumors of the possible use of chemical weapons by the Russians in areas where the Ukraine resistance was strongest. Of course, the United States, a signatory to the United Nations International Chemical Weapons Convention treaty, has no chemical weapons. But that fact didn't dissuade the alarmists. White House spokespersons quickly explained that "...what the President *meant* to say was that if the Russians escalated to the point of using chemical or other special weapons the US sanctions would be escalated to an appropriately equivalent level of harshness."

Just a day later, after emotional visits with Ukrainian refugees at the Polish border, he told assembled members of the US Army's 82nd Airborne Division that they would, "...see the resolve of the Ukrainian people when you're there!" This electrifying, off-the-cuff comment implied to the world that the 90,000 plus US troops in Europe could be used in some undefined role in Ukraine - maybe even combat - a direct contradiction to the promise made to the American people that US troops would not fight in Ukraine. This time the White House spokesperson also blundered the clarification, stating, "There are no plans for the United States or NATO to send troops into Ukraine at this time." Equally confusing; if not now, maybe later?

The very next day during a speech outside The Royal Castle in Warsaw, the tongue-tied President added the impromptu remarks, "For God's sake, this man cannot remain in power" with regard to Putin near the end of his speech. The mere hint of embracing a regime change policy shocked people at home and around the world, forcing yet another clarification from the press secretary that the President meant "President Putin cannot be allowed to exercise power over neighbors in the region and not within Russia itself" - whatever THAT meant. The bottom line was that while the US President looked to demonstrate unity amongst the allies in their support for Ukraine, the man himself nearly undermined the cause at every turn with a series of shocking presidential gaffes.

A prominent news commentator was prompted to say that the President, "...could gaffe his way into World War III."

109

The people assembled in the Situation Room were here to consult with the jet-lagged President about his trip and to offer advice for the treacherous days ahead. But the President was surrounded by a hand-picked, left-leaning cabinet, and most of them were primarily concerned about threats to the upcoming midterm elections. They could fill meeting agendas for hours to discuss domestic social issues, the benefits of the Green New Deal, the need to suppress conservatism in Congress and on the radio, printing trillions of dollars to pay people not to work, or extol the value of WOKE training on the proper use of pronouns. But most of his extended staff (and even members of the National Security Council) had little to no experience in international affairs, let alone warfighting.

Thankfully, not everyone there was inexperienced in the violent ways of the world. Standing quietly in hushed conversations, distant from the histrionics on display elsewhere in the room, were the half dozen chiefs of the nation's defense and intelligence agencies and their senior advisors. Most prominently among them, the Chairman of the Joint Chiefs of Staff and the Director of National Intelligence, who are the senior advisors to the President on military and intelligence matters, respectively.

To his credit, the President had been listening intensively to these men and women in the months leading up to the crisis. Together, the people in this group held decades of cumulative experience in the world of warfighting and intelligence gathering and interpretation. Their professional but intense purpose was to guide the President on the way ahead, over and above the economic sanctions already in place. And that's where Skip came in. He was responsible for all CIA officers' clandestine and covert operations around the world. The Director owned the Agency, but Skip oversaw all the operations. At six feet tall and a trim 195 pounds, with an erect bearing that spoke *confident*, Skip cut the picture of a highly fit, dominating Type A male, with an unknown but threatening skill set. Blunt and highly intelligent, he avoided politics whenever possible (that was the Director's job) and spoke directly, uncomfortably for some listeners, about operational facts and data. He was not interested in opinion - public or otherwise. He aggressively kept the details of black operations very close to his chest and found that most people agreed with that approach. With more than 30 years of field service and operations leadership, few people at senior levels knew the history behind the current situation in Eastern Europe better than he did. Where he was barely tolerated by the sensitive crowd, he was a hero by reputation and action to his officers and the agency.

Despite months and years of warning from US intelligence and DoD officers, many in the administration were caught flat-footed when Putin moved over 100,000 troops to surround Ukraine on three sides: by land from the north through Belarus, from the east through the contested Donbas Region, and by sea from the previously seized Crimea.

In their defense though, even the Ukrainian President downplayed the threat right up until they crossed the border. Despite our warnings.

Thinly disguised as "war games" with Belarus, this was the largest assembly of forces and military exercises in Eastern Europe since the Cold War. All aspects of Russian warfighting components were deployed or exercised - including the

Strategic Rocket Forces. This brash and reckless display of nuclear weapons capability was met with anger and incredulity in the West - that anyone would dare rattle the atomic saber and threaten world peace with it was shocking. But altogether, in the days leading up to the invasion, many did not expect Putin to act, and when he did it was convenient to explain away the lack of foresight and action by claiming him to be insane and the situation therefore unpredictable.

He had to say though that President Biden listened to the experts, and tried to convince Zelenskiy that it was coming.

And since the Russians invaded Zelenskiy's performance has been stellar.

Putin's war of aggression was a long time coming. In November of 2013, Ukrainian President Viktor Yanukovych decided (at Putin's urging) not to sign the hugely popular political association and free trade agreement with the European Union, instead choosing to build closer ties with Russia and the Eurasian Economic Union. He did this despite the decision by the Ukrainian parliament earlier in the year to move aggressively toward the European Union. In reaction to that decision, growing protests throughout the country evolved into what became known as the Revolution of Dignity, culminating in deadly confrontations with government security forces which killed more than 100 people and inflamed the discontent further. Protesters occupied government buildings throughout the country and finally on 21 February President Yanukovych agreed to the formation of an interim government and the security forces yielded the cities to the protesters. The next day he fled Kyiv and then left the country. Soon after, three-quarters of the assembled parliament voted to remove Yanukovych from office by 308 to nothing, paving the way for a new government with a rejuvenated turn towards the West, a blatant move away from the legacy of communism, and a succession of democratically elected leaders up to and including today's President Volodymyr Zelenskiy.

But Yanukovych's exit was not without consequence. He declared the vote to remove him from office to be unconstitutional and asked Russia for assistance. Putin, in turn, declared the overthrow of Yanukovych to be an illegal coup, and the Russian government chose not to recognize the new government of Ukraine. Demonstrations of support and protest of the new government occurred throughout Ukraine, with the most objection occurring in the eastern Donbas region, namely in the oblasts of Donetsk and Luhansk - areas that have large populations of Russian-speaking peoples, many with Russian citizenship.

In the 1920s and 1930s, the General Secretary of the Communist Party of the Soviet Union, Joseph Stalin, forced the collectivization of farming on the rural peasant farmers in the wealthiest grain-producing republics. In addition to the desire to efficiently feed the people of the USSR, he did this to generate revenue through international grain sales to fund his planned industrial revolution, and to liquidate the prosperous peasant farmers.

The collectivization concepts failed miserably resulting in famines that killed more than 5 million people in the Soviet Union - but nearly 4 million of those were Ukrainians who died after Stalin purposefully deprived them of the limited available food. Known as the Holodomor, or Terror-Famine, it is still thought by many ethnic Ukrainians and others to be genocide. Subsequently, Russian citizens were encouraged to emigrate to eastern Ukraine by the Soviet government where they took the land and established pseudo-Russian satellite states in Donetsk and Luhansk that exist to this day.

Communism was not kind to the Ukrainian people.

The protests in the Donbas against the new government in Kyiv began in earnest with Russia's successful annexation of Crimea in 2014. The separatists in Donetsk and Luhansk increased the level of protest to include armed conflict with Ukrainian forces in the east. Instigated by the leadership of the Russian Federation, Russian volunteers soon augmented their ranks. Then it escalated into a more open and organized armed conflict when Russia developed a disinformation campaign and falsely claimed genocide of Russian-speaking peoples by the Ukrainian government. They also provided irregular and some regular Russian troops, along with logistical support, to further destabilize the region.

Ukraine launched the so-called Anti-Terrorist Operation against these forces in the east in April 2014. Russia, sensing the failure of the separatist movement, invaded the Donbas with regular troops in August of 2014 and escalated the fighting that has continued right up to the full invasion of Ukraine this last month.

Perhaps, Skip thought, most people were lulled to sleep by years of inconsequential fighting in the Donbas. Maybe that explained why the Western allies were slow to recognize that it was the preamble to the current fight - everyone chose to be blissfully ignorant. The combat in the east should have lent credibility to the growing threats of invasion early enough to provoke more aggressive negotiations and sanctions before the invasion itself.

But inaction prevailed and now we have the "Crisis in Ukraine" as the news networks call it, right on NATO borders where an accidental incursion by Russian or Belarus forces could draw the 30 allied nations into the fight.

He heard the *DING* of the elevator chime, and looked up to see the Deputy Director of Oval Office Operations, Kaylee Williamson, appear at the door of the Situation Room and announce, "Ladies and Gentlemen, The President of the United States."

18

WATCHING OUR EVERY MOVE

The room quieted and everyone moved to their chairs, stood upright (military at the position of attention), and in walked the President, followed by the Secretary of State Antony Blinkin, and then the White House Chief of Staff Cheryl Templeton. The President waved his hand to relax the crowd, greeted those close to him, and then took his seat at the head of the table.

Skip huffed quietly and thought to himself, "We have our work cut out for us tonight."

The President said, "Good evening," as his eyes went around the table, nodding and smiling to those with whom he made eye contact. He made some opening remarks about the European trip (without referencing the gaffes), then looked at the Director of National Intelligence, Ron Minard, and said, "Let's get started."

Director Minard said, "Sir, we have a briefing to bring us up to speed on the conflict in Ukraine. You remember Andy." Analyst Andriy "Andy" Bondarenko moved to the podium.

The 54-year-old DIA analyst, slightly under 5 foot 8 inches tall, heavyset, non-athletic, with thick glasses and a slight accent, was born a US citizen to Ukrainian immigrants who fled the Eastern Block in the 1960s. A smart man, with PhDs in International Affairs and Russian History and Government, he stated, "Good evening Mr. President."

"Hi, Andy - been seeing too much of you lately. What have you got for us today?"

"Sir, as Director Minard said, I'll start with the current military situation in and around Ukraine, then I will discuss President Putin and his regime - what we think is his present state of mind and the weaknesses and potential exploitations of his advisors, and I'll end with a look at the Russian population concerning the latest polls regarding their support of the regime." All of this, of course, was listed on the first PowerPoint chart displayed on the many monitors around the room.

"Let's not overuse the word *regime* today if you don't mind. Rather sensitive to that." Nobody laughed. Skip hoped nobody noticed the frown on his face.

"Yessir." And with that, Andy got on with the briefing.

For Skip, the briefing droned on without any new content. After all, most of it had come from his team or his counterpart's team over in the Defense Intelligence Agency, Deputy Director Susan Black. Not surprisingly, Skip and Susan shared information frequently - he was on the Sectera vIPer Universal Secure Phone more often with her than he was with the Director of the CIA herself, Ms. Angela Harkin.

Susan's and Skip's primary goal in this meeting was to ensure CIA Director Harkin and the Director of the Defense Intelligence Agency (DIA), Lt General Scott Barry, emphasized the agreed-to conclusions and supporting evidence presented

117

to the President. Sometimes, these briefings can be overwhelming, leaving the principal and his or her audience overwhelmed by bullshit, and accomplishing nothing in the process. Can't afford to have that happen here.

Andy presented the facts and data surrounding the deployed Russian and defending Ukrainian forces. For a country supposedly wary of the West and fearful of its existence it was revealing to note that fully 70-75% of Russian combat power was engaged in the conflict - maybe up to 200,000 soldiers, with over 2,800 tanks (outnumbering the Ukrainian tank numbers by three to one).

Since the fall of the Soviet Union, the Russian Armed Forces enjoyed the privilege of peace to draw down, design new equipment and technology, and rebuild without a legitimate fear of attack. This decades-long truth highlights the absurd notion posed by Putin that Russia is at risk. If so, why wasn't Russia overrun by the Western hoards during all that time they were so weak?

Unfortunately, too many people continued to mistakenly model and assess Russian capability to be world-class. This may have been due to old Cold War habits, or a reflection of dollar chasing by the many-faced complexities of the congressional-military-industrial complex. For decades, these high assessments of Russian power presumed that good equipment would perform in accordance with the specifications, that the crews or troops using that equipment would be well-trained, and that adequate logistics would provide the needed petroleum, oil, and lubricant products, along with ammunition, water, food, and other gear to keep the combatants fighting.

Logistics, always under-sung by the ignorant, was key to success no matter the technical capability fielded. And in this case, the Russian forces have failed miserably. They never were Supermen, Skip thought - and they're proving they aren't logisticians either.

Andy continued, "Perhaps the biggest factor is the individual soldier's skill and motivation to fight. As with their Soviet fathers and grandfathers, the average Russian soldier knows nothing about the plan, where they are going, who they are fighting, and most importantly in Ukraine, he does not even know why they are fighting. They - the regular soldiers and conscripts alike - found themselves involved in a war with their cousins who were supremely motivated to fight back."

Cheryl Templeton, the Chief of Staff, asked, "I thought these guys were 6 foot 5, 225 pounds of muscle, and superbly equipped - what happened?"

"The Russians are poorly motivated," Lieutenant General Scott answered, "They are demoralized by losses and abandonment, they wonder where their next meal will come from, and they are disillusioned with their leadership. There is no will to fight. And we expect that they will only continue to lose combat efficiency as casualties continue to rise past what we estimate today to be as high as 15,000."

Angela Harkin, Director of the CIA added, "Caution is warranted here though. It seems that Putin is poorly informed by his most trusted advisors concerning military capability and their performance in Ukraine. Though we see many problems for them we don't see the poor performance reducing his desire to continue the fight." Skip found himself nodding his head in agreement.

Andy advanced to the next charts, pointing out that apparently, the Ukrainians didn't believe the superpower myth. While their forces are largely equipped with Soviet-era tanks, armored vehicles, artillery, rocket launchers, aircraft, and associated weapons, their motivation to fight is enormous.

The Chairman of the Joint Chiefs, General Mark Milley, pointed out to the President that, "The will to fight - defending your home, your family, your country, is way more motivating than any political purpose or ideal. And it is a universal truth that the fight favors the defense by a good margin if they are well equipped and prepared and motivated."

Andy went on. "Though Ukrainian forces are relatively small (with a total of 200,000 active duty troops) the concentration of those forces in key defensive positions measures up well against the Russian linear advances. In addition, many of the Ukrainian forces, especially special forces, artillery, and tactical aircraft and air defense forces have been training with Western military operational teams for several years."

"And," he said, "they are joined by perhaps thousands of volunteers - including internationals. And the West is providing them with billions of dollars of superb defensive surface-to-air and anti-tank missiles and other weapons."

He continued. "Though some of their weapons are old, many tanks and armored vehicles went through refurbishment and refit since the loss of Crimea and during ongoing combat in the Donbas. Much of this was completed before the invasion, and the remaining equipment is undergoing that process now, during the war. Some equipment, like the S-300V surface-to-air missile system inherited from the Soviet Union, is superb and deadly against even newer stealth aircraft."

The Chief of Staff asked, "Do the Russians have any stealthy kinds of airplanes or helicopters?"

"No," said Andy. "They don't have any stealth aircraft operational, and helicopters do not have stealth capability. Though probably not engaged by the S-300V, they are suffering many losses to US and British MANPADs."

"What's a man pad?" she asked, quietly.

"Man Portable Air Defense system. Like the FIM-92 Stinger missile or the British Starstreak missile. Perhaps you've seen the video recently of the Russian Mil-26 helicopters being shot down and crashing in the field - those were knocked down by MANPADs."

"Oh yes, of course. On TikTok."

Without missing a beat, Andy continued, "The Ukrainian Air Force is doing well - and still in the fight. Though aging, the MiG-29 Fulcrum and Su-27 Flanker aircraft and their air-to-air missiles are very capable in the hands of well-trained pilots. Not only have the Ukrainian pilots been training with Western forces for several years they also fly nearly double the number of hours that a Russian pilot gets each year. And the Ukrainian tactical training is much more complex and combat-oriented than the Russian's."

"Like the Ghost of Kyiv," said Ms. Templeton.

"Actually, we're not entirely sure that the so-called "Ghost of Kyiv" isn't wishful thinking by some Ukrainian social media hack hoping to ignite some national pride."

"Oh."

Andy went on. "The ground forces are bold, aggressive, imaginative, and very resourceful. They took possession of inexpensive camera drones from Turkey..."

"Wait," interrupted Vice President Harris, "aren't they still trading with Russia?

"They are playing both sides," said CIA Director Harkin. "It pays well. It also puts them in a perfect spot to act as an intermediary for future peace talks. It is a wise regional power move by President Erdogan."

"The Ukrainians," Andy continued, "use the drones and commercially available satellite imagery to locate Russian forces - whether they are stuck in 40-mile-long columns or deploying to fight - and use that data to improve the effectiveness of their artillery as they engage and kill those targets in great numbers. They have also started using the US-supplied AeroVironment Switchblade drone to loiter over Russian avenues of advance, locate targets, and attack them."

The Russian forces have no place to hide, thought Skip. Sucks to be a Russian soldier right now.

"We think this aggressive fighting has resulted in a full stalemate in the attacks on Kyiv and other cities in the north - and the losses, in personnel and equipment, are forcing Putin's hand to find a suitable solution to save face by repositioning his forces to the east - to reinforce the fight in the Donbas and claim that was his goal all along."

"Mr. President," Angela Harkin again, "we cannot stress enough that we honestly believe that Ukraine can beat Russia in this fight - or similarly, that Russia can fail to win. We strongly urge that we do all we can to support them in this effort."

"But the nukes! Putin is crazy - what if he gets backed into a corner and does the unthinkable?" asked Templeton.

Ron Minard, DNI, piped right up, "Mr. President, we have coexisted, and fought proxy wars and near conflict on the open oceans and in the air for decades with nuclear weapons always in reserve but never used. We cannot dismiss them. But there is no reason to think Putin or his inner circle is so irrational to allow decisions to go nuclear in this conflict. Their recent clarification that "nuclear weapons would only be used when the nation's survival is at risk" is proof that reflects this way of thinking. It is your intelligence agencies' combined opinion that their use is highly unlikely."

President Biden nodded, then turned to Angela and asked, "So you don't think we are doing enough now?"

"No sir, that is not what I said," Harkin replied. "I only mean to emphasize that we must continue to provide Ukraine every possible chance to succeed using every type of conventional weapon, surveillance, intelligence, and logistical and humanitarian aid that doesn't escalate the situation in such a way as to cause Putin and the rest to fear for their national survival. We cannot let the fear of his nuclear forces deter us - we must do all we can short of threatening Russian territorial integrity."

"But how will his inner circle advise him when push comes to shove?"

"We have more information on that effort when this meeting convenes, Mr. President," said the CIA Director. She fully intended to talk to the President about increased actions against the inner circle surrounding Putin. But not in this audience.

Biden just looked at her as the Vice President and the Chief of Staff looked blankly at each other.

"Ok, after this meeting," he said.

The Chairman of the Joint Chiefs, General Milley, spoke up again, "Mr. President, I think they are right. Don't let anyone sell the Ukrainians short - they can win this fight." Skip couldn't tell if the President was sold or not.

Ending the pause, the DNI prodded Andy with a wave of his hand.

"Mr. President, concerning Mr. Putin, it is easy to claim he "is insane" but that does not appear to be the case. Egotistical? Yes. But crazy? No. Personality studies recently conducted by researchers at St. Benedict and St. Johns University find his particular blend of personality patterns suggests a foreign policy orientation best described as that of a *deliberative high-dominance introvert*. They also claim his personality-based strengths in a political role are his *commanding demeanor and confident assertiveness*, while his personality-based major shortcomings are identified as *uncompromising intransigence, lack of empathy and congeniality, and cognitive inflexibility*." Thank goodness, Skip thought, these things were spelled out for everyone on the charts.

"Taken together, he is arrogant, a loner, driven to success, uncompromising, not interested in what you think, and dutifully bound to concepts of greatness and achievement. But he is not insane."

"He surrounds himself with people who agree with him. For the President of the Russian Federation, it is the siloviks and the oligarchs - those wealthy people of privilege and power from the military, the intelligence organizations, and from

124

industry and business, who may or may not influence Putin. As one contemporary author recently put it, they are opportunists, the most successful of which keep their cards close to their chests, trust few, are careful not to make enemies, and operate within carefully constructed coalitions. Though few break with him (a personally dangerous thing to do) they too are egotistical and ultimately interested in *their* self-preservation."

Andy's PhD-ness and penchant for history lectures were just reaching full speed now. "Even the most powerful leaders in the Soviet Union found their power was subject to the combined will of the politburo whose withdrawal of support often led to new leadership through their consensus. After Stalin died, many thought that the obvious choice to succeed him was Lavrenty Beria, once head of the NKVD, the previous Minister of Internal Affairs, and the sitting First Deputy Chairman of the Council of Ministers. But the politburo had him killed so that Nikita Kruschev could take power. That was a *consensus decision* of the politburo - the Soviet leadership's inner circle. But Kruschev too fell from grace after the Cuban Missile Crisis and was deposed and then succeeded by his most trusted deputy, Leonid Brezhnev - again through the *consensus* of the politburo. Politics at the highest levels of the Russian government are decided behind closed doors - in seclusion and by consensus when someone chooses to act against the leader. It is usually not clear what succession plan is in place until one falls and another rises. It is uncertain how this works now in Putin's Russia without a politburo and no clear definition of a succession plan."

The DNI again, said, "Mr. President, we have identified several individuals that might lead towards a consensus to persuade Mr. Putin to change direction - or even to remove him from office. We need to act aggressively to support the former and "influence" the latter."

Ms. Templeton asked, "Mr. President, you seriously can't consider the latter suggestion - we cannot possibly be seen supporting or enacting regime change." The President winced.

DNI Minard said, "There is a distinction between taking action to remove someone and encouraging others if they are so inclined, to follow through with their plans. Concerning our role, the key there is plausible deniability."

Harkin added, "One key person on the "influence" list was Yuri Demonov, the Chief Advisor to the Russian President. He helped author the 'Putinism' political ideology and was the chief architect behind selling the Putin brand to Russia and the world. He may not have been a silovik but he certainly had more influence on Putin than anyone else. We learned recently that he has been killed."

"What?" asked Secretary of State Blinkin. "Who killed him, and on whose authority? You know we are not doing wet ops without..."

The DNI interrupted, "I'm sorry Antony, let me state that we had nothing to do with it. And we don't know who did yet. But we can confirm that he was killed right after the special military operation started."

At this point, Skip leaned forward, caught the approval from his Director, and then said, "Mr. President, as a result of his death we have taken possession of Demonov's laptop, his secure access card, and cell phone which we have been able to exploit."

Everyone in the room looked at Skip, stone-faced, wanting to know more, but nobody dared to ask how we came to possess those things.

Harkin followed up, "At this point, there are several potential killers. It could be a Ukrainian operation - though they have not indicated that they have been involved. Another choice might be the opposition - followers of Navalny; but his organization is more noise than violence and he is currently in prison. It could be a member of the inner circle who was jealous of Demonov, or some other person posturing for advancement. The trail may lead to the Wagner Group - the Paramilitary Company fighting with the Russian Army, or people associated with that organization."

The President said, "I want to hear more soon on that please Angela."

"Yessir."

Back to Analyst Bondarenko. Thankfully, Skip thought, only a few more topics.

"We cannot focus solely on the Ukraine situation - bad actors on the world stage arc flexing their muscles as they watch how the West responds. Though the United Nations voted 141-5 in support of the "Aggression Against Ukraine" resolution, there were 35 abstentions and four predictable nations voted with Russia: Belarus, Syria, North Korea, and Eritrea. Since the invasion began we have seen Russia sortie the Northern Fleet into the Atlantic prompting significant NATO naval force deployments."

"Russia also sent 10 warships of the Pacific Fleet through the Tsugaru Strait between Honshu and Hokkaido and into the Sea of Japan for the first time in decades, prompting diplomatic objections from the Japanese. China not only refuses to condemn the Russian invasion, but they also continue to significantly strengthen defenses in the South China Sea on the contested Spratley Islands, and they sailed a carrier battle group through the Taiwan Straight just 45 miles off the coast of Taiwan causing that country to raise its defense status to the level just below wartime."

"Meanwhile Kim Jong-Un announced the development of additional nuclear weapons capabilities and test-launched a true intercontinental ballistic missile for the first time. And his sister has openly threatened South Korea with nuclear annihilation if even one ROK soldier crosses into the communist country."

"What is the point?" Andy asked. "It is this: we are being tested everywhere by our enemies that sense weakness. They are watching our every move against Putin."

International geopolitics is no puss game, mused Skip.

Finally, Bondarenko's focus moved to the political climate in Russia and the opinions of the Russian people.

"Recent polling shows that 80% of the Russian people support Putin since the war started. That shouldn't surprise anyone considering the polling is controlled by the Russian Ministry of Information. Unlike our political polling, the people in the Russian Federation are given no alternative answers to subject questions. But there is no denying they do support their government - but why? Because for them, life is better under Putin than at any time in history. They have food without lines, modern conveniences, good schools that lead to meaningful work, housing, and an environment that enables the average person to marry and raise a family without threat. But the sanctions are already having a punishing effect on banking, commerce, utilities, transportation, and even food supplies. The Russian citizens will be tested hard."

Skip thought what an interesting juxtaposition of motivations: on the one side nations doing all they can to assist the citizens of the invaded country of Ukraine, and on the other, imposing sanctions that cause severe pain with a potential long-term negative impact on the quality of life of a peaceful Russian population. Sucks to follow a bloody tyrant.

Bondarenko continued, "Despite the polling, many Russians are not taking the Kremlin's story of military action in Ukraine as the state-controlled press explains it. After all, many have relatives in Ukraine, and they don't associate them with threats to the nation. We are seeing many examples of protests and arrests and detention of dissidents. These are people who Putin calls, "traitors and scum" who he openly calls for elimination from Russian society - much to the pleasure of those ultra-nationalists cheering under the Red, Blue, and White flags of Russian imperialism assembled at Putin's rally in Moscow."

Bondarenko went on, showing several charts of pictures of protestors holding signs and screaming as Russian security police put others into handcuffs.

As he brought up the chart that tells the audience what he told them, the Vice President asked, "What did that sign mean there in the last photo?" Skip smiled.

"It was a protest sign, ma'am," Bondarenko said as he reversed the presentation to the picture of the protesters. The 3x5 foot white sign with red letters, held aloft on a pole by a screaming man, was written in Cyrillic: "Пу́тин – хуйло́!" It says, "*Putin Khuylo*!" Red-faced, Bandarenko tried to advance to the final chart again.

"I can see that, but what did it *mean*?"

Several in the room looked uncomfortable. But undeterred, she repeated, "I shouldn't need to remind you that I am the Vice President, and when I ask a question I expect to get an answer - what does it mean?!"

Without hesitating, Skip said, "Putin is a dickhead. Or dickwad, or just a dick - the translation is not literal. Ukrainian soccer fans dreamed it up as a chant during matches after his forces invaded Crimea in 2014. I guess it has caught on in Russia."

The Chief of Staff looked stunned. The Vice President was speechless. Skip thought maybe he had gone too far.

The President nodded, then said, "Ok then," looking at Minard, Harkin, and General Barry, "I want to see the three of you in my office in 30 minutes for a short meeting. Alone."

To everyone, he said, "I am hopeful we will find a way to persuade Mr. Putin to end this war without starting a bigger one. We cannot allow ourselves or our allies to be dragged into a shooting war with Russia. But we must do all we can to support Ukraine and democracy against this action. Now go home and get some sleep."

19

PUTIN'S CHEF

The curtains were drawn in the Oval Office and the late hour was evident not just by everyone's fatigue but also by the hushed atmosphere they experienced as they walked there through the night-shift White House. It was a small meeting - the President, Mr. Minard, Ms. Harkin, and Lt General Barry. No one else.

The President looked very tired. No, exhausted. It had been a long week filled with public appearances. His tie was unknotted, and hanging down, his top shirt button undone. His jacket hung open and loose on his frame as he took his seat behind the Resolute desk. This desk was salvaged from the British ship-of-the-line HMS Resolute and donated to President Rutherford B. Hayes in 1879. It adorned the oval office for seven presidents before Joe Biden chose it again last year.

Looking at Mr. Minard, the president said, "Ok Ron, what do we have here?"

"Mr. President, as we alluded to in the previous meeting, we have been able to exploit media taken from a deceased member of Putin's inner circle that may shed some light on things - as you know, this is Top Secret/SCI" (referring to the special compartmented information and its extreme sensitivity).

Ms. Harkin started, "Mr. President, a CIA officer in St. Petersburg came into possession of Mr. Yuri Demonov's computer, his security badge, and his cell phone..."

"And how exactly did this officer stumble across these things in St. Petersburg?" asked the President.

Mr. Minard, "You don't want to know all the details, sir. Yet."

"Oh, ok. For now."

"The officer found him dead in his study and his mistress dead in the connecting bedroom. At first, we did not know the killer (or killers). But now we do."

"In a related development, the German Federal Intelligence Service, the Bundesnachrichtendienst, has shared data from their very successful communications monitoring program in Ukraine and Russia. They have been monitoring the extensive use of cell phones in the combat zone. Between our officer's information and the data provided by the Germans, we think we can now identify the actual leader of the PMC Wagner Group and begin to understand their role in the Russian military and anticipate some of his intentions."

She continued, "The intercepted telephone calls are between a senior leader of the Wagner Group, fighting with the Russian Army near Kyiv, to a person in St. Petersburg who we have identified as Mr. Yevgeny Prigozhin. You may have heard of him before."

"Yes, I've heard of him. A petty thief turned businessman and cook or something like that. More like Russian mafia in my opinion."

"Very close, sir. He would be more like what Andy referred to as an oligarch. He became incredibly wealthy on exclusive and excessive government food services contracts for military and civil agencies - and other business dealings. He is close to another old St. Petersburg resident - Vladimir Putin himself. He is known in some circles as Putin's Chef."

"Isn't there a picture somewhere of this guy serving dinner to Putin and George W?" asked the President.

"Yessir, there is," said Director Minard. "I've also read that it was an excellent meal."

The President chuckled. Then seriously, "Go on."

Ms. Harkin continued, "Prigozhin has a criminal record. He was arrested in 1981 and sentenced to 12 years in prison for robbery, fraud, and for involving teenagers in a crime. What goes unsaid in the indictment is that the crime was prostitution. He was a small-time pimp."

"The officer that found Demonov dead also got personal information on his mistress. When we ran her name, Natal'ya Medvedevora, we discovered that she was one of those teenagers. Our Russia Desk Officer recognized Prigozhin's name in her records. As it turns out, we think Prigozhin and Medvedevora maintained a life-long relationship, despite his marriage and two grown children. We don't know why, but we think she was placed as Demonov's mistress some time ago by Prigozhin or his people. Perhaps specifically to gain insight on the inner circle for future exploitation or maybe to facilitate his murder."

"Ok," said the President, "and?"

"The transcripts we got from the Germans record him talking about the murder of Demonov and complaining to the

Wagner leader about the death of the girl." She handed him the highlighted portion of the transcript and he read silently.

The President studied the transcript, handed it back, and asked, "I suppose, but...?"

Director Minard intervened, "While there is nothing of significance to us about the girl's death, the connection to Prigozhin is important because it points to two things: first, Prigozhin took bold action to remove a key official in Putin's inner circle; second, these calls identify him almost certainly as the founder and financier of the Wagner Group, something he and Putin have denied for years. We believe he may be posturing to survive whatever becomes of this war - perhaps even be so bold as to try to succeed Putin if the opportunity arises."

"But how do we know that?" asked the President. "And what do we do with this information, if it is true?"

"Like usual, we don't know for sure yet," Angela said. "But we have high confidence that it is so and it warrants watching. We may be able to exploit this - at least in a defensive manner in our support for Ukraine."

The President kept his thoughts to himself. Then said, "Talk me through this Wagner group again; are they really a fighting force or are they more like Blackwater?"

The Director of the Defense Intelligence Agency, Lieutenant General Barry, picked up the dialogue.

"There are similarities. The Wagner Group, or PMC Wagner, is a private military company - not a mercenary organization like the press repeatedly calls them. They are present or registered as a business in over 20 countries worldwide. They have business offices in Buenos Aires, Hong Kong, and St. Petersburg."

"Mercenaries are soldiers who sign on to fight other countries' wars for profit. Neither the United Nations nor the Geneva Convention recognizes the rights of individuals to fight as mercenaries. They specifically say those individuals who choose to do so are not protected by laws of war. Though those bodies discourage participation, many countries allow their citizens to participate at their own risk. We do not prohibit it - but largely because we don't want to cause any prohibition on the use of legitimate Private Military Companies, such as Blackwater."

"Go on," said the President wearily.

"A PMC is a private company that provides armed and combat-capable services to a host nation for company profit. The members are paid individuals within that legal entity. As such, they are not mercenaries. But the line is blurry for those companies - they are supposed to be providing security and other protective services. Normally, they fight when they have to, and integrate with the national military which is the primary combatant force. However, PMC Wagner is engaged in full combat duties in the Donbas - Donetsk and Luhansk - and in Northern Ukraine, even though this role is specifically forbidden by Russian law. They are said to operate beyond the law, probably embraced by Putin to allow plausible deniability. Because of this, and the fact that international law says they are supposed to provide support and services only and not conduct combat operations, we view them as "*not quite Russian military*" and of lesser risk on our part if we interfere with their ability to fight."

He paused to see if the President fully comprehended that position.

The President asked, "You mean that if we confront them somehow we are not confronting Russia the same as if we interfered with their legal armed forces?"

"That's exactly what I mean, sir. Though it is in our best interests to keep any actions very covert or clandestine." Covert, with operators acting undercover to conceal their origins, and clandestine operations performed in secret and meant to stay secret.

The President looked at all three directors to look for any sign of disagreement. There was none.

Lt General Barry continued, "Wagner is a fighting force, composed originally of combat-proven veterans from fighting first in Libya, Syria, the Central African Republic, and Mali, and in Crimea and the Donbas in eastern Ukraine. They operate within the military structure, and benefit from a close, almost suspect, relationship with the Russian Ministry of Defence. They are organized in battalion strength, similar to the regular army structure, but with top-of-the-line weapons and support equipment. But they appear to take their real orders from someone outside the military chain of command, who we have long suspected to be Yevgeny Prigozhin."

He glanced down at his notes.

"We assess that The Wagner Group soldiers are proving to be more adept and competent than the Russian Army we are seeing in the field right now. While they are suffering from similar logistics issues as the army, they are not the ones sitting down, disobeying orders, killing their commanders, or abandoning their equipment to return to the border. They appear to have a role of "steeling the nerves" of the Russian Army itself."

"They also seem to pair frequently with the Kadyrovites - a paramilitary organization named after Akhmad-Khadzhi Kadyrov, the previous leader of Chechnya; they now serve his son Ramzan Kadyrov, the current Head of the Chechen Republic. The 141st Special Motorized Regiment is fighting in the areas west and north of Kyiv right now. They are historically involved in assassinations and anti-terror operations - they are especially known for their brutality in carrying out their orders. Wagner forces appear equally comfortable in those roles."

Director Minard wrapped things up with, "Sir, PMC Wagner has been a part of Russian military and political action around the globe for more than ten years. They are probably financed and led by Yevgeny Prigozhin, a corrupt, extremely wealthy oligarch with direct access to Putin, and he probably has ambitions of his own regardless of how this conflict turns out. He and his PMC Wagner organization are violent and capable of extreme action and unpredictable behavior in the conduct of this war in Ukraine. We suspect their direct involvement in the atrocities against military and civilians being discovered and reported by the press in areas to the west and north of Kyiv. This organization represents a threat to keeping this war under control."

The President sat back in his chair, placed his hands behind his head, and took a deep breath. Then lowering his arms and leaning forward, he said, "I am not opposed to confronting PMC Wagner wherever we find it in ways unseen by the press or the public. I desire us to keep this war regional without putting Mr. Putin in a position from which he cannot back down. No matter what it takes."

The meeting broke up soon after that.

20

RIGHT TO KILL

Skip stood in front of Director Harkin's desk. According to her executive secretary, she would be here momentarily. He always marveled at how clean her desk was - the absence of clutter of any kind spoke volumes about her intelligence and her ability to work something, finish it, and put it away - both figuratively and literally. She even kept her classified "In" and "Out" baskets on a rack by the door, out of sight.

The room itself was remarkably clean of clutter as well. A couple of family pictures behind her chair on a small set of glass shelves with a polished metal decorative frame, set beneath the picture window with views of the leafless trees of the woods on the building's south side and the gray skies overhead. Two well-stuffed leather chairs sat in front of the desk but he did not sit down.

There were some obligatory CIA Director-type national decorations and awards from various sources attached to the sidewall to the right of the desk, hung in a line over a few armless chairs, their backs snug to the wall. On the opposite side wall were three large TVs, mounted above a multi-level security classification control system situated on top of a cabinet the length of the displays above. Placed perpendicular to the media setup was a moderate-length polished wood table (matched the cabinet) with three chairs on each side and one - hers - at the end. There were the usual electrical and network connection wires, rolled up nicely, protruding from the black metal-covered wire tunnel centered along the midline of the table.

The left and right TVs were blank. The image on the center monitor was muted, while the UN Security Council awaited the start of President Zelenskiy's speech to be delivered from his Palace in Kyiv via video teleconference.

He knew this same image was on throughout the building, on desks where the occupant's role involved anything to do with Russia, Ukraine, Belarus, Chechnya, or anywhere in NATO or its immediate neighbors.

It would start precisely at 9pm EST. In 12 minutes.

Nearly every chair at and behind the rounded security council table was filled. The large video screen above and behind them showed only the UN blue map of the world, a polar azimuthally equidistant projection surrounded by two olive branches. The olive branches were a bit ironic given the circumstances of the upcoming speech.

"Hello Skip, sorry I'm later than planned," said Director Harkin as she breezed into the room carrying only her cell phone and a small handbag.

"Good evening ma'am. We still have time."

"Have you read the advanced transcript?"

"Yes, I have, but I haven't had time to get the opinions from anyone at the Ukraine desks yet."

"That's fine with me. Allows us to listen and discuss it from our gut without everyone else's input."

She sat at the head of the table and Skip took his seat to her right. They had a great working relationship - rare sometimes in Washington. And he was grateful. She offered great leadership, provided excellent cover for him and operations, and allowed him to make decisions and act on his own - as long as they maintained excellent communications. It doesn't get any better than that.

"Have you seen the video?"

"No," Skip answered, "but I have seen many satellite images and more recently a lot of cell phone pictures. It looks as bad as we've been hearing."

"I do understand how exhausted and frustrated soldiers make errors in judgment and commit crimes during a war. Not saying it is justifiable - just saying that I understand how that comes about. What I don't understand is state-sponsored criminal behavior - and the balls to openly lie and deny that it even happened. I'm sure this will be disappointing tonight."

The video screen overlooking the security council members blinked several times and changed to a blue over yellow background with the gold Ukrainian Trident displayed in an azure rectangle centered in the image. Angela reached for the remote and turned up the volume in time for Zelenskiy's image to replace the trident and to hear the UN moderator announce the guest.

Zelenskiy, his familiar lightly bearded and mustachioed face looking weary, and deadly serious, was dressed up for this occasion in an open-collared, green button-up shirt, with two pockets, and his sleeves rolled up to the elbows. If he intended to show the gravity of the situation, the actor-turned-president certainly accomplished it. After the salutations, Zelenskiy jumped right into the gruesome story, in Ukrainian, pausing dramatically between each point for the translators.

"Yesterday I returned from our city of Bucha, recently liberated from the troops of the Russian Federation.

It is difficult to find a war crime that the occupiers have not committed there.

The Russian military searched for and purposefully killed anyone who served our state.

They executed women outside the houses when approaching and simply calling someone alive.

They killed whole families - adults and children. And they tried to burn their bodies.

I am addressing you on behalf of the people who honor the memory of the deceased everyday. Everyday, in the morning.

The memory of the killed civilians.

Who were shot in the back of the head or in the eye after being tortured. Who were shot just on the streets.

Who were thrown into the well, so that they die there in suffering.

Who were killed in apartments, houses, blown up by grenades. Who were crushed by tanks in civilian cars in the middle of the road. For fun.

Whose limbs were cut off, whose throat was cut. Who were raped and killed in front of their own children.

Their tongues were torn out only because they did not hear from them what they wanted to hear.

How is this different from what the ISIS terrorists were doing in the occupied territory?

Except that it is done by a permanent member of the United Nations Security Council."

Skip looked up from the English transcript and glanced briefly at Angela - she was listening intently already aware of the message from the translation but focused on the man's every word as if to wrangle the truth from the tenor of his voice, the look on his face, and the gravitas with which he presented it all.

She felt his look, and said without looking at him, "I know he is an actor, but I see great sincerity and burden in his presentation. It is like even he cannot believe what they've found there and he seems to wonder aloud whether he will be heard and if anyone will do anything about it."

He nodded his head in agreement as Zelenskiy continued.

"...the massacre in our city of Bucha is just one, unfortunately, of many examples of what the occupiers have been doing on our land for 41 days.

And there are many other such places that the world has yet to find out the full truth of: Mariupol, Kharkiv, Chernihiv, Okhtyrka, Borodyanka and dozens of other Ukrainian communities, each of which is like Bucha.

I know, and you know very well, what the representatives of Russia will say in response to the accusations of these crimes. They have said this many times. The most illustrative was after the downing of a Malaysian Boeing over Donbas by Russian forces with Russian weapons. Or during the war in Syria.

They will blame everyone, just to justify themselves. They will say that there are different versions, and which of them is true is allegedly impossible to establish yet. They will even say that the bodies of those killed were allegedly "planted", and all the videos are staged.

But. Now is the year 2022. There is conclusive evidence. There are satellite images. It is possible to conduct a full, transparent investigation.

That is what we are interested in."

Angela said, "The President will call for complete, international investigations and will be pushing our media to go to Ukraine and report on what they see. The Russian ambassador, meanwhile, has already said that everything Zelenskiy says is a lie - that all the evidence they provide are scenes that the Ukrainian war machine created. The Russians claim that the Ukrainians are killing their own people for propaganda purposes."

Skip said, "Those kinds of crazy claims have been part of the dialogue from Russia since they seized Crimea, shot down Malaysian Airlines Flight 17, and invaded the Donbas. It always amazes me that those kinds of distortions of truth can go on for so long without consequence."

"Some people, some countries, buy into it. The Russian people certainly have. And it feeds the guilt complex of other nations who do similar things. They hide together in plain sight, behind their lies and misinformation and atrocities."

"...they abducted more than two thousand children. Simply abducted thousands of children. And continues to do so. Russia wants to turn Ukrainians into silent slaves.

The Russian militaries are openly looting the cities and villages they have captured. This is looting of the highest scale. They steal everything from food to gold earrings they just rip out with blood.

We are dealing with a state that turns the right of veto in the UN Security Council into a right to kill."

Skip said, "It appears that the Russians are transporting all the kids - be they orphaned by the war, or living in orphanages - back to Russia under the guise of humanitarian aid."

"Nothing gets otherwise docile, non-committed people energized faster than the abuse of children. And the rampant looting simply reflects the gross lack of professionalism of these forces."

"If this continues, the finale will be that each state will rely only on the power of arms to ensure its security, not on international law, not on international institutions.

Then, the UN can simply be dissolved."

Angela said, "Here comes the part that is most interesting to me. Will the Security Council react at all?"

"It'll be a cold day in hell before those 193 ambassadors change anything about the charter," Skip said, "let alone a complete redesign of the Security Council itself. No matter how well deserved."

"And now we need decisions from the Security Council. For peace in Ukraine. If you do not know how to adopt this decision, you can do two things.

Remove Russia as an aggressor and a source of war from blocking decisions about its own aggression, its own war. And then do everything that can establish peace.

Or show how you can reformat and really work for peace.

Or if your current format is unalterable and there is simply no way out, then the only option would be to dissolve yourself altogether."

"Sometimes, I think I would vote for dissolve yourself altogether," Skip said.

Angela didn't even react. "He is winding down now; let's look at the video." She shut off the feed, pulled up the file, opened it, and clicked on the play arrow.

The video's few minutes offered nothing the two of them hadn't seen before in horrific places in many conflicts. Suffering and violent death are the same the world over. It respects no language, no culture, no society, no race, nobody. The line between peace and violence is too easily crossed by those who choose to do so.

The two of them shared the hope that fewer would die if they did their jobs well. It kept them sane in such a challenging occupation.

Labeled sequentially with city names (Motyzhn, Irpin, Dymerka, Mariupol, and finishing with Bucha) all the images were consistent with the stories they'd heard from numerous sources.

A man's body, sitting upright in a cistern covered to his waist in bloody water. Four bodies covered in sand. Eight people lying dead in a courtyard - still in the grotesque positions in which they fell. Two of them with hands tied behind their backs with plastic of some kind. An elderly couple shot dead outside the back door of a house. A dead man lying on the curb with his bicycle overturned next to him. Dead bodies, burned.

A family of four or five, including a small naked child, bound hands, shot dead, and tossed against the wall in the corner of a basement. Angela paused the video at this scene and stared silently at it. Blue and white striped underwear, a cream sweater, dark pants; normal clothes worn by a normal family.

Then the worst in Bucha. Dead in the streets, hands tied and murdered, burned bodies (one with pink fingernail polish brightly contrasting with the char), an old man dead, again with hands bound behind his back. A dozen bodies or more in black plastic bags in a ditch.

Angela closed the video and shut down the media system. Skip said nothing.

"Interesting to note that none of those bodies shown had large wounds indicative of artillery or tank rounds - large shrapnel. They all seemed to be gunshot wounds given that you couldn't always see the wound itself and there was no gross disfiguration like you would see with heavy weapons."

Skip ventured, "That does seem to point to murder, versus noncombatants killed in the crossfire or during some kind of bombardment."

"So, is this sanctioned Russian cruelty, directed from the highest levels? Or is this, in its basest form, just poor discipline from hungry, desperate, angry, abandoned troops? Or something else?"

He said, "The Ukrainians haven't split it out. They are calling out atrocities against civilians. I suspect it is everything you said and more."

"Our friends PMC Wagner?"

"And their partners, the Kadyrovites."

"I think we need to find more compelling evidence," she said. "Can you talk to your counterparts in the Ukraine intelligence agencies and see if they will share more information? If that doesn't work, will they take visitors - you know as well as I do that sometimes a face-to-face meeting is more productive."

"I'll make the calls, and I will set that up. I know just the person to send."

21

PAPAL CONDEMNATION

Every morning Angela received the CIA Daily Update compiled by the various senior leaders of the divisions within the Agency. The desk experts, and the analysts, scoured their sources, the regional chiefs reviewed and elevated noteworthy subjects, and the division chiefs and their respective staffs compiled the electronic drop box for executive review. In reverse order, her meetings with the President and other Cabinet members would signal interest in certain areas, which in turn would flow back to the desk experts for added emphasis. The drop box included sometimes dozens of folders for review - both Word documents and videos.

She clicked on the third video file in the Ukraine folder. Pope Francis, formerly the Argentine Cardinal Jorge Mario Bergoglio, stood wearily before the podium to address the General Audience assembled in the great hall. Hundreds sat on the chairs before the papal platform, and a thousand more sat in the raised seats behind them. Conspicuously, a group of children and a few adults sat in folding chairs to the left of the stage, near the Pontifical Swiss Guard in his blue, red, orange, and yellow dress uniform who stood alert with a halberd in hand just in front of the first step.

Dressed splendidly in his white robes, with the silver chain and pectoral cross hanging in front and his mitre on the back of his head, Pope France was visibly pained. With his wire-framed glasses perched forward on his nose, he read his remarks from a paper handed to him by his attendant.

"The recent news about the war in Ukraine, instead of bringing relief and hope, attests instead to new atrocities, such as the Bucha massacre; increasingly horrific acts of cruelty, carried out even against defenseless civilians, women, and children. These are victims whose innocent blood cries out to heaven and implores: End this War! Silence the Weapons! Stop sowing death and destruction!"

And then he led the congregation in prayer.

After which that same attendant handed him a cloth-wrapped bundle, which when unfolded revealed a tarnished, dirty, Ukrainian flag. It was marked up by hand with a Cossack Cross in the center surrounded by the words "Cossack Hundreds of the Maidan."

She knew that was a reference to those killed in the 2014 Maidan Revolution - considered heroes of modern Ukraine.

But the flag he held there represented the sadness of war - and the victims of the atrocities in the city of Bucha, just 14 miles northwest of Kyiv. And you could see the sadness in the Pope's eyes as he unfurled it and partially held it aloft for the crowd to see.

In a quiet voice, he said, "This flag comes from the war, specifically from the tormented city of Bucha. And there are a few Ukrainian people here who are accompanying us. Let us greet them and pray together with them."

The few adults and the children sitting in the folding chairs near the colorfully dressed guard got up, mounted the 10 grand marble stairs, and walked across the large platform to the Pope at the podium where they all gathered around him and prayed together.

Angela knew that most in the East would view this as another Western propaganda ploy, particularly in Russia where the Russian Orthodox Church dominates religious affiliation. The Patriarch and the Pope may have signed a Joint Declaration at a meeting in Cuba in 2016, but neither they nor the two churches were particularly close.

Within Ukraine, where only 1% of the total population identifies as Roman Catholic, Protestant, or Evangelical Christian, she didn't expect his remarks to be particularly influential. But, the Pope's remarks would appear to be an independent validation of their claims of Russian atrocities being uncovered in dozens of cities as their forces withdraw from around Kyiv and other places.

Though the Pope openly opposes the war and has been especially critical of the political forces on each side of the fight, these remarks by themselves will be seen as support of the Ukrainian cause. And in Russia, the leadership almost certainly will think the remarks are another jab at Putin and his dirty little war.

The accompanying remarks in the Word file added three additional observations the analyst thought worthy of consideration:

1. The Pope was recorded later that day as saying: "We are witnessing the impotency of the United Nations over the inaction of Ukraine;" and saying, "...a 'potentate' was fomenting conflict for national interests."

So, she thought, his thoughts on the UN seem to echo those of Zelenskiy. And the Pope called Putin a potentate. Interesting. To be certain, she typed that in the search box: "a monarch or ruler, especially an autocratic one."

An autocratic ruler. Solid word choice. She knew the Pope to be very particular, choosing his words carefully in both spoken and written communications. He knew that his words carried weight and one could presume that the words he chose had a purpose. Papal condemnation perhaps.

2. The Pope had plans to travel to Kyiv but the trip has been canceled. The Vatican quoted the Pope as saying he, "...planned to go to Kyiv but he would do so only if he could travel to Moscow as well and that was *denied at the highest levels*." EMPHASIS ADDED by the analyst.

Hmm, she thought. Was that a slap in the face to Putin, an implicit criticism? Another jab at the potentate. That too probably won't go over well in the private offices of the Kremlin.

3. The Il Nuncio to Belarus, Cardinal Eryk Jablonovski, had been in Poland visiting relatives. Upon return to Belarus, he was denied reentry to that country as the Catholic churches in Belarus were "...showing radical anti-government

behaviors." The Belarus State Security Committee determined that their Church members and some priests were caught participating in citizen protests against Russia's special military operation in Ukraine in the streets of Minsk and other cities. It is unclear where the Nuncio will go as he works to regain access to his priests in Belarus.

Does this represent an emergence of anti-Catholic thought in Belarus - and given the puppet nature of President Lukashenko's relationship with Putin does it spell similar thought in the Kremlin? One has to wonder.

Especially when you consider the role of Patriarch Kirill with his support for the invasion and his influence on Putin, she thought.

Kirill claimed all along that unidentified forces were trying to turn Ukrainians from being part of the holy united Rus into a state hostile to this Rus, hostile to Russia. He also insists that Russia has never attacked anyone. Right, she thought sarcastically.

Angela remembered that Pope Francis' response to these and other comments regarding the war was to caution Kirill against becoming Putin's altar boy.

Will need to keep an eye on this.

She sat for a moment. Something about this write-up caused her concern and she couldn't quite put a finger on it. Reaching for the mouse, she closed the file and moved on to the next folder. There were many folders left to go before the mid-morning meetings with her deputies.

22

WAYS TO PUNISH WAGNER

C arlos settled himself in the comfortable chair at 7:50pm, Eastern European Standard Time, in the Embassy Conference Room in Helsinki and watched the techie finish setting up the secure, encrypted video call with Langley. It was her job to ensure the call went smoothly so that the principal could concentrate on the subject matter.

Finally, a call with Deputy Director Walker.

The room had one large screen and a couple of cameras at the far end of the table - one wide angle and the other a steerable zoom camera (pointed directly at him today).

Electronic clocks (red-dot lights on black backgrounds, nicely framed) were arranged on the walls with local Helsinki time in the center and Washington DC and others to the left, and Moscow and other eastern cities to the right. Luckily, his need for perfection was satisfied as he was seated facing north.

There were microphones embedded in little coaster-like fixtures arranged in specific places around the table. The chairs were leather, and comfortable. It was nearly 1pm in DC. The live feed came up on the screen showing nothing but the Seal of the CIA on a plaque behind the opposite head of the table where he expected deputy director Walker to sit any time now.

Which is exactly what happened next.

"Helsinki, how is the feed? I show system SECURE TS/SCI here." Skip's booming voice.

The techie leaned over the table and replied into the nearest microphone, "Video and sound are good. The system here is also SECURE TS/SCI. I'll be leaving the room momentarily." With that, she turned, nodded her head to Carlos and went through the door behind him, and closed it securely.

"Carlos, good to see you. Sorry, I haven't been in touch much. I trust you are comfortable there?"

"Yessir. Anxious to leave though."

"I'm sure you are. Hope your bags are packed."

"Yessir."

"Ok, let me bring you up to speed on what we found from the items you left at the train station. It took only five days to get full access to the computer; less than that to enter his iPhone via the backdoor. His Contacts List reads like a Who's Who at the Kremlin. Everyone, except some key people's direct lincs. As you would expect. But this by itself justified the trip as it gives all of our listening teams access to current phone numbers as opposed to fishing uncountable phones and calls."

Carlos was relieved to hear the words "justified the trip."

"Best we could tell from the time stamp of events on both devices was that they arrived at the palace only four hours before you did. He had his laptop open almost immediately and locked it up about 45 minutes later. Based on the way you found him and the woman, the analysts presume the hit team (and we think it was only two people) were there and were in place well before the Demonov party arrived. They were pre-positioned in the bedroom assuming that both people would go there right away, then when that didn't happen they killed her quietly and waited for the right time to kill him. Then left. That's the story anyway. Doesn't matter much - except for the guards. There has been no message traffic about any of them. So the team thinks they were turned by whatever party did the hit. More on that later."

Skip continued, "The Bundesnachrichtendienst shared transcripts with us of phone calls they intercepted between a PMC Wagner leader in the field northwest of Kyiv, named Dimitri Utkin, and his boss back in St. Petersburg."

"I know of him. I got a look at him through a Lapua rifle scope in Niger when I was there. You can find stuff online about him and his Wagner fighters."

"Too bad you didn't shoot him."

"Funny. The EOD Captain I was supporting there said the same thing. Sorry, ROE."

Carlos had two military encounters with Wagner before his Agency adventure in Africa. The first time in Niger and his last run-in with Wagner in a US Army uniform was at the Battle of Khasham, in Syria. Just before his assignment to Monterrey and the Language School he was serving as a sniper in elements of the 75th Ranger Regiment, alongside some Special Forces and US Marines, and allied with the Syrian Democratic Forces in the fight against ISIS. They held fortifications in an old Conoco oil facility on the east banks of the Euphrates River. Forces of the Syrian military, supported by the radical

Shia militia group Liwa Fatemiyoun, and augmented by up to 100 PMC Wagner soldiers, moved on their position with tanks, APCs, and smaller vehicles. The US force commander warned the attackers not to advance, but they shelled the complex and did not heed the warning to stop. As the lead Syrian vehicle crossed the bridge, Carlos took one very long shot with the M82A1 .50 caliber Anti-Material Rifle destroying the radiator and engine block and halting the column in place.

From there, US air power responded with overwhelming force provided by AC-130 gunships, F-22s, F-15Es, MQ-9 armed drones, and AH-64 attack helicopters, and capped it all off with a B-52. It was an amazing display. Nearly all of the vehicles and more than 100 opposing forces were killed. Though the number of Wagner fighters killed was not confirmed, the press called it "the first deadly clash between citizens of Russia and the United States since the Cold War." So all-in-all, Carlos thought he had a long history with PMC Wagner.

"Wagner forces, like so many in the Russian Army, have been using open cell phone lines to communicate. Apparently, nobody bothered to check their keys or whatever the Russians call it for using their secure radiophones. This tool Utkin was talking to his boss, and the boss was using burner phones so nobody could ID him until he slipped one day during a brief discussion about the Demonov murder. Turns out not only did we learn that PMC Wagner almost certainly did the hit, but this mystery man complained on the phone to Utkin about killing the woman - like he knew her. An analyst saw that and ran the data on Natal'ya and sure enough she has a history with Yevgeny Prigozhin. Ex-Con, Restauranteur, buddies with Putin, huge government food contracts, immense wealth, and an oligarch is born. And *bingo* the head of PMC Wagner gets outed."

"Interesting," said Carlos. "Question: do you have anything else on what happened to the security detail?"

"The analysts theorize that Wagner turned them. That's the only thing that explains no sign of them and no news of anything happening to them from our few friends in the FSB. Perhaps they are in a lake somewhere. But it seems money talks louder than loyalty for many in Russia these days."

"But more insightful is we think that Prigozhin has an agenda of his own after years of hiding in the shadows. The consensus is that he is exercising bold power by flexing Wagner's attributes amongst the Ministry of Defence. He can only be acting this way with Putin's blessing - Wagner has long given Putin the ability to reach out and make things happen while retaining some level of deniability. But you can't tell who is loyal to who in the Kremlin these days. History shows that people there offer support until they don't, then *WHAM* it is time for a new guy. Could Prigozhin be solely supporting Putin, or posturing to help place a new guy, or even working to be able to place himself? Only conjecture but worth watching."

Skip took a long drink from the water bottle he'd been crunching in his hands and then said, "You saw Zelenskiy speaking to the UN about atrocities. Not all are verified but they are finding many examples of atrocities in the occupied areas - by civilian reports and pictures, by satellite imagery, and by Ukrainian Ground Forces personnel as they reoccupy territory. Long story short - the Ukrainians lay the blame on the Russian Army, PMC Wagner, and the 141st Special Motorized Regiment of the Kadyrovites."

"Ah, I have personal experience with the 141st, also in Syria. They're a particularly nasty bunch."

"There have been at least six and as many as a dozen assassination attempts on Zelenskiy. Kudos to the Ukrainian security teams. Helps that some of those friends in the FSB made some phone calls too. But the place is hardly secure. And the SecState and SecDef are secretly going there to meet with him in two days."

"Do I sense a role in this meeting?"

"Yes. The G6 will be there in Helsinki tomorrow midday to fly you to Lviv via a round-about flight plan through Germany and Poland. Get your list of gear to the team there in Helsinki tonight and they will make arrangements. Dress up a little. You are traveling with some VIPs once you join them on the train from Lviv to Kyiv."

He continued, "You will accompany the Secretaries and their security teams to the meeting with Zelenskiy. You will be on the roster of the SecDef security team. I want you to meet personally with the Ukrainian Deputy Directors of the SBU and ZSRU after the meeting. You will be taken to them. You are to learn all you can about PMC Wagner and their role in the war to date. Prigozhin is a loose cannon and more worrisome than Putin's and Lavrov's blustering lies. We are looking for ways to punish Wagner in future endeavors - wherever we find them."

"I'll get online today and see what the Russia Desk Analyst can provide."

"Great. Now, get to work."

23

UNINTENTIONAL LONER

It was cold in this place, but warmer than the office space he occupied with the other officers of the unit. And more private. Captain Luka Pavloff sat all bundled up in warm winter gear, hunched over the broad desk he had assembled here, away from prying eyes and from the constant negativity of a unit in disrepair.

His refuge was in the small office outside the entrance to Nuclear Weapons Storage Bunker number 1B, sitting just outside the steel blast door enclosing precisely 40 RDS-9U tactical nuclear weapons in a climate-controlled concrete vault. Close enough to the administrative building and the barracks to be available if he was needed, but far enough away to prevent others from casually wandering out here to disturb him. Particularly in the ice and snow of March.

Belgorod-22 is one of the remaining 48 nuclear weapons secure storage facilities in Russia - one of 12 west of the Ural Mountains. As recently as 1991 there were 507 such sites. Like all National Level Sites, this one is under the direct control of the secretive 12th Main Directorate (GU MO) of the Ministry of

Defense, a partnership of sorts with the Strategic Rocket Forces (RSVN) of the Russian Federation.

This site was special for several reasons (not the least being it was just 12 miles from the Ukrainian border). First, even though it is a National Level Storage Site it does not contain any strategic nuclear weapons. Those are located close to missile bases and their vast missile silo arrangements, or the ports that are home to the ballistic missile submarines of the Military Maritime Fleet. The weapons stored here are non-strategic - tactical nuclear weapons - of lower yield than the big bombs and meant for Russian Army delivery systems like artillery and surface-to-surface missiles.

Second, this site was no longer active. It still housed the bombs and was still home to hundreds of Army security guards, civil engineering and administrative support personnel, and his small engineering component. But most of the weapons were obsolete, the last version of the RDS-9 being built in 1992 and, in most circumstances, no longer considered a valid battlefield option.

Except for these, he thought, as he took his eyes off the half dozen RDS-9U technical manuals in front of him and adjusted the electric heater at his feet.

The third reason Luka knew this site to be special was unacknowledged and largely unknown (or at least no one cared): it was rundown and poorly maintained, a disgrace really, and staffed by incompetents and drunks.

Except for himself, of course.

His career started brilliantly - an honor graduate from the prestigious Peter the Great Military Academy of the Strategic Missile Forces in Balashikha, Moscow Oblast, with five years of study culminating in a BA in Physics and a Specialists Degree in Nuclear Engineering. Upon graduation, he was commissioned as a Junior Lieutenant and then immediately enrolled in the resident Masters Courses program, spending two and a half more years in the school's Nuclear Weapons Studies program and successfully composing and defending his thesis regarding the *Design Modifications and Maintenance Requirement of Aging Nuclear Weapons*, whereupon he received his Master Qualification in Nuclear Weapons.

He got into the Academy at 17 years old only through his academic credentials. Tested at 15, he was categorized as Highly Gifted with an IQ of 149. The school administrators championed this as if they made it happen. He only knew that learning came easy - and performing academically was his salvation from the bad people.

Short, underweight, scrawny, with pale skin and dark eyes and hair, he thought he looked more like a cadaver in the mirror than alive. And always the glasses - with ever-thickening lenses. His clothes hung on him - and to this day he looks lost in a uniform. Throughout his life this view of physical inferiority was reinforced by others - on the playground, in his neighborhood, and later in physical fitness classes, and basic combat skills training. He was physically pathetic.

And it didn't help that he was a loner. He didn't know if he was a loner because of the bad treatment or if being a loner brought on the bad treatment. As a child, the doctors called the condition Unintentional Loner Syndrome (as if anyone would choose this disposition). Growing up, he desperately wanted to socialize with others and to be accepted, but it never seemed to work out. Yes, he looked awkward, but he acted awkward as well. And it made him angry inside to be rejected by everyone. He tried to bury it, but it bothered him, a lot, and he couldn't help but think bad thoughts about himself and others. The kids made fun of him, attacking him relentlessly with jokes and ridicule, even physical pranks. Academic performance was his escape.

After nearly eight years of academia, the RSVN career development personnel decided he needed an operational assignment. So he completed UR-100N intercontinental ballistic missile command and control training and was posted to the 13th Red Banner Rocket Division at Yasny, Orenburg Oblast as a new Captain. 968 miles east-southeast of Moscow. The town was incorporated in 1961 in the middle of nowhere to support the missile base - it was of the Soviet design style complete with a lack of comforts and entertainment. It was hell.

He was good at his job, though. Nobody else in the unit knew more about the weapon or the command and control system - or launch procedures. He quickly became the acknowledged expert in the unit.

The technical science was fascinating to him. This 88.5-foot tall, 8-foot wide, 105-ton silo-based, liquid-fueled missile could launch six Multiple-Independently targeted Reentry Vehicles, and cause them to be delivered within 1000 feet of the target located over 6,200 miles away. Each thermonuclear weapon yields 400 kilotons of explosive blast - equal to 400,000 tons of TNT. And he, along with the other junior officer in the silo, held the launch keys.

Unlike most missile crews, his life was at its best down in the launch control bunker in the missile fields on alert. He was miserable back at the squadron. He found nothing in common with his peers, and his commander was a tyrant. The man was constantly berating his officers, probably due to his unhappiness about living in that place, and Luka became a prime target.

One day, during a higher headquarters inspection, he dared correct his commander in front of the inspector and other officers about the rules surrounding the authority to launch nuclear weapons. Though he was right, it almost ended his career. In a way, it did.

Along with formal administrative punishment for insubordination, he was moved from the unit and assigned to the Belgorod-22 weapons storage site some 37 miles west of Belgorod, near the small village of Antonovka. His job was to oversee the maintenance of the facility and storage of the outdated weapons kept indefinitely at this godforsaken place. He'd been here long enough now to be passed over for promotion to Major. Disgraceful.

The complex was not impressive. It had deteriorated steadily since it was completed some 50 years ago. Like most projects subject to Soviet-era and New Russia economics there was no money for maintenance - even for something as sensitive and valuable as nuclear weapons.

Storage site? Yes. Secure storage? Hell no.

There were six underground storage bunkers buried in the woods (the area above each was clear-cut and covered in unkept grass). Each was connected by decayed concrete service roads that went around the perimeter, just inside the triple ring of electrified fencing (that rarely worked), interlaced with rusty barbed wire, and more recently added silver concertina wire at the base and top of the middle fence. Eight guard towers, complete with lights and machine guns, encircled the site, every single one viewable from the one before or after around the perimeter. They weren't always manned - staffing did not allow for that. Particularly now with the special military operation going on in Ukraine. But each tower was used at some point every day, managed through three shift changes, to ensure that each one remained operational in case the rare inspection came along.

Also inside the wires, there were two administrative buildings (one each for engineering and the combined security and support teams), and a large barracks for a full complement of Army security police. Partially filled. The command section had offices in the engineering building but they were rarely occupied. The staff tended to stay near the 12th GU MO offices in their headquarters building on the other side of the Vorskla River, southeast of Antonovka, past the small highway towards Belgorod in the east or to Kursk in the north. Which was fine with him - it allowed him to practically rule the storage site.

The bunkers themselves were simple, long rectangular holes dug two meters deep into the tundra, waterproofed, then fitted with walls and ceilings of steel-reinforced concrete (a full meter of steel and concrete on top). They were sealed by the heavy steel blast door with a large outdated combination lock securing the bunker. The locks were tested periodically to ensure they functioned. Each bunker was climate controlled, the wheezing, ancient heaters and air conditioners toiling away on the roof of each bunker in freezing winters and roasting summers. Next to the ramps which descended slightly towards each steel blast door for every bunker was the small office building he sat in now. Most were near derelict, rarely occupied by anyone since the only reason to go there was to prepare for the movement of weapons out of or into the bunker. And the only one holding any usable weapons was Bunker 1B. 40 weapons on racks - 20 on each side.

He pushed his glasses back up against his forehead and focused again on the documents. He had to be prepared for what was coming - if there was a need.

The RDS-9U (U for uluchshen, or improved) was a marvelous yet comparatively simple piece of technology. Simple compared to the thermonuclear, fusion weapons, or hydrogen bombs, carried on the ICBMs or dropped from aircraft. This was an old-school, fusion-boosted fission bomb. Relatively small, the implosion-type weapon functioned when an exquisitely timed conventional explosive surrounding the fissile material (like the Plutonium-239 in this device) is detonated, compressing the Pu-239 to critical mass, thus initiating the nuclear detonation. First theorized in the late 50s and 60s, the use of a small amount of deuterium-tritium gas mixture, injected inside the fission core, would result in a fusion reaction that increased the release of neutrons, thereby boosting the overall yield of the weapon. In practical terms, this allowed smaller-sized weapons to be more powerful than simple fission weapons, and still fit on smaller delivery vehicles like inside the nosecone of the new 9K720 Iskandr-M surface-to-surface missile.

Luka's banishment to this prison improved somewhat when some of the older RDS-9s were taken out and then returned as RDS-9U weapons with the necessary modifications to fit on the Iskandr-M missiles. These changes included revitalized electronics and electrical wiring bundles, replacement of the old radar altimeter with a newer, more reliable model, and addition of revised external frame mounted fasteners that allowed for the conical weapon case to fit and easily fasten securely on top of the missile body and into the aerodynamic nosecone. Like the proverbial hand in a glove. All the weapons engineer had to do was remove the nosecone from the missile, disconnect and extract the conventional weapon, load and connect the RDS-9U, run a systems check to ensure communications with the missile guidance system, then secure the nosecone. The job would not be possible without the right support equipment - and that is stored in the third building inside the complex, a small steel-framed aluminum storage building situated next to the administrative buildings and adjacent to the large concrete parking lot between it and Bunker 1B.

And the job of mounting those weapons to an Iskandr missile will not be possible without the ignorance of most of the unit and the cooperation of a very few.

He adjusted his glasses again and scooted up to the books. He lived for the history - the heritage - of the science, and the technical fascination he had for the engineering of the weapon.

It.

Nuke.

Bomb.

Blivet.

Device.

Gadget.

Weapon.

Use the name of your choice - they were all effective and very common descriptors. As the sole person beneath the commander with access to the bunkers and all of the technical data, with an insatiable interest in nuclear science, Luka liked to think of himself as a self-defined second Igor Kurchatov - the Russian Oppenheimer. Though he never did actually "tickle the dragon's tail" like his predecessors he did feel close to that every time he opened up one of the RDS-9U weapons for inspection. The Reaktivnyi Dvigatel Specialnyi - chisel Devyat' (Uluchshen) is an exciting thing to gaze upon with the case opened. Externally conical in shape (unhardened and with no heat shield), the interior was a series of concentric spheres, starting with the unseeable core of Pu-239 in the center, a protective shield, then covered by the cylindrical surrounds of the conventional explosives with its two dozen electrical wires connected to the trigger device (which was barometrically initiated by the radar altimeter).

At the right height, the bomb is detonated. The altitude differs for an airburst - where the resulting fireball does not touch the ground - and for a ground burst (with this delivery vehicle it will detonate before hitting the ground but altitude could be chosen that allows the fireball itself to touch the ground). The former may be desirable for troops and non-bunkered buildings across a wide area; the latter would be used to cause more serious destruction to hardened buildings and shelters. Having said that, the contact with the ground results in significantly more radioactive debris as the ground itself is disturbed and lifted into the fireball to be carried away in the wind. That may not be desirable.

When triggered, supremely timed electrical signals are sent via the electrical wire harness to the two dozen conventional charges so that they detonate simultaneously, their energy converging on the plutonium core just as the tritium-deuterium gas is injected. The small, two-pound ball of plutonium is compressed to a critical mass - the pressure needed to split atoms - and the fission chain reaction begins, releasing excess nuclei to combine with the nuclei released by the fusion of tritium and deuterium, and the explosion becomes even more powerful. The product of this reaction is energy - and lots of it - in the form of heat, radiation, and blast.

The predicted yield of the RDS-9U is 20 kilotons or the equivalent of 20,000 tons of TNT. The Little Boy bomb used at Hiroshima was only 15 kilotons. Even a tactical nuclear weapon is a significant thing.

Luka opened up the modeling tool on his standalone engineer's laptop. When he entered all the parameters using a likely target, it quickly revealed the effects. If the weapon detonated over a city (Kyiv?) at 1600 feet elevation, the 540,000-degree Fahrenheit fireball would not reach the ground. But it's diameter will be wider than a city block, radiating vaporizing heat and 20psi of overpressure on the surface below out to a full half-mile radius and causing heavy blast damage within that distance - sturdy steel and concrete buildings will be severely damaged or destroyed. Radiation is lethal - predicted to be 500 rem - out to two-thirds of a mile radius, causing most people not killed by the blast and fires to die within one month. Moderate damage occurs out to a mile and 3rd degree thermal burns will be present out beyond a mile from ground zero. Everything combustible will burn out to those distances and beyond.

People within a half mile or even a mile of the blast, unprotected and outside, would simply vaporize, reduced to basic elements like carbon.

The modeled effects, integrated with known population center data for Kyiv, predict that 104,780 people will die and 172,410 people will be injured. Worse numbers if the city was swelled by refugees.

He knows the bombs will work. Whether they should be used or not is above his pay grade. In the big scheme of things, what are two more bombs? The nuclear nations have conducted over 2,000 nuclear detonations in tests since 1945 - more than 500 of those were at or above ground level or air bursts. An under-appreciated environmental disaster.

He wondered if the effects of those tests contributed to his social disorder. Whatever.

Frankly, he was beyond caring. His brilliance was long marginalized and overlooked; beaten down, suffering from professional failure and embarrassment, a missed promotion, and years of isolation in this hell hole. More than anything he wanted to get even somehow. To show them he was better than any of them. And Yevgeny Prigozhin is providing that opportunity.

24

HEADED DOWNTOWN

It was only two hours from the Helsinki airport to Lviv in peacetime. But this afternoon, the Gulfstream G650 (known worldwide as the G6), was routed out of Finland to the southwest over the Baltic Sea, then west nearly to Denmark where they turned south into Germany and then made to land at Berlin's Brandenburg Airport. Only they didn't.

Just as it was about to touch down, the pilot advanced the power, raised the gear, changed his IFF transponder code, and picked up a previously filed flight plan as a regional airliner en route to the John Paul II International Airport in Krakow, Poland. Once there, they repeated the illusion of landing only this time on departure they left the gear and flaps down and stayed very low (under 500 feet) and slow and headed directly to Lviv's closed airport in the west of Ukraine. The IFF code on this leg showed a small aircraft operating under visual flight rules. The subterfuge turned the normally two-hour flight into a four-hour experience.

Not that the Agency jet couldn't handle the extended time - fuel capacity was a whopping 48,000 pounds, providing a trans-oceanic range of over 7,500 miles for those special assets needing to go somewhere quickly and inconspicuously.

As they approached the border, the pilot contacted Ukraine Western Air Defense Agency traffic control on VHF 131.8MHz and declared their intention to land.

"Western Traffic Control, this is Hotel Bravo - Alpha Romeo Charlie, VFR, squawking 1200, 10 miles west of Przemysl, Poland, request airspace entry and navigation direct to Lviv." The Swiss registration, especially the Romeo Charlie letters at the end of the callsign, might allow someone listening or watching to believe it was a Red Cross airplane.

Without missing a beat, Ukraine's Western Traffic Control answered, "Hotel Bravo - Alpha Romeo Charlie, cleared as requested, contact tower on 128.0." They, of course, were briefed ahead of time by the Foreign Intelligence Service of Ukraine to expect this aircraft.

Carlos watched the dirty white countryside slide by outside a lot slower than passengers in this airplane were used to seeing. Small villages, dirt roads, some two-lane roads to larger villages and towns, and lots of farmland. Pretty country - and peaceful just inside the Ukrainian border.

Lviv airport sat in the southwest sector of the city with some industrial facilities clustered in the areas west of the airport and continuing across the highway to the western perimeter of the field. The pilots maneuvered the G6 to land straight-in on runway 13, pointed to the southeast, starting the descent from their already low altitude just one mile out from touchdown.

As they descended to the runway, Carlos noted from the right side of the aircraft that the airport had suffered damage sometime in the recent past. What looked like the remains of at least several dozen MiG-29s and older MiG-23s and -27s littered the parking ramp on that side of the field. A closer look showed damaged, if not destroyed, buildings, a large hangar, and a smaller bare aluminum hangar with a yellow light flashing above the open doors. That all went by in a flash as the G6 touched down smoothly, decelerated using just about half the runway, turned off to the left, and taxied back on the parallel taxiway to a remote parking ramp at the approach end of the field. The pilots rapidly parked the jet in parking space N3, facing southeast again, as close to the buildings off the tarmac as possible as the N4 and 5 spots appeared to be severely holed.

The engines quickly shut down, the door was swung open, and the air stairs deployed. Ukrainian security police came up the stairs, did a quick check of identification (they too had heard from the Foreign Intelligence Service), then left as quickly as they'd come. Carlos picked up his bag holding a change of clothes and other basics, his weapon, several clips, and his combat knife, then started for the door where he met the US embassy station chief who came up the air stairs to greet him.

"Welcome to Lviv, Carlos, long-time no see." They vigorously shook hands. They partnered on an Op in Africa right before the station chief switched from being a field officer to take up a desk job.

"Good to see you again Leo. I trust you've been dodging incoming well while you're here."

"Not hard to do in Lviv. Except for the damage you see on the west side of the airfield, there has been little need to duck and cover here. But we do need to get moving - there is an air raid alert right now and we don't want to miss that train."

At the bottom of the jet's air stairs, the embassy SUV driver stood practically at attention as he watched the perimeter carefully waiting for them to emerge. When they began to rattle down the stairs he led the way to the vehicle.

But as Carlos reached the bottom of the stairs he heard for the first time the unmistakable *AHOOGA* sound of an alert Klaxon horn blasting away somewhere behind him. Moving quickly toward the tail of the aircraft he emerged to see the miraculously intact aluminum building with the flashing light on top. Its doors were fully opened and a Ukrainian Air Force Su-27 was just nosing its way out from within. Fully armed and in a hurry, the jet turned left towards him, navigated a short taxiway at a fairly high speed, and turned right onto the runway. Without stopping, the noise increased suddenly to a tremendous chest-pounding roar as the pilot selected afterburners, accelerated past him, took off, made a slight left turn, and disappeared to the east.

Leo reached over and grabbed Carlos by the elbow, saying loudly, "Come on Carlos, we don't have time for this - let's get headed downtown." And with that, he pulled Carlos around and directed him towards the waiting black SUV at the edge of the deserted tarmac. En route to the car, the wailing, sorrowful sound of the air raid sirens became apparent as the jet noise faded. Then, before they even got to the SUV, the G6 engines started up as the Agency crew raced to get airborne and away from the area before whatever was coming got here.

Welcome to Lviv.

25

SINGLE-SHIP BANDIT

Shawski felt fortunate to be alive. A month ago he might have said it was skills and cunning that would see him through this difficult time. But now he knows better because though you do your best to fly and fight as you train, luck plays a huge role in determining who lives and who dies.

Many friends were gone already. With 12 years of flying in the Ukrainian Air Force, it was not uncommon to hear of an aircraft accident that claimed a pilot or two a year. As awful as that was, you would mourn the loss, consider what lessons could be learned, and then go on about flying again as if nothing had happened. Like most of his contemporaries, newly-promoted Mayor (Ukrainian for the officer rank of Major) Maksim Shcherbakivskiy always thought, "Zi mnoyu ts'oho ne stanet'sya!" It won't happen to me! Always the other guy.

The first month of combat brought reality. But the first four days were particularly unsettling as the UAF lost 54 aircraft of all types - many of them fighters (and three of them were Sukhoi Su-27s like what he sat in now). Considering there were only 34 of what NATO called the "Flanker" in the inventory before the Russian Orcs came to fight, it was a loss rate that cannot be sustained. Some of those were lost on the ground, but the many air combat losses made you stop and doubt your chances.

After all, he thought, "How many hundreds of Su-27s and its derivatives do the Russian possess?" Too many to worry about today, but knowing there will be more tomorrow and the day after that and the days and weeks after that was not comforting. The Russian Air Force was huge.

After that first week, both sides sat back and licked their wounds a little. The Soviet-designed S-300 and S-400 surface-to-air missile systems were too good no matter which country was shooting them. Especially against older aircraft like his with insufficient electronic countermeasure systems. If an aircraft is detected and is within the engagement range there was little you could do but vainly hope aggressive maneuvering, dispensing old chaff (designed to fool old radars), and diving for the deck might cause the missile to lose radar contact with you. But probably not. And luck won out.

He had been sitting "five-minute cockpit alert" now for 40 minutes, waiting on a launch order. He didn't even know if there were targets out there. He, his crew chief, and the assistant crew chief had "hot-cocked" the jet earlier (an American phrase) when he came to the alert facility after a short eight-hour rest period since yesterday's missions.

Looking around the inside of the hangar, he thought, "Some alert facility," and laughed. With the Russians attacking all the UAF bases with surface-to-surface missiles, and air-to-ground missiles and bombs his 39th Tactical Aviation Brigade operating out of Ozerne Air Base in Zhytomyr Oblast frantically dispersed the surviving aircraft to other airports with limited support. Most of them (Shawski included) landed at an airport, taxied to the ramp, and shut down with no support on-site yet at all. His crew chief team drove to Lviv's Danilo Halytskyi International Airport using their personal vehicles with their tool kits loaded in the trunks. Luckily, he went to an airport that included a piece of real estate near the north end of the runway that was home to the depot maintenance facility for the older MiG-29 fighters. Most of those hadn't flown in decades. And many of those were blasted to bits when Russian weapons found them in the first days of the war. The attack also damaged the work centers and the main hangar - but left standing this small, aluminum structure with doors in front and back that was just big enough to house his Su-27P1M fighter.

Luckily, the Russian attack failed to damage the UAF stock of air-to-air missiles that were maintained here, so his aircraft could be reloaded with missiles whenever he managed to return.

The Su-27P was an old version of the Soviet air superiority fighter. But these UAF aircraft went through a thorough upgrade in 2012, including new communications, navigation, and some radar modifications that made them more compatible with NATO design specifications. Hence the P1M suffix to the Su-27. They even got a new digital, hexagonal, multi-blue-colored paint job. On the side of his jet, just aft of the huge gray radome (and on the vertical tails) was painted the large blue number 09, outlined in white. His callsign was BORT-09 - literally, "the number on the side of the aircraft." Nine just happened to be his lucky number.

"New weapons would have been a nice part of the upgrade, too," he thought. His two Vympel R-27ET and four R-73E missiles (both models had infrared heat-seeking sensors) were not bad - they were just outclassed by newer models of the same missiles carried by the Orcs on their more modern aircraft. That, and their better radars gave them a huge advantage in detecting and shooting at UAF aircraft usually before our systems could be employed. Especially when they shot the long-range autonomous self-guided radar missiles. At least he had the OLS-27 Infra-Red Search and Track (IRST) system, a bowling-ball-sized glass protuberance mounted just in front of his windscreen, and a helmet-mounted sight that allowed him to employ the R73s visually just by looking at the target and shooting it. He didn't always have to maneuver the aircraft in a close fight to point his aircraft at the enemy to use the missile.

Starshyi Maister-Serzhant Josef Chewbenko, normally in charge of the Aviation Brigade Weapons section, but in these crazy times his crew chief, came up on the intercom, "Shawski, sir, is everything alright?" The crew chief was responsible for the overall condition of the jet. Despite the hardships, his uniform was perfect - as was his aircraft.

"Other than being a little bored, I'm good," Shawski answered. "I guess we're just waiting on a target." And waiting, and waiting.

"Do you need anything?"

"No thanks chief, I'm fine. Just make sure Andrei is ready to get the back doors open as soon as that klaxon goes off." There was no way those flimsy doors could accommodate the thrust even at idle speed from these powerful Saturn AL-31F afterburning turbofan engines.

Up through engine start the aircraft was connected to a portable electrical power cart - a generator, powered by a gas engine, and connected by a long, heavy-duty cord to the aircraft. This allowed them to talk on the intercom and for Shawski to listen on the radio without depleting the aircraft battery. After the engines were started, assistant crew chief Andrei would pull that connection and close and fasten the access panel.

Shawski. His callsign was not that old. In 2018 he was first disappointed that he would not be participating in the special training exercises with the US Air Force and other NATO countries called "CLEAR SKY 2018." But that disappointment soon evaporated when he was told he'd be traveling instead (along with one other senior captain) to the famous Nellis AFB outside Las Vegas, Nevada, for a month-long opportunity to fly with the F-15 Fighter Weapons School. In the squadron that first week the Americans were having trouble pronouncing his last name. And then Friday night, in the squadron bar, the Commandant of the Fighter Weapons School (a full Colonel) announced, "Henceforth, Major Shchababo-baloff-sky, or however you say your name, will be known as Shawski!" And with that, and a round of applause and lots of yelling and laughter, they drank a toast and he was so named. The Colonel took him over to a row of pictures across one side wall of the bar and pointed out a tall individual, third from right in a lineup of the six graduates of the F-15 Fighter Weapons Instructor Course, Class 86CIN.

"He was my first F-15 squadron commander back in 1999 when I was a lieutenant and just a wingman in Alaska. Best commander I ever had. His call sign was Shawski - I want you to know how highly he was thought of by the pilots, and I want you to use that callsign with pride."

Along with the new name, Shawski was exposed to training scenarios he'd only dreamed about before. Though relegated to the back seat of the "tub" - the F-15D two-seater - the learning curve was steep. He flew exhausting, high-G, one-versus-one basic fighter maneuver sorties against another F-15, two-versus-one advanced combat maneuvers flying first in the two-ship tactical formation and again in the single adversary aircraft - called the "bandit." He didn't know it at the time, but his most valuable experiences were gained flying in the back seat of the F-15Ds assigned to the famous 64th Aggressor Squadron in the final week. There he saw bandit tactics against large-force employment scenarios comprised of multiple sets of opposing formations at all altitudes. Including at very low altitude.

Little did he know it at the time, but those wild "low and fast" single bandit scenarios were to become the method of operations against the Russians in Ukraine. Traditional combat formations went out the window in this high-threat SAM and missile environment. The UAF quickly learned that the only way to stay alive long enough to engage the enemy was to fly as low as possible, as fast as possible, and be invisible. Make it harder for the Russians to detect you by staying out of the radar detection envelope of the SAMs and down in the ground clutter to complicate the radar performance of the fighters. With luck, they thought, this would allow Ukrainian fighters to close to a range where we could employ weapons before the Russians even knew they were there.

That also meant being completely passive - no electronic emissions at all. No transponder, no communications, no radar, no radar altimeter, nothing that would reveal your presence electronically to any kind of sensor designed to pick it up.

Luckily, the large IRST located in front of the windscreen allowed passive infrared detection of aircraft out to 54 nautical miles in front of the aircraft without the use of the radar. A critical piece of this technique was broadcast control - ground-based radar sites communicating target positions in Ukrainian airspace by referencing a specific ground or geographic reference which is called the "bullseye." In this way, ground controllers could broadcast the target position by calling out the direction and distance relative to the bullseye for the UAF fighters to reference. The pilot could then "point" his aircraft at the referenced location and allow his passive IR sensors to detect the target when he got within range. The controller could also declare the airspace "weapons free," meaning that there were no friendly aircraft in the area and the targets were confirmed hostile, enabling the fighter pilot to engage freely with IR sensing weapons without fear of hitting anyone but the enemy aircraft and without his hands tied by strict rules of engagement. Like those missiles loaded on the aircraft now.

Underneath him, attached aft and beneath each engine inlet hung the long-range R-27ET IR missiles. The R-27 is big (just over 13 feet long and weighing 767 pounds) and it has four prominent trapezoidal butterfly moving control fins mounted a third of the way back that makes it look even bigger. Most importantly, it had long legs - he could shoot it at a target 28 nautical miles away in a head-on engagement. The continuous rod warhead contained 86 pounds of high explosive charge, activated by proximity or impact fuzing. He could carry semi-active radar-guided versions of the missile, but what was the point of that when the IRST and the fire-and-forget IR missiles let you maneuver without concern for a radar lock after the shot that the semi-active missiles required him to maintain?

Shawski looked left and right at the R-73E missiles on the outermost two stations of the wings, noses covered by the red, magnetized covers that protected the IR seeker mechanism. Though it had a shorter head-on 16 nautical mile range, the nine-foot-long, 232-pound highly agile IR missile was highly respected around the world. It carries a 16-pound warhead with the same type of dual fuzing as the R-27. This was the close-in missile that could be employed with the helmet-mounted sight.

Then there was the gun. The GSh-30-1 was buried in the right wing root and carried 150 rounds of high-explosive-incendiary ammunition. The single-barrel cannon fires 30mm shells at a rate of 1500 rounds per minute (25 rounds per second). At just under a pound apiece, each round carries a lot of destructive energy when it hits the target at 2900 feet per second velocity - made worse when each round blows up! He had yet to shoot the gun in combat.

It was cold in the cockpit, despite wearing several layers of clothing. He was connected to the aircraft by no less than five umbilicals (anti-G suit hose, communications cord, oxygen hose, and the smaller emergency oxygen hose connected to the high-pressure bottle fastened to the Zvezda K-36 high performance, zero-altitude, zero-speed ejection seat, and finally the cord powering the helmet-mounted sight). He was further restrained in the seat by a lap belt, two side fasteners that attach him to the survival kit in the seat pan, two leg-restraint straps that activate during ejection, and two shoulder fasteners that connect his harness to the parachute buried in the top of the seat. Almost no skin was visible as he was fully clothed in his flight suit, G suit, combat boots, winter flight jacket, combat vest (with 9mm pistol and other survival gear), and the seven-pound ZSh-5 helmet and visor, helmet mounted display, and oxygen mask that now dangled down next to his face. He favored one item of unorthodox gear to complete the ensemble: the white leather flying gloves he got as a gift from one of the Thunderbird crew chiefs he met when visiting the demonstration team at Nellis.

He was part of the jet. He loved the smell: a pervasive aroma of metal, plastic, epoxy, paint, hydraulic fluid, ozone, and other scents accumulated over the past 25 years of service.

Mission planning for air defense was not complicated: takeoff, get fast, stay low, and fly east towards the bullseye (in this case it was centered over the city of Vinnytsia nearly 110 nautical miles southwest of Kyiv), then listen for the broadcast radio reports of the target relative to the bullseye and navigate to detect and then engage the threat as a single-ship bandit just like an Aggressor pilot. Sweet.

The cockpit was spacious compared to many other fighters. In front of him, on a pale blue panel, sat the primary analog flight instruments and engine performance gages, and to the top right, just under the glare shield, was the heads-down display (HDD). That display portrays pre-loaded tactical navigation points (like the bullseye), as well as radar returns, or as in his case today, targets detected by the IRST (shown as "T" symbols on the displays). Those are generated by the onboard computers and placed on the screen relative to the bearing and range from his aircraft; it also shows the target altitude in two digits next to the left of each symbol. Simply put, that was his "picture" of the battle space in front of him.

Below the HDD, and to the right, is the radar warning receiver (RWR) showing surface and airborne radar signals detected by sensors on the aircraft. Those signals are shown on a circular presentation around his aircraft representation in the center. A radar signal detected in front of the aircraft at a long distance would be represented by a symbol on the screen at the top of the outer ring - at 12 o'clock on the display. Lights illuminate and a tone is played in the headset when the signals are picked up by the defensive system.

On top of the glare shield is the heads-up display, or HUD. Between that and the helmet-mounted sight, the pilot in a maneuvering visual fight with an enemy fighter need never look inside the cockpit. Altitude, airspeed, radar target data, closure velocity, weapons choices, engagement envelopes for missiles, and use of the gun are all presented in the HUD. The helmet-mounted sight allows him to look anywhere in a 45-degree cone around the nose of the aircraft - wherever the target can be seen from the cockpit within that cone - and the sensor in the nose of the selected R-73E IR missile follows those helmet-mounted commands when enabled by one of the many multi-function switches on the two throttles.

The advanced fly-by-wire flight controls - pedals at the feet controlling the twin rudders, a center-mounted control stick with six switches or buttons and the trigger on the grip, and two throttles on the left console that controlled the Saturn engines...

Suddenly, in the headset, "BORT-09, launch immediately," followed within seconds by the Klaxon horn sounding. Startled, the two crew chiefs jumped up from their seats along the front wall just left of the open door and rolled up and secured their blankets. The assistant then ran past the left side of the aircraft to open the back hangar doors.

Shawski slapped the cold oxygen mask up against his face and fastened it to his helmet, smelling and tasting both the antiseptic cleaning fluid and the stale air from the air conditioning system.

He keyed the mic switch on the right throttle with his thumb and acknowledged the launch order, "BORT-09 launch."

Then on the intercom, he said, "Say *CLEAR*, ready start number two."

After a few moments, the back doors were fully open and Josef said, "*CLEAR*, ready for start," from where he was positioned at the front right of the aircraft so Shawski could see him. The assistant crew chief manned the fire bottle for the engine start sequence, his breath visibly puffing rapidly from his mouth in the cold air after the strenuous effort to open the doors.

Shawski spun two fingers over his head, said, "Starting Two," and pressed the starter button for the right engine, engine number two; he then immediately brought the right throttle up out of the cutoff position to idle. This commanded the digital engine control to perform the automatic start sequence: it energized an electric motor to spin the engine, introduced fuel into the combustion chamber, and then ignited it, all without pilot action. With a thump and low growl, the right engine lit off and rapidly started howling, a shrieking whine as the engine accelerated to peak start revolutions per minute then reduced in pitch slightly as it settled back to routine idle RPMs. He waved his hand again over his head with one finger extended as Josef hustled to the front left of the aircraft, said, "Starting One," and repeated the sequence of events, adding more noise to the small shelter. Instruments and lights indicated a normal startup sequence with nearly two dozen indications of the aircraft coming to life all around him.

Quickly he lowered the canopy, the huge reinforced plexiglass laminate enclosure swinging down and locking with a *THUNK*, followed immediately by audible airflow noise and pressure in the cockpit as the aircraft air conditioning and pressurization system activated. The engine noise faded for him. He turned on the pre-set inertial navigation system (the hot-cock procedures allowed for an abbreviated alignment of the INS without degradation of accuracy) and confirmed again all switches in the proscribed settings for a no-emissions launch.

Meanwhile, Josef said, "Happy hunting sir," disconnected his comm cord from the aircraft, showed it to Shawski, and ran over to stow it at the base of the hanger wall. The assistant crew chief parked the fire bottle aside, removed the landing gear pins, pulled off the magnetized protective covers on the six IR missiles, and signaled to the crew chief that all tasks were accomplished while he waited to pull the chocks from in front of and behind the main gear wheels. The crew chief showed "good to go" with a thumbs up to Shawski, and after the three minutes needed for alignment, Shawski selected the navigation mode on the INS, held the brakes by pressing his feet on the tops of the rudder pedals, released the parking brake, and signaled for chocks to be removed. Josef signaled Andrei and the chocks were pulled out of the way.

Shawski then wound his hand in a circular motion in front of his face and pointed forward. The crew chief signaled for power and pointed out the door. He was moving in less than five minutes since receiving the launch order. Excellent work!

Careful with the power (after all, this wasn't a strengthened shelter), Shawski advanced the throttles slightly then retarded them and heard the rising and falling whistle sound as the nozzles' circumference first closed some and then opened fully again to the normal idle setting. Rolling forward he engaged and checked the nose wheel steering, then tapped the pedals to check the brakes, and returned Josef's salute as he passed through the door out into the late afternoon pearl-gray sunlit winter day.

Standing to his right on the taxiway he was surprised to see perhaps 15-20 civilian depot workers, all cheering inaudibly and shaking their arms and fists above their heads in a show of support. He gave them a thumbs-up and then turned left onto the patchy snow-stained taxiway towards the runway, disconnected the nose wheel steering, kicked the rudder pedals left and right, and watched in the mirrors on the canopy frame as the rudders on the large vertical tails swung first left then right appropriately. He re-engaged the steering and carefully added power again to boost the 51,000-pound combat-loaded jet to a fast taxi speed. He quickly cycled the control stick first to the left, then right to drive the ailerons up and down on each side, then stick fore and aft to see the large horizontal tails deflect trailing edges down then up in the mirrors. All good. He switched the radio to the tower frequency and then looked for a green light signal from them for a comm-out takeoff and departure.

There it was.

He visually cleared the final approach on the left, crossed the solid and dashed yellow hold-short line at the end of Runway 13, slowed slightly, turned right to align with the centerline, then advanced the power first to max unaugmented power, checked the engine instruments (looked the same as always), and then selected full afterburner. With a significant kick in the back, the engines spun up through every stage of afterburners and produced 55,200 pounds of combined thrust. Always exhilarating.

BORT-09 rapidly approached 100 knots where Shawski pulled back slightly on the stick and raised the nose approximately 10 degrees - careful not to strike the extended centerline tail boom containing the defensive countermeasures, chaff, and flares. With a positive rate of climb, he reached left and pulled up the gear handle with the tiny white "wheel" on it, whereupon he heard the nose gear retract and gear door close followed closely by the large main gear and doors thumping closed underneath, warning lights out (wary of the big engines in this cold air pushing him past the gear door limiting airspeed before they were fully retracted). Reaching 480 knots - eight nautical miles per minute - he pulled the throttles out of afterburner, leveled off somewhere near 200 feet altitude, and turned carefully left to approximately 090 degrees, putting the bullseye symbol in the HUD squarely at 12 o'clock.

He breathed deeply and then thought to himself, "Please Lord, don't let me screw up." Something else he learned in the bar at Nellis.

26

A CLOWN ACT

Some officers get promoted by virtue of their performance. Too many get promoted because of who they know, or how well they kiss ass. His commander is one of the latter.

Grigoriy was angry and scared. His pilot (also his commander) was clueless. This was not going to end well.

Captain Grigoriy Sokolov was a weapons operator, combat-qualified in the right seat of the new Sukhoi Su-34 twin-engine, twin-seat, all-weather supersonic fighter bomber aircraft. It was a fabulous machine. Too bad most of the leadership in the 38th Fighter Regiment had no idea how to employ it properly.

The problem was easy to see from his point of view: people with long-time flight experience in older Soviet-era aircraft like the Su-22 and Su-24 dominate the regiment's leadership and they simply don't understand all the modern equipment. As a result, they default to using tactics and procedures developed for those older aircraft with their poor flight characteristics, rudimentary systems, and archaic weapons, even though this aircraft they are flying today is superior to most attack aircraft anywhere. And because they are senior and arrogant, they refuse to take inputs from junior officers - even those who graduated from the Su-34 training program with honors.

Like him.

And now, at 30,000 feet over southern Ukraine, the commander just slapped his hand - he reached across the cockpit and hit him and told him to, "Stop interfering and let me fly!"

Grigoriy was stunned - he was doing his job!

The airplane is complex; that is why there are two crew members. At 76 feet long, with a wingspan of 48 feet, it shares design characteristics with the Su-27 in the aft fuselage, wings, intakes, engines, and horizontal and vertical tails. But forward of the wing line, it is quite different - most obviously in the flattened, larger cockpit area allowing for the two-person crew to sit side-by-side, designed to increase crew interaction and effectiveness. Called the "Duckbill Nose" by the designers (and Hellduck or Platypus by the crews), the cockpit is spacious and filled with the latest in Russian technology - large color displays with almost no traditional, analog flight instruments or weapons controls. Just aft of the cockpit, one on each side of the fuselage were large maneuvering canards - wings that increase the static instability of the aircraft thereby providing improved maneuverability. Though slightly slower (top speed Mach 1.8) than their cousins, the Su-27 family of aircraft, the larger Su-34 (weighing 50,000 pounds empty, and over 85,000 pounds loaded up) can still sustain 9G turns at the right altitude and airspeed!

But Grigoriy learned that some pilots just do not share responsibilities well. And this one was a gem. He was a top graduate of the lofty Gagarin Air Force Academy, went first to a post-graduate study program, and then through training and an operational tour as a Su-22 pilot for six years.

He was an imposing figure, tall and well-built, poised and handsome, with a loud voice and an ego that suggested he knew all of that. As a new podpolkovnik (lieutenant colonel) he acted more like a senior lieutenant. A party animal and a ladies' man in his own mind.

At the end of his Su-22 tour (where he was a basic flight leader only, never upgrading to instructor pilot) he was assigned to a mid-level Air Force staff position at the Ministry of Defence in Moscow, and after a year there he was "chosen" by senior officers to be a Military Aide to the Deputy Commander in Chief of the Russian Aerospace Forces. Promoted early, first to major and then to podpolkovnik (lieutenant colonel) with no recent operational qualifications whatsoever, he was specifically placed by the generals to command the 38th Fighter Regiment ahead of many more qualified officers. He arrived at the unit, a recent graduate of the Su-34 conversion training program, with fewer total flying hours than most captains and majors in the unit.

Arrogant, intolerant, and stubborn, he was not revered, to say the least. No fighter pilot (or weapons officer) ever admired someone's staff skills. And they did not trust him.

The 38th Regiment had been at Belbek Air Base in Crimea for nearly three months now - since just before the start of the special military operation. Initial combat sorties had mixed results, with a couple of unexpected losses. It turned out that the Ukrainians were better prepared and equipped than the Division-level Intelligence officers let on in the pre-mission briefings. As it turns out, the S-300 and S-400 were just as effective in Ukrainian hands as they were in Russia's air defense units.

After the losses, the unit took some downtime and regrouped. Senior leaders in Moscow placed additional pressure on commanders to show results. There was a very strong emphasis to lead from the front.

So today was his commander's first combat mission. It started badly during mission planning in the days prior. At first, other than telling Grigoriy and the other crew of their two-ship attack formation the target location and description he did not take part in any of the other work to prepare. Then, when he did show up to review the plan he rejected it, ordered them to do it all differently ("In the Su-22 we used to do this..."), and sent them back to the vault to work another plan. Hours later they completed the task but he had gone to quarters for the night. So the next morning they reconvened, went over the general plan, and got his approval, whereupon he then conducted an abbreviated mission briefing and left for his office. He would meet his weapons officer at the jet.

Grigoriy was able to brief tactical formations with the other pilot and weapons officer - unit standard rules and practices and such, but they didn't know what to expect from their flight lead.

This was going to be a clown act.

At the aircraft, Lieutenant Colonel Mikhail Balakin, Commander of the 38th Fighter Regiment made it clear who would be in charge during this flight.

"I'm the aircraft commander. You will do as I say during this flight - I need immediate obedience for us to succeed. Is that clear?"

"Sir, respectfully, I have much valuable experience with the offensive and defensive systems on this..."

"That is all fine. I expect you to do your job, but I will tell you what I need from you and when I need it." And with that, he turned and went up the ladder in the nose gear well and into the cockpit without performing a walk-around preflight inspection of the aircraft.

"I guess he meant to tell me to do the inspection," Grigoriy thought to himself.

Once he joined Balakin in the cockpit, the weapons officer soon found that the commander followed no standard procedures. Not in the cockpit, not during ground operations, nor on the radios, and even the departure from the airfield was complicated by poor coordination with the tower controllers and their wingman. Once safely airborne (Balakin would have exceeded gear airspeed limits if Grigoriy hadn't said, a little too loudly, "Airspeed!") things did not change. As they climbed through 5,000 feet on departure he was relieved to see the wingman join up on their aircraft on the right side; Grigoriy used hand signals to tell #2 (callsign BORT-44) to check fuel amounts and to perform the pre-combat checklist since his pilot forgot to do so.

The pilot and the weapons officer in the second aircraft were not the best in the unit. The pilot was a "yes man" - and afraid to contradict a senior officer. The weapons officer was a new graduate from the training unit and not yet confident with his equipment. But Grigoriy couldn't do their jobs for them. Hopefully, they would not collide with his aircraft during the mission.

Grigoriy first set up the displays so that he would manage the weapons systems - offensive and defensive. He wanted to be able to see the images from the Leninets V-004 Passive Electronically Scanned Array radar and to monitor the navigation tracks, but his pilot kept "stealing" the displays from him through purposeful switch activations to put those before him along with the electronic flight instruments. He was berated for complicating the display presentations.

Luckily, what the pilot could not control was the six Kh-59MK2 cruise missiles carried two each on the left and right, on the farthest outboard underwing hardpoints, and the last two on the centerline of the aircraft. Those required timely action on his part to enable or arm the systems before release.

The pilot also kept putting the radar in standby mode - it was passive yes, and was designed to work in a manner that wasn't easily detected by enemy aircraft. But ignoring that, he insisted on using the ground-mapping mode of the radar to "double-check the navigation system" - a technique necessary in Su-22s before they had satellite-assisted navigation. And when he wasn't doing that it was put in standby mode.

Technically, Grigoriy also owned the countermeasure systems (the metallic chaff that caused problems for ground and airborne radars, and the flares that confused infrared air-to-air missiles), but the commander ordered him not to select Auto-Dispense as he did not trust it to work properly. Instead, they would rely on Balakin's ability to deploy countermeasures promptly via a push-button switch on the left cockpit wall.

Right. This guy is going to manage our countermeasures better than the computer.

30 minutes into the flight they turned more to the west, to a heading of 285 degrees, following the course set in the navigation system, one of the few things displayed in front of both the pilot and the weapons officer.

Grigoriy busied himself with preparing the cruise missiles for launch. He reached for the Master Arm switch - the last item on the checklist, and that is when the pilot struck his arm.

"Stop interfering and let me fly!" Then the pilot moved the Master Arm Switch to ARM. Tensions were high.

Grigoriy was deeply troubled - they were 100 miles south of Kyiv, en route to the release point to fire on the NATO weapons storage sites west of Lviv, and he had absolutely no picture of the battle space. Luckily, his L150 Pastel radar warning receiver showed no enemy fighter activity.

27

FLYING LOW AND FAST

There is something about flying low and fast that is never comfortable. Exciting, yes, but extremely dangerous. Only several seconds of inattention can mean the difference between skimming above tree tops and the ground and plowing into the ground or some other obstacle with enough destructive force to turn his titanium, steel, and aluminum fighter aircraft into fire and bits and pieces - and death.

At 480 knots, Shawski was traveling through the air at more than 800 feet per second - the equivalent of two soccer pitches in every blink of an eye. At this low height, the flickering effect of the changing terrain going by underneath looked surreal. It was as if he was traveling so fast that the near-space went by faster than he could focus. A disciplined visual "cross-check" of flight instruments, the outside, and the HUD and its altitude display were critical. The Aggressors said to watch for the near rocks, then the far rocks, then the threat, and repeat. After all, the rocks have a very high "probability of kill" if you hit them.

Since the Lviv airport was located on the southwestern extremes of the city limits his left turn took him just around the Sports Arena Complex and then into more rural country. But he was sure there were some shaken souls living behind him as his jet must have rattled windows as he went past the various housing neighborhoods. Also soon after takeoff, his RWR came alive with search radar signals detected from airport traffic control and near and distant Ukrainian surface-to-air missile (SAM) sites shown from 11 o'clock on the RWR display all the way around left to his aft 6 o'clock. Alerted to his departure by the same command network from which he received the launch order, there should be no threat from them. But it was still unnerving to be "lit up" by very capable (Russian-made) S-300 and S-400 SAM search radars. You had to trust in the teams' fire control discipline and just press on.

"BORT-09, two targets, bullseye, 130, 125, angels 30, heading 310," ground control radar broadcasted on the tactical frequency. First picture: the targets were southeast of the bullseye 125 miles, at an altitude of 30,000 feet, and they were flying to the northwest on a 310-degree heading. No response was required.

The bullseye was 150nm in front of him. At this speed, it would take him 18 minutes to near that point if the tactical situation allowed him to get that far.

"BORT-09, targets hostile; weapons free." He thought, "They've probably been tracking them since takeoff out of Crimea, and the controller just confirmed there were no friendlies in front of him." He could fire his weapons without restrictions when the situation presented itself.

He allowed himself a slight climb for safety and then he checked his fuel (16,000 pounds of fuel left from the 20,000 pounds he had onboard when he taxied out). Then he double-

(triple?) checked his various systems for silence: radar in standby, navigation system INS only, radar altimeter off, aircraft lights, and rotating beacon off. He reached out with his left hand, flipped the red cover, and moved the Master Arm switch from SAFE to ARM, enabling the use of the GSh-30-1 30mm air-to-air cannon and the six IR missiles. He flicked a switch repeatedly on the left throttle that sequenced through the missiles hung on stations 1, 2, 9, and 10 to test the IR seeker heads and the symbology in the HUD for each R-73 missile, then moved on to check the two long-range R-27 missiles mounted on stations 5 and 6 - one on the outer edge of each massive air intake below and behind him. All missile seeker heads behaved as expected, and each one emitted a decisive high-pitched tone in his headset indicating they were "seeing" ambient heat. Next, the IRST: ON, and operating properly (with appropriate symbology displayed in the HUD and the heads-down display). Finally, radar and IR missile countermeasures systems are set to MANUAL (vice automatic). He didn't want those kicking out defensive flares and highlighting his position unless he felt threatened by a known enemy missile launch. Back down under 200 feet.

"BORT-09, two targets, bullseye, 130, 60, angels 30, heading 310," was called out by ground control radar - an update of the enemy position relative to the bullseye. Shawski considered the unfolding geometry. Their heading would have been further north if they were headed to Kyiv. On this heading, it looked like they may turn the corner and head more for Lviv and its surrounding areas. There were many lucrative targets in the area (like NATO weapons delivery sites). As if watching from overhead - a God's-Eye View - he could picture them flying from the 5 to 6 o'clock position relative to the bullseye upwards and to the left towards 9 or 10 o'clock. He wanted to run a very hot intercept, directly at them from far below. So he estimated their position and steered slightly right of the bullseye.

Fuel check - 14,000 pounds. Fuel burn as expected, but he would burn fuel far faster when he accelerated to engagement speeds and if he had to maneuver in afterburner in some kind of visual fight. Near rocks, far rocks, navigation. The system showed that he was 100 miles from Lviv; 162 miles south of Kyiv. Near rocks, far rocks; the terrain had changed from suburban, rural to farmland and open tundra - a mixture of dormant brown and partially snow-covered wheat fields and scrub with some isolated forests of what he knew to be evergreen trees. Occasionally, he raced over rivers and streams crisscrossing the flickering scene. Otherwise, it was all just a dirty brown gray white brown gray white smear at this altitude and this speed.

"BORT-09, two targets, bullseye, 140, 50, angels 30, heading 285," came the calm, low voice of the ground controller. There's that left turn pointing them more towards Lviv. He pushed it up to 540 knots.

Suddenly, a tone. Near rocks; he climbed slightly. RWR clear. The IRST symbology in the HUD showed first one, then two target "T" symbols at the top of the HUD field of view. 60 nautical miles and approximately 30,000 feet high. Slightly left of his nose (he had overcorrected to the right previously). He turned to put the symbology directly in front of him at 12 o'clock. He knew that as the distance closed, given the altitude of the targets, the symbology would be augmented by a green arrow with an associated number to the left of each T symbol indicating that the targets were outside the field of view of the HUD at a certain angle off of the aircraft boresight or centerline. Essentially, if Shawski stayed low he would have to look above the HUD and even above the canopy bow to see them. And he knew at some point he would have to pull the nose up and climb.

Steady heading, back down low. Near rocks, far rocks... The RWR suddenly buzzed in his headset and he saw one air interceptor search radar indication at 12 o'clock on the outer ring of the display - then it faded. The style of the symbol represented that of a newer Leninets V-004 electronically scanned radar as fitted out on a Su-34 - the latest Russian air-to-ground attack aircraft.

Another call from ground control and the data just confirmed the indications he had in the HUD for the same targets. The controller will continue to talk but as far as Shawski was concerned he was on his own. Inside 10 miles the controller would look for trailers - any enemy threats following from the south that could interfere with his intercept. For now, the area south was "clean" - no other Orcs coming.

Su-34s! That didn't ease his mind any - this was a variant of the ancient Su-27 he was currently flying, but with a two-person crew, a better suite of avionics, and more modern weapons. It even had a feature that would automatically launch R-73 missiles at threats autonomously detected behind the aircraft! The pilot and a weapons systems operator sat side-by-side in a large modern cockpit with multiple nine-inch color displays and an astonishing array of air-to-air and air-to-ground free-fall and guided munitions. One thing they didn't have though was the outstanding visibility he had from his single-seat fighter - and he thought sure that the Russians weren't "dynamic" enough to work together effectively as a team in a fast-moving tactical environment. At least he hoped so - he hadn't faced any of these yet.

They were closing, almost head-on, at a combined rate of nearly 20 miles per minute. It looked on the HDD that they were flying an offset tactical formation with the second aircraft as much as a half mile back and 45 degrees aft of the leader's right wing. At 60 miles, Shawski selected the first R-27 long-range missile from station 5 and it gave the high-pitched tone in his headset, and when he selected the trailing IRST "T" symbol of the second aircraft it growled at him to indicate that it saw a heat source at that location too. Distance now 55 miles - just outside optimum employment range. Give it another 10-20 seconds. A gentle climb to quit looking at the rocks.

He pressed the red, second button on the top left of the control stick and there was a loud *THUMP* as the 750-pound missile was ejected from its mount and then the sound of a freight train as the huge missile roared by the left side of the cockpit and arced suddenly up in front and out of sight trailing a huge white smoke plume; the system automatically selected the second R-27 on station 6, gave a good tone on the same target, and he pressed the launch button again and was rewarded again with the vibrations and noise of another freight train going past, this time on the right side of the cockpit, and up out of sight. He let the jet continue to climb gently, keeping the targets at 12 o'clock, and selected the first R-73 on station 2, then targeted the leader on his display.

Immediately, the missile screamed out that growling tone in his headset. At 8 miles range he began a 4G pull to point at the targets, then relaxed the G to hold the leader dead center in the HUD, saw both aircraft now, waited, and then pressed the button once, then a second time as the system auto-selected the second of four R-73 missiles. The missiles blasted off stations 2 then 9 in sequence like bottle rockets, with a much higher pitched vibration off the launch rails and a terrific hissing sound and they were gone. While the rocket motors burned you could see both missiles violently pull lead on the target, flying well out in front of its flight path before they burned out and Shawski lost sight of them.

28

ENGAGED, DEFENSIVE

Grigoriy was just about to say, "10 minutes to weapons release, armed and ready," when he heard a broken radio call that sounded like their wingman's callsign, then nothing. He turned right in his seat and looked 45 degrees aft expecting to see the #2 aircraft still parked there about 3000 feet out only to see a fireball falling back and down. Holy shit, his mind screamed, as he involuntarily stared at the sight. BORT-44 was gone.

Frantically he looked back inside and searched the radar warning receiver display - and found it void of any symbols. No warning tones. No blinking lights.

In as calm a voice as he could muster, he shouted, "Sir, we just lost BORT-44!"

No response.

Then before the commander could react there was a loud metallic BANG, and the aircraft spasmed as dozens of pieces of metal rods and other debris peppered the fuselage behind them. This was immediately succeeded by a red warning light, a right engine fire light, a right side hydraulics failure light, and numerous other yellow caution lights glaring at them from their black-framed Caution Panel display matrix.

Balakin announced, "We have a right engine failure," while simultaneously pulling the right throttle to idle and then to cut off, and pulling the RIGHT FIRE T-handle to discharge the fire bottles into the right engine bay. One look at the dual left/right engine RPM gauge showed that it was already fully stopped. It had eaten itself.

Grigoriy announced, "We are engaged, defensive!"

"Nonsense, we had an engine failure," said the clueless pilot, as he reached up and pushed the Emergency Jettison switch. Grigoriy then heard and felt three distinct *THUMPS* as the three pairs of cruise missiles fell away on their multi-carriage racks. Then the commander moved the Master Arm switch to SAFE and started an easy left descending turn to return to base. Apparently, he was unaware (unable to handle?) all else that was happening around them.

Flabbergasted, Grigoriy looked again at the radar and the radar warning receiver and found nothing on either. He squirmed around to the left, forcing his left elbow against the seat to help him twist around while pushing off the instrument panel glare shield in front of him with his right hand, struggling to stretch as high as he could to see over the back bulkhead. He was looking inside their easy, descending left turn, when suddenly he heard the screaming tone of a close-in threat from the radar warning receiver. Then, much to his horror, he saw it settling into position - an Su-27, nose in lead, speed brake stood up on its back and then closing, and he shouted at Balakin to, "Break left, break..."

29

HUNDREDS MORE OUT THERE

Shawski let his jet's nose move slightly aft of the leader - just in time to see the detonation of the first R-27 as it passed from above, down and directly through the center of the trailing aircraft, reducing it to a roiling, ugly fireball of debris as it disintegrated and began its long descent to the ground below. He thought he saw the second R-27 as it went right through the debris and detonated somewhere inside it all. Time seemed to slow down as Shawski noted the low western sun's rays from behind him reflecting off the ticker tape waterfall of pieces as they fluttered through the air.

Meanwhile, the leader was smoking now with a puff of smoke visible at his six o'clock indicating where one of the R-73s must have detonated. There was no sign of the second. As Shawski selected afterburners and laid into a high G turn to continue the intercept on the leader he noted the smoking target had suddenly begun to roll over to the left in a lazy descending turn towards him. The third R-73 was growling but the two aircraft quickly closed to inside the minimum employment range, so he continued a vertical high-G turn that passed just aft of the leader who continued his easy descending left-hand turn. As he pulled through over the top of the looping turn, he couldn't believe what he saw happening, as the Orc's lower-G turn put him in a perfect place to continue his turn to arrive tight in a gun solution for the kill! Pulling the nose down and inside the turn of the big ground attack fighter, he moved his left thumb forward against a switch on the right side of the right throttle which brought the radar out of standby and commanded a radar lock on the smoking Su-34 for a gun-shot. He closed to 1000 feet range at 30 degrees off the tail inside the Russian's turn, pulled out of afterburners, quickly fanned the big speed brake behind him on the spine of the aircraft to control his speed, steadied the aiming circle on the cockpit and pulled the trigger on the front of the control stick.

The three-second burst of 30mm cannon fire sent 75 high explosive incendiary rounds at the target. It sounded like a jackhammer on the right side of the aircraft. Most of the rounds appeared to hit as the aircraft was carved apart in front of him.

If any other threat was out there, nothing would attract their attention faster than two flaming wrecks falling out of the sky. Shawski quickly pulled up and rolled right, then sharply put the nose down to minimize drag, and selected full afterburners again to accelerate away from these airborne "The Fight Is Here" signs. Once again he would return to the low and fast world as he headed home. After sweeping the airspace in front of him and finding it clear he put the radar back into standby mode. He checked his fuel and it was good. He turned on his IFF transponder in the descent - both for the radar ground controller and to show himself to friendly SAM sites as he returned to the airport.

"BORT-09, Positive IFF, southeast clean," came the call from the controller indicating he was visible on their radar and that there were no threats behind him as he pushed it up well above the Mach - going through 720 knots - in his descent to the low-level environment. His RWR stayed clean - nobody chasing him. He could hear the roar of the wind passing over the canopy bow and around his cockpit. Oh my God!

He was soaking wet, and suddenly cold in the chill of the blowing air conditioning and pressurization system. Shakily, filled with adrenalin, he reached up and moved the Master Arm switch to SAFE, then closed the red cover over the top. He had never fired the gun at anything before other than in a simulator. The entire HUD and instrument panel vibrated. Two kills - one with the gun! He would feel good about that except he knew there were hundreds more out there against his air force's few Su-27s and MiG-29s. It was still one versus many - and those aren't good odds in the long run. And the Orcs would not always be so stupid. But luck was good to him today.

30

THE UKRAINIAN EXPRESS

The embassy driver sped through the streets of Lviv like they were his private race course. But they were nearly empty - with the air raid sirens wailing, the traffic was quite sparse. Embassy Station Chief Leonard "Leo" Goodwin hardly noticed, talking throughout the drive about what he hoped to get out of the meetings tomorrow with the two Ukrainian intelligence agency deputies.

"You have to be careful with these folks. Ukraine broke away from Russia in 1991 and became a separate State but they are not that far removed from the Soviet Union. You will notice it with these guys more than any other agency as they trace their heritage to the KGB. And sometimes they still act that way."

"Do you trust them?"

"Let's say that I have a good relationship with them. This is a good opportunity to pick their brains. But my experience has been that even though I thought I was there to learn from them I usually leave wondering who interviewed who."

Carlos smiled slightly. "I intend to let you do most of the talking. The less people know about me the better."

"I understand - I will help keep you on the down low."

Carlos had to laugh to himself. Leo and his word choice. Some people never change.

They left the airport area on Liubinska Street, then right on Horodotska for several miles, bypassing the left turn you would normally take to the Kyiv Railroad Station, then finally turning left onto a series of lesser streets of some indeterminate names until they pulled up to a security cordon within sight of the tracks. The driver, Leo, and Carlos all showed the guards their IDs and they were waved through to park next to the first of a series of three small red-roofed buildings where several Secret Service-type people were waiting outside on either side of the sidewalk headed to the door.

Carlos said, "Thanks" to the driver, stepped out of the vehicle after grabbing his bag off the seat next to him, and walked to the front of the building where Leo joined him. They were whisked inside and shown to a small room to wait along with some other people.

Luckily, they arrived before the Ukrainian Express did. It wasn't called that, of course. But Carlos picked up the term when Skip flippantly likened this VIP train to the storied Oriental Express train from Paris to Istanbul. He hoped there'd be no murder mystery on this train.

In the room were several men and women in suits, some other obvious security types in bulky jackets with "equipment" hidden poorly underneath, and a man on the far side dressed impeccably in the black robes of the Catholic Church. People were talking.

Carlos said to Leo, "Obviously, that must be the Papal Nuncio to Belarus, Cardinal Eryk Jablonovski." Skip told him he would travel on the same train as the secretaries but meet with Zelenskiy separately.

Leo nodded his head. "Yeah, not a happy man there. The Belarus President, Lukashenko, kicked him out of the country. The Pope is throwing up his hands on the matter and leaving the Catholic priests there to care for the flock by themselves. Allegedly, the Nuncio is here to reach out to Zelenskiy to show support while at the same time explaining why the Pope is begging off on his planned trip here in a couple of weeks. He'll probably head back to Rome afterward."

Carlos looked questioningly at Leo and said, "The Pope was planning to come to Ukraine? Really?"

"Oh yes. Very hush-hush, of course. A little too hot for him here I suppose."

"It does seem like a big risk."

"No, that's not the point. As the leader of the Vatican, there are diplomatic reasons for him to come here just as other heads of state are doing. But as the head of the Catholic Church, it is turning more dangerous - he is receiving many more death threats than usual."

"Why is that?" Carlos asked.

"There is quite a power struggle going on in the eastern countries between the Churches - Roman Catholic and Russian Orthodox. The eastern countries who are leaning towards the West, and who support Ukraine, are turning their backs on the ROC and that crackpot Patriarch, Kirill. His role as the head of the Orthodox Church has strayed away from preaching and way more towards propaganda as he justifies Putin's crazy special military operation amongst his followers, and fans the flames of their shared mystical view of the return of the Russian Rus to its proper place in the world. And then there is the Iranian influence."

"Iran is threatening the Pope? I thought he made some kind of notable peace visit there not too long ago and met with the Ayatollah."

"Oh, he did. And they are not the threat. But elements of the Shia religion are scattered throughout the Caucasus and frequently march to their own drum. Enter the Kadyrovites and their pairing with PMC Wagner."

"But Kadyrov declared Chechnya to be Sunni only."

"Yes, he did, while at the same time thousands of his Shia people, ostracized and persecuted at home, joined the ISIS ranks and gained combat experience in Syria and Iraq. You probably ran into them at one point or another."

Carlos turned and looked out the window at the empty tracks as he digested that information.

After a few moments of silence, Leo saw him looking and changed the subject, "The airspace has been closed since the start of the invasion (well, except for certain G6 aircraft into and out of Lviv). As a result, the train has become the best way to travel expeditiously in Ukraine."

He continued, "The westbound trains have taken thousands of refugees to safety in Europe and beyond. Then the returning eastbound trains carry weapons and other supplies. Occasionally, they also secretly carry closely guarded VIPs as they travel to the capital. You won't find today's train on a public schedule."

Suddenly, Leo raised his left hand in the air slightly, pulled out his vibrating phone with the other hand, and said, "Be right back," then stepped away to take a call.

Though Ukrainian Railways does everything it can to be discreet, the trips are not without risk. They even play a shell game with the trains themselves, changing the overnight or maintenance locations of the engines and cars to avoid sitting too long in one place and attracting the attention of satellites and then Russian missile targeting teams. Several times now train stations have been attacked coincidentally with trains arriving or departing with tragic loss of life. To date, no VIPs have been killed.

It isn't easy on the travelers - most of whom are used to fast, efficient air travel. In this case, a trip to Kyiv always involves first traveling to Przemysl, Poland, just eight miles west of the Ukrainian border. Once in Przemysl, they go to the border and then travel the remaining distance on Ukrainian Railways as the track width difference prevents western trains from continuing into Ukraine. It is an 11-hour journey to Kyiv - done with VIPs only at night.

Once onboard, the VIPs are well cared for by a professional service staff and an excellent chef. The special cars - the last five on the train - were originally built in 2014 for wealthy tourists on long trips to Crimea, but that soon stopped with Russia's illegal annexation. Since then they have been enhanced for the comfort and function of the guests.

The car at the end of the train is the VIP private quarters. There are two private bedrooms, each with a queen-sized bed, nightstand, closet, and restroom.

The second car from the end is the conference room, equipped with a long mahogany table and deeply padded leather chairs, big screen TVs on both the front and back walls, and all of the windows are draped luxuriously in heavy decorative cloth curtains for noise suppression and blackout purposes.

The third car forward is the kitchen and dining area, with two private booths seating four in the back, the kitchen in the middle, and a longer centerline table seating 10 in the forward part of the car.

The fourth car accommodates the security personnel and others traveling with the VIPs, each person getting a reclining seat and side table. Bags go in an overhead rack. There are two restrooms at the front of the car. Everyone not traveling with the VIP party will board the fifth car from the end - a luxury coach.

Leo put his phone back in his pocket and stepped over to Carlos just as a tall thin man dressed in the blue uniform of the Ukrainian Railways stepped into the middle of the small room and raised his hand for attention.

"Ladies and gentlemen, may I please have your attention," he called out.

Once the room became silent, he continued, "Welcome to Lviv and our little embarkation annex. As you may know, tonight's train will be carrying some VIPs for business in the capital. I tell you this for your awareness and to ask you please not to try to wander the train as the aft four cars will not be accessible. Remember too that the window shades are to remain drawn for the entire trip - no sightseeing please as we don't want the train to be easily seen from the air."

Finally, "The train is expected here in 10 minutes. It will be a quick boarding and departure. Please be ready. We hope you will have an uneventful trip with Ukrainian Railways tonight. Ask the attendant in each car for anything you might need." And with that, the man went to the doors facing the tracks.

One of the security men from out front appeared at Carlos's side, motioned his hand towards that same door, and said, "Mr. Pombar, Mr. Goodwin if you would please come with me."

The three of them walked forward to the door, which was held open by the tall man who just spoke. They passed through and then moved left down the ten-foot wide platform to the very end where they took up station to wait for the train.

"You will board here sirs, into the fourth car from the end of the train," the man said. And then he left them standing in the dark.

While he waited, Carlos thought that Lviv looked remarkably well two months into the war. But then given how far west it was on the map it did not surprise him that there was no visible damage (except the damage to the aircraft and buildings on the west side of the airport that he observed during landing). This was a large city of 721,301 according to his pre-mission study material - a population that recently swelled to well over a million as they tried to manage the refugees and families of those people moving to safety in Poland and other Western countries.

He'd met the Secretary of Defense, Lloyd Austin, just last year. Carlos thought he was a fine man - tall, large, imposing - all appropriate adjectives to describe the previous Army 4-Star and current civilian leader of the Department of Defense. He was also very intelligent. He was lucky to be assigned to his security team.

The meeting last year came after a significantly dangerous mission in Africa he did in support of US forces that could not be seen to participate in force-on-force activities. As it turned out, the other force included PMC Wagner personnel helping the bad guys.

Africa, and our involvement there, was a sensitive subject not covered well in the press and not well known at all to many Americans. In the last 10 years, American forces saw some level of combat in at least 13 African countries, from Burkina Faso to Chad, Niger to Somalia, and Tunisia. All places frequented by PMC Wagner "assistance" forces. There were casualties on both sides.

The Secretary of State was a different animal from Secretary Austin, Carlos recalled. Smart, yes, but Skip said he could never get a grip on exactly what Secretary Blinkin was thinking or which way he would go on a subject. Where Secretary Austin was used to considering input and making tough decisions on his own, Secretary Blinkin appeared to seek counsel and consensus on every subject before representing the group's opinion as his own. Protecting them both is important on this trip, but knowing he was under Austin made him feel better about it all.

While he appreciated the opportunity to attend the beginning of the meeting with President Zelenskiy, his real purpose here was talking to the deputies of the two intelligence agencies face to face. Things were changing so rapidly in Ukraine that it was thought they could get current information on the status of the war - and Wagner's role -

direct from those whose job it was to assess those things for their own country.

Looking back along the expansive parallel rows of tracks towards the actual Lviv Holovnyi Railway Station, he noted the normally brilliantly lit station and its Art Nouveau architecture were simply lost in the darkness. He heard it first, but coming into the train yard from the west was a single, bright engine headlight mounted high atop a flat-front diesel locomotive, with two, less powerful ditch lights, one mounted on each side of the lower right and left front of the engine. The three lights grew larger as the train continued right past the grand old station, and then began to slow only as it approached his position. The rest of the passengers were now out on the platform nearer the other end. With the brakes protesting noisily, the diesel-electric engine (Ukrainian blue with a yellow stripe) decelerated past the small annex until the fifth and fourth cars from the end were abreast of the platform when it came to a stop. The last three cars trailed out beyond the platform to his left. The crowd queued up at the door of the fifth car from the end. After a few moments, the door at the aft end of the fourth car opened and they were beckoned inside by a Diplomatic Security specialist, his coat barely concealing the larger-than-normal weapon underneath.

"After you sir," Leo said. Then to the imposing figure at the door, "Good evening Specialist Daniels, how are you tonight?" The specialist smiled slightly but didn't say a word as they climbed the steps and entered the security car.

31

TREACHEROUS GROUND

Carlos placed his bag in the rack over his seat and then he and Leo got a short briefing from the Chief of Security, Specialist Scott Milton. The train was already moving, picking up speed as evidenced by the sway and the increasing double clack-clacking rhythm of the wheels traveling over the rail gaps. After covering basic safety procedures, Milton went over their security responsibilities while traveling with the Secretary of State and the Secretary of Defense.

"First, the Diplomatic Security team is responsible for VIP safety on this train - not you. We know you are armed - keep your weapons in your bags until we arrive in Kyiv. No offense, but we can't have well-intentioned, highly capable people going rogue on us here. Be alert, and talk to people if you see something, but do not act on your own. We've got it."

Head nods.

"Second, when we get there, Mr. Goodwin, you are attached to the Secretary of State's detail, and Mr. Pombar, you will be attached to Secretary Austin's detail. We understand you will separate from the team after the meeting with President Zelenskiy and proceed on business of your own."

"Finally, get settled. It is easily seven hours from here. You can get something to eat soon, then rest up. You are expected to attend the first part of the Executive Meeting starting at 7pm tonight. Someone will come for you."

"See you around," and with that, he turned and walked through the door in the back and disappeared.

Carlos looked around and acknowledged that he'd had worse accommodations and sat down. Leo had a seat across the aisle.

The meal that night was better than expected

At precisely 10 minutes to seven, Specialist Daniels appeared between their seats and asked them to follow him to the conference car, again with hardly a trace of a smile. They moved aft, into the dining car again, and through the gangway connection to a frosted glass door that provided access to the conference room. It was as elaborate as he'd heard. He and Leo took seats on opposite sides of the forward end of the table. There were no tablets of paper or pens on the table.

There were several other members of the secretaries' staff already seated at the table, surrounded by laptops and the orderly contents of the briefcases set behind them against the car walls. The TV screens at each end showed a State Department PowerPoint title page, titled unimaginatively, "Ukraine Visit" on a light blue background. After a few moments, Secretary Austin and Secretary Blinkin came into the car from their private quarters at the back of the train along with their Chiefs of Staff.

They all stood.

"Sit down, please."

"Please take your seats," they said simultaneously. Blinkin took the seat at the head of the table, and Austin and the two chiefs sat in the remaining empty three seats.

After some pleasantries with their senior staff members, the meeting got started. Secretary Austin and his staff were seconded to the Secretary of State on this visit, so Blinkin's Chief of Staff, Susanna Burns, led off.

"Sirs, I think you know everyone here except for our two guests from the CIA at the end of the table, Mr. Leo Goodwin, the US Embassy in Ukraine station chief, and Mr. Carlos Pombar, an...er...an...an *associate* of Mr. Goodwin's," she finally spit out.

Everyone said hi all around. Secretary Austin locked eyes with Carlos, smiled, and nodded.

"Ok," Ms. Burns started, "Next chart." And the person seated to her left on Carlos' side of the table tapped a button on the computer to reveal the agenda:

- Overall Objectives of Visit
- Current Situation
- Schedule of Events
- Closing Remarks

Carlos wondered why that needed a PowerPoint chart.

Secretary Blinkin started. "We have two primary objectives for this meeting with President Zelenskiy. First, to show him, his country, and the world that we stand with Ukraine in this fight with Russia. And second, to allow him to tell us exactly what he needs to succeed. Behind all this, of course, is

President Biden's desire to do all we can do but to have no US Forces involved in the conflict. This is treacherous ground - we cannot provoke Russian actions against us or our allies that will invoke Article 5 of the NATO charter and brings all the alliance members into a shooting war. And we cannot do anything to provoke Mr. Putin to go beyond reckless saber-rattling concerning his potential use of nuclear weapons. We will stay on the periphery as we provide the weapons and supplies to the Ukrainian Armed Forces, all the while trying not to escalate the fight beyond the current borders."

Secretary Austin added, "There is another aspect of these discussions that we must keep in mind: we cannot let the desire to provide weapons turn into an endless drain on our warfighting stockpile and make us vulnerable to the kinds of challenges other bad actors are showing us around the world. Regardless of what happens in Ukraine, the security of the United States is paramount, and putting that security at increased risk for noble causes is unacceptable."

The staff began discussing various complications and variables associated with those objectives, but it didn't interest Carlos much. His objectives were simple: do what he could to learn about the true situation on the ground in Ukraine and then do whatever he could to hinder the effectiveness of PMC Wagner and anyone else who qualified as a target. Pretty simple.

Soon, bullet number two: the Current Situation. A DIA staff member spoke up, addressing the two secretaries.

"As of today, Russian forces to the north of Kyiv show signs of overextension and loss of inertia. They have stopped advancing and are still taking horrendous casualties from

Ukrainian artillery and drone strikes. They are demonstrating an inability to execute in any aspect of modern warfighting and they have completely failed to achieve any of their objectives as they did not capture Kyiv and they also failed, after multiple attempts, to decapitate senior Ukrainian leadership."

Austin asked, "What kind of numbers do you have?"

"Preliminary, only," the DIA staffer said, "but we think as of this month Russia has suffered over 40,000 soldiers killed, wounded, or missing on all fronts. We know from intercepted comms that at least seven general officers have been killed at the front trying to improve tactical control or properly communicate orders and such."

Austin: "Let me put that into perspective for everyone. We lost more than 58,000 troops in ten years in Vietnam; after two wars with Iraq and 10 years in Afghanistan, we lost just over 7,200 killed total. There is significant bloodshed in Ukraine."

"Is that common to have so many generals lost in combat?" asked Blinkin.

"No sir. We think it reflects the realization that their tactical and secure communications systems are not working properly - why, we don't know. They have demonstrated modern command and control equipment and infrastructure at various Arms Fairs and the like, but they aren't showing that they work in combat. They are using privately owned cell phones to communicate between units and with headquarters."

"The loss of vehicles of all sorts numbers in the thousands. First, they didn't take enough trucks and other equipment to sustain an operation for longer than 5-7 days, and then as they lost vehicles they also lost the opportunity to resupply the deployed units. They are stuck, getting attacked continuously, and running out of food, ammunition, and supplies. We are seeing the beginnings of a tactical retreat from the north."

Blinkin asked, "And the Ukrainians?"

"Well organized and capable - we think the Russians are genuinely surprised that the resistance is so strong. It is uncertain how long that can last. Fighting spirit only lasts so long - this is where we think the Ukrainians will be focused during our visit: they will be asking formally for more weapons and a commitment to stay with them."

Austin asked, "What about in the east and south?"

"Though there is combat there, and some Russian successes in both areas, the bulk of Russian forces are in the north. It is as if there is a holding action in the Donbas while the fighting rages north of Kyiv. Intelligence suggests that as the northern forces are withdrawn they will almost certainly be repositioned to the east to further the cause of liberation in the Luhansk and Donetsk Oblasts."

Austin summarized for the group, "Putin intended a quick war to capture the capital, decapitate the leadership, and install another puppet government on his western doorstep similar to the arrangement hc has with Belarus. In his view, Ukraine leaning west is a threat to Russian security - whether it is or not does not matter as that is his story. He and his forces have gotten their teeth kicked in and we expect them to retreat. But he isn't throwing in the towel - he is pissed off and more belligerent than ever. While Ukraine has done admirably they cannot do this in the long run without dedicated Western support as Russia is just too big, with too many expendable military resources. Weakness in the west will spell the end for Ukraine if they have to stand on their own."

"There is a new development that is worthy of mention," continued the DIA staffer. "There is satellite and HUMINT intelligence that points to significant Russian atrocities committed against Ukrainian military personnel and civilians in the regions they occupy. We aren't just talking about the obvious indiscriminate bombing, artillery, and missile fire on non-military targets. Towns west and north of Kyiv are reporting people disappearing, beatings, torture, rapes, and murders against their populations by Russian forces. In this case, this includes regular forces, but we are also hearing about PMC Wagner soldiers, and members of the Chechen Kadyrovites' 141st Special Motorized Regiment."

"Who are the Kadyrovites?" This was from Ms. Burns, Blinkin's Chief of Staff.

"They are a special security force under the command of Chechen President Ramzan Kadyrov. Essentially, his personal protective service. They are "on loan" to Putin where they do particularly onerous things for him that allow him to maintain plausible deniability - similar to PMC Wagner. Only even more vicious and less professional. For years they've been accused of all kinds of human rights abuses such as kidnapping, forced disappearances, torture, and murder wherever they are deployed."

Silence except for the continued, rhythmic banging of the wheels on the tracks underneath them. The car continued its relentless gentle swaying.

The staffer continued, "Both Wagner and the 141st are embedded in Russian forces west and north of Kyiv - and they have suffered tremendously in the Ukrainian counterattacks. Inevitably, in undisciplined forces, such losses seem to result in extreme violence and atrocities committed against anyone seen as a threat - even as retribution for their suffering. With these two organizations, it appears to be part of their standard method of fighting."

Ms. Burns, transitioning to the next topic, said, "Concerning the schedule, it is pretty simple. We arrive in Kyiv at approximately 7am. From there, Ukrainian Security Forces will take us to the Palace and down to the bunker, where we will meet with President Zelenskiy at 9am. Meetings will continue afterward for the rest of the day with various state and defense officials, and then we'll return to the train under escort and depart for Lviv at 7pm. Any closing remarks?"

Blinkin shook his head no.

Austin frowned, then said, "I don't mean to be an alarmist here, but let's not forget we are riding into a combat zone. You could find yourself suddenly in a very threatening environment. Trust your security detail and do what they say if something happens. Be alert."

Once they returned to the forward car, Leo and Carlos talked to Austin's security specialist, made arrangements to leave the party after the presidential meeting, and then got some shuteye.

7 hours is a long time to be on a train.

32

HIGH-STEPPING STAMPEDE

The 333-mile train ride from Lviv to Kyiv was uneventful. While they passed through eight significant towns and countless villages during the seven-hour journey, there was something about the rocking and swaying and the steady clacking of the wheels on the rail gaps that made it restful. Carlos wasn't even tempted to open the shade to see any of those places.

Upon arrival, the train moved to a remote section of the yard - still in the predawn hours - and stopped at a platform that allowed for the quick exit of secretive passengers. From the cold air of the platform, they were herded through a door that led down to a lower level and into a room that opened up on the other side to an uncompleted underground parking garage - the only cars visible through the windows being the four SUVs for the American party, and another assemblage of cars for the rest of the passengers.

A Ukrainian Security Police team met the passengers in the subterranean room and explained the procedures.

"Good morning. I hope you all slept well on your journey. Welcome to Kyiv."

Then, "There will be two separate convoys this morning - the four vehicles directly outside these windows will convey the United States Secretaries, their staffs, and their security details. Our Security Police will drive the vehicles to the palace."

He continued, "The first and fourth cars will carry the American security details, except for two specialists - one each will ride in the front passenger seat of vehicles two and three with their principals. There is one change this morning - Il Nuncio, Cardinal Eryk Jablonovski, will ride with the American Secretary of State."

Carlos noted no surprised reactions so he figured it must have been prearranged with the SecState staff. He looked at Leo, who then whispered, "Blinkin invited him when he heard he would be on the train."

"Outside and to the left, behind the first four SUVs, are the vehicles for the second convoy containing the remainder of the visitors. Those vehicles are all going to the Ministry of Defence building - if you are not with the American party you may take any seat in any one of those five vehicles."

"There are restrooms, better appointed than most, to my left. We will leave to go to the vehicles at 08:00 hours."

Very scripted - Carlos approved. It provided the maximum opportunity for Ukrainian security to arrange to close certain roads and to provide the best protection for their guests.

At the appointed time they all moved to the vehicles and climbed in (Carlos was asked to ride in the second row with Secretary Austin, the staff behind them; he looked through the windshield and saw Leo seated in the way-back of the SecState vehicle). It was cold and damp - near freezing in the early morning air in the garage.

As they wormed their way through the long-ignored construction equipment and supplies, a Ukrainian military police vehicle cut in line to lead them out and a second one waited for the four cars to pass before bringing up the rear. Smooth.

The convoy drove up the ramp to the street level into a gray, smoky morning, navigated around the large traffic circle, and headed east into the low morning sun and out of the station complex. It was only two miles from the station to the Mariyinsky Palace as the crow flies, but the round-about route (traveling only on major roads) would be more than three miles overall. The Ukrainian driver provided a few tour-guide remarks as the group passed notable sites. At one point they were driving northeast on Khreschatyk Street when he pointed out (purposefully?) the Maiden Nezalezhnosti - the square that saw the many 2013-2014 protests turned violent that led to the removal of then-President Yanukovych. On the right side of the car, opposite the square, was the Independence Monument, a 203-foot tall, marble-sided column built on a Christian-style pedestal with a gold-clad figurine of a woman holding rose branches in her upheld arms - looking both celebratory and appropriately defiant.

She was left behind as the convoy took a right at that intersection and proceeded the last half mile southeast on Mykhaila Hhrushevskono Street before turning left into an open-gated (with manned sentry boxes) one lane road, and drove northeast through the woods to another gated entrance on the right - the entrance to the rear of the palace. Once through the gate, they followed a long horseshoe-shaped driveway to stop at the grand back entrance. There were three arched passages, and the whole rear face of the entrance was flanked on either side by stone stairways doubling back halfway as they continued up to the second-floor balcony.

When they got out of the vehicles, Carlos noted there were armed guards in the uniform of the Ukrainian Ground Forces on the top floor above the balcony and at the arched entryway. They were surrounded by dense, black conifer woods backstopping the gate from which they entered, and on the left (to the east), beyond which he knew flowed the Dnipro River. As they were ushered through the center arch and into the initial enclosure, they found it to be as wide or wider than the three framed arches themselves and approximately 50 feet deep into the palace. At the back of the room, they were funneled through a single large doorway with a metal detector. Almost comically, but as directed, each member of the security team placed their weapons in plastic trays and then went through the detector as innocently as a traveler placing his or her computer through an X-ray machine at the airport expecting to retrieve it on the other side.

Through the machine (shoes and belt on), Carlos picked up his bag and placed his two spare magazines in the small pouch with elastic retaining straps on the right side of his TacWear Belly Band holster which he wore under his black tactical winter jacket (the weapon was easily accessed via mini-tabs of Velcro used as fasteners for the jacket). Each magazine carried 15 Underwood 8.74 gram/135 grain jacketed hollow point rounds. Though there are heavier rounds out there, the high velocity of 1,400 feet per second results in a lot of hitting power - 588 foot-pounds. People tend to stay down when hit with these.

Then he pulled the Glock 22 Gen4 .40 caliber automatic pistol from the plastic tray, checked it clear and safe, inserted the 15-round magazine that laid next to it, smoothly cycled the slide to load a round in the chamber, and returned it to the pocket on the holster. This was a standard configuration with one exception - instead of a vertical carry, the pocket was angled somewhat sideways so the barrel-end was pointing down about 45 degrees from horizontal, and it was mounted on the left front of his body so a cross-body reach would comfortably catch the grip for quick draw situations. The pistol was stock too, except he had the techs take a full pound out of the trigger pull. Well placed, the weapon was easily reachable when needed.

At the back of the room was a long floor-to-ceiling concrete wall that served as a secondary barrier to the elevators - solid protection against vehicles and projectiles. It extended nearly the entire width of the room save for about 10 feet of opening on each side for people to navigate around to get to the lifts. In an overall clockwise flow, those headed to the elevators moved to the right and around, and those leaving the elevators moved to their right and around the other end of the long wall to access the main chamber. There were no signs as there would be no unescorted persons wandering about wondering where to go.

On the elevator side of the long wall, there was about 20 feet of room between it and the elevator doors mounted in the face of the room's back wall. Finally, there was a perpendicular concrete wall attached to the middle of the long wall that sat between the two elevators, stopping ten feet short so people could go either way when necessary. It helped flow foot traffic to the selected down elevator on the right (and it moved those exiting from the left, up-elevator to their right, and around the wall to the exit).

By the time Carlos got around the wall the first elevator load - with both Secretaries, their immediate security details, and their Ukrainian escorts, had descended to the bunker level below. The remaining members of the staff, one Ukrainian Security police officer, and the Nuncio, Cardinal Jablonovski, were standing before the elevator doors, the latter standing aside by himself some distance past the short wall aimed between the two elevators. Apparently, he didn't make it in with the crowd on the first trip. People talked casually while they waited.

Suddenly, from outside, Carlos was positive he heard several single distant gunshots, and then what sounded like the detonations of two grenades. Usually, the sound of AK-47s and -74s meant bad guys, but in Ukraine, everyone had them.

He quickly withdrew his pistol from underneath his jacket, smoothly taking off the safety and had it up in a ready position as he moved back toward the opening through which they'd all come. Before he could get there the distinctively short, sharp, loud, "beat on a table with a sledgehammer" sound of the Kalashnikovs became very close, with yelling and then the cracking thuds of rounds impacting the concrete walls - and bodies. There was a crashing sound from what he assumed to be the X-ray scanner getting knocked aside or down.

Stopping at the edge of the long wall, he quick-checked around the corner and saw mayhem in the entry hall.

Ukrainians down, some still firing, with rounds going everywhere, and some attackers fell and laid where they'd fallen. He looked further around the corner just as the first of two filthy, bearded, camouflaged soldiers rounded the far end of the wall; the firing started soon after that.

He stepped out around the wall and fired three quick rounds at the trailer - before the second two rounds found his torso the first round took off the top of his head and painted the far wall with a grisly gray and red spray while his Kalashnikov crashed noisily to the floor.

Checking the entryway and finding no other "filthy" soldiers heading his way he sprinted along the wall, nearly skidded to a halt, and came around the corner to find the first attacker arriving in front of the elevator doors, standing over what looked like the security guard and the Nuncio lying inert at his feet. He was raising his AK to fire on the staffers cowering on the other side from the noise and the violence they just witnessed.

As he ran, Carlos shouted in Arabic, "Ansur khalfak!" and saw the man hesitate and start to turn slightly to check behind him. Worried about the ricochets in that enclosure Carlos held up just a little longer than he would have liked, steadied up, and fired once to the head hitting him square in the temple and then again that hit behind the shooter's right arm penetrating around the 4th or 5th rib and in front of the scapula. He collapsed hard to the floor and did not move.

The survivors screamed as one at the sight. The elevator *DINGED* then the doors opened causing a frantic high-stepping stampede through the mess for the relative safety within. The doors closed right away as someone inside determinedly mashed at the opposing arrows of the DOORS CLOSE button on the elevator control panel with both thumbs.

Carlos checked behind him, ran forward through the area just vacated, cleared around the corner, and returned to the fallen. The attackers were dead, he knew that. Unfortunately, so too were the Ukrainian security policeman and the Papal representative.

33

CALM DOWN

It was surprisingly calm by the time Carlos got downstairs to the bunker. People were clustered into small groups talking nervously, some hugging, and several crying quietly. Secretaries Austin and Blinkin were both on the phone looking very serious. Leo was sitting comfortably on a chair by a table in the corner.

When Carlos approached, Leo said casually, "I heard you were busy. The Nuncio?"

"Not a chance. But it was quick. I can't say they singled him out because the shooter was about to fire on all the rest when I got him - but killing the Pope's representative is pretty bold."

Leo nodded.

After a moment, Carlos resumed, "People here look better than I thought they'd be after nearly getting killed."

"Well, *General* Austin gathered everyone around and had a short rally-the-troops talk and told 'em all in no uncertain terms to calm down. He can be very persuasive."

So true, thought Carlos. After a moment, he asked, "Are the meetings still on?"

"Yes, of course. The Palace Security Chief left right before you got here. He said that his unit engaged some Russian soldiers at the back gate who came out of the woods, and with them focused there some half-a-dozen others came out of the woods from the east and ambushed the guards at the entrance. He suspected they may have been in the woods for a while. Told me that this is the 10th assassination attempt on the President they have defended since the war started - though this is the first one that got to the palace."

"I'm afraid it isn't pretty upstairs," Carlos said. "Will be a while before it is cleaned up enough for these people to leave for the follow-on meetings."

Carlos was searching the pockets of the two dead attackers when Ukrainian Ground Forces troops appeared, uncertain of what they would find. Consequently, Carlos spent the next 30 minutes with them explaining what happened. Ukrainian casualties were not light - but none of the attackers survived as far as they could tell - including the two that got through to Carlos.

"They weren't all Russians Leo."

"What do you mean?"

"I knew the two guys I dealt with weren't Russian the moment I saw them. They've been in the field for a long time, but no Russian wears a beard like a soldier of radical Islam."

"Any patches or other ID?"

"Their uniforms were sanitized - no rank and no patches. But they each had an ID card in their left breast pocket - Chechen 141st Special Motorized Regiment. Kadyrovites."

Leo thought about that a moment, then said, "Well, that isn't too surprising. We knew they were in the region, allegedly fighting alongside Russian and Wagner forces."

"True. But check this out." And with that, he dropped a small brownish-tan, 4-inch diameter circular tablet on the table, with wear marks on the raised temple rendering and Arabic script.

"What is this, a souvenir?"

"It is a Turbah - a clay tablet representing the purified earth used in daily prayers by some Shia Muslims. Specifically, they put their foreheads on these when they prostrate themselves during prayer."

"And your point?"

Carlos paused, forming his thoughts more fully, and said, "Chechen President Ramzan Kadyrov rules a country that he and the Head of the Spiritual Administration of Muslims, Salakh Mezhiyev, proclaimed would only tolerate Sunni Muslims in their country. The 141st is a very political and extremist organization fighting to protect the President and execute his orders. It seems strange to me that they would knowingly harbor Shia members - especially given that Chechnya is at odds with the biggest Shia nation in the world - Iran."

"Ah, yeah, this might be worthy of follow-up."

"Especially when they succeeded in killing a representative of the Catholic Church. I already sent photos of the turbah and the IDs to Langley to see what they make of it all."

Just then, the large doors at the end of the room opened and in stepped President Zelenskiy, dressed in his usual war-time olive drab pants and "formal" sweater with the Ukrainian insignia at the collar in front. The room went silent as he stood there gazing solemnly, but confidently, at the crowd.

Immediately, he said, "Please, given these circumstances, let me walk the room and shake your hands and assure you we are safe."

And he walked to every person in the room, shook their hand and said a few kind words, and moved to the next. He did not let on in the slightest that he knew what Carlos did upstairs. At the end of the line, he went and stood with the two secretaries, shook their hands, and turned to face the whole room.

"Today we lost people again while defending our democracy. We grieve our soldiers, and His Excellency, Il Nuncio, Cardinal Jablonovski. I'm sorry this happened, especially coincidental with your arrival for these important meetings. But perhaps you see with how much heart the defenders of Ukraine live every day to win this illegal war brought upon us by Putin's Russia. Secretary Blinkin and Secretary Austin and I will retire immediately for private meetings without the planned informal, open discussions. Thank you all for coming to Ukraine. I hope your meetings with our people are fruitful."

And the three turned and left the room.

Leo said, "So much for getting the upstairs cleaned up before these folks depart."

Several of those who ran for the elevator earlier approached Carlos to express their gratitude. It was uncomfortable but appreciated.

Leo and Carlos soon picked up their things, said some goodbyes, and found their handler from the Security Service of

Ukraine waiting in the back of the room. He would ensure they got to the SBU building for the planned visit with the deputy leaders of the Ukrainian intelligence community.

34

DEATH AND WANTON MURDER

Once Leo, Carlos, and the handler settled into the passenger and second-row seats of the SUV in the back of the palace, the Ukrainian Army driver left for the headquarters building of the Security Service of Ukraine located just a third of a mile west of Independence Square. It took only minutes to get there. Traffic was light.

Technically, the host of the meeting today was the Deputy Chairman of the separate Foreign Intelligence Service of Ukraine, Mr. Mykola Voloshin. But the SBU building was closer to the palace, and as Carlos would soon learn, there was somewhat of an ongoing power struggle within the intelligence community here.

The SBU building (SBU for Sluzhba Bezpeky Ukrayniy - Security Service of Ukraine), was an imposing gray, six-floor concrete structure, highlighted by four columns appearing to support a Greek-style pediment jutting out from the fifth floor. It featured a grand front entrance save for the dungeon-like solid wood, windowless, double front doors surrounded by filled sandbags.

In fact, the entire first floor was either windowless - or significantly protected by iron bars. Given the history, Carlos wasn't sure if those bars were fixed in place to keep people from breaking in, or to keep those inside from getting out. It had an appearance as cold and unwelcoming as the Lubyanka prison itself in Moscow. The blue and yellow banner flew brilliantly over the pediment as if to dress it up.

The SBU traced its history back through the Ukrainian KGB, to the Russian KGB, and before that the NKVD and its predecessor, the Joint State Political Directorate. A sinister lineage thought the officer from the CIA.

In 2003, the SBU sub-unit responsible for foreign intelligence was split off and subordinated directly to the Office of the President. That new agency, the Sluzhba Zovnishn'oi Rozvidky Ukrayniy, or SZRU, held a higher rung on the hierarchy ladder. Unless you were old school.

And most of the SBU was made up of old-school operatives from the Ukrainian KGB (or their direct hires) who operated by that infamous acronym up until the dissolution of the Soviet Union in 1991.

Mr. Voloshin on the other hand liked to think of himself and the SZRU, chaired by a political appointee named Valeriy Kondratzuk, as more enlightened. Unburdened by the dark past. And certainly more powerful given the direct link to the President.

Their SBU handler took them through the front doors, into a large vestibule, face-to-face with an armed guard. On the right was a glassed-in enclosure that contained the security administrative staff and sign-in, badging, and discussion of escort requirement rules common to every classified military or industrial or intelligence facility he'd ever been in anywhere. After processing they were taken directly to a first-floor, moderate-sized conference room with a bunch of photos of scowling military uniformed senior citizens who undoubtedly were prior leaders.

Motioning to the chairs, their handler disappeared.

But before they could sit down, in walked Mykola Voloshin, comfortably dressed in appropriately warm civilian clothes, tall, average build, light brown hair thinning slightly on top.

"Dobroho ranku, panove," he greeted them in Ukrainian, "But perhaps we should switch to English."

His handshake was firm, vigorously shook, and he looked them right in the eye as he did it.

"Good morning to you too, Deputy Voloshin," said Leo. "Nice to see you again. This is my associate, Carlos Pombar." Carlos nodded hello.

"It may not surprise you but I am familiar with both of you." Interesting, thought Carlos. He did not respond.

"I expected my counterpart, the Deputy Director of the SBU, Bryhadnyi..., excuse me, Brigadier General Danilo Martinovich to be here already. Please have a seat," he said, indicating two chairs on the side of the table - he took one of the two chairs on the opposite side as they sat down.

"I understand your visit to Kyiv has been...eventful so far."

Leo smiled slightly and said, "More eventful than expected perhaps. But we are glad to be here meeting with..."

And in walked General Martinovich. The Americans stood.

Dark featured, with dark hair, speckled gray at the sides. Intensely dark eyes. He was immaculately dressed in military green uniform, the SBU security service patch on one shoulder, an SBU metal and ceramic badge (blue cossack cross with centered gold trident and wreath) over his name tag on the right breast pocket, a single row of ribbons over his left breast pocket, and notably, the Alpha Group Spetsnaz patch on the other shoulder. He wore brigadier general shoulder boards with a single embroidered diamond set inside the crossed bulava, or scepters, which bordered the outside edge.

He immediately sat down. At the head of the table, as opposed to the chair next to Deputy Voloshin.

"Good morning General," started Voloshin, "may I introduce..."

"I know who they are. Welcome, Leo. And this must be Mr. Pombar." No warmth whatsoever.

"Thank you, sir," Leo replied. "We are pleased to be meeting with you two today."

Curtly, Martinovich asked, "Do you not get our intelligence summaries which we release daily to your leadership in Washington?"

"Of course we do," said Leo. "But as within our organization, we know that sometimes there are things omitted from written reports that might be more easily discussed in person."

"Then perhaps we should ask our guests..." started Voloshin.

"Mykola, please, we know why they are here," said Martinovich. "Pardon my abruptness, but I do not have time to wait through the preamble."

"Alright then, Danilo, I'll get right to it," said Voloshin. "President Zelenskiy asked me to pass you the same message he is conveying to Secretary Blinkin and Secretary Austin. He wants you to know that we have spent the time since 2013-2014 preparing the best we could for this inevitable invasion. Putin has made his intentions clear, and despite those of our politicians who might have been slow to see it coming (wishful thinking, perhaps?, he asked, and shrugged his shoulders), the intelligence and military and logistics branches have been doing all they can to upgrade processes, to accomplish training, and to modify old weapon systems and acquire new ones. Perhaps more than anything else we have well-trained and motivated people to put in this fight and we are doing so. But, we want you to go away from here UNDERSTANDING that what we need most is more, more, and more advanced weapons systems to beat the Russians."

Martinovich added, "In my blunt way, let me say that we want to ensure that our messaging about any subject we discuss today does not interfere with that presidential desire."

"Yessir," said Leo. "You have made that clear."

"I understand you came here specifically to learn more about, what should we say, certain elements of the Russian forces. Is that correct?"

"Yes, it is."

Voloshin started to talk but General Martinovich held up his hand, and said quietly, "Mykola, please."

Leo had explained the separation of powers between the intelligence agencies to Carlos on the train. Since the separation of the two security services, the lasting disagreements have centered primarily on turf. The SZRU focuses on international intelligence gathering and evaluation - in politics, economics, military, scientific, technical information, and ecological areas. They look outside and try to assess what information out there might be exploited or defended against for the good of the nation. Similar to the Agency at Langley.

The SBU is focused more internally. They are charged with the protection of national sovereignty, constitutional order, territorial integrity, and the economic, scientific, technical, and defense potential of Ukraine. Now that the Russians were *in* Ukraine the first-hand knowledge of the fight resided in the SBU (in partnership with the MoD intelligence teams). Resembling a very militarized FBI.

"Please continue Danilo, I didn't mean to overstep."

"The only persons who might know this topic better than me, or who might be more appropriate to talk to about it, would be the soldiers and civilians within our borders being beaten, tortured, raped, and awaiting their turns to be murdered while they watch helplessly as the fucking Russians kill their comrades."

Silence for a moment. Blunt but well said, thought Carlos.

After a deep breath, the general began his assessment of the forces arrayed inside Ukraine.

"First off, let me say that I will not focus on the Russian Strategic Forces, the Army, the Air Force, or their Maritime Forces except to say that they appear to be poorly led, poorly trained, poorly supported, and the soldiers themselves are struggling to perform the most basic combat tactics. The Russians are doing nothing well, with the possible exceptions of embracing the old Soviet practices of wasting soldiers' lives without concern, and employing voluminous artillery and aerial bombardment - even if that is indiscriminate."

"We are better trained and better equipped already than those we meet on the battlefield. But, as we said in the beginning, we cannot keep up with the Russian military might over time without more weapons."

Neither Leo nor Carlos wanted to interrupt.

Martinovich continued. "What causes us the most concern is the non-traditional military forces we see in this war. Primarily for their unpredictability. The paramilitary presence, particularly the Wagner Group, is significant in the east and also in the forces invading from the north."

"PMC Wagner is a serious fighting force composed of many Russian and international, combat-experienced personnel. They have been fighting for years in places in Africa and the Middle East. They are present in countries as "teachers" in military assistance roles where they are known for doing things the resident forces won't do to control local populations or to ensure the success of illegal or immoral businesses. Of course, this is on the books as a legally legitimate company - it employs personnel to do work for a profit. Regardless of the work they do, you cannot dispute they gain experience along the way. And in recent years, we've seen relatively small numbers of them fighting in Syria, Libya, the Central African Republic, and Mali - basically fighting with governments aligned with Russia. They fought in the annexation of Crimea, and have participated in the years-long fight in the Donbas; in Luhansk, and Donetsk. In every instance, there are internationally documented cases of human rights abuses and war crimes. And now they are here."

He poured a drink of water from a decanter into a glass, took a drink, and then went on.

"We are certain that they operate with the blessing, if not under the direction of, Vladimir Putin. As you may know, PMCs are outlawed in Russia, so how else could they operate except with his blind eye? And we now know, from our signals intelligence gathering, that after years of suspicion, the oligarch Yevgeny Prigozhin is the overall master of PMC Wagner. Somehow - via Putin, we don't know - he has access to the Russian Ministry of Defence budget, equipment, supplies, training facilities, and planning. His forces are embedded in the fight to the west and north of Kyiv. They are certainly responsible for many of the atrocities we are seeing in dozens of recaptured cities and towns."

"They are accompanied here by Chechnya President Ramzan Kadyrov's security forces, the 141st Special Motorized Regiment. This security force for hire is popular in places where you want to enforce discipline in your own forces and instill terror in the local population. While the Russian forces can be equally brutal, the Kadyrovites are particularly heinous and vile, taking enjoyment from the killing of innocents. They post their excesses online! They were personally tasked with decapitating the leadership of the Ukrainian government. I am proud to say they have not succeeded." An SBU responsibility.

Leo asked, "Do they both fight as intact units under Army command or are they executing orders from another leadership source?"

"We've seen evidence of both. They were embedded with the Army as they moved south out of Belarus and occupied towns along the way to Kyiv, like Ivankiv and Bucha, and Irpin; they even maneuvered independently and tried to get to Hostomel and other areas where the Russian Airborne was so badly mauled. But as I said, at times we see small elements of them running missions such as the assassination attempts, or performing security details for other Russian units bogged down along the way."

"There is another aspect to them that I do not believe is well known or commonly understood to be true. Interrogation of Wagner captives - frequently, financial incentive works well - has revealed that there are Wagner elements in many organizations not associated directly with their fighting units in the field. In addition to access to everything from personal weapons to armored vehicles, to aircraft and helicopters, and even to artillery and missile batteries, we know there are Wagner supporters in the active duty military units. Are they sleepers? Are they just there as part of the Wagner boss's desire to know everything and influence things his way? We don't know. For example, a *retired* Russian Air Force general was recently killed when he was shot down flying an Su-25 air-to-ground attack aircraft in the Donbas - allegedly under the employ of PMC Wagner. How does a Wagner employee get access to an Air Force jet?"

Leo asked, "Is this sanctioned by Moscow or independent of the Kremlin?"

"Every single instance we find of these sleeper Wagner personnel appears to be without the knowledge of their supervision. In fact, those we know of appear to have never done anything outside of their normal job description, yet we know through gathered intelligence findings that they are in Wagner's employ."

After a quiet pause, Leo asked, "Can you provide more information about the atrocities you are uncovering and who you think is behind it? Even in his remarks to the UN, some feel the President was holding back a little."

Voloshin sat forward and said, "President Zelenskiy knows how to work an audience. He knows that numbers - even each horrific number we are talking about here - can be mind-numbing to some. He wanted to expose the truths without losing the sympathy he wanted due to overstating the numbers."

"I will be blunt again," said the General. "Even if you discount the indiscriminate artillery fire, the reckless aerial bombardments, the errant cruise missiles, and the surface-to-surface missiles, there are thousands of dead Ukrainians that did not have to die. I'm not talking about collateral damage. I'm talking about the reckless death and wanton murder of civilians in every area occupied by the Russians. And the worst of atrocities are directly linked to Wagner and the 141st Regiment."

"We won't dwell on the images and the stories, the bodies we found in wells, stacked in the cellars, the tied up victims executed at close range - sometimes blown up with hand grenades fastened to them. The children. This murderous rampage must be stopped however we can stop them. I understand bad decisions made by hungry, demoralized, angry, and undisciplined soldiers. Sometimes these things happen in the best of armies. But the world cannot tolerate the purposeful detention, abuse, torture, rape, disfigurement, and murder of innocent civilians. You and I have seen combat in the uniform of our countries. Bad things happen. Accidents happen. Trying NOT to kill non-combatants separates the good soldier from the bad ones - but trying to kill as many as you can, to rape and to torture and to murder them, is what makes those soldiers all criminals."

They felt, and the clock showed, that it was time to end the meeting.

The General stood, followed by Voloshin and the Americans. They somberly shook hands and bid farewell. Then the Ukrainian driver took them to the train station to ride the nighttime Ukrainian Express in reverse back to Poland.

35

JUST BIGGER BOMBS

Dimitri Utkin sat uncomfortably on the adjustable seat in the commander's cupola of the Wagner Group's BTR-80 command vehicle. It was uncomfortable - even when they weren't bouncing on these roads worn out by too many armored vehicles and trucks.

All now going the wrong way.

Well, he thought, his soldiers may not agree with him saying they were going the wrong way as none of them have died since leaving Bucha behind. For them, this may be exactly the direction they prefer to be going.

Despite Prigozhin's desires to get out as soon as possible and save as much of the Group as he could, they were unable to do so. First, elements of his and the 141st forces, those that hadn't already been destroyed, were extended well south and they took a long time to reconstitute and move north. Second, even Prigozhin would have to admit that the only disciplined force capable of providing a rear guard for a large Army in retreat (or a "strategic reposition" as the Kremlin called it) was PMC Wagner.

Once they were moving on the roads north of Bucha to Ivankiv and points beyond, it was comforting to finally realize that they outran the Ukrainian's ability to pursue them. No doubt because the khokhols were also exhausted after putting up such a fight.

Thankfully, we've run farther than the longest reach of their artillery, and now we are safely under the umbrella of our surface-to-air missile defenses which will keep the enemy's air force off our backs.

From inside, the radio came alive with the announcement that the last elements of his Group were only miles away now. About time, he thought.

His vehicle was parked on high ground in the middle of a roundabout on the P-35 highway to the town of Chornobyl (as the Ukrainians call it) which was lying visible just 2 miles to the east.

Vehicles were going by in front of him, noisily clanking and rumbling and belching diesel smoke one after another on the trek north. It was a motley collection of battered tanks, APCs of various sorts, supply and troop trucks, fuel bowsers, and other staff and utility vehicles. They were all festooned with dirty, ill-equipped, exhausted soldiers, clinging glumly to their souvenirs which they had collected from Ukrainian homes and businesses. They looked defeated.

There was none of that hanging off of his vehicles. Inside, maybe. But not dangling on the outside like a damn gypsy parade.

There was no unit cohesion to speak of either - all the various vehicles from numerous regular army groups were intermixed in the convoy. Elements of armored units, engineers, mechanized infantry, and even some of the surviving airborne troops from down south. Their only common traits were filth and exhaustion.

But his unit collected and moved as one. The remains of PMC Wagner Group were lined up on the shoulder of the road in front of him to the south-southeast, all around the top of the turn-circle behind him, and nearly all of the way to the Pripyat River to the northeast. He sat here waiting on the arrival of the last of his vehicles, and then for all of the army stragglers to pass before the Group could move as one another 20 miles into Belarus to bed down for the night and take stock of our remaining forces.

A blue and yellow highway sign behind him pointed an arrow to the right with directions to the "Monument to Those Who Saved the World" - a tribute to the heroes who worked the runaway reactor at Chornobyl nearly 36 years ago to the day. This place made him nervous.

The only reason he allowed the Group to proceed this far into the Chornobyl Exclusion Zone today was that it was overcast and raining - light but steady. He reasoned that the water would keep the radioactive dust down. When it was time to move he would order the Group to button up as best as they could - close and seal up the hatches, doors, windows, and canvas flaps - and they would transit the area and cross the river as quickly as possible.

He was not eager to get the status reports of the units - it would not be pleasant given the losses they'd suffered.

This special military operation was planned poorly and executed worse. He was spoiled - in past operations, his relatively small group of professional soldiers were well-motivated, superbly equipped, and successful as independent operators in smaller scenarios. In this case, while his core cadre was still well equipped and motivated, the expansion in the last year had brought a lot of new soldiers who, despite rigorous training, were not quite so competent.

That was typical of any organization that tries to grow quickly.

But by far, the worst part of this experience was trying to work as an integrated part of the immense Russian Ground Forces. The army (and the air force and the navy) performed poorly - from the very top down. Not that he can say that in front of anyone.

By now a laughing stock in the international press - the biggest army in the world had been defeated, yes defeated, by a third-rate military using a flood of superb weapons provided by the West. Without NATO interference there was no way this would have turned out so badly.

Dmitri glanced at his watch. He was expecting Prigozhin to call at the top of the hour and it was nearly time. He connected the earpiece to the phone in the unlikely event that someone in the vehicle could hear over all this noise.

When the phone vibrated in his hand he pressed the green button.

"Dimitri here."

Listening.

"Yessir," he replied.

Prigozhin talking again.

"We expect to be at the camp by nightfall - it is only 20 more miles or so."

Long pause.

"There is only one left of the whole battery."

Longer pause. Dmitri frowned. He shifted in his seat and then stood up and turned around, looking along the line of Wagner vehicles to the north. He jotted down some things on a small notepad.

"I can see the last Iskandr and its trailer from here. I know it is fully functional. But the crew is exhausted - they need the break."

He flushed a little red in the face.

"Ok. I will have them fueled and then send them east later tonight. There will be three vehicles that will need fuel at the other end to return."

Waiting.

"Yessir. I will send a third escort vehicle with ten soldiers. There better be food and showers at the site." He made some additional notes.

He nodded. Frowning.

Finally, "Are you sure you want to do this?"

He closed his eyes and bowed his head slightly.

"Then it will be done."

Pause.

"Yessir," he said with a heavy voice, punched the red "End" button, disconnected and rolled up the cord to the earpiece, and put everything back in his pocket.

He looked up in time to see the Wagner flag on the whip antenna of the last vehicle in line headed his way. His command sergeant was out front waving the three vehicles to his right to park behind the rise inside the back of the turn-circle.

The BMP with the flag on the whip antenna was soon passing slowly to his right when the officer in the cupola stood up straight and snapped off a perfect salute. Dimitri allowed himself a tired smile and returned it.

Two Mi-28 attack helicopters flew over and headed south-southeast along the road to sweep it, looking for stragglers and especially for Ukrainian units.

PMC Wagner would stay here for an hour to ensure no other vehicles were coming. And to give some room between the last of the fleeing gypsy vehicles and the lead elements of his Group.

Then he thought about the phone call.

Though he and Prigozhin had talked about this possibility before, he did not expect to be told to make it happen. He understood the motivation - and frankly, didn't much care about the consequences. It will rattle a whole bunch of governments but in the end, they are just bigger bombs. And Russia will look stronger.

There was no doubt in his mind that the West wouldn't do anything as long as no NATO forces were harmed in the process of using them. And, he had to admit, in addition to hindering the shipment of more arms from the West for a while, it will make a huge statement to the West regarding their actions: stop helping the Ukrainians.

Then, of course, there was Prigozhin's primary purpose - to demonstrate his power to the inner circle and show his ability to get things done in these difficult circumstances when regular army leadership could not. And it would partially erase the humiliation of the defeat suffered here.

"Dominick," he shouted down to his radio operator. "Get Captain Sidorov on the net and tell him to run down here immediately. Alone. And hand up something to eat and drink."

"Yessir," Dominick shouted up at him. And immediately Dimitri could hear him on the radio doing what he was told. Another soldier passed up the rations and water.

When Captain Sidorov arrived, somewhat winded, Dmitri put down his midday meal on top of the vehicle, got out of the cupola, walked to the side of the armored deck, turned around and stepped backward off the side to put a foot on one of the huge tires, and lowered himself to the muddy ground.

"Alyosha, let's take a walk," and he guided the Captain around the back of the vehicle, across the turn-circle, and into the field on the far side. Away from idle ears no longer bombarded by the noise of the parade of vehicles.

After some brief discussion about the long ride, and the typical comments about discomfort and army leadership, Dmitri asked him, "What is the status of your battery?"

"Sir, we only have one TEL, but it is fully loaded with two missiles and combat-ready."

"What about the transloader? Where is it?"

"It is parked further up the road - closer to the head of the column. It is functional - also carrying two missiles."

"How is the fuel supply on the transloader?"

"Fairly low - but enough to get to today's destination"

Dmitri paused, looking up at the helicopters as they headed back their way.

Then he said, "Listen to me carefully. We have been chosen for a very special mission. Your transloader needs to be at Weapons Storage Site B-22, outside of Belgorod, by sundown the day after tomorrow. When you arrive at the site, your men will be cared for while as they assist with the completion of special maintenance on the weapons. You will leave as soon as that work is complete and return to today's bivouac location. Here are the coordinates of site B-22." He handed the officer one of the pages from his notepad.

Continuing, he said, "Access to the site is already arranged for you - there will be no need for orders or passwords - just have your normal IDs available."

Captain Sidorov was looking very serious.

"I will see that a fuel bowser tops off the transloader and your two escorting GAZ vehicles when we stop today. You and your soldiers will leave as soon as the supply truck provides a full replenishment kit for all of your men."

Finally, he said, "I want you to take every kind of maintenance person you might need to keep the transloader fully functional. No empty seats - take soldiers from the TEL personnel, if needed. I will provide a BTR-80 with ten soldiers to accompany you. Major Navikoff will be in charge. He will seek you out during replenishment."

He paused for a moment, looking carefully at his Iskandr Battery commander. Then he said, "Do you have any questions?"

"No sir," Alyosha nearly shouted. Of course, he does, thought Dmitri. I will check up on him again later.

"You will do fine. Now go prepare - and say nothing to anyone outside your soldiers."

Captain Sidorov stood up straight, saluted, and started the jog back to his vehicle.

Dimitri headed off to his vehicle to talk to Major Sacha Navikoff, his deputy, about what he just told Alyosha they would be doing for the next couple of days.

36

MISFORTUNE OF ONE KIND

P rigozhin sat in his private study considering his call with Dmitri. He seemed to take it as expected - another order to execute. As always, an outstanding leader and loyal subordinate.

But he had another call to make.

This decision was probably more difficult than what he had just discussed with his PMC Wagner leader in Ukraine. Though he was certain it had to be done.

The Pope canceled his trip to Ukraine, and only today did the Vatican place a small notice on The Vatican News website that the available time would be spent in Buenos Aires - the place of his long residency as the Archdiocese before being named to replace Pope John Paul II in 2013.

This opportunity could not be missed. After years as a staunch opponent of Russian nationalism, and especially after the recent public denunciations of President Putin and the War in Ukraine, he could no longer be tolerated.

He was especially harsh on the atrocities uncovered in Bucha and led the West in condemnation. His recent propaganda display at the Vatican with the Ukrainian children was particularly offensive - especially holding up the Ukrainian flag for the cameras and insulting the military leadership and the President in the process.

During a joint video conference in March, the Pope chided Kirill, the Patriarch of Moscow and the Primate of the Russian Orthodox Church to "...read from that piece of paper you are holding in your hand all the reasons that justify the Russian invasion," thus humiliating the Patriarch in front of the many participants.

Then there was the public display with the refugees and the flag regarding the atrocities in Bucha.

In reaction, Kirill went nearly apoplectic with rage. How dare this man, whose Church has centuries of bloodshed on its hands, admonish Russia during its rightful pursuit of the restoration of the Kievan Rus' in the territories historically held by the Russian empires?

He had barely calmed down when Prigozhin dined with him at one of Moscow's finest restaurants. A wealthy man like him, Kirill did not deny himself any of life's creature comforts. But he hardly touched his food as he went on about the threat posed by the Vatican to his vision of Russia's future. After all, he said, Putin's ascendancy to the Presidency was a gift from God and all who spoke against it, and the invasion should be eliminated as enemies of Russia and God.

Enough of that, Prigozhin thought.

He picked up the phone and dialed the 0054 number for Argentina, then 9 for cell phones, then the unlisted 9-digit number for the PMC Wagner Site Manager in Buenos Aires, Sergei Miloslav. The Wagner office there had just opened.

Miloslav was an interesting man. Dark, sadistically violent, he was long thought to be the up-and-coming PMC Wagner leader - Prigozhin's deputy - but things turned south for him in Syria. The United Nations Commission for Human Rights is so...inconvenient sometimes. Sergei picked up on the other end.

"So, Putin's Chef calls the exiled soldier. What do you want today Mr. Prigozhin?"

"Sergei, there is no need to be this way. Consider Buenos Aires a temporary assignment for rest-and-relaxation."

"While the serious leaders of PMC Wagner fight in Ukraine, I just sit here setting up an office and wasting my skills."

"Nonsense," Prigozhin said, "standing up the new office there is important to me. You will get your chance. And I have an *opportunity* for you now."

"Do tell," said Miloslav.

"Perhaps you've seen the news about the Pope's intended trip to Argentina?"

"You can't miss it."

"Well, it is in the interests of very senior people here that he suffers misfortune of one kind or another on this trip. And I've been asked to make that happen."

There was a pause, then Sergei drew a deep breath and then asked, "Are you ordering me to assassinate the Pope?"

"If it has to be said, then yes, that is what I want you to do."

"Very well. I would think we can expect significant financial incentive to do this thing you ask."

"Of course."

"Then do not bother me again until it is over. The secure phone system will be operational soon. Call us at that number on Monday following the event. We cannot risk these kinds of calls again."

"Good luck."

"Yes. That would help."

They hung up. Prigozhin thought Sergei would have come unglued if he had to rely on cell phones like Dmitri.

37

SAFE HAVEN FOR WAGNER

Carlos just completed a long workout in the gym in the basement of the George Bush Center for Intelligence in Langley, Virginia, and set his bag down next to the hoteling cubicle he was using when his SatPhone disguised as an iPhone vibrated in his shirt pocket. The caller ID showed it was Skip.

"Good morning."

"Are you in the building?"

"Yes."

"Then get up to Angela's office on the top floor. Right now," said Skip, and then he ended the call.

It was a short walk to the bank of four elevators, then a fast ride to the sixth floor. The elevator opened into a large foyer with a security desk set in front of a floor-to-ceiling bullet-proof glass wall with electric-powered sliding glass doors. You could see the entire length of the expansive hallway and the office doors of the Executive Wing but you could not enter without clearing security.

Which happened quickly as Skip was there waiting.

As they walked the long hallway to the Director's office at the end, Skip filled him in on what was happening.

"The Germans just dropped another set of cell phone transcripts on us. This one involves our friend Prigozhin, his Wagner office in Buenos Aires, and Pope Francis's upcoming trip."

"Really? I knew he canceled his trip to Ukraine, but I did not know he was headed to Buenos Aires."

"Apparently, he has not been back since he became Pope in 2013. Some wonder if he might soon retire."

They were waved through by the Executive Secretary, who nodded her head at Carlos and said, "Good morning."

Upon entering, he saw that the wooden conference table was nearly full - the Director sitting in her usual spot at the end, Skip sitting to her left (where he motioned to the next chair for Carlos), and three analysts were sitting on the right side of the table, and one person in a spare chair against the wall behind them with several files and loose papers. Carlos sat down next to Skip.

"Good morning Carlos. Welcome back. I apologize for not meeting with you after Kyiv but things have been quite busy, as I'm sure you understand."

"Good morning ma'am."

"The Secretaries both reached out to me to thank you for your work there." Carlos just nodded.

Skip said, "Right. Carlos, I believe you know almost everyone here: Andy Bondarenko from the Ukraine desk, John Volkoff and his assistant, Alex Laskin, from the Russia desk, and Greg Gomez from the Argentina desk."

They all nodded, several not making eye contact as was not uncommon for analysts. The only one Carlos did not know was the new guy Alex. Fairly young, slight build, fair hair, and blue eyes, with thick glasses. He looked at the floor a lot.

Angela led off by pointing at the screen and saying, "Carlos, we just got this transcript from our associates in the German Bundesnachrichtendienst. It records an open line call between Yevgeny Prigozhin, the assumed leader of the PMC Wagner Group, and an associate of his in, of all places, Buenos Aires."

Skip said, "Prigozhin is the long-time presumed financier and leader of Wagner. But now we have SIGINT that confirms it."

John Volkoff, the Russia analyst, offered, "As you may know, the Wagner group has various levels of forces in more than 20 countries around the world."

"I'm aware of that," Carlos said.

"You can presume that Carlos has extensive experience with the Wagner Group," Skip said.

Without missing a beat, John continued, "Technically, despite how they are represented in the news, these people are not mercenaries since PMC Wagner is a registered business within Russia. They have a Group Headquarters due to open this year in St. Petersburg - a large six-story polished metal shape nestled in amongst more traditional businesses downtown. Complete with the stylized capital W symbol etched into the double glass doors at the entrance."

He took a drink. Then, "They also have an office registered in Hong Kong though we haven't established whether it has opened yet, or not."

"And they do have an office that just opened in Buenos Aires. The Site Manager is Sergei Miloslav."

"Really?" asked Carlos. "Last I heard he was in Syria."

"That is right. He and his group of "soldiers" rounded up a bunch of civilians they accused of aiding forces of the Islamic State, tortured the men, raped the women, and then killed them all - including children. It was very gruesome - and it was caught on film and released online. The United Nations started investigations and he and some key members of his team disappeared. Apparently Argentina is still a safe haven for wanted men."

"Not so fast John," said Greg the Argentina desk analyst. "He entered the country legally on a work visa." Some turf pride showing.

Angela said, "Move on please."

"In any case, Miloslav has overseen the design, contracting, and construction of the office in Buenos Aires. As I said, it just opened for business, hoping to attract Argentine and other South American countries' interest in contracting various types of security assistance work."

John continued, "There is a huge power struggle - more like continuous maneuvering to attain power, associate with power, or retain power - in and around the Kremlin. We can't always say that Putin or Medvedev or even Shoigu originate or condone many of their policies as so many other hands are in the mix. One of those ambitious and cutthroat sets of hands belongs to Yevgeny Prigozhin."

"We have linked him not only with Wagner but also with some murders, including that of Ivan Rostov. He was a MoD attorney who was objecting to the Defence Ministry diverting money away from regular forces to pay for the outfitting of PMC Wagner in Belarus as they awaited the start of the Invasion of Ukraine. Apparently he died for his objections."

He continued, "We now know he had Demonov killed outside St. Petersburg." And with that, he looked up again and made eye contact with Carlos, who just nodded.

"We suspect he is behind some other death-by-falling-off-tall-building events around the country and maybe even abroad. In any case, he is ambitious, innovative, imaginative, persuasive, and ruthless. And he has a penchant for doing things impulsively, allegedly for the good of Russia, but especially for the good of himself."

"That brings us back to the transcript on screen," he said. "It looks like he intends to assassinate the Pope."

Carlos took the time to read through it all thoroughly.

Caller 1: Sergei Miloslav, Buenos Aires, Argentina
Caller 2: Yevgeny Prigozhin, St Petersburg, Russia (originates call)

—————————

START CALL
GMT 19:02:13

CALLER 1: SO, PUTIN'S CHEF CALLS THE EXILED SOLDIER.
WHAT DO YOU WANT TODAY MR. PRIGOZHIN?
CALLER 2: SERGEI, THERE IS NO NEED TO BE THIS WAY.
CONSIDER BUENOS AIRES A TEMPORARY
ASSIGNMENT FOR REST-AND-RELAXATION.
CALLER 1: WHILE THE SERIOUS LEADERS OF PMC WAGNER FIGHT IN UKRAINE, I JUST SIT HERE SETTING UP AN OFFICE AND WASTING MY SKILLS.
CALLER 2: NONSENSE. STANDING UP THE NEW OFFICE THERE

IS IMPORTANT TO ME. YOU WILL GET YOUR CHANCE. AND I HAVE AN OPPORTUNITY FOR YOU NOW.

CALLER 1: DO TELL.

CALLER 2: PERHAPS YOU'VE SEEN THE NEWS ABOUT THE POPE'S INTENDED TRIP TO ARGENTINA?

CALLER 1: YOU CAN'T MISS IT.

CALLER 2: WELL, IT IS IN THE INTERESTS OF VERY SENIOR PEOPLE HERE THAT HE SUFFERS MISFORTUNE OF ONE KIND OR ANOTHER ON THIS TRIP. AND I'VE BEEN ASKED TO MAKE THAT HAPPEN.

CALLER 1: ARE YOU ORDERING ME TO ASSASSINATE THE POPE?

CALLER 2: IF IT HAS TO BE SAID, THEN YES, THAT IS WHAT I WANT YOU TO DO.

CALLER 1: VERY WELL. I WOULD THINK WE CAN EXPECT SIGNIFICANT FINANCIAL INCENTIVE TO DO THIS THING YOU ASK.

CALLER 2: OF COURSE.

CALLER 1: THEN DO NOT BOTHER ME AGAIN UNTIL IT IS OVER. THE SECURE PHONE SYSTEM WILL BE OPERATIONAL SOON. CALL US AT THAT NUMBER ON MONDAY FOLLOWING THE EVENT. WE CANNOT RISK THESE KINDS OF CALLS AGAIN.

CALLER 2: GOOD LUCK.

CALLER 1: YES. THAT WOULD HELP.

GMT 19:03:43

END CALL

————————

"Andy?" said Angela.

Bondarenko looked up from his notes.

He said, "We think this is motivated by some of the Pope's negative statements concerning the war and overall Russian behaviors dating back before Crimea. For example, the Pope went out of his way to host Ukrainian refugees during one of his General Audiences earlier this month. He also had some tough words for those who committed the atrocities in Bucha and other cities, for Putin, and even for Kirill, the Patriarch of the Russian Orthodox Church. There are videos and stills of him online holding up a Ukrainian flag allegedly from Bucha."

John Volkoff, the Russia Desk Analyst added, "This decision is shocking and obscene. We think it cannot be coming from the Kremlin, though sometimes leadership there tends to turn a blind eye to things that may benefit them if accomplished in an unacknowledged way. And PMC Wagner is frequently used in actions that can be plausibly denied. There is another aspect of this which we don't fully understand."

Andy spoke up again, "After the assassination attempt in Kyiv, you picked up a Turbah from the assailants. You were right to question the presence of that *clearly Shia* holy artifact on the person from a country that is supposedly, and legally, wholly Sunni, and especially a person in the President's 141st Regiment."

Then John added, "Like so many other things about this war, there are constantly unpredictable elements, unforeseen actors, and unanticipated consequences of decisions to consider. In this case, we have to ask if there is a Shia element behind the scenes with Chechen forces, and also within Wagner. Could those elements further disrupt the chaos we know to be part of Prigozhin's plans? If it exists, does he even know of their presence?"

After a moment to consider that uncertainty, Greg Gomez, the Argentina analyst spoke up.

"PMC Wagner is new to the Buenos Aires business scene. To date, we know of no roles in the Argentine government, its military or security forces, or in the rest of South America. We believe the office is meant to establish a foothold in the region much like they've already done in Africa."

He continued, "But a preliminary analysis of the employment records indicates it is more like a safe haven for Wagner fighters who may have gotten too hot overseas. Having said that, it makes them even more threatening - perhaps some of their worst actors in Syria and other countries are on the payroll there. This adds to the concern about Prigozhin's ability to carry this out. We think it is a viable threat."

Skip said, "Tell him about the Shia statistics you discovered."

Greg continued, "After we saw your pictures of the Turbah and their IDs, we did a deep dive into the demographics of Buenos Aires, and alarmingly, we found that while there are only about 400-500,000 Muslims in all of Argentina, fully 22% are estimated to be of the Shia faith, and most of those live in Buenos Aires. So there may be a connection here."

"Most of us are familiar with the differences," Greg continued, "but at risk of oversimplification, let me remind everyone that Sunni and Shia Muslims differ in some significant ways going back to the formation of the religion itself. The Sunni faith (representing about 85% of the total Muslim population) believes that leadership of the religion is not a birthright - the leaders should be a caliphate elected from among the most capable. The Shia branch on the other hand believes that leadership of the faith is passed to a member, a descendent, of Muhammad's family. While not always violent, their differences are always there under the surface. The most obvious example at the state level is Iran (Shia) and Iraq (ruled by a Sunni minority) in the 80s."

"But, he continued, "there is another distinct difference between those two branches amongst those who choose to be terrorists. Sunni terrorists tend to be motivated to act impulsively, to attack frequently against any element of the opposition; the Shia extremists are more calculating - striking less impulsively, with a preference for targets of significance who have a huge impact. Like killing the head of the worldwide Roman Catholic Church."

A moment of silence.

Angela said, "So, now you know why we called you here. We want you to go to Buenos Aires and interfere with Prigozhin's plans."

"When do I leave?"

Skip said, "The G6 will take you to Buenos Aires tomorrow. The Pope arrives two days later, on Friday night. He will convoy to Villa 31 on Saturday, then perform Mass Sunday at the Cathedral, and return to the Vatican on Monday evening."

Greg said, "You will be met at the executive terminal by a new Agency field officer from the embassy who will take you there, where you can draw equipment and get the latest intel and an in-depth briefing on the Argentinian efforts to host the Pope in Buenos Aires."

Carlos thought quietly for a moment.

Then he said, "I want to meet privately with Greg after this meeting before I go home to pack."

"Of course," Angela said. "Good luck."

38

IT'S ALL GOOD HERE

Alone again, studying. As he liked it. Luka had just finished another bunker inspection - routine steps to ensure the temperature and humidity within the bunker were providing the right kind of atmosphere for the valuable weapons inside. He hardly checked the older weapons in the back of the bunker anymore. Only the newer RDS-9U versions - the 40 updated tactical nuclear weapons in his possession.

He allowed himself to think of them as his. No one else in this command ever did anything to manage this storage site - only he. Leadership (inappropriate word, he thought) was usually absent, negligent, drunk, or some combination of the three. But that left him alone to prepare.

Though the snow was finally gone, it was still cold and damp out here in the woods tonight. And it wasn't nearly so climate controlled in his sanctuary, the small office outside the bunker, as it was inside with the bombs. The electric heater at his feet was going full blast with little apparent effect.

He looked up from his inspection log and noticed it was completely dark out - his cold fingers fumbled at the heavy coat's sleeve as he pulled it away from his wristwatch on his left arm and saw that it was already nearly 22:00 hours. Another two hours or so before he could head to his cot back in the engineering office in the administrative building.

After pouring a cup of hot coffee from the thermos, he opened up his classified laptop and selected the file containing the 9M723 Iskandr-M Operations, Maintenance, and Weapons Procedures manual.

Though he knew he would never have a role in the operations of the missile - planning the strike, programming the computer, enabling the weapon, or firing it - he found the Operations section fascinating. After all, he used to be a highly qualified ICBM launch control officer before he was sent here to be the nuclear weapons engineering officer for this weapons storage site in the woods.

The General Description paragraph of the manual defined the weapon as a mobile, short-range ballistic missile. It is called a ballistic missile because, for most of its flight, it is unpowered and falling freely - much like an artillery shell - and exhibits ballistic characteristics subject primarily to the force of gravity.

He read that the overall Iskandr-M system was designed by the KB Mashinostroyeniya State Defense Enterprise. The missiles themselves were manufactured by the Votkinsk Machine Building Plant, and the ground equipment (the 9P78 transporter/erector/launcher (TEL), the 9T250-1 transloader, and four other support vehicles) were built by the Titan Barrikady Defense Company.

He read in professional publications that the missile system equipped 11 missile brigades in the Russian Army - each brigade having 12 TELs and the same number of transloaders. The TELs and the transloaders each carry two fully ready-to-launch missiles, complete with warheads.

Usually a conventional weapon.

The missile itself is 24 feet long, 3 feet in diameter, and it weighs in at 8,400 pounds. It has a single-stage solid propellant rocket engine that will boost a 1,500-pound warhead up to a velocity at rocket engine burnout of Mach 5.4 - over 4,000 miles per hour. It can travel its maximum range of just over 300 miles in only 4.5 minutes.

He had to sit back a minute and take in those numbers. It was unstoppable.

The magazine he'd read said that the 448th Missile Brigade southwest of Kursk is one of those 11 brigades equipped with the Iskandr-M. He had learned from associates (he did not have friends) that half the brigade was deployed forward during the special military operation. That meant there are six TELs, the same number of transloaders, and more than 24 command and control, mission planning, and other vehicles in the field. Then add in the trucks and supplies to support the many hundreds of personnel needed to maintain and operate the equipment.

And there were at least 24 missiles in the field. Hard to determine that, he thought, as he had no idea how many had been launched against targets in Ukraine.

During combat operations, as each 9T250-1 transloader transferred its load of two missiles to the TEL, it would rotate back to a rear area to get more and return to the brigade's position. With any operations at all transloaders were constantly on the road between the front and the supply depot. While they could be forward deployed, they required special handling equipment and storage capabilities - so most operations relied solely on the transloader for storage and resupply efforts.

In a typical combat scenario, the brigade would get targeting information from higher headquarters and then allocate those details to one or more batteries. The planning crew would do their work in the purpose-built planning vehicle, then transfer the needed targeting information to the launch crew at the TEL via a hardened data transfer cartridge. Once inserted into a reader device it was plugged into the missile data port, then powered on, and the data would load into the missile's flight computer. Though it required no work from the crew, that is where the magic happens.

The guidance computer would control the missile from just before launch, during the launch itself, through rocket engine burnout, then navigate during Iskandr's relatively flat ballistic flight (it never leaves the atmosphere), and finally, guide the missile to the target during the terminal phase.

Inflight, the computer has both onboard self-computing inertial navigation, GLONASS, and radar terrain correlation guidance. From 300 miles away 50% of the shots fired will land within a circle around the aim point of no more than 16 to 32 feet in diameter. That is called Circular Error Probable, or CEP. If the other 50% of the missiles fired doubled the miss distance it is irrelevant - particularly for tactical nuclear weapons like the RDS-9U targeted at open storage sites.

But, he thought as he reached to refill his cup, it is the actual targeting mechanics that is fascinating. How did the Germans do it with slide rules and chalkboards?

The German V-2, the grandfather of all ballistic missiles, was nearly twice as long and twice as wide as the Iskandr-M to accommodate the liquid propellent and oxidizer tanks - and to carry a 2,150-pound warhead. Overall it weighed more than 27,000 pounds compared to Iskandr's lightweight 8,400 pounds. Its combat range was up to 200 miles. But when they launched towards London its CEP was a circle 40,000 feet in diameter - 7.5 miles - a circle bigger than all of London today - including Hyde Park and Chelsea in the west, up through the London Zoo, then to Victoria Park and nearly to Greenwich in the east and down to past Peckham in the south. And even that accuracy was amazing for the time.

There are many factors to take into account when targeting whether your old missile is controlled by simple gyroscopic accelerometers or a new one with various onboard and off-board guidance sources - not to mention being maneuverable at the end game.

Luka thought out loud, "Just the fact that the earth rotates requires consideration."

In the simplest terms, the target moves from where it was at launch during the time of flight of the missile. Even snipers know that!

He thought to himself, the earth rotates 360 degrees every 23 hours, 56 minutes, and 4.04 seconds. In his head, he calculated that the approximate rotation speed of the earth is - approximately 1,000 miles per hour at the earth's equator. Let's say you aim at a target on the equator from directly north and the distance is such that the time of flight is 10 minutes. In the time it takes to reach the target's position that target would have moved 160 miles to the east! So, like a good duck hunter...

The old dial-a-number phone rang, *RING-RING*, startling Luka from his scientific distractions. He picked it up before the second double ring. He cleared his throat.

"Allo, Captain Pavloff here."

A pause, then, "Are you alone?"

"Yessir."

"What is the status of your possessions?"

"All my possessions are ready. Everything is in place."

Another pause. He could hear him breathing on the phone. Deep breaths, steady.

"And your supervision?"

"They will not interfere - they never come out here."

Quiet.

"Very well. Expect delivery in the next two days. You will be notified before arrival on this phone. Two of their possessions need to be modified as soon as possible. The delivery people will assist with security."

"It's all good here. I am very..."

"Enough Luka, it is time and you will have your chance to contribute in a major way to our situation here. You are in charge there. Be ready, perform well, and you will celebrate in the riches and recognition that will follow."

The line went dead. Thank goodness he didn't go back to his quarters early tonight. Quickly, he pushed the Operations manual aside and picked up the Weapons Procedures manual and began to study the load instructions in earnest.

He will be ready. He will get even.

39

BREAKING NEWS

Ron Minard waited for his secretary to close the door on her way out before turning the key on the secure phone. He saw the SECURE text appear in the window, followed soon after by the letters DirNRO.

"Good morning Chuck," he said, into the fuzzy background noise that came with knowing you had an encrypted line. Chuck was the Director of the National Reconnaissance Office - whose satellites the government relied on for imagery intelligence.

"Yes, it is a good morning Ron," came Director Chuck Higgins' voice as if speaking through an air purifier, "what can I do for you today?"

Pretty chipper for 5:30 am, Ron thought.

"I'm holding in my hand yet another German SIGINT transcript of a call made late last night from Prigozhin to a previously unknown recipient in an unknown location. But we suspect he is in Site B-22 near Belgorod."

"This guy seems to have lots of friends in strange places."

"Yes, he does. I'm sending it to you right now, but I wanted to get you on the phone first so you could expedite narrowing the search areas for your satellites. Let me know when it pops up."

A few moments went by.

"Got it. Opening it now."

"As you can see, it was recorded about 12 hours ago our time. So, what you read here has advanced in the real world about half a day."

"Looking at it ..."

Caller 1: Luka Pavlov, Captain
Caller 2: Yevgeny Prigozhin, St. Petersburg, Russia (originates call)

———————

START CALL
GMT 20:41:17

CALLER 1: ALLO, CAPTAIN PAVLOFF HERE.
CALLER 2: ARE YOU ALONE?
CALLER 1: YESSIR.
CALLER 2: WHAT IS THE STATUS OF YOUR POSSESSIONS?
CALLER 1: ALL MY POSSESSIONS ARE READY. EVERYTHING
IS IN PLACE.
CALLER 2: AND YOUR SUPERVISION?
CALLER 1: THEY WILL NOT INTERFERE - THEY NEVER COME OUT
HERE.
CALLER 2: VERY WELL. EXPECT DELIVERY IN THE NEXT TWO
DAYS. YOU WILL BE NOTIFIED BEFORE THEIR ARRIVAL ON THIS
PHONE. TWO OF THEIR POSSESSIONS NEED TO BE MODIFIED AS
SOON AS POSSIBLE. THE DELIVERY PEOPLE WILL ASSIST WITH
SECURITY.
CALLER 1: IT'S ALL GOOD HERE. I AM VERY...
CALLER 2: ENOUGH LUKA, IT IS TIME AND YOU WILL HAVE YOUR
CHANCE TO CONTRIBUTE IN A MAJOR WAY TO OUR SITUATION

HERE. YOU ARE IN CHARGE THERE. BE READY, PERFORM WELL, AND YOU WILL CELEBRATE IN THE RICHES AND RECOGNITION THAT WILL FOLLOW.

GMT 20:42:13
END CALL

When he read through the transcript, Chuck said, "This is helpful. Since we got that previous message of him talking to the Wagner team leader in the field we were able to locate their bivouac area where they spent the night before sundown and accounted for the Iskandr TEL, the transloader, and the support vehicles. But since we saw that the transloader was gone in the next morning's images we've been searching every road since with no luck."

"Like the proverbial needle in the haystack."

"Yes, but a big needle - not happy we couldn't find it. The good news is that we think we've accounted for every surviving TEL/transloader tandem set from the Russian 448th Missile Regiment and ruled them out as players."

Ron said, "Well, given that they've been on the road 24 hours, maybe not traveling in the daylight, they should be turning the corner around northeast Ukraine and be headed in a southerly or southeasterly direction towards Site B-22. The operators will know best, but it seems to me the search could focus on radiating out from the weapons storage site in the direction of approach - probably within a 100 miles or so. Anyway, they should be at the site today."

"Makes sense to me. I'll get this right down to the operations center."

"Good. Thanks - best people on it, please. Immediate notice when you find them, as the President is waiting."

"Of course." Then Chuck added, "It reads like he turned someone inside the site. Did you all consider that this might not be a national leadership-sanctioned thing?"

"Yes. But since they won't talk to us we have no way of confronting them. And we aren't going to share this with anyone else but Ukraine. And Germany, of course."

"How did that go down with ZSRU?"

"They said, "Thank you very much" and we agreed to keep monitoring the situation. But, in my opinion, they are already planning to take action. They were very serious."

"As they should be. I'm headed down to current ops now. Will be in touch."

40

WELL-AIMED AK ROUNDS

This is a long ass flight. Even in the Agency's Gulfstream VI, flying just over 0.9 Mach, it was a bit of an endurance test. But Carlos had a lot to think about during the eight-hour flight to Buenos Aires.

His time with Greg Gomez, the Argentina desk analyst was not encouraging. He was fine - but the information he had was not good. He felt like he would be on his own.

His mission:

1. Go in with an incomplete picture of the threat.
2. Prevent the assassination of the Pope.
3. Expect no help from the Argentina government.
4. Work with an understaffed embassy.

First, the embassy. The Ambassador was assigned but had not yet reported, and the Deputy Chief of Mission was on travel. Worse, there was no Station Chief, though his assistant, Jackie Rapp, was there and said to be exceptionally competent. Better yet, the embassy had an excellently equipped special missions supply section that primarily assisted Drug Enforcement Agency activities in the region.

"Excuse me, sir, will there be anything else tonight?" asked the steward/security guard. He looked more like a security guard though the service was pretty good.

"No, I'm good. Thanks."

"The flight deck advised me that we'd be starting down in about 10 minutes. We'll be landing just after sunset. Weather is clear and about 72 degrees."

Nothing like autumn in Buenos Aires he thought.

The thing he couldn't understand was the low level of interest shown by the Argentina government. Granted, the Pope did surprise everyone with the announcement of this trip just 10 days ago, but normally these things require a lot of planning and effort from the host country to ensure everything goes well. Particularly for a leader like the Pope that will be getting out and about to tend to the flock. But in this case, Greg said that the government planned a very low-level amount of crowd control and escorts. They decided that since it was a late-notice visit there would probably be a smaller crowd. So they will close the roads surrounding the plaza out front of the Buenos Aires Metropolitan Cathedral to all vehicular traffic the morning of the convoy to Villa 31, as well as block off the access roads to Diagonal Norte Avenue between the cathedral and Avenida 9 de Julio (leading to the white Obelisco monument at the intersection).

The convoy would be led and trailed by the Buenos Aires City Police on motorcycles and in patrol cars. Police would also control traffic all along Avenida 9 de Julio from just before the Obelisk all the way past the Retiro district to Villa 31.

Carlos' childhood stomping grounds.

But other than that, nothing more. Even after the Agency approached the Secretaria de Inteligencia with concerns about the Wagner Group there was no response. Very odd.

Looking out the right side of the aircraft, somewhere over Paraguay or Uruguay, he could see the beginnings of a brilliant sunset off to the west as they started their descent.

Then, how to prevent the assassination of the Pope? As usual, the Pontifical Swiss Guard (the ones dressed in suits with bulges and sunglasses, not the colorful medieval dress of those at the Vatican itself) were closed lip about papal security procedures. Except to say that they would protect the Pope in every imaginable situation. This meant that the Pope would be traveling in one of the many choices of security vehicle - anything from the famous Pope-Mobile to small white rental cars used on some occasions. His actual convoy would be made up of approximately three limousines following the papal conveyance taking other church leadership, dignitaries, local politicians, business leaders, and perhaps civilian members of the church advisory board.

Like his Abuela, Lilia Pombar used to do. At least he hoped it was past tense.

The Swiss Guard would provide the vehicular and foot patrol security for the convoy, usually made up of five vehicles - two in front of the Pope-Mobile, one behind, and one on either side of it. In an emergency, those security vehicles would alter the route, or escape the area with the Pope's vehicle securely surrounded by those large black SUVs. The rest of the convoy would be left to local authorities for protection.

One of Carlos' concerns is doing his best to protect the Pope but then being misidentified as a threat by his security forces and or the local police. He would have to leave concerning himself with *how* to prevent the assassination of the Pope to later after he had thoroughly scouted the probable areas of attack.

Changing engine noise, accompanying hydraulic sounds, and various *DINGS* signaled the aircraft was on final approach - landing to the southeast based on what he could see out the window.

Greg owed him significant research on the PMC Wagner office setup, the building, the personnel, and any other background information that might be useful. He totally got it and promised to work all night on it with other members of the South American desks to provide a decent assessment of the threat sometime tomorrow.

They landed, smoothly, taxied off the runway to the left at the end, and followed the parallel taxiway part way back before turning off to the east. The turn took them on a circuitous taxiway, past the limited airline service hangars, and around to a fairly large, isolated, parking ramp. It was nearly dark outside, with only a few lights in the random buildings surrounding the parking ramp. They took a final left turn and parked on spot 42, finally shutting down the engines.

The door opened, the air stairs dropped open, and up came two people - the US embassy representative, and the minimally interested Argentina Customs official.

"Hello Mr. Pombar, I am Jackie Rapp from the embassy. I'm here to pick you up," she said with a faint smile. 5 foot 3, if that, blonde hair and green eyes, wearing a perfectly fitted green top under a light jacket, and jeans.

After a short pause, Carlos said, "Hello," and at the same time, absentmindedly, handed his passport to the customs agent who looked briefly at the picture, looked at him, and then handed it back and left the aircraft.

"Let's go," Jackie said and went out the door, blonde hair bouncing lightly as she walked. Carlos picked up his bag and followed orders. Somewhere they were doing an aircraft engine run - on a test stand nearby.

Outside, a young man in shorts and a dark, collared shirt, sat at the wheel of a small golf cart type vehicle. He mouthed the words "buenas noches" amidst the noise.

They got in and he took the two of them around the front of the aircraft toward the hangars then turned right onto an access road, then across a two-lane road to a small parking lot that held perhaps 125 parking spaces, about three-quarters filled. It was quieter here than on the ramp. One light dimly provided minimal illumination from the center of the lot.

They got out, watched the cart drive back to the ramp area, then walked toward the parking lot, Carlos on her right.

"We are parked in the third row, about five spots down," Jackie said.

But Carlos wasn't listening to her now.

Two men stood in the shadows, under the trees, at the far end of the rectangular lot by the exit, nearly diagonal from the corner they just entered. One took a last draw on a cigarette before tossing it to the ground and stepping on it. The second looked over his shoulder at them and then they split and walked out of sight.

Carlos noted a third man on the far left of the lot, about midway down, when suddenly a bearded man in black rose up from behind the Toyota Tundra pickup they were passing and lunged out at Carlos, amateurishly, holding what he immediately identified as a Russian Bopoh-3 fighting knife, a six and a half inch blade favored by Russia's Spetsnaz forces.

"Kiai!" he shouted for Jackie's benefit as he dropped his bag, ducked slightly right, threw his left arm up and made contact with the inside of the attacker's knife arm to deflect the blade, then slid down to firmly grasp his wrist while his right hand grabbed the assailant by the front of his black sweatshirt. He shoved him off balance and then slammed the attacker's extended right elbow down upon his rising left knee, hyperextending and then breaking the elbow, causing the released knife to clatter on the blacktop. He set his feet, released the man's wrist, and twisted with all his might to deliver a left-handed chisel fist punch to the attacker's exposed throat - just above his Adam's apple - permanently collapsing the man's trachea. The man then fell hard to the ground with only a short time to live.

Carlos drew his Glock 22 from the Belly Band holster, dropped to a crouch, and turned to look the new field officer in the eyes.

To Jackie's credit, she hadn't made a sound, and was now crouched down with one knee on the ground, and had a Beretta drawn and held 45 up and left.

He had a stern combat face on when he said, "There are three more at least. Go back to the entry point and make yourself small. I will be back. Go now!"

Staying low and looking towards the parking lot, she backed slowly between two parked cars and disappeared.

There was no sign of the two he had seen at the far end, but he could hear steps fast approaching from where he had seen the single man across the lot. He quickly slid across the open space to row two and then moved further away down the row and dropped between two vehicles.

The second attacker came hurtling out into the open about 20 feet away and rushed toward his fallen comrade's position. Bad decision.

Carlos shot him, once, in the back right side of the head as he kneeled over attacker number one. He too had a beard. Then he shuffled back between the cars, moving across the nose-to-nose parked cars of row two and ran, low, across to row three.

That sprint drew three well-aimed AK rounds from the third attacker at the other end of the drive, one of which hit him in the right foot causing him to stumble forward to the ground. As he scrambled to safety between a parked car and another pickup, many follow-up rounds crashed through the metal and glass of the couple of vehicles around him. Car alarms blared.

It was dark, but a quick check with his fingers showed that only the heel of his right boot was damaged. He had blood on his forehead from hitting the left rear of the car as he fell.

He quickly crawled to the end of the second car in the nose-to-nose parking row and saw the feet of attacker number four, much closer than his partner, walking towards him down that last driveway between rows three and four. Carlos rolled away from him, under the pickup truck, and waited on his belly.

The fourth attacker walked cautiously towards his position and turned into the row on the far side of the car parked next to the pickup. When the man cleared the back tires, Carlos shot him twice in the feet from under the truck, causing the man to lay on the trigger and fire off a dozen rounds into the ground and neighboring vehicles as he dropped to the ground, where Carlos promptly shot him twice more in the upper body. The man exhaled fully and lay still, staring sightlessly in Carlos' general direction.

Number three was running down the drive between rows two and three, toward the AK sounds, when he came around the back of the car and looked down at his dead partner. He looked up just as Carlos shot him in the face from around the tailgate of the truck he had been hiding under.

He quickly searched them both and took their IDs.

Cautiously, he visually checked out the parking lot, first up the drive between rows four and three, then three and two, and then two and one as he moved back to where they started. Four bodies. Lots of noise. Time to leave.

He walked carefully to the corner where they entered the lot just a few minutes ago and called her name.

"Here." Jackie emerged from the brush at the end of row number two, holding his bag in her left hand and her Beretta in her right, and walked carefully towards him. She looked even more attractive than she had on the plane.

"That was a first for me," she said, breathless.

"You did good. Let's get going."

41

EYES IN THE SKY

On the 4th of October, 1957, the Union of Soviet Socialist Republics launched the first artificial Earth satellite into orbit on the world's first Intercontinental Ballistic Missile. It was doubly terrifying for many.

Sputnik-1 was a polished metal sphere of 184 pounds, measuring just 23 inches in diameter. From the sphere sprang four long antennas, with a simple single-watt transmitter powered by three silver-zinc batteries that broadcast a continuous *BEEP...BEEP...BEEP* signal heard by radio operators around the world.

And it was launched into orbit by the 280-ton R7 Semyorka rocket, firing 20 engines, and feared to be capable of boosting the latest Soviet atomic bombs into space to fall who knows where on Earth.

That event spawned the Sputnik Crisis and led to the Space Race between the Soviet Union and the United States which played a key role in the Cold War.

Sputnik decelerated, fell out of orbit, and burned up in the atmosphere on the 4th of January, 1958. Though the satellite was in orbit for a short three months, its impact lasted decades.

In the months and weeks leading up to Russia's invasion of Ukraine, the US National Reconnaissance Office (NRO) employed the latest generation of electro-optical digital imaging satellites in existence to provide decision-makers with information needed to do their jobs - be they political, intelligence, or military in nature.

The NRO is known as one of the "Big Five" intelligence agencies in the United States. It is on equal footing with the CIA, the DIA, the National Security Agency, and the National Geospatial Intelligence Agency. Its Director, Chuck Higgins, reports to both the DNI and the Secretary of Defense.

According to the mission statement, the NRO is responsible for developing, building, launching, and operating space reconnaissance systems and conducting intelligence-related activities for US National Security.

In the headquarters building in Chantilly, Virginia, the National Reconnaissance Operations Center, or NROC, operates 24 hours a day, all year long, where the men and women run daily operations and execute time-sensitive space-borne intelligence reporting. Located just 23 miles due west of the White House, their leaders and analysts are used to being "on call" to work emerging crises. Or, as in the case of the war in Ukraine, enduring crises.

Their state-of-the-art electro-optical digital imaging satellite is called the KH-11 KENNEN, or Improved CHRYSTAL, depending upon the block number. Built by Lockheed, there are six operational satellites, two each of the Block III, IV, and

V versions of the assets in orbit today, operating around the clock.

In technical manuals, its purpose is defined as "earth observation." In popular lore, they are spy satellites - America's eyes in the sky.

These are big satellites, put into orbit by the heaviest-lift rockets available. Luckily, the latest models are designed to last 15 years or more in space.

The satellites, weighing approximately 40,000 pounds fully fueled, are comprised of a cylindrical barrel body 64 feet long and three feet in diameter, open on one end. The opposite end is connected to a cuboid, a rectangular box, that houses the hydrazine-powered maneuvering rocket motor and its fuel tanks, an electronics section, and communications equipment.

There are two pairs of large solar panels on each side of the barrel that provide all the electoral power.

Inside the cylinder is mounted the seven-foot-ten-inch diameter primary mirror. It has exemplary image resolution capabilities. Mathematically, from a satellite orbit of 160 miles, the mirror provides a diffraction-limited resolution of 0.05 arc seconds - yielding a 2.4-inch ground sample size - or the ability to distinguish details of that size or bigger from space. In the real world, atmospheric complications distort the ground sample size upwards by a couple of inches. It is not good enough to recognize a face but it could sure locate and track a missing Iskandr transloader.

Four hours ago, the orbit track allowed operators to program the KH-11 to look for the objective vehicle on the roads from a general area southwest of Kursk to Belgorod. That exercise yielded electro-optical images of the transloader in a south-bound convoy of four vehicles - a GAZ-type truck in the lead, followed by the transloader vehicle (armored roof closed), then another GAZ truck, followed by a BTR-80. They were about 35 miles south of Kursk on the E105 highway.

The next pass showed the vehicles parked inside the facility known as B-22, near Antonovka, Russia.

The satellite operations specialist completed his report, attached the set of photographs (all properly marked TOP SECRET/SCI), and forwarded it up to his supervisor, who then sent the report immediately to the Director.

Fifteen minutes later, the Director of the NRO, Chuck Higgins, had a secure video teleconference with Director Minard (DNI) and Secretary of Defense Austin.

"Thank you both for responding so quickly," Higgins began. "I just sent you two the report and the photos of the Iskandr transloader we've been looking for in Russia."

"As you know, analysts noted two days ago that an Iskandr-M missile battery, including the transporter erector launcher, or TEL, its transloader, and the associated support vehicles were located just inside southeastern Belarus, off of highway P35 in a clearing near the town of Kirovo. It appeared to be part of a bigger force that bedded down there for the night. Then yesterday we saw that the transloader disappeared that first night, leaving the TEL behind. See photos one and two."

He continued, "There are other Iskandr batteries located on the highways headed east, but each of the TELs is traveling with their transloaders."

"During the satellite pass overhead nearly five hours ago we found the missing transloader, two utility support type trucks, and a BTR-80 about 35 miles south of Kursk, southbound on

293

highway E105 - see photo three. Then the final pass about 40 minutes ago captured these several images of the vehicles in the B-22 tactical nuclear storage facility near Belgorod."

Director Minard said, "Well, this is pretty convincing to me. Lloyd, I'll contact the President right away. Do we need to alert anyone else yet?"

"No, let's see how the President wants to react before we pull everyone in. The role is his, and Zelenskiy's."

"Agree. I'll get on the phone with him immediately. Thanks so much, Chuck - tell your guys they did great."

42

EXACTLY AS WE FEARED

Ron Minard waited impatiently for the White House to put him through to the President. Apparently, there was an important reception of some kind - a birthday party for one of the staff - and he couldn't be interrupted. Ron told the staffer, "I suspect he'll wish you'd interrupted when he hears what I have to tell him."

But the assistant to the Chief of Staff was adamant, saying, "Director Minard, I'm sorry but he gave explicit directions not to be interrupted. I will get him on the line as soon as I can." And then put him on hold. Nearly 15 minutes ago.

There was a lot that needed to be done, quickly and smoothly, and they were dependent upon several people making the right decisions. Lots of variables here to be confident of success.

"Standby Director Minard," the assistant came on the line and said to him, "the President will pick up when he gets to the Oval Office."

Priceless minutes went by.

"Ron, good afternoon. What have you got for me?" At least the assistant conveyed the DNI's urgency well enough for him to forgo the preliminary niceties.

"Sir, are you alone?"

"Yes, Ron, I'm alone."

"I was just contacted by the Director of the NRO, Chuck Higgins, and he passed satellite imagery taken in the last several hours that confirms the presence of the Iskandr transloader and other vehicles arriving at the weapons storage site called B-22 near Belgorod. This appears to be going down exactly as we feared."

"OK, so what do we tell Zelenskiy?"

"Sir, as we discussed, the main points are: 1) We have confirmed the presence of an Iskandr transport trailer at the tactical nuclear weapons storage site near Belgorod in a state of maintenance - people are working on the two missiles."

He paused a moment to let that sink in. Then, "Point 2) We strongly believe this trailer belongs to or is under the control of PMC Wagner whose northern forces are in southeastern Belarus at this time."

"Point 3) We have SIGINT - telephonic intercepts - provided by German Intelligence that indicate Prigozhin's intent to use special weapons in Ukraine."

"Point 4) The Russians are not talking to us. This intelligence is not going to be shared with third parties. It is up to him to either a) Attempt to contact the Russians to stop this activity, b) take decisive action to end the threat, or c) do nothing and hope we are all wrong."

Silence on the other end.

"Mr. President?"

"I'm here Ron. Don't want to be, but I am. Will you come over here right away?"

"Yessir."

"I'll compose my thoughts and we'll call him together when you get here."

"Do you want anyone else to join us, sir?"

"Hmmm. Not yet. We'll bring in a few key people after the call. No sense crowding the room here. There will be time."

"Alright, sir. I will be there soon." He was glad he typed up those talking points already.

He hung up, rapped on the soundproof glass, let it roll down slightly, and told the driver, "Let's go."

They pulled away from the rare parking spot the driver had found in front of the Old Ebbitt Grill on 15th St, headed north, and turned left onto Pennsylvania Avenue, and from there to Executive Avenue for access to the White House.

There won't be much time, he thought.

43

A TERRIBLE SITUATION

President Biden sat behind the Resolute desk, staring at the talking points again. Director Minard sat on the president's right on one of the two wooden-framed, armless chairs beside the desk. Thankfully, the cushion was soft.

They waited on the White House switchboard operator to make the connection with the Presidential Palace in Kyiv. Protocol would have President Zelenskiy on the phone before President Biden is brought on the line.

The phone rang, the President selected "speakerphone" and the operator said, "Mr. President, President Zelenskiy is on the phone." And she dropped off the call.

"President Zelenskiy, thank you so much for taking my call so late at night." It was 5:45pm in Washington and 11:45 hours in Kyiv.

"It is my pleasure, President Biden. We get very little sleep here these days."

"Volodymyr, we have something very serious to discuss."

"Then you will not mind if I have my interpreter present?"

"Of course not. I encourage you to do so."

Without hesitation, Zelenskiy said, "He is here. Please begin."

President Biden took a deep breath, quickly, and said, "We have confirmed the presence of an Iskandr trailer, with two missiles at the B-22 site near Belgorod."

In the background, they heard the translator's voice provide some remarks of clarification - some minor exchange between the two.

Then from Zelenskiy, "Go on."

Biden continued, "We have tracked this trailer from southeastern Belarus to the B-22 site near Belgorod. We strongly believe it belongs to or is in the control of PMC Wagner forces."

Another brief exchange between Zelenskiy and his translator, then then Biden continued, "As we shared through intelligence channels before, we have telephone transcripts that indicate Prigozhin intends to use these weapons."

This time, with no sound from the translator, President Zelenskiy said bluntly, again in English, "Are you sure of this?"

President Biden hesitated, then answered, "Are we ever really sure at times like this? We must balance assurance of what we think against the risk of inaction. The transcripts tell us, and the satellite imagery shows us, things are happening which we know he has set in motion."

There was some muffled conversation on the line, indecipherable in the Oval Office, followed by a moment of silence.

"Continue please," said Zelenskiy, again in English.

"As you know, the Russians are not talking to us. We can't share this information with third parties to help resolve it.'

The translator started to say something but Zelenskiy cut him off, and said quietly, "This is very disturbing. I hoped it would not be so. What do you recommend?"

President Biden paused again, then said, "I am not going to tell you what to do - that is up to you and your government. But it looks to me like you may have three choices."

"And what are they, Mr. President?"

"Attempt to contact the Russians to stop it - they probably have no idea it is happening."

"Or?" Zelenskiy said quickly.

"Take action to eliminate the threat."

"And the third?"

"Do nothing and hope we are all wrong."

A long pause.

"Thank you for sharing this information with me. I am very grateful. It is a terrible situation. You will know our decision soon."

They said their goodbyes and the President disconnected the call, his hand visibly shaking over the button. Adrenalin, understandably.

44

THE GEEK SQUAD

Leytenant Artem Vasko - superman! Flying the Baykar Bayraktar TB2 combat drone was the best thing he'd ever done. Including competing in and nearly winning the *Call of Duty* World Championship (Infinite Warfare version) in August 2017.

Of course, they didn't get to go to Orlando - college students the world over could barely afford to eat. Especially when all of your spare change (and some of your father's money) went into the exquisite gaming setup they designed and purchased for themselves.

There was no doubt however that their four gaming centers were the hottest dorm rooms in the whole of Ivan Franko National University of Lviv. There were variations, but each guy had a great setup with five monitors, realistic throttles and control stick, and even some up-front controls.

One of his favorite memories of the whole World Championship competition - especially given what was going on now in Ukraine - was that no one in the *Call of Duty* gaming organization spoke Ukrainian, and no one associated with the production of the championship itself bothered to google the team name, "Platov Khuylo!" so over and over the moderator kept yelling it out in the arena and online never knowing he was insulting the President of the Russian Federation.

Cool.

They all managed to graduate in the spring of 2018. But since taking Crimea by force back in 2014 Russia had ramped up the separatist fighting in the Donbas region. And though he and most of his friends hardly paid attention to anything but gaming, girls, and classes (in that order) none of them considered how those events might change their lives. That is until the Ukrainian Air Force recruiter showed up at their doors. Literally. Apparently, they knew who they were. Artem and his friends didn't know whether to be flattered or scared.

It turned out that the UAF was one of the first purchasers of the Bayrak Company's new drone. It was designed by another gamer - Selcuk Bayraktar. Someone Artem had never heard of until he learned the name from the recruiter and looked him up online. He is the chairman of the board and chief technology officer of the Turkish technology company Baykar.

Bayraktar has a list of credentials a mile long, including an engineering degree from Istanbul Technical University, and two master's degrees, one from the University of Pennsylvania, and the second from the prestigious Massachusetts Institute of Technology. He led the development of Turkey's first Unmanned Aerial Vehicle (UAV) project - the Bayraktar Mini UAV. And, he was the architect of the unmanned combat aerial vehicle (UCAV) Bayraktar TB2 project. The model purchased by the Ukrainian Air Force in 2019.

The type Artem was waiting to fly tonight if directed. He and his payload operator Marko Krasinski were sitting in the operations lounge of the squadron by themselves, sunk into some large lounge chairs provided by a local furniture company. Marko was playing a video game on the big TV in front of them. Artem was just watching the clock tick down anxiously awaiting word about the mission.

He had "flown" many air vehicles in *Call of Duty,* the best video game of all time, and a myriad of other games, both manned aircraft and unmanned drone simulations. Who knew that those hours (days?) of time spent in front of the screens or with goggles on were essentially primary training for flying the real things?

He and all of his friends signed up with the UAF with very little pressure. After all, the war in the East was heating up and they needed technically savvy people like him to fly these machines. And who was better than a bunch of gamer geeks? They called themselves the geek squad.

After completing the obligatory military training (physical fitness, military history, rules, and regulations, uniforms, decorum, etc.) they were each commissioned fairly quickly as melodshyy leytenants - the lowest lieutenant rank in the UAF. Then they all got orders to attend academic and flight control training in Istanbul, after which they were posted to the 383rd Unmanned Aircraft Regiment for operational training, located in the city of Khmelnytskyi, in the Oblast of the same name. It is located 173 miles west southwest of Kyiv and 135 miles east southeast of his home and family in Lviv. And it would be a long way from anywhere he wanted to live if he had time to be bored - but combat operations started within months of arrival and there hasn't been time for anything else.

Artem had to admit that it didn't seem right to call it combat operations since he wasn't personally at risk. In fact, to date, no one in Khmelnytskyi has even seen any evidence of the war first-hand except through relatives and friends who went away to fight. It was all way out east and up north of Kyiv. There was extreme seriousness to this work. Not only were they pressured to do their best work for the Ukrainian Ground Forces, but they also have the emotional burden that comes with killing people. Often unsuspecting people that don't even know your weapon is overhead and who cannot put you at risk. He preferred attacking parked armored vehicles as opposed to attacking troops - he was glad he didn't fly the small drones with the grenades.

The 383rd Unmanned Aircraft Regiment had several aircraft types - from those small drones dropping grenades to the largest aircraft in the fleet, the TB2.

His was the 3rd Squadron of three in the regiment. They possessed approximately 12 TB2s - well, there were 12 on the books but with combat losses (more lately) and constant resupply, the numbers on the flight line varied from week to week. There were four flights within the squadron, with each flight owning a single ground control station (GCS) and three TB2s along with other vehicles, and all the soldiers to maintain them or employ them.

Each climate-controlled GCS is the size of a medium-sized shipping container with an access door at one end. It holds two large computer racks and a desk with three workstations for the vehicle pilot, the payload operator, and a mission commander. Each workstation employs cross-redundant architecture to display flight and weapons employment data on dedicated screens for each position whenever anyone needed to see it. It allows them to command, control and monitor the drone during the mission.

The GCS can be moved from site to site via a moderately sized flatbed tractor-trailer, or it can be placed on the ground at a semi-permanent site. They haven't had to deploy anywhere as the range of the drone extends way past Ukraine's borders.

They'd spent the first day since being put on notice in the mission planning room in the secure vault next door. The room was crowded with large tables with varying scales of maps of Ukraine and the border regions under plexiglass, pens, pencils, and preprinted forms with matrices for all the data associated with flying a mission - mission number, callsign, weapons load, flight planned altitudes and navigation points arrayed down the card through the destination (target area) and return. There are several computer stations - one each in three corners - for the pilot and payload operator to load the mission data into the cartridges they would take to the GCS. Once loaded there, the data would be used to fly the drone.

They could do all of this from anywhere actually. They didn't even have to be near the aircraft itself as long as someone could pre-program the automatic launch sequence and get it airborne. From there, the crew in the GCS would "acquire" the TB2 and take control. All via radio communication and satellites.

"Yeah!" shouted Marko as he blasted demons in the fast-paced *Metal: Hellsinger* game, the booming soundtrack driving his head up and down but the sounds were undistinguishable through the padded headset he wore.

Believe it or not, Artem hadn't played that game yet.

He walked to the window to try to see the weather. The biggest issue tonight might be the cloud layers. They expected to fly to the target at a very low altitude to try to avoid detection. Not assured, he thought. But at some point, the weather has to allow them to climb to employ the weapons using the laser tracker. He couldn't see the clouds so he went back to his seat.

The aircraft was awesome. First, this was no remote control model aircraft - it was the real thing. It was 21 feet long with a 39-foot wingspan, and weighed, fully loaded, just over 1,500 pounds. It was a blended wing and body design with an inverted V-tail structure on two booms extended aft of the wing line. Its small engine in the back centerline turned a variable pitch two-blade pusher propeller that could drive the aircraft to cruise speeds of 70-100 knots. Maximum speed is 120 knots.

There was, of course, no canopy. But he was the pilot just the same. And that was made possible by the radio line of sight command linkage, or via the satellite linkages when they had access. Like tonight.

The aircraft used triple-redundant avionics and flight controls, and his "view" came from cameras in the top of the inverted V-tail that gave him the image of most of the aircraft out in front of him on screen.

Max range? A whopping 2,100 miles (with satellite links) and it could loiter in the air for 27 hours - with a crew change of course.

Marko, yelling again, stood right up out of his chair to make sure the demon that wasted him knew he'd get him next time, then he sat back down again and regenerated. Artem hardly opened his eyes to see it.

The TB2 had some great avionics. In addition to the navigation package, the aircraft was equipped with the Aselsan CATS EO/IR/LD imaging and targeting sensor, suspended under the aircraft in a ball - like the ball turret gunner on an old WWII bomber. The electro-optical and infrared sensors allowed the payload operator to find the target on the screen, identify it, and then use the laser designator to laze the target with infrared light with a wavelength of approximately 1020 nanometers for the bomb's sensor to aim at during its descent.

The bomb, (one under each wing tonight), is the Roketsan-manufactured Mini Akilli Muhimmat - a Smart Micro Munition - designated MAM-L for its ability to follow laser guidance. This small bomb, weighing only 48 pounds, carried an 18-pound HE charge of Composition H6 - 44% Hexagon, 30% TNT, and 26% powdered aluminum and bonding agents. It had quite a bang for its size - but what made it so lethal was the accuracy of the weapon.

Basically, it went where the payload operator directed it to go. The three-foot long by six-inch diameter weapon had relatively large steerable wings that guided it to the laser spot on the target.

Marko always said, "Big bombs are for the guys that can't hit the target!"

Luckily, Artem knew Marko was good at what he did. And they would need his skills tonight. The nation needed his skills tonight.

If they get the call.

45

ASSESSING THE KILL ZONE

The ride back from the airport last night with Jackie was tense. As he remembered it, there was not a lot of conversation. For him, it wasn't just defeating the ambush in the parking lot so much as the knowledge that someone, someone in the know, had to alert someone here to make that attempt to kill him. Langley has a mole.

Jackie took him to the embassy, swapped out the embassy car with hers, and then drove home. She assured him her residence was secure - and that she was fine.

Before falling asleep, he sent a quick report to Skip along with the personal information from the last attackers. This morning, he realized his message was a little blunt. He had texted, "Ambushed leaving BA airport parking lot. Four assailants, all dead. *Langley has a mole*. Pic of IDs attached. Middle East/Caucasus origins," and hit SEND.

Skip had not answered yet this morning.

He thought Skip wouldn't mind his bluntness - and he'd take the declaration seriously about the mole and stay quiet while he initiated an internal investigation.

Not his concern now. Except to assume the adversaries now know he is here and that he survived their attempt to eliminate him.

He did have one text this morning from Greg Gomez. It said, "Ready when you are boss." Carlos logged on to the embassy computer and logged in to his encrypted account.

Today was all about assessing the kill zone. He had done this type of thing dozens of times before, but this was a role reversal. On previous occasions, he was the shooter. Today he has to think like a shooter to locate the probable point of attack so he could *prevent* the kill.

Carlos called Greg's number.

Greg answered immediately. "Gomez here."

"Good morning Greg. What have you got for me?"

"I've sent you a folder with the Pope's schedule and various screenshots of the Cathedral and the area around it, the convoy route, and the destination."

"OK. At least growing up here gives me a certain advantage - I'm sure I know this city better than anyone at Wagner."

"No doubt about that."

"And because of that, I think there are some areas I can rule out for the attack without even scouting them out."

Greg said, "I'll talk and you shut me up when you don't need my thoughts. The schedule is a stand-alone document - you can save that to your phone. The Pope will arrive Friday, late afternoon, and spend the night at the Archbishop's Residence next door to the Metropolitan Cathedral."

He paused, then said, "Call up the Map1.pdf."

"Got it."

"On Saturday, around 13:00, the Papal group will assemble on the access road between the residence and the church (it's shown as point A on the map) to get in the vehicles. There will be four VIP vehicles in total. The Pope mobile will be led by two Swiss Guard SUVs, flanked by two more, and followed by a fifth vehicle immediately behind him. The other three VIP vehicles will follow. There will be Buenos Aires police motorcycles in front of the convoy and behind the last VIP car, and street cops in the area. Questions?"

"No. Sounds like standard escort protocol."

Greg continued, "Once everyone is ready, the vehicles pull out onto the street in front of the Cathedral (point B) then turn right onto North Diagonal Avenue and drive along that road until they turn right onto Avenida 9 de Julio (point C) and travel north through ten city blocks toward the Retiro District. They then depart the road (point D) to the east to circle and enter Villa 31 from the south (point E)."

Greg then added, "My thought was that each of the points was a potential ambush spot, though you, of course, may see more."

"No, this is helpful. Give me a minute."

Carlos ruled out point E or the approaches into Villa 31 - Wagner would not "fit in" there and he presumed Russian and Chechen or Muslim attackers would be uncomfortable in that environment. Too many people there would notice strangers.

He was equally dismissive of points C and D - the ten-block run up Avenida 9 de Julio - each repetitive tree-lined block along the eight-lane major thoroughfare was boxed in by high-rise buildings on each side offering no cover and no clear fire areas. It would be especially challenging as the police would have a rolling blockade going on each side of the four northbound lanes (and later the southbound lanes). There simply was no place to conceal yourself, then anticipate the passage of the vehicles, reveal yourself, and hope to have anything but a fleeting shot at a 50mph target. No. Not the avenue.

If anything, the North Diagonal Avenue was more confined than Avenida 9 de Julio. Neither of the avenues.

Carlos said, "I just don't see it happening anywhere along the drive itself. There are too many variables, all happening too fast, to give a shooter or shooters a good opportunity."

Greg stayed silent - not his skill set.

That left points A and B - the areas in and around the cathedral and the residence. Pretty tight quarters in the private drive. And the area around point B had to include the open, rectangular, park-like Plaza de Mayo.

Casa Rosada, the Presidential Palace, framed the eastern edge of the plaza. The Ministry of Economics building, a History Museum, and an eight-story office building ran the long side of the plaza to the south, then there were more high-rise buildings to the west where North Diagonal and South Diagonal avenues joined the four-lane one-way road that circled the entire plaza counterclockwise. And on the north side, from right to left, was a 12-story government building, then the Residence of the Archbishop of Buenos Aires (itself ten stories tall), and finally the Metropolitan Cathedral.

Carlos said, "This is ugly. The most likely kill zones at points A and B, are in the middle of a veritable stadium of tall buildings - flanked on the right by one of the most secure buildings in Buenos Aires, the Presidential Palace."

What was it Skip always said? This ain't no puss game.

Greg offered, "I have some measurements on the plaza. It is 700 by 300 feet - 210,000 square feet of openness - oriented lengthwise from the pinkish Casa Rosada in the east to the two diagonal avenues you see in the west. Dead center in the eastern third of the plaza is the Monument of General Belgrano on his horse. In the center sits the Pyramid of May, the oldest monument in Buenos Aires built to celebrate the May Revolution in 1810. It sits on a broad earthen mound, that rises some 15 to 20 feet above street level. The statue measures 62 feet from the ground to the peak of the Statue of Liberty's cap - but there is nowhere on the statue itself for an assassin to hide."

"But that rise does have line-of-sight to the Cathedral and to the road between that and the Residence," Carlos said.

"True."

Then he went on, "If you look closely you can see that the mound is nearly surrounded at ground level by four concrete-edged, four to five-foot deep ponds. Tourists routinely access the upper area immediately around the monument via the paths you see between the ponds."

Carlos said, "Listen. The buildings themselves are non-starters. Most of them are government or church-controlled, so unauthorized access by a bunch of unrefined tough guys seems unlikely."

"True," Greg said again.

"And frankly," Carlos said, "I have no hope of stopping anyone that chooses to poke a rifle out of some window in a tall building. If we entertain that thought here then where in the 15 or so blocks along the route do we start looking?"

313

"I suppose we could..."

"I'm sorry, that was a rhetorical question. It is a futile task."

Thinking again.

Carlos said, "No, the only opportunity I see is at points A and B. I will have to check those spots out today."

Then he closed with, "Thanks for the work. I'm headed out soon. Please stay close in case I need something more," and ended the call.

He headed directly for the Plaza, three and a half miles southeast of the embassy. The driver dropped him off at a coffee shop halfway down North Diagonal Avenue for an easy walk under clear skies again with the early fall temperature approaching 65 already.

Blending in as a South American tourist was easy here given his ancestry and comfort with the area. He walked casually, checking out each interesting storefront, pausing in several and doubling back looking for followers and spotting none. Then there were the museums and the obvious tourist spots of the Cathedral (he went in pretending he'd never been there before). When he came out he lingered on the steps looking at a tourist map, and glancing up at the surroundings for obvious vantage points on the plaza. He walked around and checked out the private drive between the church and the residence, then as if confused, consulted the map, turned around, and slowly walked back - again glancing up at intervals to "see" the plaza.

He went to the Presidential Palace (the museum was closed; there was only light activity as the president was on travel), then repeated the tourist walk across the street, past Belgrano on his horse, through the ponds, and up to the base of the white Pyramide de Mayo where he lingered to take in the sights. More so on the side facing the cathedral.

Satisfied, he slowly meandered back up North Diagonal to a taxi stand, hired a cab to drop him at the Museo de Arte Latinoamericano de Buenos Aires, then walked the last mile to the embassy.

Having walked the site, it was now time to prepare.

46

READY AND WAITING

Artem's mission commander, Mayor Borys Danyluk, came through the door into the lounge just as Marko raised his hands and shouted to no one outside the game. Looking the wrong way and with his headphones on, he had no idea the major was in the room.

Danyluk was a tiny man - but like most techno geeks he burned with energy and excitement when it was "go time."

"Get your crazed payload operator and head to the van. It looks like this mission is on - they want us up and ready when the final decision is made," and with that, he left the room.

Artem, already on his feet, walked over quickly to Marko and hit him hard on the shoulder with his open palm.

"What the...?" cried Marko loudly, looking around at him with his ears still on.

Artem signaled to take the headphones off, and as Marko did so he said, "Game's over. They're going to decide on the mission soon - let's get out to the box."

They grabbed snacks and water bottles, then headed out of the building into the cold 02:00 hours darkness to power things up in the GCS.

On the flight line, the ground crew was readying the TB2. As with any other aircraft, there were pressures to check, fluid levels to service, grounding wires to pull, panels to secure, and weapons and gear safety pins to remove. Most of this had been done hours ago - so the checks revealed nothing much to do save for the safety pins.

The last thing they would do is turn on the aircraft battery when they get the call from ops that the mission is a go. But for now, they were ready. The aircraft glistened dully in the waning gibbous moon's light.

The door to the GCS opened suddenly and Danyluk climbed unceremoniously into the box, dumped his food and water in the corner, and took his seat at the mission commander panel.

Marko looked up from his screens and asked, "Any news?"

"No. Not yet. This is not an easy call, I'm sure."

Marko nodded his head.

Artem was glad he was only a drone pilot and not on the President's staff right now. But he was a little worried - they can't delay too long and risk a daylight time over target.

At first, nobody could believe the nature of the target when the Regimental Intelligence officer briefed them on the mission yesterday afternoon.

"Good afternoon gentlemen," the officer said to the seated TB2 crew. Your target is an Iskandr weapons transloader - a large trailer capable of hauling two Iskandr missiles, recently arrived at a tactical nuclear weapons storage site near Belgorod, called B-22."

He showed a chart with pictures of the Iskandr weapons system, the TEL, and the transloader centered in the frame.

Size descriptions and specifications littered the column on the left side of the photos. They were marked SECRET, though Artem was sure he's seen them online before.

The second chart showed the B-22 site itself with an arrow drawn upon it pointing to the location of the transloader not too far from the gate, parked between what looked like the entrances to two bunkers on the right and some other buildings on the left. The satellite photo (again marked SECRET - this time understandably so) clearly showed work being done on the missiles in the open bay of the transloader.

"The Russians have withdrawn most of their northern forces from Kyiv, across the border with Belarus, and into Russia itself. There are some exceptions. Some units of the Russian force are still in southeastern Belarus. This transloader is linked to an Iskandr battery that remains in Belarus at this location here," and he pointed to a town named Kirovo.

He didn't mention the connection with PMC Wagner.

"We assess the B-22 site to be old, containing mostly obsolete weapons managed by the 12th GU MO, the agency responsible for all nuclear weapons in the Russian Federation."

"But there is evidence that some recently upgraded weapons are stored there. They are assumed to be compatible with the Iskandr system. It is thought the Russians may be intending to use these weapons as they have been threatening, possibly to destroy either a key political target or a military target such as the weapons storage and transshipment sites in western Ukraine."

"Here is a chart showing the disposition of known threats in the region," he said as he put up a third chart. "There are no surface-to-air weapons of any kind in the Belgorod area. There is, however, an S-400 site just over 75 miles north, 10 miles south-southeast of Kursk, on the southern outskirts of a town named Lebyazhensky. It has seen very little action since the invasion started. We expect them to be less than proficient and, maybe, not so alert given their forces are retreating fully towards them and action has slowed significantly in the lull since those forces departed Ukraine."

Marko said under his breath, "Makes you glad we are flying an UNMANNED combat aerial vehicle, doesn't it?"

"Shut up Marko," Danyluk said.

The intelligence officer continued, "To jog your memory, the stats on the S-400 are intimidating. The 92N2 search radar will detect you inside 120 miles when you show yourself above 500 feet. If you show yourself too early it is game over - lower altitude is better. But again, they may not be that alert in the middle of the night and we have not seen them use the auto-launch feature on any of their batteries so far. We think they don't trust their systems - or maybe their aircrews don't. In any case, from the missile site, the 4,000-pound 48N6E2 missile, traveling at 4,500 miles per hour, will take approximately 68 seconds to reach the aircraft when you are within about 10 miles of the target. As you know you can do nothing to beat it once it launches. It either hits you or the 400-pound warhead gets you - in either case, it is over. The only thing to consider is delaying the intercept so you have more time to laze the target. So, once you come up out of low altitude to drop, consider a move to the south after bomb release to give you a few more seconds. If they fire at all."

The three of them just sat there. But it was clear the seriousness of the target - the potential arming of the Iskandr missiles with nuclear warheads - warranted the suicide mission.

"Let's hope the bombs hit before we blow up," Marko again.

There was little left for intel to say. He handed the major the coordinates of the target and the S-400 site. Then they were released to the mission planning room to craft the navigation route, and the attack plan, and then to load the data in the cartridge for transfer to the GCS. That all took about an hour.

Then they sat and ate, and tried to relax. When daylight came they were released to quarters to return this evening.

The navigation routing was not difficult to develop - takeoff, fly low towards the north-northeast, avoiding all centers of population and known friendly and enemy positions. No need to fly over anxious Ukrainian anti-aircraft positions either.

Artem would be responsible for flying the aircraft at a very low altitude using the basic flight instruments and the forward-looking infrared cameras, and the autopilot. That and the radar altimeter should keep them from hitting anything. Then, with 10 miles to go to the target, he would push the power up and start a climb to 7,500 feet for the final drive on the target. This would allow Marko to use his sensors to spot the target and prepare to release the weapons one mile from the target. Upon weapons release, Artem would initiate a 45-degree turn to the right, to the southeast, to put a little more distance between the aircraft and the S-400 site in the hopes that Marko can keep the laser on target for the full time-of-flight of the bombs.

From 7,500 feet, the bomb will fall for about 20 seconds and hit the ground going 450 knots. The aim point is the cab of the trailer. Marko wasn't so sure the missiles wouldn't explode in the MAM-L detonations, but it would be best if they did not. There wasn't much they could do about that.

If the drone survived this far it still wouldn't be safe if the missile site had detected them at any time, or until they got back down to low-level to continue to avoid the missile site, or got back across and well south of the Ukrainian border. Then they'd fly it home and give it back to the ground crew. Tonight, the survival of the aircraft did not look promising.

For now, they were ready and waiting for the launch order. Again.

47

DO WHAT YOU'RE TOLD

Captain Luka Pavloff had been hustling, non-stop, since the Wagner Group arrived with the transloader and the missiles nearly 12 hours ago. It was now almost 04:30 and except for a quick snack when the sun went down he'd not had anything to eat or drink, and no rest at all.

On top of that, though Prigozhin said that he'd be in charge, it was clear that the real boss right now was Major Navikoff, and the Captain named Sidorov was his number two. The only thing Luka felt truly in charge of was his weapons and the weapon load equipment.

The group (the transloader, two utility trucks, and a BTR-80) arrived late yesterday afternoon. Drove right up to the gate as if they owned the place. Luka barely had time to grab Lieutenant Orloff, the deputy security commander, and get to the sentry box to assure the young enlisted troops that it was all good before they called the main base.

Then Major Navikoff got two of his men and replaced the guard at the gate. To his credit, Lieutenant Orloff quickly escorted him to the barracks. Then the vehicles rolled through the gate, the trucks parked by the administration building, and the transloader backed in between the maintenance building and the north side of Bunker 1B. Interestingly, the BTR-80 entered, turned around, drove back down the road, and parked in front of bunker 1A, with its armored front and the top turret's 30mm auto-cannon facing the gate.

There were eight Iskandr Battery drivers and maintenance personnel, and 21 battle-hardened, surly, tired, Wagner combat troops. About half of the latter rotated in and out of the sentry box, or stood guard over the bunker and the transloader, while the rest went into the administrative building and asserted their control. The B-22 personnel disappeared into their rooms.

Once his men were dispersed, Major Navikoff wasted no time getting things started.

"Ok, Captain Pavloff, are you and your team ready for us?" Luka couldn't help but notice the dismissive tone and the look on the major's face as he addressed him.

"Yessir. The load team consists of four plus myself. The loading equipment is in the maintenance building, but unpacked, serviced, and ready for use. The tug and the weapons trailer are already in the bunker and ready to load with the first weapon."

"What do we need to do first?"

From the Iskandr weapons load manual he'd been studying, Luka loosely recited, "The Iskandr team needs to open the transloader's armored doors on top, then prepare the missiles for service - they should be familiar with that."

Captain Sidorov nodded in agreement.

Luka continued, "There are systems to secure, then equipment to be put in place including the crane, the personnel stands, and tool bins. But none of that can happen until the missiles and their warheads are made safe and ready for maintenance."

Again, Sidorov nodded.

"Once that is all done, the Iskandr team will need to remove the nosecone and then prepare the weapon for removal. Protocol requires us to store the first weapons before we move the special weapon from the bunker."

"You can store the conventional weapons when we are finishing up," the Major said sternly. Luka understood that to be an order.

Sidorov spoke up, "There is another restriction we cannot work around, however. We cannot work on both missiles at the same time - there is not enough room with two missiles in the bay of the transloader."

Major Navikoff considered that. Then said, "So, we have a linear load process - that nearly doubles the time. Let's get started."

Luka said, "Sir, I will take my team to the maintenance building so they can pull out the equipment now and then begin the setup as soon as Captain Sidorov's team is done preparing the missiles."

"Very well. Get to it," Navikoff said, then turned and walked away.

It wasn't until after he'd watched the men pulling the equipment out that he managed to get back to the office for something to eat. Then he went back out to the transloader and watched the process. Though the team all looked exhausted and filthy, they knew their jobs and within just a few hours the doors were open, all of the equipment was in place, and they began the slow process of removing the nosecone of the left-hand missile in the bay.

At this point, Luka took two assistants and went to his Bunker 1B to prepare the nuclear weapons for loading on the trailer. They found them as Luka had left them, previously inspected and serviced a dozen times in the past week, sitting on the racks in the first two spots on the row of weapons lined up on the right side of the bunker. They used the overhead manual chain and pulley assembly to lift the first bomb and lower it carefully down onto the trailer behind the tug, then secured the bomb in the cradle, unchained it, and moved the lift assembly overhead weapon number two.

Before they could pull the weapon out of the bunker he had to go check on the progress of the Iskandr team's work on the missiles. It served no purpose to have the weapon sitting out in the open.

Out of the bunker, he went, turned right, and walked the 30 yards to the transloader to see the first nose cone, dangling from the crane, being carefully placed on a large tarp a short distance from the vehicle.

Captain Sidorov walked over next to him and said, "They should have the warhead off in about 30 minutes."

"The weapon is on the trailer and ready to move," Luka said, then turned and walked back to the bunker but chose to take a seat in his office for a few moments of quiet.

48

TAKE THAT

Artem was sweating, even though the GCS was air-conditioned. The autopilot helped, but the task of constantly monitoring the drone's altitude and looking for obstacles in the infrared image in front of him was exhausting. There was little time to think of anything else.

The navigation route carefully took into account avoiding all towns and cities (and known friendly and enemy air defense sites) but this crooked path added time to what would have been a shorter flight in a straight line.

The launch order came about 25 minutes after the three of them settled in the GCS. So that put to rest the fear of having the drone over the target in daylight. And the sun will be at our back during the return to base - which is so much easier on the eyes than staring at a sunrise on the screen.

Major Danyluk's silence spoke well to the confidence he had in them and even to his approval for the way Artem was flying. Over the last two and a half hours he had relegated himself to narrating the progress on the nav route (visible to all three of them on screen), and to verbally tracking the clock en route to the pull-up point, or PUP - that point where they will climb to altitude to acquire and attack the target.

"Ten minutes to PUP," Danyluk said quietly.

Payload operator Marko had his IR targeting device camera called up on his primary screen giving him a view of forward progress from underneath the aircraft. He quickly checked the two MAM-L bombs - nominal - and then said, "Request permission to Arm the System."

Danyluk replied, "Permission granted."

Marko move his cursor to the side panel on the display and pressed the rectangular grayed-out Master Arm icon with white letters, which immediately changed colors to a bright red image with white letters.

"Master Arm - Armed," he declared loudly for all to hear.

"Three minutes to pull," Danyluk said.

"Yessir," Artem acknowledged. He could also see that fact displayed on the nav system indicators on his forward-looking infrared camera on the pilot's primary screen.

In the center of the screen was a large circle, with a flight path marker symbol showing steady on the artificial horizon line. Each time he banks or climbs or dives the aircraft flight path marker tilts right or left or moves above or below the horizon line...when it goes up or down it does so on a ladder with each rung showing degrees of nose-up or down flightpath.

An "A" symbol in the center of the flight path marker shows the pilot that the autopilot is flying the aircraft. When Artem disconnects the autopilot to fly it himself, the symbol disappears.

The display also shows airspeed on the left, at the nine o'clock position around the larger circle, in a rectangular box with a number in it representing knots of airspeed, and another box at the three o'clock position showed thousands of feet in altitude. Beneath that box is another set of numbers showing the actual altitude above the ground as determined by the radar altimeter.

Right now the computer was flying the aircraft using Altitude Hold and NAV Steer features, steady at 300 feet above the ground and pointed directly at the target some 15 miles in front of them.

"Two minutes to PUP."

"Yessir." Artem did a last-minute check - engine instruments are good, fuel is good, Marko had us in Master Arm - Armed, radar warning receiver is on (and clean). He was ready.

"Fifteen seconds."

"Pilot ready," Artem said.

"Payload ready," from Marko.

Pause.

"5, 4, 3, 2, 1, execute."

Artem disconnected the autopilot using the thumb button on the control stick mounted on the right side of his part of the console, advanced the throttle to full power with his left-hand controller, and smoothly pulled the nose up ten degrees and held it there to perform the climb.

Passing 3,500 feet the radar warning receiver BEEPED in their headsets and placed the symbol for the acquisition radar of the S-400 on the left 9 to 10 o'clock position of the scope. Then it faded.

"Lost us?" Marko said hopefully.

BEEP again. S-400 again - faded again.

Soon, "Leveling off 7,500 feet:" Pilot.

"2 miles to release:" Mission Commander.

"Yessir," from Marko.

Throughout the climb, Marko had been watching the IR tracker centered on the target marker on his display. Already he could make out the vehicles in the target area. He zoomed in twice to reveal the building on the left, a bunker on the right, and the transloader smack under the target symbol on the display. GPS is an amazing thing.

"One mile," said the Mission Commander, "Cleared to drop."

"Copy cleared to drop:" Payload Operator.

BEEP. S-400 acquisition symbol at nine o'clock on the display, steady.

BEEP-BEEP-BEEP, with a flashing light on the radar warning receiver and a screeching alarm tone now in the headset. It was an S-400 launch indication on the radar warning receiver.

A long 30 seconds.

"Bombs gone!:" Payload Operator.

The two bombs, released milliseconds apart, started their fall to the target.

"Turning 45 degrees right:" Pilot. And Artem rolled the aircraft slowly to the right towards the new direction away from the incoming S-400 missile coming from their left, 9 o'clock.

"Laser on:" Payload Operator. He was pressing the trigger button on the front of his control stick, commanding the Aselsan CATS laser designator to illuminate the target. In the 2x zoom mode, Marko could see the windshield of the vehicle that his designator was splashing with invisible laser energy.

He could also see numerous people around the vehicle along with a collection of stands and equipment.

"15 seconds to impact," the Mission Commander said aloud, then added, "30 seconds to missile impact."

Artem glanced to the right - Danyluk was holding a stopwatch in his left hand - apparently started at the indication of the missile launch they got on the radar warning receiver. Marko was dead-serious focused on the target and the laser spot.

Artem was thinking about the upcoming turn to the south when the Payload Operator's zoomed-in image flared once and twice on the target, followed by a larger explosion.

Marko yelled without keying the microphone, "Take that assholes!" And simultaneously all three of their screens pixelated into multiple colors and then went black. Comms all showed no contact.

Though pleased with their success, they all felt surprisingly depressed about getting shot down.

49

A RIPPING, TEARING SOUND

After about 20 minutes in the office, Captain Sidorov came jogging around the corner of the bunker, slowed, saw him sitting inside, walked to the door, and knocked. Then he opened the door and came in.

"The warhead is on the tarp set well to the side of the transloader. We are ready for weapon number one."

Luka stood up and headed toward the door, but Sidorov did not move.

"Before we go, I want to say that I think what you've done here is incredibly brave. All of us in PMC Wagner work for Russia and, of course, for the money. But what you've done, not only splitting from the corrupt Russian military to join Wagner but doing this under the noses of the nuclear assurance teams, is amazing."

"Don't think too highly of me. You don't know my motivations. And we don't know how this will play out. But I've done what is right for me. Prigozhin is the first person in a long time to acknowledge my abilities."

"Well, I just wanted to mention that the team thinks this took much courage."

Luka just nodded his head and smiled slightly. Sidorov turned, and then Luka followed him out the door to go to the bunker but then decided to go out to inspect the location of the warhead for himself. Once satisfied, he'd return to open the blast door and retrieve his weapon.

They walked together toward the transloader, the vehicle surrounded by work stands, the crane, the toolboxes, and the maintenance crew finishing their last tasks before he brought the weapon out to them.

Suddenly, he heard a ripping, tearing sound high and to the left, like someone pulling apart a giant sheet of canvas. It quickly grew much louder until the night turned white. And then all was blackness.

50

ACT OF BRAZEN TREACHERY

Secretary Austin and Director Minard sat in the Oval Office early Friday afternoon with the President as he examined the morning's satellite photos. With a shaking hand, the President picked up one of the photos, studied it, turned it over to reveal the next one, studied that one, and repeated the process until he'd seen all five. The last two close-up photos were disturbing when you looked carefully around the wreckage.

He looked up at them and nodded his head.

"Ron?"

"Sir, the first two photos were taken yesterday, late afternoon, sometime after the Wagner convoy arrived at the tactical nuclear weapons storage site known as B-22, near Belgorod, Russia."

He nodded.

"That site is managed by the 12th GU MO, the same organization that manages all of their storage sites and the organization we've been working with for years as part of the nuclear safety agreements. They have a small unit nearby on the outskirts of Antonovka. It appears that security at this site has become quite lax."

"When did our inspection teams last visit that site?"

"Never. Technically, tactical nuke sites are not part of the inspection agreements. While we've been to some - probably only their best-maintained sites - this one never made the inspection list."

"How did Wagner get in?"

"We know that Prigozhin contacted someone in that site about being ready and checking on his *possessions* - we assume now it was an officer inside this particular facility. That person, acting alone or with the cooperation of another unknown person or persons, enabled the entry and access to the weapons."

"So, Prigozhin *recruited* someone inside this facility?"

"It appears so, sir."

"Does that mean Putin or Shoigu may have no role in this event?"

"That could be the case. No, I'll say that we highly suspect the Russian leadership did not know about this operation. It appears that Prigozhin ordered it, and his units sent the Iskandr transloader, and his inside contact probably made it all possible."

The President thought about that for a minute, then said, "From what I see in the last three photos, I presume we can say with certainty that their operation failed. Am I right?"

"Yessir," said Secretary Austin. "The photos of the destruction of the transloader, the other vehicles, and support equipment are about six hours old - mid-morning in Russia.

They clearly show the burnt-out shell of the Iskandr transloader vehicle right in the center."

The President's said quietly, "Attacking a nuclear storage site is a big step - scary. The potential fallout, pardon the pun, is huge. What about the bunkers and the nukes?"

Director Minard answered, "The close-up pictures show superficial, external damage to the two bunkers visible there. You can see debris on the tops of the storage bunkers and the destruction of the external offices, but the bunkers themselves seem intact, and the blast doors look closed. We don't see any evidence of the nuclear weapons or their trailers in the debris."

He nodded again, momentarily held his chin, then asked, "What happened to the missiles - I assume they burnt up?"

Austin said, "We think that even though the TB2 drone used in the attack carries relatively small, 48-pound laser-guided bombs, the secondary explosion may have been a detonation of one or both of the missile's solid fuel loads - in the zoomed-out photo, photo three, you can see a line of debris and marks on the ground ending in a fire-damaged section of the woods and what appears to be metal wreckage. That is probably the remains of one of the missiles. Perhaps it ignited, flew off the trailer, raining pieces all the way, and stopped in the woods. The remains of the other missile lie in the transloader wreckage."

He continued, "We did account for both conventional warheads, so they must have been made fully safe for the swap - one is on the ground about 30 feet from the transloader or so, and the second is that triangular shape you can see in the wreckage of the vehicle."

Director Minard summarized, "Sir, what we have here appears to be an act of brazen treachery from Prigozhin and his PMC Wagner Group, and it appears that the Ukrainian forces stopped them using a TB2 drone to destroy the missile transloader and associated equipment. It also appears to be done with inside, traitorous cooperation, and without the knowledge of Russian leadership."

"So, there are many bodies in those photographs and destroyed property. How do we expect Putin to react?"

Ron answered, "They will probably show great restraint and choose to cover it all up. After all, treasonous acts are at play here, and, at a minimum, their security was embarrassingly lax. They could cover it up, deny it happened, and let the situation pass - at least in public anyway."

"Can we suggest that to them?" asked the President.

Secretary Austin replied, "Sir, as you know, we have not had direct communications with any of their state or military leadership since just before the invasion. But I would like to try. I've met Chairman Shoigu on several occasions - I will strongly encourage him through multiple channels to take my call if you allow me to do so."

"Yes. Soon. Today if you can make it happen. I'll ask the Russian ambassador to come to the White House if you cannot get through."

"Yessir, I will try my best. But you should ask the ambassador to call you if we hope to keep this whole story under wraps."

"Good point. I want Shoigu to know that we know about this and expect them to handle it quietly. And, while you're at it, push him hard on reigning in Prigozhin and PMC Wagner."

"I will."

Then to Ron, he said, "And, as if we don't already have enough going on, I want to know the moment anything happens in Buenos Aires."

"Yessir. We are watching."

Ron expected this to be a long weekend.

51

RECOILING IN HORROR

Carlos had gotten up at 03:00 Argentina Standard Time to prepare for the day's events. No shower, no shave, only dressed in some throwaway clothes to cover his Premium Body Armor t-shirt with Level IIIA armor inserts, his Belly Band holster holding the Glock 22 with two additional clips, and his SatPhone. That and his Spyderbite Equalizer self-defense combat knife strapped securely to his right thigh were all he'd be taking to the plaza today.

He was out and gone soon after waking, dropped by an embassy employee near the Retiro district on the north end of Avenida 9 de Julio. His old stomping grounds. Even in the early pre-dawn, he could see that nothing had changed. The cartoneros were out and about, heading home after a long night's work collecting other people's garbage in exchange for pesos at the recycling centers. Many spent the money right away on booze or drugs and laid about in the alleys and along the sidewalks and curbs, and in doorways of businesses. It was not pleasant - this poverty - but today it would be useful.

It was not hard to find appropriate attire here among the desperate. A filthy, oversized shirt, baggy pants (torn at the cuffs or where cuffs might have been), holed and equally filthy, tied at the waist by a nylon rope. Shoes were the hardest part to find - both size and the right amount of decay so they looked the part but were functional for the kind of action he might see today. He left a roll of pesos in the pocket of each person who helped him out.

The worst part was getting himself filthy enough.

Luckily, his dark complexion made it easy for him to blend in - he was thankful for his father's hearty Spanish, Portuguese, southern European, African, and South American heritage. It also made it easier for rich or privileged people, or Wagner soldiers, to choose not to see him at all.

He found all he needed to look the part of a hopeless cartonero from the slop in the gutters, the sewer drains, and in the alleys - and there were bottles whose remnants added a final distinctive odor to the disguise. He was a poor, filthy cartonero - and a drunk. It reminded him of many desperate people of his childhood.

It took him most of the remaining pre-dawn hour to walk, crookedly and with a feigned limp, to the Plaza de Mayo. On the way, he noted the traffic barriers already set on the curbs and in the parks along the convoy route. When he got there, he found that in the Plaza itself, the barriers were already up on the east end in front of the Presidential Palace and already blocking the roads on either side of it.

He meandered about, checking every trash can, looking under the benches, stumbled into all the bushes, and reconnoitered every vantage point that an assassin might use later this morning. He had collected a small bundle of treasures - a broken plastic chair, a half dozen cardboard scraps bound by a series of knotted plastic shopping bags, and an old hat (with most of the brim) perched unattractively on his head but shading him from the sun. And hiding his eyes. He slowly moved the few possessions he had up onto the mound on the northwest side and stashed them partially under a bush there. And then he wandered around collecting more.

In front of the history museum, a woman handed him a coffee, a tostada, and medialunas. He looked only at the street and said nothing while accepting the food - not wanting her to see his clear eyes and healthy teeth. No one else seemed to even notice him.

The convoy vehicles arrived around 09:00. The three VIP limousines backed into the service alley first, followed by the rear guard security SUV, then the Pope mobile. The two flanking SUVs parked on each side of the street at the alley entrance, and the lead and second security SUV parked in a line, one behind the other, against the curb directly in front of the Cathedral.

There were a few cops, mostly keeping in the shade and hanging around the Cathedral and the Presidential Palace. Several groups of motorcycles were parked in various places in front of the lead SUV, ready to assume their position at the head and tail of the convoy when it moved.

Slowly, people were gathering in the streets and along the Plaza. For now, it was dominated by normal people, people you would expect to see - families, the faithful, tourists - all here to get a glimpse of the Bishop of Rome, Vicar of Jesus Christ, Successor of the Prince of the Apostles, Supreme Pontiff of the Universal Church, Primate of Italy, Archbishop and Metropolitan of the Roman Province, Sovereign of the State of Vatican City, and Servant of the Servants of God.

Put THAT on your business card, Carlos thought.

But he wasn't here to see the Pope, he was here to see that nobody killed the Pope. By himself. Outnumbered. Without a clue of the enemy's plans.

By 10:00 hours, the last of the barriers were in place along the sidewalks of the Plaza and to the right of the Residence, blocking all the streets except the outbound lanes of North Diagonal Avenue.

He was looking for things that stood out. Non-normals. Oddballs. Weird clothing choices - things that don't go together. Something that just didn't look right.

The crowds were now swelling and settling in, first lining the sidewalks, then seeking higher ground to get a better view of the Pope.

Which is where he was now - nestled in with his recently acquired possessions, near the top of the mound, near the foot of the pedestal of the Pyramide de Mayo.

A couple of young lovers on the other side of his bush, on a blanket, were not acting in a very Catholic way. A family, a father and mother, and four kids were gathered to his left, about 15 feet away, sitting on little gardening chairs spiked into the ground.

More and more people were crowding the plaza. He was beginning to doubt his kill zone identification skills. Or maybe Wagner had called this off today. Or maybe they were already here and he just couldn't pick them out.

The Swiss Guard was soon out and about the vehicles. Black suits, appropriately oversized jackets, black ties, earpieces, all wearing sunglasses. They wanted to be seen - they wanted people to be assured, and intimidated.

He couldn't quite see down the alley but could see people walking in front of the Cathedral and then turning left into the alley. People in religious attire, some obvious politicians. Some elderly people, a woman, silver-haired, walking tall, with assistance on either side, eventually trailed the others as they all passed her on the way into the alley - undoubtedly to get into the vehicles before the Pope came out of the Residence with his entourage.

The sidewalks were now full. The plaza was crowded with people, with even more moving up the hill towards him and his hide. Some came near him but moved away when the light breeze shifted in their direction.

Odd. A lone man in the crowd came up the hill, following a family a little too closely as if to be a part of them. Carlos watched from under the brim of his hat. Caucasian, dark hair, cut short, tanned - like the kind of tan you get in the desert. Could this be the man? He was carrying what looked to be a long, rectangular fabric or plastic container, about four feet long and eight inches square, for something like a foldable tent. He veered off to sit in front of a bush down below and to the left of Carlos' refuge, still in his line of sight. The man looked for no other location. He sat and put the container on his right side.

Carlos averted his eyes and looked for others without success. He kept coming back to him, seated 30 feet or so down the gentle slope of the hill.

A short time later the noise steadily rose as the crowd anticipated the Pope's emergence from the Residence, and then cheers went up as the white-robed figure appeared. Everyone who wasn't standing was now.

Except for the man with the good line of sight. Carlos turned fully around, assessing the area at the top of the hill for backup. Some kind of cover soldier. No one stood out.

The lead SUVs pulled away from the curb and stopped in line for North Diagonal Avenue. The two side escorts positioned themselves at either curb in front of the Cathedral, and then the Pope Mobile began moving forward in the alley towards the street.

There were no other anomalies, nothing out of place. Nobody else caught his eye. But for all he knew the man brought a sun shade for people who never showed up.

The Pope Mobile edged towards the intersection, then began the right turn - fully exposing the left side of the car to the crowd, with the Pope waving through the glass.

While he was looking at the Pope Mobile, the man must have unzipped the case, because when Carlos looked back he had lifted out an NLAW, and was standing up to put it to his shoulder even as Carlos was up and running down the hill.

The crowd noise was amazing. If anyone around them recognized what was happening there was no sign - and no screams of horror or shouts of protest. As Carlos launched himself bodily through the air to take him to the ground, the man was letting the sight settle on the target for the required two-to-three seconds, then the man pulled the trigger just as he hit him full-on above the right hip in the back of the ribcage, and under the rear of the weapon tube, causing him to drop the aim down as the missile soft-launched out of the tube with a *WHOOSH* sound and flew directly into the pond below them, and the mud, without time to arm. It threw up a splash of water out of the pond towards the people standing between it and the sidewalk, the spray hidden from the convoy by the crowd of people.

The two men tobogganed a little way down the hill, plowing through a couple of people until they stopped short with Carlos' left arm around the man's neck in a chokehold, and his right arm coming up from the hole in his pant leg with the Equalizer in his hand, plunging once to the kidney on the right lower back, then out and up into the side of the neck and shoving forward to sever the right carotid artery and trachea. The man went still under him. And then the crowd around them recoiled from the violence and bolted.

Carlos stood, replaced his knife in the sheath inside his baggy pants, and then ran with the crowd, most of whom were going with the surge now and not knowing why.

A glance at the convoy showed them moving as if nothing happened, the first VIP car now turning into the street. But the two cars behind were not yet in sight. Then, over the noise, he heard the unmistakable sound of an AK-47. Or several.

The crowd flowed across the street towards the Residence as the police tried vainly to control them. Carlos flowed along with them, leaning left towards the service alley.

When he came to the corner of the Residence he turned to see several cops down, blood on the street, and the first of the two remaining vehicles with its windshield blown in and on fire. The convoy continued on its route - already gone.

He ran to the chaos and saw one man just opening the rear door of the last vehicle while a second man, standing near the left front wheel, fired his AK-47 directly into and across the windshield, holing it everywhere and killing the driver.

Carlos pulled the Glock 22 from under his shirt, slippery with blood (his blood?! No), slowed to a walk, then took up a two-handed Modern Isosceles shooting stance, calmly exhaled as best he could, and put three Underwood 8.74 gram/135-grain jacketed hollow point rounds tightly grouped into the shooter's upper back.

He walked quickly forward, gun still raised in that forward-leaning posture, and when the intruder at the back looked up to see what had happened, he shot him twice in the upper body, right below the throat.

Hollow-point is a highly effective, but messy, deterrent.

Carlos kicked the body out of the way as people ran by in every direction. Unlike the white man on the mound, both men here were middle eastern or southern central European. He turned and ducked into the car and was shocked to see his Abuela, Lilia Pombar, recoiling in horror at the look and smell of her rescuer - even before she recognized that it was him. Then she passed out. She appeared to be unhurt.

The elderly man in the seat next to her was dead, as was the man in the passenger seat - both killed by the mass of rounds fired through the windshield that also killed the driver.

He heard sirens, and there way too many people coming into the alley. He quickly unbuckled her seatbelt, then pulled Lilia out of the car, and laid her carefully on the road, rolling up her coat and putting it under her head.

Then he fled the scene in slow motion, limping, staggering in odd directions, like any cartonero would when awakened from a drunken sleep into a nightmare.

52

BLUNTLY AND FIRMLY

A big man, standing slightly over six feet two inches tall and weighing more than 200 pounds, Secretary Austin was normally reserved, more comfortable keeping his thoughts to himself and letting others do the talking. Listening, learning, deciding, and then speaking. As the Greek philosopher Epictetus said, "We have two ears and one mouth so that we can listen twice as much as we speak." Austin thought that advice served him well.

His physical stature by itself commanded attention.

And no one could dispute his accomplishments. A 1975 graduate of the United States Military Academy, he entered the infantry, graduated from airborne school, then Ranger training. He commanded units at every echelon and was the first Black general officer to command US Central Command. He was the Combined Forces Commander overseeing the campaign to defeat ISIL in Iraq and Syria. Eventually retiring with 41 years of service, he has the extraordinary distinction of commanding troops in combat at every general rank from 1-star to 4-star.

So he knew how to communicate in tough situations. And he planned to speak bluntly and firmly on this call today.

He sat at the head of the table in the conference room next to his office in the Pentagon, with his Russian translator, Dr. Tricia Patterson, seated to his right, and General Mark Milley seated in the chair to his left. They were waiting for the conference room phone to ring, expecting the call at any moment from the command post at US European Command in Stuttgart, Germany.

One of 11 Unified Combatant Commands, EUCOM's area of responsibility included Europe, Russia, and Greenland - 51 countries and 21,000,000 square miles of territory.

Today, it was important because they were the Western link with Russia via the vaguely titled "Deconfliction Line" - a dedicated phone connection between senior command positions in the US Military and their equivalents in the Armed Forces of the Russian Federation.

Purposefully, the line was set up to prevent miscalculations, military incidents, and escalations from happening during tense situations. Like the invasion of Ukraine.

Or, like the destruction of an Iskandr transloader on a nuclear weapons storage site after unauthorized access to those weapons by a third party.

He knew his counterpart, but not well. Sergei Kuzhugetovich Shoigu, as the Chairman of the Council of Ministers of Defence of the Commonwealth of Independent States, Hero of the Russian Federation, was also the General of the Army. But in his case, that last title was in name only.

Shoigu was a career politician - and personal friend of Vladimir Putin.

Austin knew him to be two years younger than himself. A civil engineering graduate of the Krasnoyarsk Polytechnic Institute, he worked in construction jobs for a decade before becoming a minor functionary in the Communist Party of the Soviet Union, after which he served in the political youth organization Komsomol. After moving to Moscow in 1990 he was later appointed as Deputy Chairman of the State Architecture and Construction Committee of the Russian Federation - the same path Boris Yeltsin took in his progression through Soviet politics on the way to the eventual Presidency. Shoigu soon had greater roles - Minister of Emergency Situations, Governor of Moscow, and then in 2012 he was appointed by Putin to be Minister of Defence. Like his predecessor Anatoly Serdyukov, he had no military background - so he took to wearing the uniform of a General Officer to improve his standing and instituted many reforms desired by the military leadership. Including increased use of contract soldiers.

He thought it interesting that Shoigu directed commanders to develop professional reading lists in 2012, about the time that the previous Secretary of Defense, General Mattis, was vociferously advocating reading lists for his Marines as the then US CENTCOM commander. He wondered what Mad Dog would think of that.

He looked up from his notes and took a drink of hot tea, now lukewarm.

"Ready?" Milley asked. General Milley knew his role today was to listen. It speeds up the communication process after a meeting like this and it helps to have the Chairman listening to the dialogue in real-time.

"Yes. This is pretty straightforward. And I expect him to be...well, mostly quiet, maybe in denial...he certainly won't be willing to admit their nuclear security fell apart."

To Dr. Patterson, he said, "His English is fair, but we'll stick with the translations just to make sure our message is clear."

"I think that is appropriate, given the circumstances," she said.

It was nearly 3pm - 22:00 hours in Moscow.

The phone rang, Austin picked it up, and the voice said, "Sir, this is the EUCOM command post, I'm connecting you with the Russian Ministry of Defence in just a moment." And the line went silent.

Then again, after working whatever coordination she did with her counterparts in Russia, she said, "Sir, Minister of Defence Shoigu is connecting now."

"Good evening. Minister Shoigu is on the line," the voice of the translator.

Austin began, "Minister Shoigu, this is Secretary Austin. I know it is late there - thank you for taking this urgent call."

Dr. Patterson rapidly spoke the translation in Russian.

Shoigu spoke, then his translator, "Hello Secretary Austin. Yes, it is late."

"I will get right to the point." Dr. Patterson translated for Austin.

"Yes, please do." Shoigu's translator.

"It has come to our attention that there was an incident at a nuclear storage facility near Belgorod last night."

"Go on."

"Satellite imagery shows a destroyed Iskandr transloader vehicle near two storage bunkers."

Silence.

Austin continued, "We believe that the Iskandr transloader was there to load tactical nuclear weapons on its missiles. It is also our belief that it was there without the sanction of the Ministry of Defence."

Silence again.

Then, Shoigu said through his translator, "Ukrainian forces conducted a raid on our storage site, without provocation."

Austin countered, then Dr. Patterson translated, "Was the Iskandr transloader there with the approval of your Ministry of Defence?"

No answer.

"Minister Shoigu, the United States wants assurance that the Russian Federation is not considering the use of nuclear weapons in Ukraine, and is continuing to provide the kind of security for those weapons that we have both come to understand is necessary."

"Secretary Austin, Russia reserves the right to use nuclear weapons when the very existence of the homeland is threatened, but that threat has not yet been realized. Our security processes are sound. That site is under our control as we speak. All weapons remain secure."

"Then is it correct to say that the transloader, the two utility trucks, and the BTR-80 were there without your knowledge and approval?"

A long delay - possibly on mute.

"Those vehicles were not approved to be there. An investigation is ongoing."

"There will be press inquiries."

"We will handle that."

Another pause. Then Austin said, "We know where those vehicles came from."

"Your point?"

"We strongly encourage you to reign in the paramilitary forces under your control before they do things you cannot tolerate."

"Those forces are no different than your Blackwater forces."

"Blackwater *did* participate in combat when forced to defend itself. Blackwater did not torture, rape, and murder civilians."

Coldly, Shoigu said in English, "Is there anything else, Mister Secretary?"

"No Minister. I have made my point. Goodnight sir."

"Goodnight," he said. And the line went dead.

General Milley was looking at him. Hands folded on the tabletop.

Dr. Patterson began gathering her things, preparing to go.

Austin said, "Dr. Patterson, before you leave, I want you to comment on word choice, truthfulness, that sort of thing, based on what you heard."

She leaned back in the chair and thought for a moment. Unusual for a linguist, Patterson was also a Doctor of Human Behavior.

"I'm not surprised about his reluctance to speak. Several reasons, not the least of which is that he is engaged in a war in Ukraine that he knows is unpopular in the West - not that he cares about the West, but because he anticipates friction from you."

Austin nodded.

"He is also self-conscious. Though he leads a powerful military, he knows almost nothing practical about it - about the weapons, tactics, strategy, or how people fight. His perspective is all politics. As the Secretary of Defense, you are a threat to him because you also have extensive military experience. He knows he can't talk about military topics, alone, with you without showing his shortcomings."

"Do you think he was alone on that call?" Austin asked.

"I do not think he was alone," she said. "The pauses were not due to him thinking - those weren't difficult subjects. He knew about the events but was not comfortable talking freely. Everything with them is secretive and a bit paranoid. They are all political beasts - they never know enough about a topic, they never really know what they can say. And they never know who might be listening and how what they say might be received - by their people."

Milley piped up, "I would guess that Gerasimov was there."

"Possibly," Austin said, "though there is a rumor he was wounded near Izyum in April."

"Maybe his convalescence plan includes going to the office."

Austin continued, "Tricia, what do you make of him saying that the vehicles were not approved to be there?"

"That was an interesting statement - in essence, he held up his hands and said, "We didn't do it," and then stopped the conversation by saying an investigation was underway."

"He didn't want to say too much," Austin said.

"I'm surprised he said that at all. Perhaps they were genuinely surprised it happened."

"And no comment on Wagner."

"No," she said, "it sounded like he didn't want to go there at all. Though he supported the reforms that brought in more paramilitary forces, we know his military leadership now does not. From what we read I think the professional military *tolerates* these organizations - because they have to. The PMCs are effective, yes, but with competing allegiances and no real acknowledgment of the chain of command in the field."

"His reluctance to talk about them may reflect the fact that a senior military officer was sitting there with him during the call," Milley said.

"Exactly," she said. "On the one hand, he supports them, though their excesses of late may be making that harder, and on the other, he has to keep the allegiance of his military leaders who may not be so fond of them, or him."

"Thank you," Austin said. "You always have solid input."

Then, as she was headed out the door, he said to General Milley, "Thoughts?"

"Her comments were good - always helpful. From my point of view, I wanted to learn that the MOD didn't order this near catastrophe with nukes, and I wanted to learn that they are all secured - at least whatever that means in Russia."

"I think he assured us of that. I only hope he got the message to crack down on Wagner - and that he does something about it."

The Chairman of the Joint Chiefs got up and left the Secretary alone to talk to the President.

53

A RAT'S NEST

He had lost count. Was that his third or fourth shower since returning to the embassy? All he knew was that he felt like he needed another this morning. They put his clothes in an incinerator last night. Jackie called him and asked if he was ok and if he needed anything. He told her he was fine and left it at that. If she knew what he'd smeared all over himself yesterday he would never see her again.

He debriefed with the assistant station chief last night. It was a short meeting (he'd only had one shower). The press covered the events yesterday - on television and in print, but almost like it was a routine crime story, making very little association with the Pope and his successful visit. There was an explosive device of some kind in the crowd on Plaza de Mayo, and then terrorist violence in the alley that killed some people. Luckily the Pope's visit was a success.

He gave the truth to the embassy official: one person dead in the Plaza of a stabbing incident, and 11 people dead in the alley - two cops, four people in the lead VIP limo, three in the trailing limo, and two terrorists of middle eastern appearance. A terrible toll, not counting the wounded, and those injured when the crowd stampeded. He did not mention his grandmother.

But the Pope was alive. Carlos felt good about that.

And his Abuela was alive. But every time he thought about that it made him angrier. To think that this Wagner menace nearly killed his abuela, his savior, was unforgivable. He was surprised a little at the anger he felt.

He was logged into the agency network when he got a text from Skip, "Can you talk?"

"Yes." Send.

"Five minutes."

Soon the SatPhone rang.

"Heard you had a busy day yesterday."

"Skip, it was luck - pure luck. Like looking for a needle in a haystack, but the needle just came out and sat down right next to me."

"Sometimes these things work like that - you play your best hunches and things work out. Good job."

"I was about to get on the phone with Gomez. Please tell me you don't think he is the mole."

"No. He's been with us a long time. Worked the field before he went to the desk. A good man. Some of the other people around here - particularly some of the new analysts - worry me. They have skills so important we just have to hire them, only to find out later that they may have other motivations."

Skip continued, "How did Ms. Rapp do at the airport the other night? I imagine it made quite an impression."

"She reacted great - she had her shit together."

Then Skip launched right into the next topic, "While you were saving the Catholic World, there were developments in

Ukraine that further implicate Wagner. Turns out Prigozhin tried to put a nuclear weapon on a surface-to-surface missile and almost got away with it. Ukrainians struck the missile trailer at the weapons storage site."

"Is this something he did on his own?"

"The story I got from Angela was that SIGINT and IMINT both pointed to an independent operation. And Austin called his counterpart yesterday and they discussed the situation. The assessment from that call is that the MOD had no clue about the attempt until afterwards. Never said that of course, but the conversation seemed to lean that way."

"What was the target?"

"We don't know, but the launch site was going to be in Belarus, north of Kyiv. From there it could have been a major city such as Kyiv or Lviv, or even the NATO weapons storage and distribution sites west of Lviv. Probably will never know."

"But PMC Wagner remains a huge threat."

"Yes, it does. Now, when will you be back?"

"I have some cleanup work to do here. As a minimum, I want to see what is going on at the Wagner office - maybe I can reduce some of that threat for us."

"Alright. And by the way, the director sends her thanks."

"Ok. I'll be in touch."

"See ya." And he rang off.

Carlos went to the news sites and searched [russia news release ukraine attacks] and hit ENTER.

Up popped a slew of articles and videos.

Right on top: Ukraine Drone Shot Down, TASS, 12 hours ago. Russian forces successfully shot down a Ukrainian TB2 drone aircraft over the Belgorod Oblast yesterday evening. The drone was conducting an illegal attack inside Russian airspace on civilian storage sites and warehouses west of Belgorod near the town of Golovchino. No casualties were reported and no damage to the facilities was incurred as the drone missed its target. It is not clear where the drone came from or what it was after as Golovchino is a peaceful small town with no military forces. Further incursions by the Ukrainian forces will be met with the same effectiveness, and consequences in Ukraine will be felt by their military in the ongoing special military operation."

Whatever.

Speaking of luck - THAT was lucky. He could only imagine PMC Wagner with nuclear weapons.

He called Greg Gomez, and the analyst picked up on the first ring.

"Gomez."

"Good morning Greg," Carlos said, "What have you got for me?"

"Open this folder," he said. Then the email *PINGED* in the Inbox. Carlos opened it up.

"Got it."

"Contains all I could find on PMC Wagner Buenos Aires. First, they just completed construction on the building about ten days ago. At least, as complete as a building ever is in Buenos Aires. There will be finishing touches for a while, I'm sure."

"We got access to the permits, the design documents, and the tax documents. Those are all included in the folder. Along with another map, Map2.pdf."

"Excellent."

Then Greg continued, "If you open the map, you'll see that the Wagner building, point F, sits on the northwest corner of north-south Avenida Paseo Colon and east-west Avenida Independencia, on a corner lot. That is just eight blocks south of the Presidential Palace and half a mile from the Argentina Ministry of Defense. It is an old district. The city demolished the original building a few years ago, then Wagner bought the empty lot and built new."

"You can see from the permits and the design documents that the city authorities approved construction of an "office building" - owned and to be operated by PMC Wagner (registered in St. Petersburg), to conduct Security Assistance Training."

"It is a two-story brick building of 29,600 square feet, with a 12,000 square foot basement for storage and other purposes."

"That looks like an indoor shooting range in the basement to me," Carlos said.

"The front entrance is set back from the corner - 45 degrees to the west and south walls. The second floor is a full rectangle with that southwest corner overhanging the entrance below. There are no windows on the first floor, a couple of windows on each side of the southwest corner of the second floor."

"There is another entrance in the back off of the service alley. Overall, the drawings show a reception desk, then entry through sliding glass doors to the interior, a stairwell and elevator on the left, then a series of open-air office-style cubicles on the south side of the floor, and some small conference rooms on the north side of the floor."

Greg continued, "Upstairs, you step out into a long hallway that runs the length of the floor to the east, with private offices along the north wall, a large office on the south wall, followed by a large formal conference room in the southeast corner. A second stairwell in the northeast corner drops down to the first floor and the exit to the alley."

"Tax records show an employee count of 20: a site manager, two other managers, finance and technology/security leads, and 15 technical experts."

"So, no local employees in the building - all operators on the Wagner payroll?"

"That is the way it looks - a rat's nest."

"Security?"

"First of all, they have a limited system - nothing fancy. Their full-up security system is not here yet. So in the meantime, they have a pretty weak arrangement similar to what you would get with a cheap home security system. There are two cameras - both WiFI - with motion sensor activation, one above the back entrance oriented to see the alley and the door, and another inside the main entryway near the reception desk, oriented towards the entrance. There are no other cameras inside. When activated, videos get recorded on an internal computer at one of the desks upstairs - probably the technology lead's computer. When an alarm is triggered by the cameras, the service provider calls the security lead. Given that the windows are high and isolated in the front of the building, there are no glass break detectors. As I said, overall, it is weak."

"Exterior locks?"

"It specifies a Keyless Entry push-button lock at the front doors. Regular old key lock and key deadbolt at the back - no entry card readers."

"Exterior connectivity?"

"They have standard coax landline and cable TV and internet service through Telecom Argentina."

"Anything else?"

"I remember from the transcript that the site manager said his Russian ERA cryptophone would be operational by Monday - if that is what he meant by the Monday after the event."

"Yes. See if you can get me a schematic for that."

"Ok. Oh yeah, one more thing. Wagner posted online that their office hours are 09:00-16:00, Monday through Friday."

"They have a website?" Carlos asked.

"Hey, they are a business."

"Ok, Greg, excellent work. Gotta go."

On the way out of the building, Carlos stopped by the special-equipment manager and gave him a list of things he needed for tonight. Twelve hours ought to be enough time for him to find everything.

54

PERSONAL BUSINESS

He'd been sitting in Eva Peron Park for about half an hour now. Nice little chat with an old lady who remembered Eva. She had a nice dog. They sat on the bench in such a way that he could talk to her, pet the dog, and watch the Wagner building through his Maui Jim sunglasses at the same time. Worked nicely for all of them.

When he walked by earlier there was a fair amount of activity with several men - all dressed similarly in non-military but uniformed clothing - going in and out.

They wore black boots, dark gray cargo pants, and black collared shirts with the Wagner patch atop the left pectoralis major, red and black with the grinning white skull in the center. And white lettering that said "Wagner Group" centered at the bottom, and proclaimed "Nothing Personal, Just Business" in an arc around the top.

Well, Carlos thought, it might be just business to them, but it's personal business now for me.

They all looked a little harried - like something was going on. Or had recently gone on and they were scrambling to address it. He figured he probably had something to do with that.

After the old lady left with her dog, he got up and crossed the street to wander down Independence Avenue towards the water for a while. He was dressed casually, looking nondescript, like some of the other tourists and locals wandering about. He considered asking Jackie to attend as couples attract less attention than a solitary man, but he felt he'd probably given her enough entertainment for a week. Or longer. Besides, she'd be distracting.

After an hour or so of wandering around the waterfront, looking at the boats and the buildings surrounding the area, he started back - hoping to see how they closed up for the day. He observed from the south side of Independence that some were already exiting the building and walking away to various forms of transportation - some nice cars starting up and roaring away in the low-traffic Sunday afternoon.

He turned left on Colon Avenue, walked out of sight, and then doubled back to return to the park, now in shadows. He pulled out his tourist map and watched over the top of it as a tall man, suntanned, dressed similarly to the others (though without the logo shirt), came out, turned around, checked the lock on the front doors behind him, and then got into a BMW 7 Series and drove away north on Colon Avenue. He sat there for a while to make sure no one doubled back to check him out, then got up, wandered by the front of the building, and kept going up Colon to walk to the nearest taxi stand on North Diagonal.

They might have desk space for 20 in the permit but there were probably only a dozen or so in and out of the building by his count. More importantly, the building looked fully closed up and empty for the night.

Time to go back and prepare for the next steps.

55

LATE NIGHT HANDIWORK

The black backpack rode comfortably between his shoulders, slightly low. It blended right in with his black, rubber-soled shoes, flat black Tru-Spec tactical pants, and black cotton jacket. Underneath he wore his standard Premium Body Armor t-shirt, the Level IIIA armor inserts, and his Belly Band holster and Glock 22 and extra clips. Along with his SatPhone.

The backpack held his black gloves and watch cap and the complete wish list of supplies rounded up by the specialist at the embassy. A minor miracle, that.

Jackie had dropped him off in a side street two blocks south of Eva's park, wished him luck, and drove off in another direction.

There was almost no traffic at this hour. Walking on the east side of Paseo Colon Avenue, sticking to the shadows, he made his way up to the corner with Independence and turned right, stepping into a doorway about halfway down the block, almost to the alley. He looked carefully for pedestrians, lights on in windows, people on balconies - or security guards in alleyways - and then he donned his gloves and hat, pulled it down over his face, and slowly walked across the street just short of the entrance to the alley behind the Wagner building.

He reached into the backpack and pulled out the first piece of equipment on his wish list: a CTA-7875 Wireless Camera Blocker. He turned on the power (indicator lights already taped over so only he could see the feint green power LED), set it down on the sidewalk, and carefully slid it out into the alley until it had line-of-sight to the wireless security camera. He heard the faint *DING* through the taped-over audio port signaling the tri-band jammer had found the camera and was transmitting appropriate interruption code frequencies rendering the connection ineffective without alerting the base station.

Trusting it to work as advertised (it had before), he stood up and quickly entered the alleyway, checking for guards - dogs or humans. There were none. He had 90 minutes on the jammer battery to be out and away before it was exhausted.

At the door, he retrieved a 12-piece lock pick set from the backpack and quickly inserted the one he expected to work on the typical metal door lock and deadbolt. It fit. Carefully, applying medium torque, clockwise, he felt the first pin release and moved on to the second, and third, until the whole shear plane was clear and the lock popped free. He repeated the process on the deadbolt, returned the set to the backpack, and slowly opened the door.

As expected, there was no door sensor and no audio alarm.

He went in and closed and locked the door behind him. All the lights were off, the only illumination being the green EXIT signs over the door behind him and the one at the front door 150 feet or so in front of him.

Walking quickly down the hall, he paused only to check each conference room on the right and the cubicles on the left to ensure he was alone, then moved to the stairwell door and started up. More EXIT lights in the stairwell.

He opened the door on the second floor, peered carefully inside, and found it equally empty. He stepped in and started down the hall, checked the offices on the left, the boss's office on the right, and then went into the conference room in the far southeast corner of the building where he approached a large table, oriented east to west, left to right, in front of him.

The room was dominated by the table - he quickly counted eight chairs on each side, the larger boss chair at the left end, and multiple armless chairs against both sidewalls. At the right end of the table was a computer cabinet and then mounted on the wall was a large flatscreen television. Sitting squarely in front of the boss's chair, about three feet in on the table, was the Russian ERA Matryoshka phone - a very expensive, cryptophone system introduced in 2021.

The secure communications system that doesn't work in a combat zone!

It turns out that the designers put together a system that depended upon 3G and 4G cell phone towers to operate on, as opposed to satellites. And when the Russians knocked down all those towers as they invaded Ukraine to deny the enemy the ability to communicate, they ended up denying themselves that ability too. Hence their utter reliance on personal cell phones. And the catastrophic consequences of open communications.

As Miloslav had told Prigozhin on the phone call, the amber light on the panel indicated the secure phone system was operational for tomorrow's meeting.

Carlos first pulled out his LED flashlight and set it on end to illuminate the new white tiles of the 10-foot-high ceiling, giving him plenty of light.

Then he pulled out the ERA schematic he got from Greg, the electrician's tools, and the wire and the tape and got right to work. He carefully turned over the box, unscrewed the back panel, removed it, and set it aside. He then found the keyhole on the left (upside down) side of the box and pulled out the small wire bundle.

The key was what made the system secure - insert the plastic T-shaped key into that hole, with its encoded sensors embedded in the plastic thick comb-like serrations on both edges and turn it to engage the encryption software. It had to be done on both ends of the call, in a specific sequence - first the caller who initiated the call, then the caller on the other end. When both boxes showed ENCRYPTED in the display window then the parties could talk freely, assured that no one else could listen.

Provided you had access to a 3G tower or better yet, a direct phone line as they have here in the conference room.

He found the right wire, the wire that carried the power when the key was turned, and very slowly used a petite wire stripping tool to lay back the rubber insulation coating. Then, from the tabletop he retrieved the end of the roll of wire, pulled it through the wire exit hole alongside the cable, and wound the naked end around the exposed section of wire five times. He laid back the rubber surround and then used the black electrical tape to wind the splice.

Next, he slowly stuffed the wire bundle back into its small retaining clips inside the case, picked up the back panel and screwed it on, and set the reassembled cryptophone back on the table by the end chair.

Now he measured off the length of the table to the computer cabinet, added six more feet for good measure, and snipped off the length of wire with the wire cutters from the backpack. He ran that length of wire down into the hole in the tabletop, pulled it tight with the telephone coaxial cable, and threaded them into the hole together as he moved the phone box back to its original position over the top of it.

Under the table, he securely taped the wire to the under-surface so it was tight along the whole length, then got up and moved the backpack down to the end of the table, pulled out the remaining items from the wish list, and meticulously completed the work.

15 minutes later, he dusted and cleaned the table top carefully, and placed the rag and the tools and wire, and other items into the backpack. He arranged the chairs perfectly - just as he found them. Then picking up his flashlight he backed out of the room doing a final sweep for anything disturbed or dirt or debris or other marks left on the carpet.

Then he left the room and looked at his watch. Not bad, 13 minutes left. He decided to check out the boss's office.

Typical office of a retired - or exiled - military person with artifacts and photos and other relics of his past scattered about on tables and shelves and the walls. Seemed a bit arrogant.

A closer look at the pictures hardened his face. It was like a who's-who of those who committed atrocities in Syria. He recognized several, including the man from the plaza, and knew the others to be guilty by association. Other pictures on the wall showed the current team - with many of those same faces. They were all Caucasian. Odd. They'll have to work on the Chechen connection later.

Wagner Buenos Aires was like a murderer's retreat.

Time to go. He accounted for all his things, put the backpack on his back, went out into the hall, then a right turn, down the back stairway, and out the first-floor door and into the alley. He looked around the corner, in both directions, looked up - no one - and stepped out and around the corner, leaned back and picked up the jammer, turned it off, and put it in his backpack. Late-night handiwork complete.

Walking down the street he removed his hat and gloves, then texted Jackie: On the way - SEND.

56

DROPPED CALL

Morning came quickly. Another beautiful fall day, with clear skies, and temperatures expected to be above 60 degrees (or, as they would say here, above 15 degrees). At first, he didn't think he would go to watch, but then when he thought of all the innocents killed in Africa, in Syria, in Ukraine, even in Chechnya and Georgia and Crimea, he decided he owed it to all of them.

Not to mention payback for nearly killing his Abuela.

So they went. Up early, light breakfast (Argentinians rarely eat a large breakfast), and then two tourists out to see the sights in the embassy's local car. It was unremarkable, with faded paint, fake plates with current tabs, and fully functional. They would blend right in. She drove.

They headed off southeast, past the Museum of Decorative Art, the Plaza Dante where he sometimes went as a child with his mother, past the monument to another leader on a horse, Carlos Maria de Alvear, then a right turn, south on Avenida 9 de Julio for the ten block drive to Avenida North Diagonal and on to the Plaza de Mayo.

He talked about the attempted assassination and pointed out the key points as they drove around the plaza once, without a lot of elaboration. Then they drove on past the Casa Rosada and headed south via Avenida Paseo Colon, past Eva Peron Park, and turned right onto Avenida Estados Unidos, where they parked in a rare street spot in front of the Cafe Rivas. They went in for a cappuccino while they waited on the clock.

At ten to the hour, they walked to Eva Peron Park and sat on the same bench he did the day before with the old woman and the dog. It was better company today, though now he regretted letting her come along.

What he thought might be the last of the late-comers were hustling in the front door, kitty corner across the street, as they sat there. He grew even quieter as time slowed and he imagined each step in the sequence.

Precisely, Prigozhin would call that number at 09:00 hours.

"PMC Wagner, Miloslav here."

"This is Prigozhin."

"We will use the ERA cryptophone today."

"Of course. I have my key, encrypting now."

Then, "Buenos Aires encrypting now." And Sergei Miloslav, surrounded by his criminal employees in his new office building inserted his crypto key and turned it clockwise a quarter turn.

The key enabled the encryption software and sent a 9V burst of energy through the wires to the original caller, which, when received causes both devices to display ENCRYPTED in the LED window on the ERA box.

Before the display illuminated, the same burst of voltage went through the splice, along the wire under the table, to the Russian-designed NM Electrical Initiator that Carlos had screwed into the bottom of the green plastic case of the concave/convex Mina Oskolochnya Napravlennogo-50, the Russian equivalent of the US Army's M18 Claymore anti-personnel mine, attached to the far underside of the table by two velcro straps. In milliseconds, the electrical charge reached the initiator, energized the igniter, and fired the firing pin which impacted the detonator in the base of the MON-50. In less than a heartbeat (nearly the last for everyone in the room), the RDX-based explosive device expelled 540 steel balls in an arc under the table in a deafeningly destructive shotgun blast of death and destruction. Those not killed instantly would bleed out from their massive injuries in just moments.

Instead of ENCRYPTED, the screen would go blank and Prigozhin would probably wonder why they experienced a dropped call. Another failure of the cursed encrypted system.

The only indication on the street was a muffled *BOOM* and then the windows surrounding the southwest corner of the second floor starred, the cracks wandering crazily like a spiderweb etched into the glass.

Carlos glanced sideways at Jackie. Her mouth was hanging open - then she quickly recovered, closed her mouth, and looked at him. He shrugged his shoulders briefly, then he looked around the park and the surrounding sidewalks. There were no pedestrians at the time - luckily - and the noisy Monday morning rush hour vehicle traffic just kept going as if nothing happened.

"It's time to go."

"You said that the last time I went out with you."

He smiled slightly and they got up and walked back and got in the car in front of the Cafe. There were distant sirens.

She started the engine, pulled away from the curb, and continued west on Avenida Estados Unidos, then turned left onto Avenida de 9 Julio, until she merged onto westbound Highway 25 de Mayo, headed to the airport.

"Won't there be evidence?" she asked.

"There better not be. I swept the area thoroughly and I wore gloves. It was like I wasn't there."

"I've heard you can trace the explosive residue."

"That is true. That is why I used the Russian MON-50 with PVV-5A RDX explosive. It works just like the Claymore, but all of the evidence is Russian. It won't fool the Russians. But it might fool everyone else - and there is always the plausible deniability to consider."

She drove for a mile without comment.

"Do you ever have regrets?" she asked.

He was quiet for a moment. He wasn't used to questions like this. Or this kind of company either.

"Yes. I would be lying if I said no. Do I think they deserve it? Yes. Did I ask to kill them? No. Their actions caused our government to consider them, as an unsanctioned and illegal military organization, fair game. They are helping prosecute an illegal war against another democracy, and committing acts of atrocities against innocent people. And they got what was coming to them."

It was probably the most he'd said to her so far. Not very personable.

She was quiet for a moment. Then she said, "I agree with you."

He said, "There is one part of today that I find rewarding. Prigozhin caused their deaths by telling them to encrypt the phone. When Miloslav turned the key the bomb went off."

"Boom," she said softly.

"Boom."

At the airport, she said, "I'll ensure the embassy checks in on your grandmother again. She will be looked after until you or her son can get here."

"My father." He realized it was the first time he'd said that to anyone. Then he said, "And she'll probably shoo you all away long before that happens."

He got out, got the bag out of the back seat, walked around to the driver's window and bent down to say goodbye. She was shading her eyes from the low morning sun. Her eyes were particularly green.

"Do you have to leave so soon?"

"Yes."

"What, do you have a family reunion or something?"

"No. I'm expected back at Langley. And it's a little too hot for me to hang around here for a while."

"Well, you know where to find me if you need backup." And she put the car in gear and drove out of the parking lot. He turned and walked out of the lot, across the street, along the access road to the tarmac, and over to the G6. The air stairs were brought up as soon as he was inside and the first engine started as he sat down.

He called the hospital to say goodbye.

57

IN THE BOX

This session of the President's Cabinet Meeting was fully attended and in full swing at the White House. Everyone on the roster was there - wouldn't miss it - to hear and discuss the current events in Ukraine, Russia, and Argentina.

Skip Walker thought that sometimes it is easy to forget that normal, sometimes awful, things happen that keep the President busy during crises like the war in Ukraine. It wasn't the only thing the person in the Oval Office was concerned about.

He was here today representing CIA Director Harkin as she was unable to attend. Besides, Skip mused, she already knows all of this. Unfortunately, he had to sit closer to the President than normal. He made people nervous.

The first 20 minutes of this meeting were spent discussing natural disasters in Brazil and South Africa, tornados in the south of the US, failed votes in the Senate, another racist attack in Buffalo, and the ever-rising inflation rates. They also discussed the makeup of the next aid package for Ukraine.

Skip was grateful he only had to worry about intelligence gathering, analysis, moles, wars, and stuff like that.

The Chief of Staff, Cheryl Templeton, wrapped the table lightly and said, "Ok, let's move on to the war in Ukraine. Director Minard the floor is yours."

"Let me start by reminding everyone here that we will be discussing several very sensitive things today. There is to be no discussion outside this room until you hear otherwise."

Right, thought Skip.

"There was a serious nuclear incident prevented in Russia this past Saturday night. Intelligence sources discovered a plot by certain individuals in the employ of the Russian government to equip missiles with tactical nuclear weapons and most likely to employ those weapons somewhere in Ukraine."

Those who weren't already "in the know" looked shocked, and there was uncharacteristic chatter around the table.

The President said, "Calm down people. Please. The man said the incident was *prevented*."

The room hushed and Director Minard went into the details, omitting things that the Director and the President and the Secretaries of Defense and State decided didn't need to be shared yet. Like tying Prigozhin to the Wagner Group, or tying the Wagner Group to the nuclear incident that was prevented, or the actual attack on Russian territory by Ukraine forces.

Instead, Director Minard focused on vague "intercepted phone calls" and satellite imagery and supposed treasonous acts within the Russian military. He mentioned the contact between Secretary Austin and Minister Shoigu - and the assurance that Russia had the situation under control.

Not the whole truth, but certainly all true.

Then he moved on to the more publicly known event in Argentina.

"As you saw in the news Sunday there was a tragic attempt on the life of Pope Francis in Buenos Aires Saturday afternoon. Luckily, the primary assailant was subdued before he could fire on the Pope, and the convoy itself went on according to the schedule without any knowledge of the event until arriving at their intended stop in the north of the city. The Pope continued the rest of his schedule, including conducting Mass on Sunday in the Metropolitan Cathedral. He flew home today."

"The tragedy covered in the news occurred at the end of the convoy - the last two vehicles - which were attacked by unknown terrorists who were supporting the primary assailant. Unfortunately, 11 people were killed, and many were wounded, including local politicians, dignitaries of the church, and police officers. One American citizen was involved and admitted to the hospital. I'm told she is recovering fine and will be released today. The Argentina government is promising a full investigation and we've offered to support them in any way we can."

Again, Skip thought, truthful. He just omitted all the good parts that can't be told in this crowd.

Then the questions started, and Skip fell into his normal role of protecting sensitive information and sources. Luckily, Director Minard needed no assistance.

In the end, the President cleared his throat and said, "As we've said all along, this fight in Ukraine is not theirs alone. Whenever things like this happen, we are pressured not only

378

by the specific events and the key players but also by everyone else on the world stage who thinks they can get away with something while others are engaged."

"The purest realpolitik advocates will tell us that we should let the chips fall where they may, that this isn't our fight, that the Ukrainians somehow deserve this and it is none of our business to interfere. Yet sometimes realpolitik doesn't reflect reality and the need to do what is right in the real world. This will probably last a long time. It has lasted this long only through truly heroic actions taken by individuals both in and outside of Ukraine. Those people caused Russia to fail in this first phase of the war. "

He lowered his head briefly, raised his hand, and looked up again.

"It has been incredibly challenging these past several months. We are doing the best we can. This will not be easy. It will affect all of our jobs and all of your departments. Perhaps our national security. And after all that has happened, I can tell you that I am very pleased to see that so far, despite all the threats and crises, this war has been kept in the box and remains regional. Let's continue to assist Ukraine as they do all they can to restore peace to the region."

He looked slowly around the table. When he came to Skip, his gaze lingered for a moment. Then he finished the visual assessment of the audience, moved to get up and everyone stood. He had more meetings to attend in the Oval Office.

58

OLDER VERSION OF HIMSELF

Denver was an interesting place in late May. A stranger might think that the closer you get to Summer Solstice the more likely you could count on having warmer weather. But any resident of the Mile High City knows that you can wake up to sunshine, walk to work in shorts, and come out in the early afternoon to overcast skies and six inches of snow.

Thankfully, today was seasonably warm and clear.

Carlos took a high-priced limo from the airport to his father's neighborhood for two reasons. One, he thought he'd earned it. And two, the higher-priced limo drivers tended not to talk and ask all kinds of prying questions.

For once, he got back to the States from an operation without suffering the effects of jet lag - sure he was tired and sore, but not having to fight the impact of flying across multiple time zones and its interference with your ability to sleep was a rare pleasure.

He hadn't been here before. It was an interesting ride, gliding out of the modern airport westbound toward the city. The airport sat virtually alone out on the plains, in the extreme northeast of Denver's city limits. Noise complaints certainly weren't a problem as there were no neighbors in its remote location. But it did make for a long drive.

The limo passed through open prairie, then more and more suburban housing areas and small towns like Green Valley Ranch, and Montebello. Each was surrounded, fortress-like, with brown or tan cement walls with neighborhood signs differentiating it from neighboring fortresses. Each seemed to have a nearby strip mall. They drove on towards the urban skyline of Denver itself - at first dwarfed by the Rockies in the distance and then growing into an appreciably modern and sizable downtown.

Leaving I-70 and turning south on I-25 it wasn't long before the Denver Broncos stadium loomed up large in front of them. Growing up in Buenos Aires, Carlos never developed a passion for American Football - football for him would always be soccer.

He didn't share that often with his American friends.

Before reaching the stadium, they left the highway at North Speer Blvd, turned northwest and very shortly afterward turned south onto Clay Street. He had given the driver an address near the intersection of Clay and West 23rd Avenue. They arrived just minutes after leaving the highway.

He got out and stood there on the northwest corner of the intersection, holding his bag, and watched the limo disappear back towards the interstate. Can never be too careful - this was the first time he'd been without a weapon in over four months.

Crossing the street, he wandered along the dirt path in Jefferson Park, the Broncos stadium standing high just three blocks to the south. The sun was pleasantly warm on him as he navigated under the blossomed shade trees, new leaves rustling in the breeze. He went past the playground in the park, then continued along the path back to the sidewalk further west than he started on 23rd Avenue. He stood there composing his thoughts for a minute. Or was he working up the courage? Then he crossed the street and headed up Maxwell Street on the right side of the road. He was looking for a fairly new walk-up, a zero-lot-line home about halfway down the block on the right. As he walked, he saw the glossy black Chevy Silverado first, parked out front along the sidewalk.

1983 Maxwell was a three-story home, made up of lighter and darker red brick, with a burnt red front door at the top of a flight of stairs with 10 steps. An Air Force Academy sticker was in the tall but narrow window beside the door.

He paused at the bottom, wondering how this would go down. Then he slowly walked up the stairs, rang the doorbell, and waited. A dog barked an alert inside, too lazy to get up off the mat in the hall.

The door soon opened and he felt like he was looking at an older version of himself.

He took a breath, and said, "Lilia asked me to tell you she misses us both."

Then his SatPhone buzzed in his pocket.

ACKNOWLEDGMENTS

Alan Bennett, an English actor, author, playwright, and screenwriter, reportedly said, *"A book is a device to ignite the imagination."* I would amend his declaration to read: *"A book is a device to ignite the imagination, but nothing demonstrates the limits of our imagination like trying to write one."*

Unlike the fictional fighter pilot flying into combat alone in Chapter 25, writing a book is no solo effort. It certainly would not have been possible without the support of many experts, friends, and family.

First, there were countless numbers of people who, sometimes unknown to them, loaned their own experiences through many stories that provided me with the breadth of knowledge to attempt this effort. I must also thank the hundreds of authors for their books of a similar style as *Glory* for their lifelong entertainment and influence.

To Hoss, Sheila, Bill, Roger, Mark and Jody, Chris, Scott, Kato, David, Rooter, Will, Randy, Ryan, Mark, Matt, and Paul - thank you for the time you gave to read the various iterations and, most importantly, the honest reviews.

I must give a special thank you to the true-to-life Francis (who never had an affair in Buenos Aires). He dared me to write a book off and on during our many recurring texts and conversations about world events. When I surprised him with the first attempt with snippets of his family history in the plot, he expressed great support after overcoming his initial shock. I am grateful to him for allowing me to complete the story, and I am pleased to know that he is proud of his fictional son.

I dared not write about air combat without the consult of an F-15 Fighter Weapons School graduate. Bill did not disappoint. Thank you, Shawski, for our long friendship and your assistance. (And, my apologies to anyone who is part of what I thought was the fictional Shcherbakivskiy family - and for the alleged inability of Americans to pronounce what would be a glorious name!).

Glory's fictional DNI, Ron, provided unwavering support and encouragement. I probably would not have revisited the first short story that preceded this book without his reaction to reading it and his persuasive arguments to complete it. Thank you very much, Ron.

And to my green-eyed, blonde, wonderful spouse, who became my biggest supporter many years ago and is my biggest supporter still. Saying thank you does not begin to acknowledge all the good you do for me and our family.

Finally, I want to offer a salute to the brave people of Ukraine. Regardless of political persuasion, there is no denying the incredible fortitude and acts of bravery that defied the odds when they beat back the Russian Army in the late winter and spring of 2022. Sure, there was technical aid, but nothing would have gone their way without a proud national identity, strong leadership, and the resolution and courage shown at every level. I intended to honor them in this story. I hope I succeeded.

Glory to Ukraine!

Glory to the Heroes!

Made in United States
Troutdale, OR
06/11/2023

10554669R00219